HURTMOOR

TIM PRESCOTT

Published by The Robinson House Writers
Arthur Robinson House
13-14 The Green
Billingham TS23 1EU

For Keith

ONE

IT WAS an unexpected moment in Sarah's life, sitting at her dying friend's bedside. She was back in Stokesley, at the Sanderson house, and feeling light-headed. It wasn't just the effect of alcohol, although that was a big part of it. Her intention had been to share the bottle of Newcastle Brown Ale with Mark but he was so thin and frail. He'd pointed out that it might not mix well with the morphine, so she'd given him a thimble full – enough to wet his tongue, but too little to trouble his bladder. And, in a moment of social incompetence, she drank the rest herself. Alcohol was an occasional indulgence for Sarah and she hadn't eaten since breakfast. She was drunk.

Mark seemed to have drifted off and she could look at him now. He looked peaceful, but she was shocked by his withered body. It had been too long, more than forty years since they had last spent time together. She'd felt some discomfort about that as she'd driven over to the house, worrying that she'd ignored his life only to re-engage for his death.

Images from her school days invaded her memory, vivid although uninvited. Sarah hadn't enjoyed her time at school. She was never properly accepted by her peers and without

1

Mark, she would have been isolated. Yes, it had been a long time, but she remembered him fondly.

He'd been healthy at their previous meeting, a young man with his life before him. At that time, she was newly married to Alexander, unsure about her future and perhaps quite naive, hoping that her new husband and her oldest friend would be well met. But there had been some tension between the two men and, as it turned out, it had been Mark's first and last visit to Hurtmoor, Sarah's marital home. From then on, she and Mark communicated infrequently, with years between letters. Then, for a while, email reconnected them, and for a few months they had exchanged trivialities, but there was always a degree of discretion, each of them held in check, Sarah by her timidity and Mark by his impeccable manners. And now, all of these years later, she was with him again, to witness his death, to hear his confession.

Death and distant memories had combined to bring Sarah's invitation. Mark's older sister, Cheryl, had brought news of Janey North's passing. Janey was another of his former classmates. He hadn't spoken to her for many years, but somehow news of her demise had awoken something in him. Suddenly, he was confronted by the finality of death and the terrifying quickness of time, and he needed to see Sarah.

Cheryl had contacted Sarah a few days earlier, telling her that Mark had asked to see her and that his life expectancy was reduced to just a few weeks. That had been an insufficient preparation. Once she had entered the room, she had been stilled by the sight of him. She'd stood for a few seconds just inside the bedroom door, just to look at him. His eyes and his smile were mostly unchanged, certainly recognisable, but he'd become an old man and very frail.

He'd greeted her with a smile, found enough energy for three minutes of conversation and then slipped away into a deep sleep. Sarah drank the brown ale while he slept. Now, as she sat waiting, with the alcohol's encouragement, she felt her own eyes closing. They were sleeping together.

• • •

"Sarah, you've fallen asleep." Mark smiled. His voice was soft but he persisted, repeating his call and gradually increasing the volume until he saw her head jerk as she regained consciousness.

Sarah repositioned herself as she reoriented in unfamiliar surroundings. "Mark, I'm so sorry, I must have dropped off. One is one too many. Please forgive me."

Mark was amused. "Are you driving home today?"

"No, I'm in no fit state. I'll booked a room at The Lion."

Mark's grin was overtaken by a more serious expression. For the words that he was about to speak, he wanted to be upright, to sit with a straight back, to be on the same level as his companion. He wanted to deliver his message with dignity, but he couldn't find the strength to raise himself. "This bloody lung cancer has taken everything from me. I know that I'm ill and close to death. I don't complain, but there are moments when I want a few minutes of good health. I asked you to come to see me because there's something I need to say to you. I wish I had the strength to sit up. I wonder if you would help me?"

Sarah stood up. "Yes, of course." She moved awkwardly, leaning towards him and then reaching beneath his arms and placing her hands against his back. She winced as she felt the loose skin at the back of his rib cage. He was skin and bone. She lifted him easily to a more upright position and rearranged his pillows to give him comfort and support.

"I'm sorry that I've been an absent friend," he said. "It wasn't my wish."

"It doesn't matter, Mark. Anyway, we were both absent friends. I'm sorry too."

Mark was clearly hesitant, in position now to look across at Sarah, but still not ready to deliver his message. He'd held his secret for decades, always sensing alarm whenever he'd considered the impact of telling Sarah what had happened.

3

He had no clear vision of what might follow his revelation, only a vague impression of giving release to something dangerous. Somehow he felt that his discretion had held the danger in check, and for a few moments he felt trapped, pushed forward by a wish to shed a burden, but still fearfully aware that he would have no control over the repercussions. "I'm in two minds. I want to tell you why I never returned to Hurtmoor, but I don't want to cause friction."

Sarah became curious and tense, sensing the discomfort of her friend's dilemma. She was fully aware now that her presence in time and place had a purpose that she was about to discover.

"Say what you need to say, Mark." She gave her encouragement freely, disguising her own growing tension.

Even still he hesitated while he searched for the right words, but as he looked into Sarah's eyes he realised that an intensity had developed, and he found his voice. "Okay. I don't know whether you can remember, Sarah. It's such a long time ago. You were cooking lunch. Smoked haddock, if I remember correctly. Alexander invited me to one of the outbuildings, the middle barn, to look at his collection of guns." Mark sensed Sarah's reaction and he hesitated again.

Sarah felt the fine hair on her arms prickling. She was receiving the communication viscerally, ahead of Mark's verbal delivery. Already she was starting to feel angry, and impatience pushed her good manners aside. "What happened, Mark? Just tell me, it's fine."

"I guess that Alexander saw me as a rival for your affection." Mark's cheeks flushed. He'd avoided admitting to himself that Alexander may have seen something in him that he hadn't acknowledged himself. "He unlocked the gun cabinet. I wouldn't know one end of a gun from the other and I wasn't at all interested but he described the qualities of several pieces. You know, this one's perfect for shooting rabbits, another was accurate over great distances. Then he picked up a small pistol wrapped in a black cloth and he said

4

that was the gun he'd use if he had to murder someone. He qualified the remark, pointing out that there would have to be a good reason, before he'd take such action. He showed me how to load the gun and drew my attention to the weapon's power and accuracy. He said that if any man tried to steal his wife, then he'd shoot them. He lifted his arm slowly and pointed the loaded gun at my head and he stared, watched the fear rise in me. Then he told me never to return and he asked me if I'd understood what he'd said, the pistol still aimed at my forehead. He smiled and nodded, then he put the guns away. I watched him lock the cabinet and then he walked back to the house, leaving me alone in the barn to consider my future." Mark looked up to assess the impact of his words, wondering, as he had done a thousand times before, if continued silence might have been a better option. He saw that her head was bowed and her eyes closed. "I must confess that Alexander frightened me. I was shocked. I didn't know him well enough to judge the situation. I've never forgotten that moment, left standing alone and wondering if I could walk back to the house and eat lunch with the two of you. My thoughts were scrambled. I found myself inspecting the gun cabinet. It was bizarre. I'd been threatened and I took the time to admire the cabinet maker's craftsmanship."

Sarah watched him. He seemed to disappear from the room, fully absorbed into his memory. "Mark?"

He was jolted back into Sarah's company. "I would never have neglected our friendship voluntarily. I needed to tell you that. It wasn't my choice, Sarah. You were only just married and I decided that it was better to stay away rather than risk causing friction. And I told myself that he might shift his position as he grew more secure about your relationship, but he was very clear in his message and time hurried along. The months became years. It's a selfish confession. I've often worried that you'd think I'd lost interest, that you might not know how deeply I cared about you. Your friendship meant something to me, Sarah."

5

That was the secret that he'd kept for forty-five years and which he now felt unable to take to his grave.

Sarah remained silent. She could remember the weekend of his visit all those years ago. She and Alexander had indeed been newly married. She felt tears running fast down her cheeks. And she felt somewhere deep inside, that she'd divined the truth long ago.

Although she was appalled by her husband's behaviour, she wasn't surprised and in a way she was glad to learn what had taken place between her husband and her friend. At least she knew the truth. As she'd settled into married life, Alexander had controlled everything. He'd vetted her friends, laid down the house rules, given Sarah clear instruction.

She and Mark were alike in some ways, neither of them had appetites for confrontation. Mark had appreciated the sensitivities and tactfully withdrawn. Even now, on his deathbed, after so many years, he was still hesitant telling the story, afraid that he might stir up trouble.

"I know. I always knew that our friendship was genuine. I did sometimes wonder whether Alexander had said something. I never blamed you, Mark. Anyway, thank you. It's good to know for sure what happened and I think you're right, Alexander was insecure." Sarah was troubled, disturbed to a degree that she wanted to hide her feelings from Mark. She took a deep breath and found a smile. "We can't change things now and I'm so pleased to see you again."

Mark nodded. He'd unburdened himself, completed his uncomfortable task and he was keen now to find distraction. "It's Janey North's funeral today. She was in our year, Janey Tasker back then. Do you remember her? A quiet girl, but pleasant. Another cancer victim, poor Janey."

Sarah recalled an image of Janey Tasker. They'd been classmates but not friends. "Yes, I remember her well. Did she stay local?"

"Yes, lived here all of her life. She was friends with Greg Whitehead. You'll remember him, he fancied you."

She was momentarily unsettled, wondering how many more of her former classmates were in town for Janey's funeral. Long forgotten names and faces suddenly looming large, crossing her path, blowing cold air on to the back of her neck. She felt herself unsure of what to say. She'd steeled herself to face her dying friend, and she'd found the courage to speak with him about Alexander, but she was unready for Greg Whitehead. She became self-conscious, uncomfortably aware of her muted response, and she pushed herself into a flustered and unconvincing denial. "No, he didn't, I don't know where that came from, Mark. Certainly not."

Mark smiled. The prospect of imminent death held little appeal for him but there were one or two compensations. The promise of his demise had emboldened him. Finally, he'd revealed his encounter with Alexander and he'd formed a clear understanding that the death bed is no place for shrinking hearts and tactful silence. It was the last chance saloon.

"He certainly did, Sarah. You remember how we all went out for drinks at the Mucky Duck after our 'A' levels were finished? Greg insisted on walking you home that night. We all watched with raised eyebrows when the two of you disappeared together." Mark watched her proceed from mild agitation to the beginnings of a blush. He was on a roll now, enjoying himself, ready to name the elephants in every room in England.

Sarah was caught off guard. Mark's memory was as sharp as ever. She had nowhere to hide. She'd always liked Greg at school. He was one of the few who would recognise her existence, always happy to exchange greetings. As they'd progressed through their teenage years, a sexual tension had developed between them. There'd been a period when they had shared brief but nevertheless heavily loaded glances across a corridor. And then, right at the end of their school careers, he'd walked her home and they had kissed. She'd been eighteen years old, inexperienced and desperately

7

unsure of herself. It was her first kiss. She'd never told a soul but she'd never forgotten.

She glanced at Mark. He was sleeping, out like a light. She felt relieved. But she was pleased to be with him again, with all of his messages and mischief. She and Mark had repaired their friendship, the years apart didn't matter. They'd never find the time to catch up properly, to fill in more than forty years of blank space. Perhaps that was best. Neither of them had experienced fulfilment, both of them disappointed by lives half lived.

And as she watched him drifting in and out of sleep, making brief excursions into his waiting death, starting to explore his new and future place of residence, she cherished their late show of friendship. Then she cursed her husband, wondering at the same time what on Earth might have happened to Greg Whitehead. And as she sat, Newcastle Brown Ale dancing across her brain, she wondered if she'd ever find the courage to confront her husband.

TWO

GREG

GREG COULD REMEMBER the moment when he'd stood in his porch to open the funeral invitation, appreciating the physicality of a real card delivered by Royal Mail through his letter box. He'd been forewarned and already he knew what was inside the envelope. Nevertheless, he'd winced. Poor Janey.

But today it was the funeral, the good bit. Not for the first time, Greg was looking forward to a funeral. He was an enthusiastic cyclist and he hardly ever used the car, but thirty miles in a suit and tie on a cold wet day, with alcohol to be consumed, was a bridge too far. So he'd planned two unusual deviations beyond the parameters of his normal habits... he decided to drive and he booked overnight accommodation.

As he approached the crematorium, he anticipated a decent turn out, a few almost familiar faces brought together by death. The sadness wasn't to be forgotten or even pushed aside. Greg would pay his dues and then he'd enjoy the company, the reconnection with old school friends and distant memories in the warm embrace of a well-funded wake. It would be fun, there'd be goodwill, nostalgia, a bit of a spread, and drinks at the bar.

Greg had recently celebrated his seventieth birthday. He'd spent the entire day at home, watching old films on television, but indulged himself with a full bottle of Pinot Noir during the evening. So began his eighth decade. He didn't speak to a soul all through the day although Amy, his daughter, had sent her good wishes by text and three unknown Facebook friends had also wished him a happy birthday.

He lived alone. It wasn't just that he was the only occupant in his semi-detached house in the Middlesbrough suburbs, Greg actually lived his life as a solitary figure. Once or twice each week, he'd meet a friend for coffee or speak to someone on the phone, but mostly he enjoyed his own exclusive company. In truth it had become a defining aspect of his identity – he chose to live alone. That's what he kept telling himself. There had been no element of sadness about his birthday. Living alone, free from the demands, complications and compromises of a close relationship, was a considered life choice, a preference. What other explanation could there be?

Although Greg was able to describe his approach to life with an easy air of confidence, he was often occupied by self-doubt. Everyone needs a paradox, Greg was no exception. He would state clearly and often that he didn't want to be in a relationship, and he meant it each and every time. Socially and emotionally, he'd become self-reliant. It was a philosophy, a lifestyle and a choice. But despite his frequent claims of being content with his own company, the prospect of a social gathering was already provoking excited anticipation. He'd been to a couple of funerals in the previous twelve months and had a great time at both of them. The prospect of a good funeral cheered him up no end. Funerals were so much better than Christmas.

But first there would be the service at the crematorium. That was a different prospect. That was going to be an experience of sadness. The raw pain of the loss. Funeral wakes were fun but the tickets were frighteningly expensive.

Greg found something beautiful in the union of grief and celebration. He appreciated the ceremony, the cultural practice. This process, the progression from desperate and respectful grief, from hollow loss, from isolation, to community and the beginning of acceptance. Greg loved every element, even the sadness.

And he was amused by his predicament – his favourite social events were the funerals for his dead friends and relatives. And as luck would have it, this was his third one in little more than a year. Greg paid his dues in the grief phase, he felt the sadness. He and Janey had been at school together, right through from day one until 'A' levels. Now he was seventy, ready for the sadness. She was obligingly dead.

He cried easily, a thousand things could move him to tears. Any poignant story about human connection would leave Greg in pieces. It had been different when he'd been a young man, when he'd seen displays of emotion as weakness. But as the years passed, he became ever more easily affected. And funerals, they were right at the top of the pile, the agony of death, the celebration of a life. Bring it on. Greg would cry for Janey. He'd already done so alone in the safety of his home, but today he'd go public. Greg could be a bit showy, performance existed in him. Today his shaking would be slight and his tears would fall quietly. No, there would be no hint of display, but there would be no hiding either.

Greg had a selected set of pastimes, although his interest in films was more than that, it was a passion. He was convinced that he'd grown up in a golden age of contemporary art, consuming a feast of ground-breaking films and music. His commitment to a single life was almost total but not quite. If Meryl Streep came calling, Greg's philosophy would change. He played games of chess against digital opponents, watched sport on television, and read modern literature. He kept fit, mostly by cycling, compensating for over-indulgence with chocolate and red wine.

The combination of divorce with the onset of the Covid19 pandemic had greatly reduced his social life. That was the truth of it. He'd adapted to his enforced circumstances – stayed home and saw no one. He got good at it, smiled in solitary confinement, became a sad and lonely man who was unhealthily at peace and in prison with himself.

He was a small-town man, not a community spirit, just a familiar face, mostly wordless. And yet for all of his practised solitude, he remained at ease in company. He drove to the funeral in good spirit, parking his car and exchanging greetings with half-familiar faces in the queue that had formed to wait for the service. He spotted and then joined Martin and Jenny. Jenny had been Janey's best friend at university. She and Martin were both recently retired after impressive careers. Greg had watched their success while they'd paid little attention to his failures. He hadn't seen them for several years and he hoped that the absence of careers might have made them more interesting.

They found their way into the chapel and took their seats in the second row. The atmosphere fell upon them all, a gathering of fifty, and the quiet voices from the queue outside reduced to whispers once inside the chapel.

Martin leaned towards Greg. "How's Alan doing?" Anything now would be better than talking about Janey.

"I've no idea, Martin. I spoke to him on the phone. He called to tell me when Janey died, but this is the first time I've seen him." Greg looked up at the photo-stream, a tribute (arguably), reminders and memories, a ghost. He was grateful for the Celebrant's distraction. As she began to welcome the seated mourners, the photos disappeared, leaving a central and constant image of Janey from maybe fifteen years earlier. And Greg lost his focus. He was weighed down by the thought of choosing just one photographic image that would be the last visual representation of a human life.

He refocused, attending to the Celebrant who gently described chosen moments… the key markers on Janey's path through her life, sixty-nine years reduced to ten minutes of highlights. And surprise surprise, Janey's eulogy depicted a fountain of love and other good things. Amongst the living, half the world were arseholes but once dead, all were angels.

Then some music and back to the photo-stream. Greg cried. He didn't mind, he was content in his weeping. He understood that his friend had died. Their friendship had bonded when they were six years old and they went all through school together, rock solid. Then they grew up and went their separate ways, lived their separate lives. Except that they wrote occasional letters, postcards and emails. And they met up from time to time, or spoke on the phone. But as the years had passed, the distance between them had gradually extended. They had lost the fibre of their bond to the merciless indifference of life and time.

The ten years prior to Janey's death had been limited to Christmas cards with a well-intended but nevertheless indefinite 'must get together' message. They never did. It wasn't so much a loss of life, more a loss of interest. No blame.

The end of the service seemed to arrive with indecent haste. Greg experienced distaste. His lifelong friend was remembered only briefly. Was that it, for Christ's sake? Right, we've all shed a tear, Janey, whatever, let's get down the boozer and do some drugs.

He hung around outside the crematorium in amongst a cluster of waiters. He walked a few paces away from the others, just an aimless wander. Or so he'd thought until he arrived at his car. He turned around to lean his back against the car and looked again at the group of mourners, trying to get a clear view of who had turned out. There were at least half a dozen people whom he recognised. And a few more whom he watched more closely from his remote vantage point.

"Jesus," he said to himself. "That's Andy Cooper." Greg had achieved at least thirty metres of separation from the group, no one could hear him speaking. But speak he must. He needed to hear it from his own mouth.

Andy Cooper had bullied Greg over a period of years. It had started when they were in primary school and although it had been patchy rather than continuous, it only ended when Andy left school after 'O' levels. Greg hadn't seen him for more than fifty years. His mood was dampened by this unexpected reunion. And he was puzzled. Andy and Janey had fallen out before they were seven years old. After that, they never got on. She hadn't liked him. Christ only knows why he'd come to her funeral.

Then Greg watched Andy wave and walk towards him. Historically, Andy's approaches had never been friendly. Greg waited with interest.

Andy made eye contact and smiled. "Greg Whitehead!" He looked triumphant. "You won't recognise me, I wasn't this good looking at school. Andy Cooper." Andy extended his inviting right hand.

Greg reacted without thinking and accepted the handshake. "I do recognise you." He looked at him now, up close. Andy had lost most of his hair and what remained had turned almost white, but he was in good shape, no excess weight and the same slightly bowed legs. But he looked so much older. His tanned face had become weathered with deep lines around his eyes and forehead.

"Listen, Greg, I'm not going to the wake. I just wanted to pay my respects."

"Okay. Well, I'll be on my way." Greg opened the car door.

Andy raised his hand. "Will you be staying in town tonight?"

"Yeah, I'm at The Lion."

"I'll come down later, I owe you a pint." Andy walked on past the car.

Greg was quite disarmed. He'd accidentally shaken hands

with Andy Cooper and arranged to meet him later for a drink. Interventions from Andy had soured many of Greg's school days. After fifty years of respite, he felt a familiar shadow fall across him. He'd set out this morning with bright expectations for an enjoyable funeral. Andy Cooper hadn't been part of the plan.

THREE

THE WAKE

GREG ENTERED the lounge at The Bridge Hotel. The rather gaudy interior seemed inappropriate but it was the only hotel in the town with a decent sized reception lounge. He'd dropped his car off at The Lion, aware that he wanted a drink. He hadn't given up all hope. Andy Cooper's appearance had bothered him but as he walked from The Lion to The Bridge, he gathered himself, quickly developing a middle-aged man's perspective on his childhood experiences. At school, Andy Cooper had been a powerful and intimidating figure. During the brief exchange at the crematorium car park, Greg had noticed that Andy still looked tall and strong, but something in his bearing seemed diminished – he was older now, less scary. And Greg had suggested to himself that he'd absorbed the passage of the past five decades rather more comfortably than his former foe. Greg had never been inclined to violence but he smiled to himself as he imagined giving Andy a kicking in The Lion car park later. It was fantasy, but suddenly he found himself walking back towards happiness.

He scanned the room, checking out the potential for more unpleasant surprises. In addition to Martin and Jenny, he recognised Mandy Thomas. She and Sue Berry had been

Janey's closest school friends. Mandy and her husband, who Greg had been introduced to more than once, were sitting at a table with another two people who looked to be in the same age range. He couldn't recall the name of Mandy's partner. He remembered him as an entirely forgettable man. Greg assumed that at least one of the two he couldn't recognise must also be an old school friend, although neither of them appeared to be Sue Berry. That was a bit disappointing. Sue had been pretty at school. Not as pretty as the unapproachable Sarah Buxton but Greg wondered what the last fifty years had done to her. He was slightly surprised by his wish to know whether Sue Berry was married or single. That was a big question for Greg. Do you have a life all to yourself or do you share your life with another. What's your choice, and why?

He made his way to the bar where he found Martin, who kindly added a pint of John Smiths to the round of drinks.

"That was good timing." Martin passed Greg his pint and then carefully pushed the stems of three wine glasses between the fingers of his spare hand. "We're over there with Mandy and Sue."

As it turned out, fifty years had rendered Sue Berry unrecognisable. Greg approached, desperately trying to work out which of the two unrecognised women had been the focus of a hundred masturbatory fantasies during his teenage years. He arrived at the table, still undecided. "Hello everyone," he said.

Sue went first. "Greg Whitehead! Amazing, I recognised you in an instant. Not bad after all of these years." She smiled.

So this was Sue Berry after all. "Hello, Sue, I recognised you as soon as I walked into the room. You've still got it, a cheeky glint in your eye." Greg was slightly surprised by the ease of his flirtation, but not displeased.

Sue blushed. "This is my wife, Eleanor."

Greg had been thirteen years old when homosexuality

17

changed its nature, no longer unacceptable and illegal. Sue appeared to have embraced this cultural progression more ably than Greg. "Hi, Eleanor, nice to meet you. I used to fancy Sue when we were at school." This day was going badly wrong. Andy Cooper, the boy who'd bullied him. Sue Berry, the girl of his dreams. Then this clumsy and untimely confession.

Mandy rescued him. "Come and sit down, Greg. I hoped that you'd come."

They settled into some memories of Janey and of each other. Mandy's bloke was as boring as ever. Greg talked mostly with Eleanor who turned out to be a blast. She could offer thoughtful and intelligent opinions and then lighten the mood with humour. She'd shattered one of the romantic dreams from his childhood, but twenty minutes later he felt determined that they stay in touch. He punched her details into his phone. Maybe she wasn't entirely lesbian. Not that Greg cared. Whatever.

Eleanor was equally pleased by her new friend. "I thought you were with another guy, you know, at the crem?"

Sue leaned forward. "That was Andy Cooper, wasn't it? I was surprised to see you two chatting. You weren't exactly the best of friends at school."

Greg had almost let it slip from his mind. He was reduced by the reminder. "No, I was going to ask you guys about that. You're still local, Mandy. What's going on there? He said he'd buy me a pint at The Lion, later."

Sue was puzzled. "Really?"

So was Mandy. "He always smiles and says hello when we pass in the street. He's usually with a woman, the same woman, but that's all. I'm not even sure where he lives anymore. So maybe he married. Who knows?"

"Yeah well, maybe I'll get to know a bit more tonight. But if he thinks he can still bully me, he's mistaken."

Sue offered encouragement. "Good for you, Greg."

Greg was encouraged. "I'll kick his fucking head in."

"Greg! Goodness me." Mandy didn't know where to place herself. She admired his spirit but not the language. "You're not young lads anymore. I've heard nothing around town, not for years. He must have changed his ways. You know, grown up. Settled down. You need to remember your age."

"I'm seventy, Mandy. I've had my three score and ten, it's bonus territory from here on in. A bit of revenge on Andy Cooper would fit the bill nicely." Greg watched his poorly judged attempt at humour fall flat. He sat back, taking a moment to examine his anger. After all of these years, it had jumped straight out of his mouth. 'I'll kick his fucking head in.' And he realised that sitting down to enjoy a pint bought for him by Andy Cooper wouldn't be easy. Voices danced around him, but he had withdrawn. Was there really anger in him, a wish to be violent? It had hidden, unseen for fifty years, and yet so easily revealed. He shook his head.

"Greg?" Eleanor's hand rested gently on his forearm. "You okay? You look lost in your thoughts."

Greg reoriented, re-entered the room. "Sorry, Eleanor. Indeed I was."

"Sue and I are staying overnight, here at The Bridge, but we could meet you at The Lion this evening. A bit of moral support." Eleanor felt his trouble.

"That's kind of you. But no, I won't be good for much tonight, not after drinking this afternoon. I'll need an early night. I don't care if he comes or not."

Eleanor accepted his refusal although she was unconvinced by his indifference. "Will you make me a promise? Send me a text tomorrow, tell me how it went."

The conversation rumbled on. Greg found an opportunity to offer condolence to Alan and then slipped away. His cousin Richard's funeral had been much more fun – no surprises. Unlike Janey's. The sadness had more substance than he could have guessed. Mandy had told him sad news about another of their old school friends. Mark Sanderson had been quite sensitive as a child and very bright. He was a kind-hearted soul, a gentle man. According to Mandy, he'd suffered poor health throughout his life and then a stroke last year. Now he had cancer and he was beyond treatment. No one had ever taken against Mark. He deserved better.

FOUR

THE LION

GREG HAD MANAGED three pints at Janey's wake. There had been food but he hadn't eaten. He got back to his room at The Lion and he felt dreadful. He brushed his teeth, drank a glass of water and went down to the bar in search of a sandwich, although he had no appetite for Andy Cooper. He decided to grab a quick coffee and a bite to eat, before returning to his room for an early night. Andy owed him considerably more than a pint, but there was neither debt nor obligation on Greg's part. If Andy came down to The Lion later, he'd have to drink alone.

He arrived at the bar pleased by his decision. Already his mood was improving. But only momentarily.

"Hey, Greg. Over here, mate."

What? It was only six o'clock. The voice was unmistakable. Greg waited a second to allow his disappointment expression, then he straightened his face and turned to locate his assailant, wondering when he and Andy had become mates.

Andy walked to join him at the bar. "My shout, what you having?"

"Oh, I'll have a coffee."

Andy placed the order and took Greg over to his table. "Have a seat, Greg."

Greg was impatient. "Listen. If you don't mind, I'm tired after the funeral. I don't know what you want to say to me but let's have it, I haven't the energy for small talk with the school bully." He was pleased by his bluntness, he'd got the first punch in, he'd found the courage to confront Andy Cooper. Much too late.

While Chris delivered the coffee, Greg looked at Andy and saw hesitation and watery eyes. There were a few other patrons in the bar but it was quiet and Greg felt conspicuous.

Andy was clearly struggling. He swallowed once and then again. He took in a breath. "I have something to say to you, Greg." Andy was holding back a force of emotion, concentrating with great effort to maintain the control he needed for speech.

Greg's head set switched back to human mode. He looked around the room, wondering if others had noted Andy's intensity. "Alright, Andy. Give yourself a minute." He spoke softly.

Andy seemed unable to speak further. He appeared overcome. He blew, the way people do sometimes, when they try to refrain from crying. His eyes closed. Another blow, and then another.

"Sorry. It's okay. I'm fine."

The hurt from the past slipped away. Greg looked at Andy who was still trying to regain his composure. But without much success. He didn't know what was wrong or what to say. Again, he glanced around the room. Still Andy's struggle continued.

"Andy, you look unwell. Get yourself home." Greg desperately wanted Andy to quietly disappear.

Andy was red in the face but he tried again. "I need to explain." Those four words had been supported by every remaining ounce of energy in his body. And with their expression, his control was completely spent. His upper body

22

began to shake so violently that the coffee cups rattled. And every head in the bar turned to face the two middle aged men drinking lattes.

They all watched with Greg as Andy pushed his seat back, the chair legs screeching against the tiled floor. Andy found his feet and ran out into the street.

Greg was caught unawares. He gestured his bewilderment to the onlookers and walked out through the same exit. He had no wish to catch up with Andy. He simply wanted to show the spectators in the bar that he was a decent and caring man. He cast brief glances up and down the street but there was no sign of Andy. He'd gone.

Most of Greg's coffee was in the saucer. He ordered his sandwich and more coffee, and asked Chris to deliver it to his room. A flat white arrived promptly. Chris was curious but not at all disturbed by the scene in his bar and now he was hungry for information. "What was that all about?"

"Thanks, Chris. I'd like to explain but I'm afraid I have no explanation."

Chris smiled and affected his unrecognisable John Wayne impersonation. "Who was that man?"

Greg tried. "We both went to the same funeral today. We were at school together. First time I've seen him since he bullied me at school. I don't know why he came to see me. He wanted to say something but he just lost it."

"That's an understatement," said Chris.

Greg had only just met Chris when he'd checked in, but already he felt comfortable in his company. Chris seemed happy to cross into a personal agenda. He was well practised in his role as barman and Greg gave his trust too easily.

"We'll never know. I'm off early in the morning. I'm glad you enjoyed the drama, Chris, but it's over now."

"Oh no, I was in the bar. I felt the atmosphere. There's more to come there, make no mistake."

FIVE

SARAH AND ALEXANDER

EVEN IF SHE'D stayed sober, Sarah wouldn't have attempted the drive back to Surrey. She rested in The Lion and commenced her journey the following morning. She'd been three sheets to the wind when Mark had made his confession. Chris, who'd checked her in the previous day and who had served her breakfast, had said farewell like an old and dear friend. Now she was sober, and yet her anger had survived a heavy sleep and was travelling back home with her.

She turned the radio off, accepting her need for quiet contemplation, and pondered. She was searching herself, examining her thoughts and her feelings. She gathered herself into an unfamiliar mixture, feeling all at once a little afraid of herself, a stirring in her soul, and a sense of anticipation. And despite some elements of discomfort, she relished the prospect of a long drive home. She had a lot to think about.

She'd been Sarah MacDonald for forty-six years but with this rare excursion back to her home town, she felt herself to be Sarah Buxton again, stirred up by Mark's explanation and a brief glimpse back to her younger self. Maiden or married, Sarah had always toed the line. She was seventy years old, a retired Consultant Psychiatrist, mother of two grown children, a grandparent, a good citizen, and she'd toed the line every step of the way. While Mark had told her what had happened between him and Alexander, she'd listened quietly, keeping her thoughts to herself. That was Sarah Buxton. She had always been a quiet achiever, a naturally strong person who'd been taught reserve. It was her father's design. He had happily paid for her two older brothers to attend a private school and initially he'd steered Sarah along a similar path, but then he changed course, and for Sarah, a mere girl with chronic ill health, the local state school became the choice. She learned uncomplaining obedience in the same way she learned a thousand other things – with attention and ease.

She'd toed the line and managed her life, without ever speaking out. Sarah was endlessly efficient in her ability to accept her lot. She knew how to make the best of things. She'd lived her life that way. But the mixture of rogue thoughts and angry feelings, her passenger on this journey, pushed and prodded, inviting revolution.

Mark had unburdened himself, offered his confession without judgement. She hadn't known how to respond and had said very little in reply. She wasn't surprised, but the combined impact of his words and his predicament was affecting her... Death and truth mixed together seemed to have formed a potent compound, and she sensed danger as it coursed through her veins. She wondered what Mark, gentle and frail, had given her – an elixir, or something poisonous.

She drove on, mile after mile, without focus or concentration, lost in her thoughts.

She thought about Mark, her kind-hearted friend taking shallow rasping breaths with inadequate lungs, about her husband's gun cabinet, and about her accidental drunkenness. The mixture of memories caused her to shudder and to smile. And she thought again about Greg Whitehead and then about Janey Tasker. They'd all been in the same year at school – the coronation kids.

Sarah could picture Janey clearly in her mind's eye. None

25

of the other girls at school had really wanted Sarah as a friend. They had reasons to view her with suspicion: she came from a relatively wealthy family, she joined the year group late, she was allowed all sorts of exemptions because of her ill health, and she was a top of the class. Her school life had been essentially academic and minimally social.

She'd watched the other children forming friendships while she was left to herself. She'd felt the hurt but she'd held her head high. The girls had softened during sixth form when Sarah had finally been allowed into a circle of friends. Before that, only Mark and Greg Whitehead had accepted her.

She drifted in her memory, almost forgetting that she was driving. Driving back to her husband. With questions and memories stirring inside of her.

Alexander MacDonald grew up with money. Old money. Held in his family through generations. He could look into the far distance across the fields at Hurtmoor knowing that that he owned it all. Land, power and inheritance. He was educated at St Germaine's College, an exclusive boarding school at the high end of the private sector, sent away to school when he was still a young child. There was no place for sentiment or for family love. His school was chosen to provide order and discipline, to build character, and to prepare him for the duties of leadership.

It was all boys. Girls were talked about, they had a place in the world, but not at St Germaine's. Even today, sixty years after Alexander had first stood at the gates of St Germaine's College, he felt reassured that there were still no girls attending his old school. He assumed that gender fluidity would simply be against school rules. Alexander wasn't a man to tolerate the intolerable.

As it turned out, the traditions of school discipline had been delivered with cruelty and ruthlessness. The treatment of younger boys by the senior students and by teachers frequently transgressed into bullying and abuse. It was a long-established culture, a test, a requirement for the boys to withstand the early years, to survive, to earn the right to be an older boy, to turn the tables, to change from the abused to the abuser, and to conserve the traditions.

Alexander suffered some dreadful abuse as he made his way through the junior years at school. He learned to take his pain with steadfast and silent forbearance, holding back the tears and the screams, earning his passage. There was a price to pay. He grew cold, built a wall around his emotional world, and allowed his instinct for human sympathy to be extinguished. He was soured but he survived and he duly earned his time as an older boy, which he relished. Alexander passed on the school values with a particularly brutal enjoyment, became the most feared of the seniors. By the time he'd reached fifteen, he'd established a reputation. Even then he wasn't to be questioned. Alexander ruled, others suffered obeyance.

He went on to become head boy, a full year of unchecked sadistic bullying. By then he'd grown to six feet, with wide shoulders and powerful thighs. Even then, when he was still relatively slim, a square jaw and chunky hands signalled a more heavy build to come as he grew into manhood. Then he went to Cambridge, rowing and playing rugby while studying agriculture, where he met Sarah, before taking his position in the family business. He accepted all of his inheritance, the material wealth and the austere values. And the power. Especially the power.

Sarah had always been a good wife to Alexander. She was well practised in the company of powerful men, able enough in the secondary roles of woman. He had liked her physicality right from the start… she was athletic and beautiful. He appreciated her tactful and accommodating manner, and paid little attention to her impressive albeit understated intelligence. But in the world of adult relationships, she was

27

inexperienced and quite naive. That suited Alexander very well. He identified his target and he was genuinely attracted to Sarah. For her part, she enjoyed the attentions and extravagance of a commanding and handsome man.

All through their many years together, Alexander had only rarely needed to chastise her. She kept the home, tolerated the angry pounding sex, and managed the children. Once the children were sent away to school, Alexander had allowed her a career. He'd chosen well, she was a practical woman who knew her place. She'd been fine until the bloody pandemic.

Sarah did change during the pandemic, or at least she began to, but for many pre-pandemic years, she hadn't been fine. She'd put up with Alexander in the same way that she'd put up with her father and her brothers, and she had allowed him his power. She realised that she'd chosen badly for her marriage, but it had been her choice. All the way through the years of raising children, through all of her working years, and even through the first years of her retirement, she'd remained steadfast and uncomplaining, a good wife. Through it all, she'd criticised herself. Right up until Covid hit, and then she'd started to change.

Sarah had enjoyed revisiting her home town. She had made the journey on a Thursday. She liked her life to be ordered, to have regular patterns and repeating schedules, and during her journey back to Surrey she resolved to visit Mark each Thursday until he'd gone. The circumstances were surrounded by sadness. Nevertheless, each of her excursions would give her a twenty-four-hour respite from the sham of her marriage. For one day a week, for the duration of Mark's failing life, she would be free. It wasn't much but already, during the formation of her resolve, she wondered where these small steps might take her. To her surprise, she'd sat comfortably enough with her dying friend. She felt that somehow she'd gained strength, enough she hoped to finally confront the hopelessness of her marriage, enough to step forward and make her complaint. She spent the last hour of her journey back home rehearsing for the difficult conversation she intended to have with her husband.

She arrived back at Hurtmoor in the middle of the afternoon. As she climbed out of the car, she felt the weight of her intentions, and she wondered if she was ready. But she steeled herself and decided to take a 'no time like the present' approach. She walked through the front door with her determination still holding, but she entered into an empty house. Alexander was elsewhere and she breathed a sigh of relief.

SIX

GREG

TOWARDS THE END of the day after Janey's funeral, Greg sent a text to Eleanor.

Greg: *Hi Eleanor I expect you'll be back in Leeds. I'm back home now. I met Andy Cooper yesterday evening. He seemed to want to explain himself, but he got upset and left. Weird.*

Eleanor: *Yes, we're home. Well, at least there was no unpleasantness.*

Eleanor: *Better than a fight!*

Greg: *Possibly.*

There's nothing like a death to highlight the futility and the brevity of human life. Greg had spent just two days away from his home but the continuity of his everyday life had been interrupted. He'd wandered outside of his safety bubble. Apart from Andy Cooper, it had been a pleasant social excursion. Nevertheless, he felt unsettled. He didn't immediately reconnect with his own habits. He felt himself a stranger in his own home while he tried to rediscover the familiarity of his surroundings. He felt that either his home or something in himself had changed.

Surely a man of such maturity couldn't be changed over a period of two days? And although Greg first considered and then quite rationally rejected such a possibility, he felt a bit different. Not a radical change, certainly not an observable change, but something that had happened during the day of Janey's funeral had altered him, and he wondered how that might play out. He'd lived the past many years feeling a secure and stable sense of his identity. The realisation was disconcerting. He knew a change had occurred but he was yet to discover its nature and its significance.

He was a bit restless, watching the news on television but losing interest. It was the same with other pastimes. After reading a few pages of a book, his thoughts would wander. His appetite was unsatisfied but he couldn't persuade himself to cook. But it was more serious than a loss of concentration – Greg was done with changes. His carefully designed and rather insular lifestyle was exactly as he wanted it to be. The appearance of Johnny fucking change on the horizon threatened him.

Ever since the break-up of his third marriage, Greg had enjoyed the luxury of retirement and the indulgences of living alone. Each and every day he felt grateful for his uncompromised freedom and the absence of demand. He could suit himself. Live every minute of every day in accord with the whims and fancies that came upon him. No one watching, free from judgement, moving at his own pace in his chosen direction.

He could manage minor disruption, and allow himself to be unsettled. He could accept his unfocused concentration without penalty. He could relax with sleepless nights. He could deal with his old friends dying. There was, however, an aspect to his unease that was more disturbing. Somewhere, far away and hidden in the dead of night, wolves were howling. Monks were chanting. He couldn't be sure what it was but he could feel it coming just the same. Each time that his concentration slipped or his thoughts wandered, he was left with the image of Andy Cooper. Andy had appeared cheerful enough at the crematorium but in The Lion later on the same day, Andy had wilted, displaying desperation, unable to regain any semblance of composure. He'd been a sorry sight and this new view of an old foe had been the seed from which Greg's sense of change had grown.

For more than fifty years Greg had maintained a simple understanding of his history with Andy. Greg had suffered at the hands of an arsehole. It wasn't a complex psychological formulation but it had been more than adequate. Andy had indeed acted like an arsehole. However, Greg's brief encounter in the bar of The Lion had placed a question mark against his own judgement. In Greg's experience, arseholes rarely explain themselves.

Andy had introduced an unexpected twist to an almost forgotten story. And worse still, there had been an intention that had been thwarted by his overwhelming emotions, something unspoken. An explanation? Greg didn't want to dwell, he wanted to forget the whole day. Andy had occupied space in Greg's inner world while he grew up. There had been a few reasons why Greg wanted to move his life away from his home town, and Andy Cooper had been one of them. It had taken a few years before he noticed that Andy had gone from his head. Of course he could recall the many instances when Andy had hurt him but the uninvited intrusive memories had stopped.

And now Andy was back, with something to say, but as yet, unable to speak.

SEVEN

SARAH AND CHERYL

IN THE DAYS following her first visit to Mark, Sarah faltered. She hadn't summoned the courage to talk to her husband and as she'd reflected on her conversation with Mark, she realised that she'd left one or two things unsaid. She needed to say a proper goodbye and she looked forward to a second visit, when she hoped to do better. Mindful of her accidental drunkenness, she had again booked a room at The Lion. Chris welcomed her back with extravagant familiarity. She checked in and then walked in the late spring sunshine to the Sanderson house wondering if this would be her last meeting with her oldest friend. It was a sobering thought and she congratulated herself for once again bringing Newcastle Brown Ale, which would surely offer an alternative perspective. Perhaps Cheryl would help her out this time and accept a glass.

She walked with her characteristic purposefulness, hesitating only when she reached the front door. For a moment, the gravity of her task impeded her and she released a sigh.

Cheryl opened the door. "Come on in, Sarah."

Sarah followed her host through to the kitchen. "It's a fine spring day, Cheryl. How are you?" As a school girl, Sarah had been able to identify Cheryl, but little else. Their eyes met and she felt warmth. She wasn't about to lose sight of her purpose but Cheryl's welcome slowed her, offered something more.

"How is Mark?"

"He's very weak. He seems to be fading away. Even since your last visit, he's deteriorated. I'll make some tea and then I'll take you through to see him."

"I'm not in a hurry, Cheryl. I've brought beer again. I hope you don't mind. It was silly really, I don't know why I bought it. I won't expect Mark to drink, but the three of us were close companions for a while – me, Mark and Newcastle Brown Ale. It was only for a few months, Cheryl, when Mark and I were trying to grow up. The beer was our mutual friend, a symbol of our unsteady progress towards adulthood. It seemed to help us. But a cup of tea sounds much more inviting."

Sarah removed her coat and walked across the hall to hang it alongside the resident garments which still included some of Mark's jackets. She turned back towards Cheryl as a shiver shook her shoulders. Somewhere in her unconscious mind, she recognised the unforgiving fact of death. Empty clothes, empty chairs, unspent money, unspoken words. As she recovered herself, she looked at Cheryl and she knew that her brief glimpse into an unknown dark and empty space, into the loneliness and the loss, had not only been witnessed, it had been shared. "We strive all of our lives, Cheryl, do the best that we can. And then... well." She bowed her head and fell silent.

Cheryl swallowed the lump that had suddenly grown in her throat. "Yes, death's a bastard. Come through to the kitchen, Sarah. I'll get the kettle on."

Sarah watched as Cheryl produced the hot drinks. Steaming mugs of tea, and seats at a kitchen table... the currency for social exchange, a declaration of intent. Today, when Sarah had come to visit Mark, she would talk with Cheryl. She was surprised by the ease and bluntness of

Cheryl's statement, but relieved and grateful nevertheless. "I'm afraid that I didn't really know what to say when I came last week. So I needed to come again today. And I must apologise, I was impolite, rushing through to sit with Mark. It didn't occur to me until afterwards that I hadn't taken the trouble to find out anything about you and your life or even to give a proper introduction. I'm Sarah MacDonald." Sarah held out her hand.

Cheryl gave both hands, adding a little warmth to Sarah's rather formal approach. "Cheryl Ward, at your service. Please sit down, Sarah."

Sarah obeyed her host. "I'm afraid my people skills aren't great. I'm trying to get better. I hope you'll forgive me. I have plenty of time today, Cheryl, and I'm interested to know how your life unfolded." Sarah vaguely remembered the Sanderson house from childhood although she had only been inside a few times. "Have you lived here all of your life?"

"No, Mark came to live here after our mother died. I moved back seven years ago to share the house with him. My husband, Graham, died suddenly just a few weeks after his retirement and Mark's health was already failing. To be honest, with Graham gone, I didn't want to live alone in the house we'd lived in together for so long. The house was full of memories. I would have enjoyed them with Graham's company but not by myself. It would have been too painful. I didn't know what to do so I came back home to stay with my little brother."

Sarah had asked her question with genuine interest and without any expectation of opening up such a sensitive topic. She felt clumsy. "I'm sorry."

Cheryl appeared accepting of her interest and her sympathy. She continued her answer. "No, don't apologise. My life flowed without difficulty, Sarah. I loved Graham, he was a good husband. I enjoyed raising my kids. I wanted for nothing. After Graham finally agreed to retire, we anticipated a luxurious lifestyle. We'd done well financially and after

35

years of being busy with work and the children, we had the prospect of spending precious time together. We planned to travel, visit our children, who have all chosen to raise my grandchildren abroad."

"All three of them?"

Cheryl sighed. "Yes, blown on the wind to the various corners of the world, old and new. But then Graham died. Left me on my own, took the future with him. Bastard. That's what I think about death." She sighed deeply. "Graham was never ill. Here and healthy one day, dead and gone the next."

Sarah remained critical of her perceived social ineptitude. Even though she had worked in the NHS as a Consultant Psychiatrist, she had never been an enthusiastic listener. Her consultations had always been brief... identify the symptoms, make the diagnosis, and write the prescription. That had been her modus operandi. Throughout her career she had avoided emotionally loaded life stories. Not because she was disinterested or cold-hearted but she had never felt able to talk about her own feelings, let alone those that arose in others. Emotional landscapes intimidated her, exposed her limitations. But she really was working to do better, trying at this late stage in her life to make emotional connections with her fellow human beings. Rather oddly, in a stranger's kitchen, she sensed an opportunity.

Cheryl had been two years ahead of Sarah and Mark at school. Sarah had known who she was but little more than that. Two years was a world away back then. Cheryl was Mark's sister, there was nothing more. She took a small sip of tea that was still too hot to drink and, despite her discomfort, she pushed herself.

"I imagine that must have been a difficult time for you, after Graham died?"

For a moment Cheryl could only nod, then she found her voice again. "It shook me to the core, broke my heart."

Sarah had managed to travel deep into unfamiliar territory and although the discomfort persisted, so too did her

36

sense of opportunity. Before today, she and Cheryl had no significant knowledge about each other. They hadn't even thought about one another for more than fifty five years. And yet now, through their respective relationships with Mark, their tenuous link strengthened. Sarah's struggle with human connection was lifelong and yet here she was, daring to trust a stranger, sharing a moment of intimacy, unbidden, thrown to her by an angel of death. The two women had walked past each other in school corridors a thousand times without recognition or interest. Only now could their conversation begin.

Sarah sipped again from her mug of tea, feeling dreamlike, somehow removed from the familiar and the worldly. She waited for the critical voice inside her head to taunt her but instead there was an encouraging whisper urging her to speak again. She gained a sense of the moment. She'd approached Cheryl's house expecting an impersonal exchange of polite greetings before sitting at Mark's bedside. But as her host briefly summarised the shattering devastation that her late husband's sudden death had delivered, she settled into her seat, aware now that not only must she listen to Cheryl's story, but that she must also tell her own.

Cheryl paused, unable to read her companion but sensing her tension nevertheless. "I know that years have passed now but I still miss Graham, I still dream about him. I wish he was with me now. I wish I'd told him more often that I loved him. I hope he knew. It was very sudden, a huge heart attack. It's completely different with Mark, a slow process."

Sarah's vague sense of opportunity began to clarify. She felt a connection with Cheryl. "I want to spend some time with my old friend while I can. I hope you don't mind, Cheryl. I know that my reappearance is terribly late in the day, but I'm here now and I'd like to be around with Mark through to the end." She meant every word. She would give something of herself to her dying friend, but there was a second motivation… she wanted to maintain her connection with Cheryl.

"Yes, of course. It's not easy, watching him die. I thought I'd have to do it alone. Your company would be very welcome."

"Well then, we'll do this together." Sarah paused. She felt no hesitation in accepting Cheryl's invitation to stand together while the bastard death went about his work. But mostly her mind was occupied by reflection as she allowed Cheryl's disclosures to penetrate. She was envious and admiring of Cheryl, who had managed to find love in her life. No shame and no blame. But in amongst all of her thoughts there had been a dark and disturbing intruder, a second provocation of envy. Cheryl's husband had died.

Sarah had offered little in response after Mark had told her about Alexander enforcing his banishment. She hadn't felt able to judge how best to consider his health. Would an honest account of her long and loveless marriage have brought anguish or release? Would Mark want to take back his revelation if he saw in her a fierce emotional response?

So she'd held back. She hadn't told him that she and Alexander walked by each other every day without speaking, that they sat in separate rooms, slept in separate beds. She hadn't told him about the pandemic. There was no need to further burden Mark with long life stories now, he was too weak. She had exercised caution, closed down, and yet now as she re-examined her withholding, she questioned herself. He was her best and only friend, always a careful curator of emotional sensibilities. And now his sister, a stranger, had opened her up.

"I'm sorry, Cheryl, that you lost Graham. Life is horribly unfair, and so is death. I experienced a shameful thought while you were talking. It was so awful that I can't tell you." She felt her temperature rising and her cheeks reddened. She was suddenly agitated, unsure of herself. She gulped a couple of large mouthfuls of tea. She needed an escape. "I should go through and see Mark. I don't suppose I can tempt you with a glass of brown ale?"

Cheryl had baulked at the prospect of brown ale, so Sarah stood the unopened bottle on Mark's bedside table, the three of them alone together again with the rest of the world excluded.

"Now come on, Sarah. You only get one visit to a dying man." He held out a weak arm, but gave a strong smile.

Sarah walked briskly into an embrace and she held him. It was most unlike her, but she'd given herself plenty of encouragement. Sarah considered herself to be a miserable failure with personal and emotional communications but she would never be able to forgive herself if she messed up today. He felt almost weightless.

"You're very thin," she said, releasing him back into a wall of pillows.

"I know, I should be dead by now. I'm doing my best, but it's not as easy as you might think. How was your journey?"

"The roads weren't too crowded, it was fine." She nodded at the beer bottle beside him. "I bought us a drink."

"I can't drink, Sarah. You'll have to drink for us both." Mark watched her smile but she made no move for the beer. "Cheers," he said, nevertheless.

Sarah settled herself. "Yes, good health." Not the best choice of phrase.

"I didn't expect you to come again."

"You won't get rid of me as easily as that. I intend to be a regular visitor."

"That would be nice," Mark replied. He could feel his own demise and he had no power to fight. He was close. "I wasn't sure if you'd want to come again after what I told you last time. I'm glad we're still friends and I hope I haven't harmed your marriage."

39

"No, Mark, you did no harm. Alexander and I aren't close. We live in the same house, but there's no love between us. I don't believe there ever was. What he did to you that day in the barn was unforgivable, although he's committed many more serious crimes. I should have left him years ago."

Sarah looked at him. His eyes were closed. She assumed he'd fallen into sleep, but he spoke.

"You still have time, Sarah. Time to go again. Do that for me. Go again."

He'd lost weight from all parts of his body, except for his eyelids which had become unbearably heavy. Mercifully, he slept.

EIGHT

SARAH, COVID19 AND ALEXANDER

HER TWO CONSECUTIVE THURSDAY EXCURSIONS, with the added luxury of an overnight stay, had given Sarah some distance from her home and her husband – a spiritual retreat and some thinking time. She'd made a commitment to visit every Thursday. That would need careful negotiation. Alexander had been irritated by her first visit and rudely objectionable to the second. He'd made himself clear in characteristic fashion.

Sarah had bent and swayed to his will for decades. She'd intended to confront him after Mark had revealed his banishment but then she had lost her resolve. Chickened out. Even for this conversation, she'd thought long and hard about what to say.

Sarah had adapted to her bad marriage. She played her domestic and social roles, she had a career. But she'd allowed Alexander to rule. There seemed nothing to gain from objection. She'd sucked it up. And now she felt the weight of her task – she must speak an intention that would rile him.

"How is the farm?" asked Sarah.

They were both seated at the breakfast table. Toast, scrambled eggs and coffee. All prepared by Sarah. Alexander could and occasionally would prepare himself some food, but only if he'd needed to eat and Sarah had been elsewhere. Up until the pandemic, that is.

Alexander was unprepared for the question. He looked up from his plate of food, looking for information. "Yes, it's all going along perfectly well. We receive so little for the milk that I wonder why we bother, but we manage."

Sarah took a deep breath. It had taken her two or three years of marriage to understand that she was unhappy with her husband. By then both of her children had arrived, Robin first, born like his father with a covering of ruddy brown hair, and then Scarlet who favoured her mother. She made the best of her situation but she and Alexander were never close. She fulfilled her roles. They moved around their living space and lived a life together, passing on the stairs, repeating well practised patterns and rituals, coldly and co-operatively coexisting.

Then Covid hit. The first Covid lockdown had been challenging. Just the two of them – 24 seven. It wasn't just Sarah, it was both of them. They couldn't stand to be together in the same room. To sit together was to confront the inescapable desert in which their relationship existed. They had become strangers. It was Sarah who removed herself. That allowed Alexander to blame her. They had a very large house and Sarah used different rooms. She continued to prepare food for her husband and to fulfil her established domestic roles, but once the food was plated, she'd take her meal on a tray into her exclusive living space.

There had been a few unpleasant arguments as they struggled to negotiate a new pattern of life for Covid lockdowns. Alexander had often become angry. He was scary and he'd said some nasty things. It was a strange time. Their already ailing marriage had disintegrated. It had been infected by Covid19 and no vaccine on Earth would offer recovery.

"Mark is very poorly. He won't live much longer." Sarah

was proceeding cautiously. She left a silent space, inviting his response.

Alexander was suspicious. His wife rarely sat with him at the dining table. He could feel that there was something in the air.

"I see." His eyes remained focused on the toast in front of him.

"His sister, Cheryl, is on her own with him. I want to see Mark but I also want to stand alongside Cheryl. I've promised her that I'll visit every Thursday. She needs some support." Sarah saw the annoyance rise in Alexander. No surprise. But she'd rehearsed and before he could voice his disapproval, she played her trump card. "Poor Cheryl. Perhaps you'd like to come with me next week? It would give you the chance to say goodbye to Mark." She braced herself, ready for the outrage, but she was smiling inside. She'd learnt how best to manage her husband. She hadn't the power to prevent his anger but sometimes she could show him where to direct it. Without the clearly ludicrous suggestion that Alexander might accompany her, he would have used his anger to prevent her from further visits. But now she hoped that her final provocation would deflect him.

Alexander tossed his toast across the table. His eyes were glazed. He was furious. "Why the hell would I want to visit him. I don't know him. Do you seriously expect me to drive half way around the planet to visit a dying a man who I don't know. The idea is utterly ridiculous."

"I'm sorry," said Sarah, quietly celebrating her small victory. "You're right."

Alexander was momentarily disarmed by the apology. He was exasperated. "Why the hell you feel the need to travel up there to see him, I've no idea." He was regaining position. "He was always a pathetic wimp." Back to full steam now. "You're a stupid fucking cow." He was red in the face.

Sarah would still accompany Alexander to social events within their circle of friends and acquaintances and to family

43

gatherings. In the public eye, she remained visible as the dutiful wife. The two of them were able to maintain their public image, but behind the closed doors of their substantial home, there was no pretence. Not after Covid.

Alexander seemed unable to contain himself. He tipped his cup high to drink the last of his coffee, then he threw the empty cup across the kitchen. Bone china shattered and splintered. Sarah knew that whatever action she might take, whatever words she might speak, would be wrong. He would pounce on her next move. So she didn't make one. No eye contact, she sat like a statue, she gave him nothing. Alexander swept his right arm across the table, collecting more dishes and some items of cutlery which landed and crashed on the floor.

Sarah remained unmoved. She'd survived and she'd asserted her intention. Result.

Alexander shoved his chair back and stood facing her, wanting her eyes. But still Sarah held her nerve.

He looked at the broken crockery. "Look at the mess in my house, it's a fucking tip. What are you for, Sarah? Get this mess cleaned up."

Sarah watched as he marched quickly from the room. She released a sigh, having divined a route through the minor items on today's agenda. If ever she wished to reclaim ownership of her own life, there would have to be more dangerous conversations. Nevertheless, she wished.

She stared ahead without focus. The silence that now followed Alexander's explosive outburst felt oppressive. He'd left the room but his presence surrounded her. She heard him striding across the hall floor and then the sound of the house door closing behind him. Her shoulders dropped and she released the breath that she'd held, unknowingly.

Sarah had recognised the impact of Covid on her relationship, but in addition she felt herself changed by the pandemic as an individual. Something had happened to her. Without the busyness of her life, the everyday occupational and social experiences, she'd bumped into emotion. It was a domain that both she and Alexander had habitually avoided.

Sarah had never been a fan of television. She could listen to music and she enjoyed books, but mostly she liked to be physically occupied. But when Covid hit, she was glued to her seat in front of the telly. It was her new connection with the world. Somewhere along the way through the pandemic, Sarah felt for the suffering people of the world. As she witnessed the separation, the pain and the loss, watching it on TV, her heart was breaking. Her own parents had already died. She'd worn black clothes but she'd cried no tears. Not for her parents, not for anyone. That was her heartbreak. She'd never loved.

NINE

SARAH AND CHERYL

DESPITE THE VIOLENCE of Alexander's objection, Sarah was driving to Stokesley again, making her weekly pilgrimage to North Yorkshire, and to her room at The Lion. It was 30th May, 2024. Mark had died two days ago. It had upset her when Cheryl had phoned to tell her Mark had gone. She had just about managed to offer condolence, then she'd ended the call, wanting to ensure that Alexander remained ignorant and that her Thursday visits were not threatened.

She wanted to see Cheryl, to continue their dialogue.

She wanted her weekly excursion into dangerous territory, post-Covid territory. So she'd kept the news of Mark's death, and her reaction to the news, hidden from Alexander. And she'd shielded herself, put Cheryl's news into a waiting area. Finally, with her journey safely commenced, she could attend to the fact that her long and mostly lost friend was gone. For two days, her well practised stoicism had served her well, guided by her instinct for pragmatism. Now, alone in her car, she allowed the shield to slip away and she could attend to her own reaction. There were no desperate regrets, but she needed quiet. She was an habitual Radio Four listener when driving, nevertheless, as the first raw feelings of grief surfaced, she turned off the radio and felt tears rolling down her cheeks. She had already joined the motorway and she criticised herself for poor timing – the inside of a car, travelling on grey tarmac. Mark deserved a better place, she thought. But she drove on, realising that although the circumstances were uninspiring, she felt safe in her small metal vehicle, alone and beyond reach, travelling. For a woman who had always been frightened of her own emotions, there could be no better place to get a first taste of her grief. She wasn't broken hearted, she didn't really understand her tears, but alone in the car, she could allow them. And she did.

The tears and the miles rolled until they ran out. It was an emotional journey.

As had become her habit, Sarah parked her car at The Lion and took her overnight case inside, even though she knew she was several hours from check-in time.

Chris appeared pleased to see her and gave a warm welcome. He accepted her early arrival without question.

"Your room's ready, Sarah," he said.

Sarah was disarmed by her relationship with Chris. She hardly knew him and yet he'd shared confidences with her, commented on her choice of clothes. "Oh, Chris, you're so helpful. I'm very grateful."

Chris put his right hand on Sarah's left shoulder. "I'm so sorry about your friend."

She had told him on the phone when she made the booking, and she allowed herself to be drawn forward into an awkward embrace. Chris was more than a foot taller than Sarah and, despite his familiar manner, they didn't know each other. She waited just a second before pulling away.

Chris was a pleasant man who broke social rules and transgressed boundaries, but his heart was in the right place, and Sarah appreciated his effort. "Thank you," she said.

Maybe she was swimming, or floating. In water, anyway. Sarah had managed her feelings when Cheryl delivered the news, kept things in check. Now for the second time, tears

47

filled her eyes. She'd assumed that her crying in the car had been the full show, and now, as fresh tears appeared, she felt surprised by the depth and intensity of her grief. But not at all surprised that she felt awkward in this emotional state with Chris, young, human, and inappropriate.

"I'll take my bag up to the room and I'll walk to Cheryl's house."

For the third consecutive Thursday, Sarah walked towards Cheryl's front door. But this time Mark wouldn't be home. He'd slipped away between visits, brought the sad process to its inevitable conclusion. She was close, right at the front door, and she hesitated, wondering how she'd feel inside the house. Maybe she'd feel warmth, maybe cold. Maybe she'd feel death.

She had no choice, not at this stage. She rang the bell.

Cheryl opened the door. "Oh Sarah."

They held each other. Mark's ghost watched on, uneasily, as they settled into their embrace. Initially Sarah experienced hesitation, almost panic after her earlier hug with Chris, but the misgiving was squeezed out of her by the certainty in Cheryl's warm arms. Cheryl was the bigger woman, taller than Sarah and with more flesh on her bones, a robust figure quite unlike her little brother who had always seemed delicate.

Sarah felt herself relaxing. For a few seconds, her head seemed to be spinning. It wasn't just that she was allowing herself to be held for the second time in one day, which was in itself remarkable, she was participating fully, gladly even, in a deeply emotional transaction that felt wholly good, and that required this physical expression. She felt safe and comforted. It was just a few seconds, that was all. But it felt like a lifetime. There was a profound and shared sense of sadness. And rather oddly, the beginning of celebration.

During the pandemic, Sarah had watched the frustration

of people forbidden from physical comfort, experiencing the pain of isolation. The same TV drama replayed each day, human connections put on hold. She'd struggled back then in her solitude, confronted by her own failure to connect, with her husband and with the world. She and Alexander had been that way for years. Long before Covid, they had established their own self-imposed restrictions. But it wasn't until the pandemic that she'd first started to recognise the coolness of her adaptation, and to feel the agony of regret. The discomfort that had grown in her during those weeks of lockdown had stirred around inside her ever since. And now, in her brief (and timeless) embrace with Cheryl, she settled. Without the need for physical restraint, Alexander had shackled her, held her back from the world. Now, in the firm hold of Cheryl's caring arms, she experienced a sense of release, and she moved a step closer to understanding her sense of celebration... she was grieving with a new and unrestrained freedom.

If she'd walked past Cheryl a month earlier, she wouldn't have known her. Two polite conversations on her way to sit at Mark's bedside, was the entirety of their relationship. Nevertheless, Sarah had never felt more connected in her life. There was both reluctance and purpose as she pulled back so that she could focus. "Hello, Cheryl."

Cheryl stepped aside. "Come on in. Let me take your coat. I'd convinced myself that you'd wait until the funeral but I'm so glad that you've come."

Cheryl was flawless, calm and composed. She made tea and gave Sarah a brief description of Mark's descent into death. The Macmillan nurse had given good support throughout but especially during the final two days. The GP had provided morphine. The three of them had led Mark peacefully to his last breath.

"I'm glad he's gone, relieved," she said as she took her seat opposite Sarah. "The funeral is arranged a week today."

"You've given generously, Cheryl. Mark was fortunate to

have you as his sister." This was Sarah's third visit to Cheryl's house. Even so, she felt intimately familiar. Even the smell of the place. Lavender, middle age and premature death.

They spent a few minutes settling, chatting while Cheryl prepared coffee and fruitcake and updated Sarah with details for the forthcoming funeral. They became quiet. There was no awkwardness or discomfort and neither of them rushed to fill the silence. They were waiting, facilitating a shift in focus and mood, getting ready to extend their dialogue.

Cheryl smiled. The update was complete and they'd even managed a brief exchange about the weather. Now she turned to a more personal agenda. "Sarah, I remember that in one of our previous conversations, you said that you had poor people skills. I thought that was a strange remark. I enjoy your company."

"Yes, in some respects I can communicate ably enough but I'm very unsure of myself with personal exchanges. All through school I always believed that people found no interest in me, didn't want me around." Sarah almost started to explain further but she bailed out. "It's a long story and not very interesting."

"I'm interested. I vaguely remember that you seemed a bit quiet at school but I thought that was because of your asthma."

"That was a big part of it, certainly my illness set me apart. My mother tried to wrap me in cotton wool, tried to protect me and she sent me to a very expensive preparatory school. I was frequently absent and I never felt accepted. It was an exclusive school, a preparation for a privileged life. I hated it. Sadly, and against my better judgement, Alexander insisted on sending our children to similarly exclusive establishments. In the end my father argued for a different approach, threw me to the lions. I don't know what his motivation was. I suspect he decided not to waste money educating a sickly child, and so he took me out of prep school and into the state system, where I knew nobody. I hadn't

50

enjoyed my time among the privileged middle classes. I was desperately keen to make friends with the local children, grateful for a second chance, but my asthma was troublesome and the other children had already found their friends. I was an unwanted latecomer, already convinced that nobody wanted me as a friend, already identified as different and so it continued… asthma attacks, absence from school and no real friends. Except for Mark, God rest his soul." A long sigh slowly released from Sarah's chest. "The asthma's not a problem for me anymore. I have my inhalers, and the modern treatments are much improved, but the psychological effect, the feeling of being excluded, is always with me." She observed that she had found herself talking openly. "This is an unusual exception to my restrictive social rules, to talk about myself. You'd have made a better psychiatrist than me, Cheryl."

"Quite possibly," said Cheryl. "I have another question. Last week you confessed to a thought so shameful that you were unable to tell me. You looked uncomfortable and I decided not to question you. I wonder if you feel able to tell me now?"

Sarah was still feeling her way uncertainly into whatever would unfold between them, but even on her previous visits, she'd sensed an opportunity. She was quite unable to explain it to herself, but she felt that her dialogue with Mark's sister could be life changing. Not for the first time, or indeed the last, she felt disarmed by the directness of Cheryl's manner. Sarah had only just got properly comfortable in her seat, Mark's dead body hadn't yet gone cold, and already Cheryl was asking for her most shameful secrets.

"Goodness, Cheryl. I'd forgotten."

Cheryl knew better. "I doubt that. I remember clearly – how could anyone forget such a significant remark." She looked across and smiled to herself as she witnessed Sarah's uncertainty. The latest episode of their Thursday ritual was underway, inescapable and compelling.

Sarah nursed her steaming tea, wondering if her prolonged silence had deflected Cheryl, and avoided the question.

Cheryl sipped from her own cup, undeterred and impatient. "Sarah, if you hadn't wanted to reveal your shameful thought, you wouldn't have mentioned it."

Sarah wasn't entirely without social skills. She'd learned how to steer conversations with Alexander and with many other friends and acquaintances, but clearly she'd met her match with Cheryl. "You appear to be perfectly comfortable asking searching questions. In my experience, that's unusual." She was still buying time, still nervously hesitant.

Cheryl was losing patience. "I don't mean to pry, Sarah. But I think you need to talk. Do you wish that your husband was dead?"

"No, of course not. Not actually dead. Goodness me, no, although sometimes, I'm so annoyed by him." She paused.

"And you wish him dead."

"No, I wouldn't say that," Sarah replied.

"I know, you're far too polite. That's why I said it for you."

The last drops of Sarah's feeble resistance evaporated, and she accepted her new best friend's understanding. She began her confession, still a little hesitant, but without shame.

"Alexander found many ways to restrict me. He didn't want me to have friends. I sit here now and I wonder how I married someone who I never felt comfortable with. It seems ridiculous. I was quite naive, lacking in worldly wisdom, unpractised with protest and self-determination. I grew up conforming to the directions of heartless men and I took my habit into the adult world. It wasn't until the pandemic that I started to change things. Even then, Alexander and I continued to live in the same house, but we became strangers."

For a moment, Cheryl considered her response. She shook her head and smiled at life's cruel irony... she'd enjoyed being close to her husband but now he was gone. Meanwhile, Sarah's loveless and inescapable marriage endured. She swallowed the bitter taste of misfortune. For both of them.

"I don't know if I can really imagine how that must feel, Sarah."

Sarah continued. "In some ways, I was equally to blame. I think I chose to marry Alexander because I didn't know how to make an emotional connection. It's taken a long time for me to work it out. Emotional intelligence was never my strength. During the pandemic, I watched images on television that disturbed me. It still pains me to recall them. Can you remember, human hands pressed against hastily erected perspex partitions, reaching out, desperate for connection. I'd shut myself away from emotions for most of my life, but when I watched those images, tears flowed. It wasn't only the pain of their enforced separation, I also saw my own shortcomings reflected, my own failure to connect."

"I can remember. They were powerful images."

"Since then, I've tried to change my ways. It's not easy, Cheryl, changing. But I'm here now, talking to you. Perhaps that's a sign of progress. I still haven't found the courage to take the final steps of separation, to get free of Alexander, to escape from Hurtmoor."

She waited for a response but Cheryl remained still and silent. "The prospect frightens me, Cheryl. Alexander likes things his own way, he won't want to hear my message. He can become fiercely angry and he has an appetite for vengeance. He once threatened Mark with a gun."

Cheryl winced as she listened, taking in this shocking revelation, sensing Sarah's fear and foreboding, and she held her impulse to offer encouragement in check. "I'm not sure what to say. You must look after your safety, Sarah. If there's anything that I can do to help, you only have to ask."

The conversation drifted. Sarah half listened as Cheryl described the arrangements for Mark's funeral. But mostly she introspected, slightly lightheaded and with a growing sense of the power of her own words. She'd said it out loud, revealed the sham of her marriage, confessed to her fear. The discontent that had lived inside her like a heavy dark fluid, had taken on a new form, become real. Somehow Cheryl wasn't just opening her up, she wanted to know what was inside. More than that, in amongst the hesitations and penetrations of their dialogue, they were forging an alliance.

They had watched Mark die. The two women, together.

TEN

GREG

GREG HAD BEEN out on his bike. As was his custom, he'd cycled for about twenty miles, listening to the Kinks through his new buds. He showered and dressed before walking down the stairs of his three bedroomed, semi-detached suburban house and into his kitchen, hungry for breakfast. As he proceeded through his daily rituals and habits he had space in his head, the capacity for thought. And there he was again. Andy Cooper.

He looked at his phone to find out what day it was... Thursday 30th May. A fortnight had passed since Janey's funeral, and on every one of those days Greg had thought about Andy, trying to find a clue, something he'd missed as a child but which might now be comprehensible. He'd reflected particularly on Janey's reactions when Andy had bullied him. Although the friendship between he and Janey had been strong, and although she had sympathised when he suffered Andy's assaults, she had not been entirely convincing in her condemnations. She'd often said to Greg that Andy was an idiot, but no matter how deeply Greg searched his memory, he couldn't recall an instance when Janey had addressed her insult directly to Andy.

He decided that he'd text Eleanor.

Greg: *Hi Eleanor. Please can you ask Sue if she thinks that Janey liked Andy Cooper?*

He was only halfway through his bowl of granola when his phone pinged.

Eleanor: *Sue's out, I'll ask her when she gets back home.*

Eleanor: *Why do you ask?*

He finished his breakfast, considering Eleanor's question. Greg was aware that he'd chosen to contact Eleanor, who he'd met for the first time at the funeral, rather than Sue who he'd gone to school with, even though it was Sue he wanted to question. That was interesting. And he sat for a while puzzling at his observation. He felt that he and Eleanor were in tune. She had seemed to be genuinely interested to know him. He chuckled to himself, identifying his talent for mismatch as the story of his life. Women with whom he felt a strong affinity, those who would be his ideal romantic partners, were either lesbians or married to Brad Pitt, or just totally out of his league. It had always been the same. The right women eluded him, and he married the wrong ones with disconcerting ease and regularity.

And Eleanor had come good again here. Her first text reply would have done fine, but in the second Eleanor had gone the extra mile, shown her interest. Greg hadn't had a great deal of experience with lesbian women. He held no prejudice but no aggressive interest either. He wondered if perhaps Eleanor might be bisexual. Quite possibly, thought Greg, but he left her question unanswered.

He watched the news on TV for half an hour, washed the pots from the previous evening, and he managed to concentrate for almost an hour as he read a book. Then his phone pinged again.

Eleanor: *Not as far as Sue can remember. She said no one liked Andy.*

Eleanor: *What on earth made you ask?*

Greg wanted to engage, immediately appreciating Eleanor's continuing interest, but it wasn't an easy question to answer in a text message. Greg had mixed feelings about texting. He felt the same way about other written communications. He felt they offered limited scope and a high risk of misunderstanding. He started to type his reply but after three long sentences, he'd hadn't managed to say anything. He deleted what he'd written. Then his phone rang – an unknown caller.

"Hi, Greg. It's me, Sue."

"Hello, Sue, how are you?" Greg welcomed the call. Actual conversation was more his style.

"Yes, I'm well. Why do you think that Janey and Andy were friends?"

Eleanor's interest had pleased him, now he enjoyed Sue's direct approach. "I'm not sure what to think, Sue. It's only that, when I think back, Janey would diss him but never to his face. That's all."

"Did anybody? You'd have had to be pretty sure of yourself to have a go at Andy. I wouldn't read too much into that, Greg. Hang on a minute, Eleanor's trying to say something."

Greg waited while an indistinct conversation took place between the two women.

Sue resumed. "What are you doing this weekend? Why don't you come across to Leeds? You can tell us all about what happened at The Lion, Eleanor will cook some fabulous food, and we'll take it from there."

Greg was unprepared for this invitation and convinced it had come from Eleanor. "Okay, I'd love to. Thank you, Sue."

They made the arrangements. Greg would drive over to Leeds on Saturday morning, they'd have a pint for lunch in a beer garden, and then dinner back at the house. Greg looked forward to his dinner engagement. He hadn't enjoyed the company of another human being since the funeral.

ELEVEN
24 HOURS IN LEEDS

GREG WASN'T AT ALL unhappy with his life. He'd split his adult years pretty well down the middle, twenty-five years trying to make his three marriages work and still found more than twenty years for a single life. He'd given up now, accepting the prospect of growing old alone. He would content himself with the company of friends and watch his grandchildren open their Christmas presents. The adventures of love had been and gone. Greg had had his moments, but from here on in, it would just be 'me time'.

He'd learned to exist in a bubble of self-sufficiency, no longer up for the challenge of human entanglement. He'd given the relationship option major opportunities. He met Mona in his final year at university. They had married three years later when she was heavily and happily pregnant with Amy. Ten years later they had had a daughter and they had divorced. He managed to meet, marry and divorce Dawn within four eventful and unhappy years. It was almost twelve years later before he got together with Sophie. They were never right together but they struggled on for nearly ten years before admitting defeat.

He sat in the garden at The Feather and Beak trying to give a brief account of his relationship history to Sue and

Eleanor. He didn't mind talking about it but he wanted to be brief. There were more interesting things to talk about.

"So, there you have it, the life and times of Greg Whitehead. Not a glorious tale. Thankfully some people live interesting and successful lives. Anyway, I'm done with all of that now. What about you two?" He hoped he'd given them enough.

"Oh, hang on a minute. I have a few questions," said Eleanor. She was a woman who asked questions.

"Ask away," said Greg.

"What was Sophie like?"

"She was a decent sort, you know, good hearted. She worked in recruitment. I've no idea why I married her, we weren't suited." Greg held out his hands and gave a shrug of his shoulders, indicating that his answer was complete.

"So as a grown man in his forties…" Eleanor paused to do the maths. "Forties and fifties, I guess, you went ahead and married unsuitable partners. Why on earth would you do that?"

Greg had asked himself the same question many times. "That's my point, Eleanor. Finding the wrong women is a speciality, a skill matched only by my talent for allowing more suitable prospects to pass me by. I'm not proud of it, but I'm bloody good at it."

"Well, I think you should try again." She turned to her wife. "You agree, don't you, Sue."

"Absolutely," Sue confirmed. "When you and I were fifteen, I considered you as a potential husband."

"I should bloody well hope so."

Sue laughed. "There were others on my shortlist, Greg. Don't flatter yourself too much. Anyway, I always knew that you had the hots for Sarah Buxton."

"Yes, Sarah's a great example. I could have loved her happily, forever. I believe she married Brad Pitt. I appreciate the encouragement but there's no chance. I've found my peace. I'm happy. Living with another is too difficult for me, living with myself is easy. It's a no brainer. Can I ask you two a question?"

Sue responded. "Go for it."

"Did either of you have a relationship with a man? You know, when you were younger, before you'd been with a woman."

Eleanor answered again. "Yes, we both tried that. I tried a few times actually. I think that's true of lots of gay women of our generation. We grew up with a clear message in the culture. A woman must find a man. I got that message. I'm sure it was the same for Sue. When we were young children, we didn't write stories about children who grew up to find a same sex partner. We wrote about mum and dad and two kids. I guess it's different now. Thankfully."

Greg nodded. "There were no stories about the kid who grew up with a determination to remain single either. I think I married Mona because I thought that was what I was supposed to do, you know, become a part of a couple, knock out a few kids. I was afraid to be left on the shelf, unwanted. A failure. Making the best of an imperfect match was a better look than being alone. Foolish really."

Sue looked at him. "Yes, I agree. It was foolishness." Sue was a woman who made statements, quick and honest judgements. She hadn't been so forthright at school.

Eleanor felt the need to soften her wife's message. "I wouldn't call it foolishness, Greg. We all take a few wrong turns. And yes, the cultural message was so loud that it never occurred to me that I was gay."

Greg felt as if he'd been waiting for this conversation for years. "Even now, seventy years old, even though my life is fine, I still judge myself as a failure in the world of personal relationships. But I'm learning to live with it, and to die with it, for that matter."

"Hmm…" Eleanor stroked her chin. "I think you should try again, Greg. You don't look seventy, you're quite handsome. Get yourself on Tinder, man."

And they laughed and talked in the spring sunshine while more beer was consumed. Greg smiled to himself, quite unsure about how he could feel so much at ease with these two strangers, more relaxed than he'd ever felt with Sophie. Or with Mona and Dawn.

Greg should've followed his hosts' example and finished the afternoon's entertainment with coffee. But the sun was shining and it felt like heaven, like youthfulness, to be out drinking with friends. So he ordered a third pint of John Smith's before a slightly wobbly walk back to the house. He went up to his room to throw some cold water across his face, trying to reinvigorate. He woke up two hours later, took a shower and went downstairs to apologise.

"I'm sorry, Eleanor. I fell asleep. Too much beer. Please forgive me."

But it was Sue who responded first. "Certainly not," she said, grinning.

Eleanor was more generous. "You're forgiven. Come on through to the kitchen. You can keep me company while I finish the cooking."

Greg followed her and found a seat at the kitchen table. "I don't remember Sue being... well, as she is now. She speaks boldly and she has a great sense of humour. She was quite timid at school."

Sue entered the kitchen as he spoke. "Yes, I was a quiet girl. When we were talking at the pub, I thought about that. I didn't know who I was. That's the truth of it. What's a young girl meant to say when she hasn't yet discovered herself? Were you surprised to find that I'm a lesbian?"

"Yes."

"Is that it?"

"I had absolutely no idea, Sue. In 1967 I assumed that everyone was heterosexual."

"So did I, oddly enough. I was in my mid-twenties before I worked out that sex and relationships went much better with women. Even then it took a long time, decades, before I

61

felt able to live openly, to accept who I was. To accept myself well enough to be able to speak boldly, and to be with Eleanor. To be honest, I had a hard time, really a period of many years when I lived an unfulfilled life. It's amazing now, at this age, that I've learned to live with myself, almost to like myself."

"Sue, you were always top drawer. But I get what you're saying. It was different in 1967. Your lot were barely legal, far from accepted."

Sue formed an expression containing a smile and a grimace, appreciating and condemning his clumsy affection. Eleanor wanted to chastise him but she didn't want to lose her thread. She gave him the sharp end of her elbow, and accepted his apologetic and over-satisfied grin. She was reflecting on their earlier conversation. "I can be a bit pushy, Greg. I don't mean to be but I get terribly frustrated with people sometimes. You don't have to go on Tinder." She thought that perhaps she'd spoken out of turn, but even in the midst of her apology, she couldn't resist a little further encouragement. "Although I bet you'd do alright." And she still hadn't finished. "I'm nearly seventy as well, Greg, and this is the best it's ever been for me. Sue's perfect for me. I've never felt so good with another human being. I think that's why I got frustrated when you said you were done. It's still possible, Greg. Don't turn your back on love."

"Okay, Tinder, here I come. I'm happy for you, guys. I really am. But I'm done. Unless you come across a gorgeous woman who understands what being seventy means and who loves to watch old movies, you can consider me to have left the game. I'm an ex-player. I tried to love and I lost. What the hell, I found a better path. I don't want to sit at home getting anxious about whether anyone swiped me on Tinder, become a sex slave to social media. I've got better things to do." Greg moved the conversation. "I don't do this sort of thing very often. Spend an evening having dinner with friends. I do it now and again, you know, a couple of times a year. And never at my house." Greg looked around him. "Your home is warm, I feel very comfortable. I think it's a combination of the environment and the fine company. The alcohol might also be a factor." Greg examined himself. The beer may indeed have helped him but even despite his rather solitary life, he was at ease in fine company, able to speak openly.

"Well, thank you, I'm happy that you're here, Greg," said Eleanor. "Were you on your own during the lockdowns?"

Greg was disarmed by her question. "My third marriage ended a few years before the coronavirus pandemic started. I spent a lot of time alone at home. And I still do, although now it's a choice, I think. I seem to be content. I don't think that I've actually had the virus, but Covid19 changed me."

Eleanor turned from the cooker to face him. She had quite an intense manner when she engaged in conversation. "Changed you how?" she said.

Greg really felt her presence, the force of her, the unmistakable human interest. "I'm less outgoing, more inclined to stay at home. I live a quieter life and quite a solitary life. It's not a sad confession, Eleanor. I have my family and my friends. I'm actually very fortunate in both respects. I choose to spend a lot of time with my own company. I don't suppose it's healthy but I seem to be doing fine." Greg had first apprehended this observation in 2021. Back then he'd expected that he'd gradually re-establish a social life. But he'd made little change, still sitting comfortably at home, while one or two of his old friends were dying.

Eleanor gained interest. "The pandemic changed us all, Greg, but not everyone noticed." Eleanor had always maintained that the pandemic had come as a gift, a chance for the human race to pause for thought. A chance missed.

She carried a large caldron across to the kitchen table, where Greg and Sue waited, both of them hungry, mostly for Eleanor's company.

Eleanor turned off the electric lights, and lit candles. Now they sat at a small square wooden table. Amy Winehouse played at a volume that allowed both speech and listening. Eleanor was without the bold honesty that Sue could never escape, but her personal skills were impressive. She was the homemaker, the listener.

Greg was distracted by the smell of the curry. "I hope that tastes as good as it smells." He helped himself, quickly filling his plate. "Well, I'll probably find my way back into the world once I get on Twitter."

Eleanor corrected him. "Tinder, Greg."

They drank wine, and created an atmosphere of conviviality. The conversation meandered through politics, art, and personal histories, with an easy flow. Eleanor had made a great curry. By eleven o'clock they'd retired to their rooms. As Greg laid in his bed, he noticed not for the first time that he felt more acutely alone when he slept in someone else's house. When there was somebody with him, a witness to his failure.

Greg enjoyed his excursion to Leeds. Even though he'd spent several hours in the company of his hosts, he felt slightly reluctant to start the journey home. He was almost half way back to Middlesbrough when it occurred to him that he hadn't spoken about Andy Cooper. The newly emerging mystery of Andy had been the prompt for his invitation to Leeds but Greg hadn't given him a thought. And right on cue his Volkswagen's unfeeling voice spoke Eleanor's text: *We forgot to ask about Andy.*

Until Andy had arrived at the front of his mind, he'd reflected positively on his time in Leeds, noting with interest that he'd felt fully at ease, happily engaged in social interaction. The coincidence of Eleanor's text with his own realisation, added to the afterglow of the whole weekend.

His phone rang. "Hi, Sue. We're not going to talk about Andy now, are we? I'm enjoying the drive."

"No. It's not about Andy. I'm afraid I'm the bearer of bad news. Mandy's just phoned me. Mark Sanderson has died. I thought you'd want to know."

"Oh, Christ. They're dropping like flies, Sue." Greg hadn't seen Mark since 'A' levels. But he'd liked Mark and sadness seeped into him. Then it occurred to him that another funeral would be coming. Greg's social life had caught fire. "Please let me know about the funeral arrangements," he said, trying to quieten his excitement.

"Yes, of course. Eleanor and I will definitely be going. Did Andy Cooper bully Mark?"

"No, I'm pretty sure that he didn't."

"I wonder if Andy will show his face again? Anyway, I'll let you go. I'll phone again when I hear about the funeral."

TWELVE
ANDY AND JANEY

ANDY GREW up as the second of six children, produced at yearly intervals, by Brian and Kath. Five of their children were well behaved. They did pretty well at school, and they had plenty of friends. And then there was Andy. Who was disliked, a bully. A bad child.

How did that happen? Why? Everyone else in the family had accepted their world without complaint but not Andy. Ungrateful little bugger. Of course, Andy's tendencies towards bullying and unsociability were not the instruction of a rogue gene or some irrational will for evil, they were the actions of a boy who carried a dark secret, a badness inside of him. He'd felt a deep sense of shame, and some anger. And as a young boy alone in the darkness, he had needed somehow to exercise some power. He couldn't tell the truth and he couldn't stay quiet. So he messed up at school, got into fights, scraped his knees and became a bully. He hadn't known what else he might do.

Greg Whitehead had been one of Andy's long-term victims. There'd been others, some of whom were bullied more harshly than Greg, but the ten-year duration of Greg's term as a target exceeded all of his fellow sufferers.

The badness in Andy was well known in his small home

town. He wasn't wanted in Stokesley. Even his own family wanted him gone. With no sense of belonging and a tendency towards violence, there could only be one destination for Andy, and the army had welcomed him with open arms. It took a while but Andy adjusted to army life, the discipline held him in place and for the first time in his life he was one of the team. He trained hard and developed new skills, learning to survive out in hostile field environments.

He served fifteen years, stationed at bases in Catterick, Cypress, and Germany, and he fought for his country in 1982. Andy distinguished himself in the Falklands conflict and he was honoured with multiple medals and awards, but his moment of glory was also the beginning of the end of his military service. He'd led a company of men through harsh country and into battle, and he fought without fear until his mission was achieved. He accepted the awards and a promotion but he'd watched some of his buddies shot to pieces, seen enough of war, had his fill of fighting, and two years later he was back in civvy street, back to Stokesley.

There was no hero's welcome waiting. Andy drifted from one job to the next, drinking heavily and finding trouble at the weekends. Until he met Polly, who managed to look past his thorny exterior, who saw his neediness and who won his heart. Polly was brilliant, strong as an ox, with the patience of a saint. She put up with more than she should have, including heavy alcohol intake during the first couple of years, but she stuck by him. She kept the house and she looked after him.

And such was their life together. Andy, somewhat diminished by history and by drinking, needed Polly's strength and stability. Through their ups and downs, Polly stayed solid and slowly she steered him to a more purposeful path, taking him for hikes in the Yorkshire dales, wild camping out on the moors. Andy got himself reacquainted with his soldiering skills, foraging for food, building fires, surviving on the land. He loved being out in the open air, wearing camouflage gear, pursuing a mission, although the only shots from Andy these days came from his camera – his constant companion.

And so it went along, until the spring of 2020 when some changes occurred. Mostly he was able to shut out the images from the Falklands, the detached limbs and the lifeless bodies, but occasionally they would come to him in nightmares. They were distressing moments but quite infrequent and he'd learned to accept them. But 2020 brought change, pictures on the television adding new weight to his post-trauma reaction. He watched an innocent young American, George Floyd, fighting for life and breath, and he watched hospital wards full of Covid patients, also struggling for life and breath.

Those news stories resonated, breached his defences, and Andy was exposed to all of his traumas, those from nearly forty years ago in the Falklands and those from much further back to the dark secrets of his early childhood. Disturbing dreams became so frequent and frightening that he tried to avoid sleep, listening to local radio phone-in shows late into the night. That was the effect of the pandemic on Andy Cooper... his insomnia intensified and he started to listen to the radio.

On the 23rd July 2020 the phone-in focused on childhood trauma and Andy made his call. He never gave his name and when his call went 'live' he didn't manage to say very much. But Janey North was listening. She recognised his voice and she knew his secret.

Andy made his call to the radio programme but several more months passed before his path crossed Janey's. They had hardly spoken to each other since school, although they had probably walked past each other in the street on several occasions. Even though they lived in the same town, they had disappeared from each other's thoughts, but once Janey had heard his voice on the radio, first stepping forwards to speak and then pulling back, she kept her eyes open. She spotted him in the chemist, in grey camouflage trousers and shirt. She'd watched him for a minute, assessing the effects of forty-five years. Her eyes had been drawn to his body, a strong wiry physique that should have belonged to a much younger man. Then she looked at a face that betrayed its age, heavy lines in leathery sun-tanned skin, and sadness branded into eyes that had seen too much.

And finally, he got her story. Janey had explained to him how she, as a very young and powerless girl, had tried to manage the situation like a grown up. Janey's information had surprised him. He'd always been convinced that he was entirely alone with his dark secret. But she'd figured it out, more or less, known at least half of the truth, and after decades of secrecy and stagnation, the story that Andy wanted to end, began a new chapter.

They sat on benches, took slow walks in the park, met in coffee shops and tea rooms, and they talked about it all. About their history, about Gwen, about Andy's violence and Janey's guilt, about Greg Whitehead, filling the dark space between them, catching up.

Andy had dared to look at himself and almost to tell the world what had happened to him. It was the beginning of healing, finally he could tell his tale. Polly walked him to the GP surgery and held his hand through months of talking therapy. The anger and the angst in Andy Cooper had cooled after the Falklands, but the burden from his childhood remained. Polly had helped as best she could but the professional help took him to a better place, reduced the self-loathing and the feelings of blame.

He and Janey became friends and they continued their dialogue until she became ill with pancreatic cancer. At their last meeting together, Janey had made her request and Andy had made his promise.

It was a hugely important series of events and he'd reflected many times, talking through it all with his therapist: the images that had triggered new nightmares, listening to the radio, trying to avoid sleep, and in the end he had regained his long lost friend and found the beginnings of self-respect. He was pleased about all of that but still he wanted more reparation. Despite his progress, he still carried recrimination and his promise to Janey was yet to be delivered.

And he'd had his chance, sat down with Greg Whitehead, but he'd blown it. What a disaster. Too much emotion had poured from him. He hadn't expected the meeting to be easy but he hadn't anticipated such a pathetic failure. Each time that he reflected on that night in The Lion, he cringed, frustrated and embarrassed. He needed Polly's strength. "I still can't believe it, Polly, I'm bloody useless."

Polly summoned forbearance. "I can. That's exactly what I expected. Well, maybe not that bad. You were the same when you phoned in to the radio station, took centre stage and then clammed up. I mean, I thought you'd finish up blubbing but I didn't expect you to run away home. You reached a new level there, love. You'll get over it."

"Maybe, but that's not the point. I missed my chance. I can't leave it unfinished."

"You tried your best, Andy."

"I owe him a bit more than that, Pol. He deserves an explanation. I promised Janey that I'd give him the full story and I thought I'd be alright. I just can't believe how I was. I thought I'd dealt with it, cried all the tears. Seriously, after all that therapy, I'd no idea I had all that left inside me."

Polly was starting to lose patience. She'd been hearing the same complaint for days. "Let it go, man. I'm sick of listening to you."

"It's playing on my mind. It's like I need to make my peace with Greg, or else I'll never… I mean, I know I've come a long way. I'm a lot better than I was. That's for sure. But I need to do this, I need him to hear my explanation. It's all I can give him."

"Andy?"

"What?"

"What about the other kids you bullied?"

70

Andy paused for thought. "I've apologised to John Storey. He was good about it. One lad, Eric Souther, gave me a good hiding. I was home on leave, and still in my twenties. He put me in hospital. Fair play to him. If I see any of the others, I'll give an apology."

Polly tried again. "Well, you've tried to apologise to Greg…" She took herself off into the living room, leaving him alone with his thoughts.

Andy was a talker. He never learned the art of quiet thinking, his instinct was to verbalise. Polly got most of it when the two of them were both home, and when she was elsewhere, he'd talk to himself. A running commentary of impressions and observations, a stream of short phrases and obscenities, mostly imitating fictional characters from the film roles played by Bruce Willis and Arnold Schwarzenegger, sometimes whispered when circumstances restricted him, and spoken out loud when he was all alone.

"Just about," he said to himself. *"There's more to it with Greg. There's Janey."*

Janey had been a home town girl. She'd spent three years living in Liverpool while studying for a degree in Chemistry but that had been her only excursion. She'd lived the rest of her life in Stokesley. Janey was an only child. She grew up in a chaotic world, surviving impressively despite inadequate care from an imperfect mother. She always had friends and she attended to her school life with great application. School had been a solid and dependable element in her childhood. Janey had needed that.

Her family life, although free from trauma, had been infected with inconsistency. Sometimes her Dad was home, mostly he was elsewhere. He'd reappear with apologies and promises, filling Janey's heart with false hope. Then the fights would start and he'd be gone again. At least her Mum had managed to be ever present, although she was always a bit wayward. Janey had always addressed her mother as Gwen. There had always been food on the table, mostly beans on toast or cream crackers with cheese. Gwen had no time for cooking and cleaning, although she spent hours helping to make Janey look pretty. And while they tried on clothes, and brushed hair, and applied make-up, Gwen had talked. Gwen had spoken to her young daughter as if she'd been much older, treating her like another adult. She'd meant well, allowing her daughter to learn from her mother's mistakes. But sometimes, quite a few times, it had been a bit too grown up for Janey, and a bit too close to home.

As a child, Janey had resented Gwen's eccentricity. Her mother had always relished the opportunity to break the rules. Gwen had been bold with her comments and with her appearance, wearing low necklines and too much perfume, drawing attention and judgement. Even as a young child, Janey had often experienced a sense of cringing embarrassment watching Gwen's extravagant and flirtatious behaviour. Such experiences brought about a resolve in Janey to be ordinary and inconspicuous, to be dressed in school uniform, to quietly follow social rules, to be invisible, beyond judgement.

There was no real ambition driving her studies in Liverpool – it was an escape from Gwen, and when Janey returned home after completing her degree, Gwen had moved on. Janey's emotional response had been dominated by relief. She had grown to become pragmatic and adaptable and she re-established herself in her home town quickly, marrying Alan within a year of her homecoming. He was steady, a solid and unremarkable man who was perfectly happy for her to wear the trousers.

Janey and Alan had two children. Alan remained steady and as the children grew older, Janey found work in the pharmacy at a local chemist. It was an uneventful life, exactly as Janey wished.

The involvement of Andy Cooper in her life, and the triangular connections with Greg Whitehead, had meaning for her. She had been a proud mother and she had no complaints about the course that her life had taken. It hadn't been an exciting life but at least Janey had made a better success of family duties than either of her parents.

But for all of that, the lingering scent of Gwen's perfume was always present and she'd pressed Andy with her dying wish, demanded his promise to bring resolution, to free her from her mother's sins.

THIRTEEN
6TH JUNE, 2024

A GOOD TURNOUT WAS INEVITABLE, Mark had always been well liked. Greg had already joined Sue and Eleanor when Mandy and her husband found the three of them waiting outside the crematorium.

"Here we are again," said Mandy.

There was a flurry of brief embraces.

Mandy spoke again. "I've seen Cheryl, Mark's sister, and Sarah bloody Buxton."

"Watch the language, Mandy, if you don't mind." Even with the mention of Sarah Buxton, Greg wasn't going to let that opportunity slip by. One all. But he could feel Sue's eyes staring hard at him and he felt exposed, certain that she could read his every thought.

Mandy ignored him. They all turned together to watch the hearse come to a halt. Everyone became silent. With practised care, the undertakers took the coffin from the hearse and carried Mark shoulder high into the chapel. The mourners followed, maybe sixty or seventy people with varying levels of enthusiasm for a traditional Christian service. Richard, Cheryl's oldest son, had flown from Bengaluru to read the eulogy.

Sue elbowed Greg and then leaned in close. "Andy Cooper's sitting three rows behind us."

"Oh right, I'll wait until we're half way through the Lord's Prayer and then I'll pop back to say hello, maybe give him a high five."

Sue seemed to have lost interest in the service. She continued people spotting. "And that's Sarah Buxton next to Cheryl, looking quite the madam. No sign of Brad Pitt, Greg. Looks like you've got a clear path. Front row, typical Sarah. What's the story there, I wonder? I mean, they did hang out a bit at school but I wouldn't have expected that to get her on the front row. You know what I'm saying?" Sue nodded conclusively.

Greg considered his response. "No, Sue. I don't know what it is you're saying. Are you suggesting that perhaps Mark and Sarah were lovers?" He'd come to realise now that Sue's appetite for scandal almost matched her talent for brutal honesty.

"Greg! Honestly, there's a Christian burial taking place." Sue grinned through her fraudulent outrage.

"Cremation."

"Whatever. No, I'm just curious. She was always a front row girl. Well, of course you have your own perspective." She glanced across at him. "She's definitely on her own, Greg." Sue was enjoying her fun. She knew that she'd already said too much but she couldn't resist. "Maybe she's one of your lot?"

"What's that supposed to mean?" said Greg, too loudly. Half of the row in front of them turned their heads to express silent disapproval. Greg blushed.

Sue chuckled.

Greg felt grateful for the chastisement, assuming that Sue would stay quiet.

But she didn't. "You know, one of your lot. One of the lonelys."

Greg made no reply, his attention was elsewhere. He

couldn't get a proper view, just the back of her head and her shoulders. The same shining brown hair, cut shorter but no sign of grey. He examined the back of her neck. Too beautiful to be touched. Oh, God, Sarah Buxton.

The service had been overly formal but the atmosphere at The Bridge was warm and welcoming. There was a string quartet playing some of Mark's favourite pieces of music.

Their gathering together at the wake was irresistible. None of them could have willed against it. They had sat together in the same classrooms sixty years earlier. They weren't students anymore but there were still lessons to be learned.

It was easy for Sue, Mandy and Greg. They had already reacquainted at Janey's funeral. But Sarah was a late comer to the reunion and she'd never been at the heart of the group when they were all at school. She circled the room twice while Mandy provided critical commentary for the others.

"Too bloody good for the likes of us, Miss hoity toity, half a mile up her own backside. Same as ever."

"I never had a problem with her, Mand."

Mandy looked taken aback by Greg's defence. "I don't know why you're bothered. She wouldn't let you lick the shit off her shoes, Greg."

Sue intervened. "We can't ignore her, Mandy. Anyway, she was much better in the sixth form."

Mandy remained unrepentant. "That's your opinion. I never liked her."

Eleanor had heard enough. "I'll ask her to join us," she said, as she walked from the table. She returned a couple of minutes later and ushered Sarah into the seat between herself and Mandy.

Mandy greeted Sarah with a smile, and Sue offered a verbal welcome. "It's been a long time, Sarah. It's a shame that it has taken a funeral to bring this unlikely bunch together."

"Hello, Sue. Yes, a bit like Harold and Maude."

Sue was immediately puzzled. "Sorry?"

"It's a movie," Greg explained. "1971. Ruth Gordon was brilliant."

"Oh, right. I must have missed that one." Sue noticed Greg and Sarah sharing a brief smile, but she was keen to move on. Andy Cooper hadn't come to the wake, and they'd all noticed. No one had said anything, but they were disappointed. She looked across to the lounge entrance and then scanned the room, but there was no sign of Andy, and her frustration grew.

Mandy followed Sue's eyes and guessed her thoughts. "I don't expect he'll come here, Sue. It's not really Andy's scene."

Sue had been looking forward to the next episode in this unfolding story and now her disappointment fuelled criticism. "The enigmatic Andy Cooper. Now you see me, now you don't. What's he playing at? Turning up for the service, then disappearing again."

Mandy was uncomfortable with Sue's judgement. "I'm sure he has his reasons, Sue. And it's not as if he was close with Mark. He'll have got himself back home."

Sue was unpersuaded. "Either come or don't bother. Don't go half way."

Sarah had immediately occupied her historical position in her peer group. She felt content to be marginally accepted and mostly she stayed quiet, but she liked Sue's fearless judgment and she responded instinctively. "Very well said."

Sue was surprised to find that her first supporter was Sarah Buxton.

Eleanor politely brought Sarah up to speed. "Greg and Andy had an awkward meeting at The Lion a couple of weeks ago."

"I know," said Sarah. "I was there."

A change enveloped them all. At school Sarah had been an outsider, almost an outcast. With this unexpected claim, her status changed. She was a woman on the inside track, a witness, an unexpected but increasingly welcome guest. Greg in particular gained interest.

Sarah went on. "I'd been to visit Mark. I'm afraid I drank too much beer. Newcastle Brown Ale. I was unable to drive home so I took a room at The Lion. A charming young man, Chris, looked after me."

Sarah had made a reference to Chris, without elaboration or emphasis. It was an aside, never a focus, not even a distraction. But it was a moment of significance. Only Greg understood Chris's charm, and he enjoyed Sarah's appreciation of their mutual acquaintance. She had articulated a shared understanding, something private and exclusive, something between the two of them. Not quite as powerful as the Harold and Maude reference, but nevertheless...

Greg looked at her, directly and in sympathy, and their eyes locked. Only for a second, just long enough for a chemical reaction. But it was enough to be a reminder to both of them, and the distance from their youthful encounter grew less.

Sarah continued her account. "I went to the bar to get coffee, trying to sober up. I recognised Andy. He was very agitated. Then you came in, Greg. I must confess that at first I didn't recognise you."

Greg absorbed the blow.

Sarah noticed the keen interest around the table. She was centre stage which had always been an uncomfortable position for her. She concluded her intelligence. "It was all over and done in a minute or two. A dramatic scene though."

Sarah sat quiet for a moment, taken aback as she witnessed the impact of her innocent gossip. Her former classmates were desperately trying to reformulate her. They were all struggling to the extent that none of them knew what to say. They'd been to school with Sarah. They hadn't got to know her back then and they had no idea what to expect from her now.

Eleanor had no history with Sarah and was able to accept her, warts and all. "Does that happen often, Sarah? Getting too drunk to drive home?"

"Goodness no, that was highly unusual." Sarah appeared keen to protect her reputation.

Greg had sat back in his seat when Sarah joined the party. He needed some time, so he sat back, listening and looking. He was careful not to stare. Her voice was recognisable although a little lower in pitch. She was older but far from an old woman. It had been fifty two years since he'd walked her home and kissed her mouth. He'd been a bit shocked by the heat of her kiss, surprised as she'd pressed her body against him. He couldn't remember how they'd prized themselves apart, only the walk back to his home with a feeling of triumph. And now he wanted to ask her – which of them had ended the kiss. It seemed important. Also, how had he missed her at The Lion? How could that have happened? She was unmistakably Sarah Buxton. He looked across at her, her facial features strong and pretty, gentle intelligent eyes. He was seventy years old now, he'd been around the block a few times, and he wished quietly to himself that one day he'd kiss her again.

Greg gave way to an involuntary shiver. There was tension in him. Finally he heard himself speak. "I think you knew Mark pretty well, Sarah. You obviously kept in touch after school."

"Yes. We were good friends at school. He was very warm-hearted. We often spent time together up until the time that I married. Then we wrote letters. My husband and Mark didn't get along very well, but we always maintained a written correspondence."

Greg worked hard to maintain his social grace although the news of a husband disappointed him. He felt relieved when Eleanor pulled Sarah into another conversation, giving

79

him the opportunity to collect his thoughts. He was unsettled. At Janey's funeral, he'd discovered the anger for Andy Cooper that had been dormant for fifty years. And today a quite different emotion from school days had re-emerged. What's a seventy-year-old man, who has embraced loneliness, who has control over his carefully designed life, who has built and boarded a sturdy ship to cruise gently to the end of the ocean, meant to do? He felt the need for some fresh air. "I'm going to stretch my legs," he said as he walked from the table.

As Sarah watched him walk from the hotel lounge, she didn't anticipate a prolonged absence. But an hour passed and she started to feel concerned, worrying if he'd gone back to his home. She reminded herself that he'd had a few drinks and guessed that he would be staying at The Lion. She tried to settle herself, gaining some comfort as she decided that Chris would help her to find him later. Nevertheless, she felt restless.

She wanted to leave but she needed to see Cheryl. Only a few weeks had passed since Cheryl had phoned her with news of Mark's failing health. Prior to that, she'd thought nothing about either Cheryl or Greg. Now she felt a sense of panic, afraid that they might fade back into the distance.

Cheryl fulfilled her social obligations, talking with the many friends and relatives who had come to the funeral. Hard work. She'd exhausted herself even before the funeral began. The telephone calls, the letters, the funeral arrangements, the invitations, the notifications and cancellations. The emptying of Mark's room, and disposing of his possessions. She'd done it all. Sarah had been a support, standing beside her while the first procession of mourners offered handshakes, stiff hugs and condolences, but Cheryl had encouraged her new friend away to find a seat and some refreshment. Finally and thankfully Cheryl found herself left alone. She wasn't sure what she needed. She picked up a few pieces from the buffet and went in search of Sarah.

"I wondered where you'd got to. My feet are killing me."

Cheryl placed her plate on the table, then sat beside Sarah. "I'm sorry to have left you for so long. I hadn't expected so many people to come." She glanced around the table but couldn't identify anyone. "Are these Mark's friends from school?"

"Yes, plus one or two husbands and wives. I hope you were able to spend some time with your children in amongst it all. They've travelled a long way." Sarah's comment was perfectly sincere, although she realised that she felt an almost desperate need to continue her Thursday dialogue with Cheryl. More so than ever after her brief encounter with Greg.

"I'll have time with them this evening at the house."

Sarah accepted this news with disappointment, her new confidante was unavailable. "That'll be nice for you after all of this." She fell quiet and wondered if she'd ever see Cheryl again. She had to steel herself as she tried to hold back the tears queuing behind her eyes.

Cheryl took hold of her hand. "Oh, Sarah. I've neglected you. Please forgive me." But before she could settle, she was distracted by a waving arm. "Oh dear, I thought I was finished," she said, already rising to her feet. "Sarah, I'm so sorry. Duty calls." She started to move away but then she turned and sat back down. "Will you come again next week?"

Sarah felt a surge of relief. "I'd like that. Will Thursday be alright?"

"Perfect." The waving arm across the room regained Cheryl's attention. She made a brief show of her frustration and then she was gone again.

The late afternoon drifted into early evening. The music favoured by Mark Sanderson had all been played. The string quartet had packed away their instruments. Both Mandy and Sue expressed concern that Greg never reappeared. The warm bubble of familiarity that they had enjoyed for much of the wake had gone, floated away like a dream, and left them subdued. They would walk from this room in different directions, unsure whether their paths would cross again.

81

Eleanor invited them all to attend her forthcoming birthday party in an attempt to hold on to something of the sense of reunion, to counter a feeling of dispersion, to avoid goodbyes and uncertainties.

Although Sarah had appreciated the accommodations from her former classmates, she found herself once again on the periphery of the group. First Greg had disappeared, then Cheryl's passing visit had been interrupted. Now she felt alone, wanting to escape and preparing for an early exit. She accepted good wishes from Mandy and Trevor, promised Eleanor that she'd attend her birthday celebration, with her fingers crossed and her heart tied in knots, and walked, solitary and slowly, back towards The Lion.

It had been Mark's funeral, although as she walked, Sarah realised that other events had occurred. She was walking alone. She'd always walked alone. She walked on. Her pace was deliberately slow. She thought about Nelson Mandela, walking away from Robben Island after twenty-seven years of incarceration, with his head held high, his dignity preserved. She thought about the many other prisoners, unknown to her, who had found the courage to accept their freedom. She thought about Mark, remembered the very last words he'd spoken to her. And she thought about Greg Whitehead, about the passion in their kiss. All those years ago.

FOURTEEN
BACK AT THE LION

GREG HAD TOO MANY THOUGHTS, more than he could hold comfortably. Andy Cooper showing his face and then disappearing again, the gang from school, and Sarah Buxton. He'd become unsettled at The Bridge and sought refuge in solitude, his safe place. He thought about driving home although he'd consumed way too much alcohol. Nevertheless, that was his instinct, to pull back from the complications of human interaction, to retreat into his own company. He found his way back to The Lion, had a quick chat with Chris, and took coffee up to his room. Tomorrow this whole episode would be ended. The thought offered him a trace of comfort, but not much. These ghosts from another lifetime had appeared before him, showed themselves. That was a bit scary. They were in position to haunt him. He remembered how he'd felt strange after Janey's funeral, experiencing a vague perception of something changing. It was coming to him more clearly now. He'd seen the ghosts. The philosophical foundation of his lifestyle had been breached, his solitude compromised. Anything might happen.

He lay on the unfamiliar bed, unable to tempt sleep or even to rest. The same thoughts running through his mind. What was happening? What did he want to happen?

83

When Sarah arrived back at The Lion, she was also unsettled by her encounter with the past, wanting to unscramble her own feelings. If Cheryl hadn't summoned her to visit Mark and to attend his funeral, she would never have returned to Stokesley. It had become part of the distant past. Yet here she was, flooded with memories, deeply affected by the power of place and people.

Chris greeted her return with his usual cheerfulness. "I've been thinking about you all afternoon, Sarah. Come on in, I'll make some coffee and you can tell me all about it."

She accepted his lies and his coffee. "There's nothing much to tell, Chris. The service was quite formal but the wake felt more relaxed."

Chris had taken every opportunity, with both Sarah and Greg, to collect the pieces of the puzzle. Even though several pieces were still missing, he'd started to put them together. "And what about Andy Cooper?"

"No. Well, yes actually. He came to the service but not to the wake. No, there was no drama. Just a few of my former classmates from school." Sarah assumed an air of casualness as she prepared her next statement. "One of them disappeared without saying goodbye. I think he might be staying here. Greg Whitehead."

"Oh right, I see," said Chris, not seeing at all. "Well, obviously I'm unable to disclose information about another guest, data protection and all that. He's up in his room. He'll come down to the bar later." Notions of privacy and confidentiality, it seemed, were for the fickle and the faint-hearted, certainly not for Chris. "I'll give you a call when he comes down."

Sarah felt that Chris could see her thoughts but she remained impassive. "Thanks for the coffee, Chris. I need to rest now."

FIFTEEN

ANDY COOPER – A MAN WITH A MISSION

ANDY HAD NEVER BEEN a friend of Mark Sanderson but he heard about his death and he saw an opportunity, hoping maybe Greg Whitehead would go to the funeral. A few of the old school group had turned out for Janey, perhaps they would do the same for Mark. He'd made his embarrassing retreat from The Lion after Janey's funeral without gaining any information, and he didn't even know where Greg lived. So, he put on his suit and made a late entry into the chapel for Mark's funeral service, scanning the rows of whispering mourners until he spotted Greg. "*Result.*"

After the service, Andy made a swift exit, drove back home and got himself kitted out, swapping the suit for combat gear and packing a few supplies into a rucksack. Andy was more comfortable with the change of clothes, and he had a mission. He'd sit in a trench, keeping watch. He'd messed up his previous attempt to explain himself to Greg but he was confident in his tracking skills. He'd find out where Greg lived and then he'd be able to choose the right moment to fulfil his promise to Janey.

He walked along the busy street nearing The Bridge Hotel, scanning in all directions and looking for a suitably discreet vantage point, but his soldiering instincts told him that something wasn't quite right and he kept walking. *"What the fuck am I looking for?"* He'd picked up something in peripheral vision. There was no clear threat, but his military experiences had taught him never to dismiss a nagging doubt, never to ignore even the smallest signal on his personal radar, but to always look a second time, check and then check again. He slowed his pace and he could sense it, there was a danger in the street, yet to be comprehended. He crossed the road just before the hotel entrance and walked away in the opposite direction, trying to identify whatever had spooked him, all antennae on high alert.

Andy was walking along a busy street in the centre of a small town, one of the many enjoying warm sunshine in the safety of an uneventful day, and he walked with practised craft, blending into his surroundings, attracting no attention. *"Come on, whoever you are, show your ugly face."* This was Andy the soldier, in his element. The urban setting made no difference. He would have felt the same instincts out in open country. He had eyes only for the enemy and he was calm. In some ways he was ill at ease with his appetite for a fight, his ability to focus effectively in the face of danger, and uncomfortable with his talents for stealth and violence. Yet these were the qualities that would serve him in this increasingly complex mission. He wished he was someone different, a better man, but for the task in hand, his flawed self was perfect.

Just a few steps after reversing direction, he identified the threat. *"Got you."* He maintained perfect rhythm in his stride and kept his eyes and head pointing straight ahead, but he'd got his man. A white male, mid-thirties, sitting in the driver's seat of a black Peugeot, browsing his phone, looking uncomfortably hot, and who had position to watch the entrance to The Bridge Hotel. *"Who the hell are you?"* This was an unexpected development. A straightforward watch and wait exercise had taken a turn. Someone else, an unknown player, had entered the game. Maybe it was nothing, a false alarm, but Andy could see no good reason to linger in a parked car on a summer's day and he could sense it in his bones, this was a figure of interest. So he adapted his approach, finding a café table outside on the street with good lines of sight to The Bridge and to the unidentified occupant of the Peugeot. He was in combat mode. Aware of the need for energy and hydration, he ordered an espresso and a glass of spring water and settled into his wait, taking the opportunity to take a couple of photos, content that he'd be considerably more comfortable than the man he was photographing. *"Another hour in your car and you'll have tomatoes growing out your earholes. Every day's a salad day."*

A couple of hours passed before Greg emerged from The Bridge, squinting in the bright sunshine as he started to walk slowly along the street away from Andy. The suspicious man in the Peugeot appeared to show no interest and Andy needed to make a decision. He waited a few more seconds until he was sure that the car's occupant was unmoved, then he set off following Greg.

Fifteen minutes later, Andy regained his table at the cafe and ordered more coffee. Greg had gone to The Lion and Andy was drawn back to The Bridge. His original aim had been to gain information that would give him access to Greg, to allow him the chance to approach in his own time, to make a more convincing apology, and to fulfil his promise to Janey. He wanted Greg's home address and he'd be parked outside The Lion early the next morning ready to follow him home. But it was the guy in the black Peugeot who'd stolen Andy's focus, the stranger who felt the need to sit in the greenhouse that his car must have become, after receiving more than two hours of unbroken sunshine. It didn't make sense, not unless there was someone in The Bridge Hotel who you wanted to keep tabs on. Someone other than Greg Whitehead. Andy sat in the shade and sipped his water, but even still he was feeling the heat. *"I hope you're worth it, soldier."*

Another hour passed before a woman stepped out from

87

the hotel doorway and this time the Peugeot driver reacted, jumping from the car as soon as the woman turned her back and began walking away. Sarah Buxton. Andy had seen her in the crematorium. Several of his old school peers had changed beyond recognition but not Sarah. Her facial features seemed unaltered, even the way she walked, nose in the air.

"Hey up."

Andy was mystified, curious and content. A fairly simple intelligence gaining exercise had led to this rather bizarre scenario: Sarah Buxton, who he'd never been interested in, not even at school, was being followed by a man he'd never seen before today, and yet it seemed to be vitally important. He didn't know why but he felt compelled to follow them both.

As it turned out, Andy repeated his previous route, following the unknown Peugeot driver as he followed Sarah to The Lion.

"All roads lead to The Lion."

Andy took the opportunity to get a good look at the man he'd followed and he took in the information: a tall man with broad shoulders and short cropped black hair, wearing dark blue chinos and a sweat-stained linen shirt, and carrying a large man bag.

"Smarmy bastard."

Andy watched him turn on his heels and start his return journey to the waiting Peugeot. He walked directly towards him and offered a cheery greeting as their paths crossed. It was a bit bold but he picked up the southern accent from the reply, paused for a few seconds, and then turned to pursue his quarry. Five minutes later, as the black Peugeot started to drive away, Andy quickly assessed his options; it was a roasting hot afternoon, he was on foot and he didn't want to blow his cover, but he wanted to know who was driving the Peugeot. He watched the car take a right turn and he started to run in pursuit.

"You daft bugger. You're seventy, Cooper, what are you doing, man?"

He got to the corner just before his lungs caught fire and in time to see the Peugeot turn left, slowly manoeuvring through the narrow entrance into the car park behind The Bricklayer's Arms. Andy was breathing fast and heavy, sweating profusely, but he smiled nevertheless. It had turned out to be a productive afternoon. He hadn't been massively impressed by the driver's stealth and subtlety but he appreciated the choice of accommodation.

"Crafty bastard."

The Bricklayer's was a pub with just three or four rooms and a car park tucked around the back. A poor man's equivalent of The Lion.

"But not crafty enough."

Andy strolled slowly towards The Bricklayer's Arms, allowing his breathing to slow down and enjoying his success. He took photos of the registration plate before heading back to update Polly. He'd get some food and check in with her, then sleep and be back out early tomorrow.

SIXTEEN

SARAH AND GREG

AFTER TWO HOURS OF FRUSTRATION, Greg gave up his attempt to rest. He showered and dressed in a change of clothes. Then he made his way down to the bar, praying that Andy Cooper would be somewhere else.

During his previous stay at The Lion, Greg had managed to spend time in the bar without seeing Sarah. As he entered today, he took a good look around. There were three patrons all seated together at one table. The rest of the room was empty, except for Chris who was on bar duty.

Chris watched Greg scan the room, misreading his surveyance. "Yes, I don't blame you, I'd be the same. No need to worry, he's not here."

"Good, I'd like some coffee, Chris, and the chance to drink it in peace."

"The coffee's a certainty, nailed on," said Chris. "I wish you the best of luck with the peace, but with your track record, I'm making no promises." He slipped out of the room to give Sarah a quick call and returned with Greg's double shot latte. He placed the glass mug in front of Greg. "Oh, by the way, a young lady was asking for you."

"Really, who?"

Sarah entered the bar. Chris pointed with his eyes. "Here

she is now." He turned towards her. "Hello, Sarah. I believe this is the man you've been looking for." There was plenty of space in the room… Chris's smile seemed to be filling most of it. He had betrayed Greg's wish for peace and he'd suggested romance between his two guests. He was delighting in his facilitation.

Sarah attempted to give him a withering look, but she liked him too much. Instead, she turned her attention to Greg. "Hello again, Greg." She gestured to the empty chair beside him. "May I?"

"Yes, please do. Would you like a drink?"

Sarah released a long sigh as she took her seat. She checked her watch. "Thank you." She addressed Chris. "Can I have an americano, Chris. No milk."

"I'll be two minutes," said Chris as he walked towards the doorway. "You two behave yourselves."

Sarah watched as Greg shook his head. "He's very attentive," she said, "although I wouldn't trust him with a secret. I asked him to call me when you showed up. I hope you don't mind. I'm glad to see you, you disappeared quite suddenly. I think that Eleanor was worried about you."

Greg accepted Chris's duplicity, forgiving him as easily as Sarah. "I just needed a few minutes to myself." Greg hesitated. "I usually enjoy funerals. But not so much today."

The conversation stuttered while they exchanged superficial pleasantries, talking about Mark's funeral and the school reunion. Rather oddly, as they ventured into more personal territory, they created a more relaxed atmosphere, accepting the silent pauses more comfortably.

It was Sarah who asked the first big question. "You came alone today, Greg. Are you married? I mean, do you have someone in your life, a partner?"

"No. I've been married. More than once," added Greg, feeling no need for precision. One, two, three, all small numbers. "But I'm on my own these days." And unusually he left it there. No supporting philosophy, no mention that living alone was a considered choice. "Sue thinks I should go on Twitter."

Sarah paused, hesitant to correct him. She smiled kindly. "Do you mean Tinder, the dating site?"

"Yes, yes, Tinder, sorry. I'm already on Facebook," said Greg, trying to claw back some credibility. He turned to face Sarah. Their eyes, their faces, their bodies, all finding alignment. And Sue's words replayed in his mind. "But yes, that's the one, Tinder. She said that I shouldn't give up on love."

"It was lovely to meet Sue today. She and Eleanor were kind, inviting me to sit with all of you. How interesting that she said that." Sarah allowed herself to sit back. She felt comfortable and engaged. "Coincidentally, Mark said something similar to me. It really hit home to me and as it turned out, it was the last thing that he said to me. His very last words."

Greg felt his interest intensify. Sarah's words stirred his curiosity.

"What did Mark say to you?"

"That I still had time to try again."

"But surely, I mean, you were talking about your husband this afternoon."

"No, I didn't mean to mislead you, my marriage isn't a success. Actually, it's a sham."

Greg reacted. He was getting sight of unexpected information and he recognised Sarah's resignation. "That sounds like fun."

Sarah managed half a smile. She raised her gaze to meet his eyes and their engagement went to another level.

Sarah had learned self-reliance, no heart to hearts, not a lot of sharing. But now she spoke openly. "I don't think I ever loved Alexander. I'm trying to find the courage to leave him." She fell silent, fully aware she had spoken candidly, given trust. She'd found some courage and a good listener. She was empowered by Mark's last words and Cheryl's encouragement. And without great effort, she revealed herself, stealing her courage from the memory of teenage kisses, from the chemistry that had survived for fifty years in a dusty, science lab test tube. Despite a life coloured by many shades of hesitation, she informed Greg of her circumstances.

Greg heard her clearly enough. She had surprised him. Who knows where it came from? A dare or a dream. Impulse or design. It didn't matter. Sarah Buxton, more beautiful than ever, wanted to escape her sham marriage. She had confided in him. Greg, the island, the man alone, felt a shifting in the sand, a question mark against his identity.

Greg closed his eyes, drew breath, slowed himself. Took some care. He didn't want to say the wrong thing. "I see. You're as bad as me. I also have a talent for marrying the wrong people."

"Oh dear, what a pair we are," said Sarah.

I wish, thought Greg.

The evening grew late. The bar became busy and music was playing. Conversation became quite difficult, but they managed to fill in a few more historical spaces. It didn't matter much that some of their words were lost, that they needed raised voices and reiterations, that they were seventy years old and carrying plenty of baggage, that they shared the room with fifty others, or that Chris had eyes on them all night. None of that mattered.

Sarah looked at her wristwatch. "It's very late. I'm driving back to Surrey in the morning."

"Yes, that's a long drive." Greg wasn't really ready to say goodbye. "Let's meet for breakfast. Eight-thirty?"

"Perfect. Goodnight, Greg." Sarah allowed her smile to linger for a second or two, just enough for each of them to remember the last time they had said goodnight, then she went off to her room.

The bar had still been full until twenty minutes earlier but now just a few stragglers remained. Chris was busy clearing empty glasses from abandoned tables. He arrived at Greg's table seconds after Sarah's departure. "Well, well, well. You'd better get yourself off to bed. You don't want to miss your breakfast date."

Chris was able to combine charm with impertinence. Repeatedly. Greg accepted his indiscretion with a warm smile. "I'm going to bed. Are you doing the breakfast shift, Chris?"

"I am now," Chris replied.

"Well, if I haven't shown my face by a quarter past eight, give me a wake-up call. Goodnight."

SEVENTEEN

BREAKFAST

GREG COULDN'T WORK out whether he was awake or dreaming. The noise was loud and unrelenting but unfamiliar, dreamlike. "Shit," was all he could manage as he fell out of the chair. Definitely awake now and desperate to stop the phone's hideous screech. He picked up the receiver and immediately dropped it again... he had neither the time nor the inclination for a chat with Chris.

There was just fifteen minutes to get washed and dressed before re-presenting himself to Sarah. He'd lain on his bed for hours, unable to persuade himself into sleep, giving up in the small hours and climbing from his bed to make himself an instant coffee. His intention had been to watch TV until it was time for breakfast, ensuring that he kept his breakfast appointment.

"Shit," he repeated as he kicked over a cup of cold coffee on his way to the shower.

Fifteen minutes later, he sat down for breakfast and checked his watch. He was bang on time. Sarah was late. He felt unprepared, despite several hours of consideration. During the long dark hours, when sleep had eluded him, he'd tried to think of entertaining topics of conversation for his breakfast with Sarah, but without success. Now, as she walked towards his table, he felt unprepared and desperately tired.

He stood to attention. "Morning, Sarah."

"Good morning, Greg. Did you sleep well?"

"Yes, out like a light," he said, hoping that he looked better than he felt.

Breakfast at The Lion. They'd both done it before. They knew the routine. But these circumstances were unique, after what had gone before: Mark's funeral service at the crematorium, the gathering at The Bridge, and then a full evening in the bar. Now, just the two of them. With uncertain glances, moments of tension, conversation and chemistry.

Last evening, in a crowded bar, with drinks, there had seemed to be acknowledgement that their teenage desires, although dressed now in middle aged clothes, might still be alive. That's how it had seemed to Greg. But after a restless night, he was questioning his own earlier judgement. And for a while he told himself he was an old fool, believing that a woman he'd kissed more than fifty years ago, when he was young and slim, would ever think about him again once she'd started her drive back to Surrey. She had other things to think about. She was challenging herself to end her marriage. And he was seventy years old, thrice divorced, two stone heavier, grey haired. He decided to make polite conversation, say an honourable farewell and then thank God that he'd sobered his thoughts before making an idiot of himself.

It took a few minutes more before he found his way. Chris was annoyingly over-attentive and too talkative. They were both up and down to the buffet, but eventually they were left alone and settled.

He urged himself to speak. "It's been great to see you, Sarah. Perhaps I could take your number? I'd like to stay in touch." He hesitated as he pulled out his phone.

"Yes, we must. I said I'd go to Eleanor's birthday party. Perhaps I'll see you there?"

Greg knew nothing of Eleanor's forthcoming birthday, but it sounded hopeful. He'd entertained an idea of visiting Surrey, maybe inventing a friend or cousin who coincidentally lived quite close to Sarah. He didn't really want to tell foolish lies, but he just hadn't been able to come up with a better plan. A party at Sue and Eleanor's, that was much easier than he'd expected.

But he needed to be sure. "I didn't know about Eleanor's birthday. When is it?"

"It's the 24th August, during the bank holiday weekend." Sarah heard her own words and for a few seconds she drifted. She couldn't imagine where she might be by the end of August. She was a woman on the move. The dissatisfaction that she'd carried for decades had first stirred and now it had spoken. She'd told Mark, Cheryl, and now Greg. And she knew, more than ever with Greg Whitehead sharing her breakfast table, that her future was uncertain. Her post-pandemic destiny was waiting. After years of stagnation, she was on the move. She was far from sure that she'd be partying in Leeds in a few weeks' time. Sarah knew the task she faced was frightening, and that Alexander would be difficult, but already she was making moves, preparing to go again.

"Actually, I'm coming up to see Cheryl next Thursday. I'll stay here again. Perhaps we could meet for dinner? If you're not too busy." Her mind was working in a way that surprised her. She felt able to recognise her interest in Greg. There was something there, a personal interest. But in this moment, she was developing a strategy, and all of that surprised her, felt unlike her. She knew that once Alexander learned of her intention to leave him, she couldn't reliably predict what might happen. She needed to see Cheryl again, and now she felt the same way about Greg. She needed another Thursday fix. So she had at least a week to think before she would talk to Alexander, a few days to further develop her strategy and to consult with her new friends.

It was several years since Greg had been busy. "I think I'm free."

They exchanged numbers and Greg agreed to phone her to arrange their meeting.

Sarah set off back to Surrey, intimidated by the agenda she faced, and Greg went back to bed, seeking sweet dreams.

EIGHTEEN
ANDY AND POLLY

ANDY HAD BEEN DISTRACTED by the events of the previous day, steered away from his original mission, but he'd re-focused overnight and got himself out early, in position to view all departures from The Lion car park. Sarah emerged first in a red Audi, no passengers. He watched her drive away from The Lion and he made a note of the registration plate for no particular reason, but there his interest ended. *"Thank you and goodnight, Sarah Buxton."* For a while during the previous afternoon, Andy hadn't known who he should follow, but he was more clear this morning. Sarah Buxton was just a passing interest, a distraction.

Greg's car registration number was all that he wanted. He had planned to follow his return journey back to his home address, but the registration would suffice. There was no sense in wasting his time. He already knew that he'd have to make a call, seek help from an old army friend. The black Peugeot had diverted his original intentions. The unknown player was probably of no interest, but Andy needed to know for sure. He'd lost touch with most of his former comrades from the army, but Major Ferguson still sent a Christmas card and Denny was always glad to catch up. Denny was twelve years younger than Andy, although he'd out-ranked him in the Falklands. The two men had both left the army in 1984, and sometimes several years passed without contact but they never lost touch. They had served together, stood shoulder to shoulder in the heat of battle, fought together. They were on the same side. The bond that forms when you learn to trust another man with your life, holds firm. Denny was nearing the end of a long and successful career in the police force and he'd never forgotten that Andy Cooper had saved his life.

Andy had to wait another three hours before Greg's departure but then his patience was rewarded. The car details were duly noted, Denny would do the rest. Mission accomplished.

Everyone had disappeared, the funeral had ended and the mourners had gone home. He ought to have felt content, but there were one or two loose ends still occupying his mind – he'd need to figure out exactly when to approach Greg and he wanted to get some clue about the identity of the Peugeot driver. He made his way home, wondering if he should just forget about Sarah Buxton and her follower, concentrate on Greg, but he'd got the numbers now and if Denny was happy to play ball, he might as well check them out.

Polly just wanted him to move on. His obsession with apology and Janey North's dying wishes were nothing more than irritants to Pol. She'd been asleep in bed when Andy had set out to The Lion. "The wanderer returns," she offered as a greeting.

"Yes, all done. I'm starving. I'll make a brew and get some breakfast." Andy dropped his rucksack onto the kitchen floor. "Then I'll give Denny a bell."

"Oh, it's a police matter now, is it?"

"Probably not, but who knows."

Polly shook her head but she was growing curious. "Why? What do you want from Denny?" Polly had grown up in a colliery village just south of Sunderland. She knew none of Andy's school colleagues. She'd met Janey but they hadn't really got along together. The truth was that Polly had suspected a sexual motivation when Janey reappeared in Andy's life, even though Janey was in her late sixties and already ill with cancer. Pol was all grit and leather on the outside but she had her insecurities, jealousy always ready and waiting for a target. She understood that it all had meaning for Andy, but that made no difference, she never liked Janey North. It was quite different with Denny. She'd always had a soft spot for him – they spoke the same language.

"I want him to get me Greg's address. I've got the car details." Andy paused, holding his next communication for a few seconds, just enough to give Polly's clock a wind. "And there are a couple of other car registrations I want him to check." Andy was manoeuvring around the tiny kitchen, preparing tea and toast. He hadn't told Polly about the Peugeot driver and Sarah Buxton.

"Why? How many cars has he got? Get Greg's address, go and tell him about Janey's message, then please, God, we can all move on."

"That's what I intend to do, Pol. It's probably nothing, but I wasn't the only person watching The Bridge Hotel yesterday. I had a bit of unexpected company. Like I say, it was probably nothing." He buttered his toast and leant back against the work surface to eat his breakfast, smiling to himself as he waited for Polly's questions. She always had to know everything.

"Oh right, who was that then?"

"That's my question to Denny. He was in a black Peugeot and he followed Sarah Buxton, who was at school with me and Greg, back to The Lion."

"Where Greg was staying."

"Exactly," concluded Andy.

This was the way of things with Andy and Polly, playfully pushing each other's buttons all day long. Some people described Polly as a 'rough diamond', while for others, 'rough' was a sufficient description. She'd never felt at ease

101

with Janey North, who seemed to think she was a cut above, but she could relax with Denny. She would have been perfectly at ease with barrack room language and she'd have fought alongside the men. She was made from tough stuff and she sparkled, harsh words and soft heart. Andy would have ruined himself without her. Polly was a life saver.

Although she complained, Polly was delighted to see her man purposefully occupied, fully aware that his mood was always elevated by activity and fresh air. So she'd tell him he was wasting his time and ask one curious question after another.

Denny and The Lion were his only resources, he had nothing else, so he phoned Denny without delay, gaining three addresses. Greg lived in Middlesbrough and the other two in Surrey. Surrey indeed, Sarah had gone down south. Andy wasn't surprised. The unknown man in the Peugeot was George Brand, resident of Guildford, just a few miles from Sarah, and he had a criminal record, with two convictions for affray. Just like Andy.

So Sarah Buxton was being followed by a man who could be violent. Andy wasn't sure what to make of it. He'd never been close with Sarah when they were at school and there was no reason for him to take an interest now. *"Who cares?"* On the other hand, he had information. He'd spotted her pursuer and now he'd identified him. Was Sarah in some kind of trouble, perhaps in danger?

NINETEEN

SARAH AND CHERYL

SARAH ARRIVED AGAIN at The Lion. For five consecutive Thursdays, she had made the same journey. She had made her previous visits with clear purpose, first visiting Mark, then supporting Cheryl, before attending Mark's funeral just a week ago. Today the agenda was different, and although Sarah wanted to extend her dialogue with Cheryl, she was infected by uncertainty.

So much seemed to have happened in just a few weeks. She was clear about her intention – she had to find a way out of her marriage – but without a method. She had spent several days quietly considering her options, offering herself choices. The 'running away' option had been her first thought. No confrontation, no shouting, and no immediate danger. Those advantages carried some appeal. She could just pack her bags and drive away while Alexander was occupied elsewhere. Leave him a note: Thank you for nothing much, goodbye forever. But she'd examined herself, and rejected this option. She couldn't hide away forever and, although the prospect terrified her, she felt that she must face him. Surely that was part of her challenge... first to stand before him, and then to walk away. Nevertheless, she struggled each day as

103

she rehearsed her lines, imagining the ferocity of her husband's objection.

And she had to think about what would follow her announcement. What next? *Go again*, Mark had said. Go where?

She thought about her children and her grandchildren, all close by and tied to the family estate. Already Alexander had them all carefully placed within his own design. It was all under his control, the property, the wealth, and the people.

Would she have to leave them all?

Would she be able to?

She walked through the rooms of the house she'd lived in for all of her married life, taking it in, getting ready to leave it behind. The possessions collected over many years, the paintings hung on the walls, and the plants that she'd lovingly nurtured in the garden. The permanence of things, suddenly ending.

She was surprised that she managed another Thursday escape without a violent scene. Perhaps even Alexander was starting to understand the hopelessness of their life together.

Chris gave his customary welcome as he showed her to her room.

Her previous visits to Cheryl's house had been for Mark. Today, although Mark was not forgotten, she felt quite different, understanding that today she was visiting a new friend. Spring seemed to have extended for almost a month, and the summer had waited patiently. But today there wasn't a cloud in the sky, and bright sunlight filled every space. Cheryl's front door was wide open and Sarah heard Cheryl's voice in the distance, inviting her into the house.

Sarah found her host in the kitchen. "Hello, Cheryl. What a lovely day."

"Yes, it's the hottest day of the year. I thought we could

have lunch in the conservatory and then we can sit out in the garden. It's my constant project and my best friend. It's always nice but this is a particularly colourful moment." Cheryl led Sarah straight through to the conservatory at the back of the house.

Sarah was drawn to the garden and she looked deep into the long narrow display. "It's wonderful. I love the yellow rose. I've never seen yellow go so deep without becoming gold."

"It's very old and quite prolific. The flowers just keep coming and they have an incredibly strong scent. Go on out and have a look while I bring the food through into the conservatory." Cheryl left the room.

Sarah opened the conservatory door and walked out into the garden. She was a keen gardener herself and she could see at a glance that this garden was the work of an enthusiast. She felt sure that she would walk away from her home in Surrey without looking back over her shoulder, but she would miss her garden. She went to smell the yellow roses and they were exactly as Cheryl had promised. Sarah marvelled at the beauty, recognising the care and the flair, the toil and the talent, and her mood ascended. It was a great place to be, a great space to have to herself, for a few minutes at least. She walked up and down the length of Cheryl's magical garden, smiling at every turn. She had approached this visit with a clear agenda, but she hadn't felt confident that she'd find the courage to open up to Cheryl again, maybe even to recruit her support. Sarah was under no illusion. She knew that the task of getting free from Alexander was hers alone, but she needed her friend, and now, she found some hope. The first real day of summer and Cheryl's garden gave comfort to Sarah. She had found a time and place where she could talk.

She looked up to see Cheryl, beckoning. They ate salad and talked about gardening. Their common interest added more strength to the bond that had developed between them. They enjoyed the food and the conversation, but Sarah wanted to get back outside, where a more important conversation was waiting. She felt relieved when Cheryl suggested lemonade in the garden.

Cheryl could feel it too... the conversation in waiting, and she wasted no time. "I've thought about you often these last few days, wondering what news you'd bring today."

"I'm going to leave Alexander. That's my task now, to get free from him. Mark told me that I still have the time to start again, and he was right. I'm healthy and able, and I know I'm much too old, but nevertheless, I want a new start." These were big statements, and already Sarah was trembling. Her chest felt tight and she could only manage shallow breaths. She felt Cheryl's eyes, assessing her. "But I'm frightened. Not about starting anew or even to be alone. I'm frightened of Alexander."

"Being on your own isn't so bad. I'm sure that you have nothing to fear." Cheryl hoped that Sarah might accept her reassurance, although she was far from convinced by her own words, and aware that she hadn't properly acknowledged the focus of Sarah's concern.

Sarah allowed her gaze to wander, exploring further into the far reaches of Cheryl's garden, and she felt the tension and fear subside, and her breathing slowed. "I met Alexander while I was still studying. He was a good looking young man, full of confidence and he seemed to be in charge. In his personality and his attitude, he was alarmingly similar to my father, although I didn't see that when we first met. I was caught up in the whirl of romance." Sarah waited for Cheryl to offer comment, but found only a silence, pressing her to say more. "I thought I'd done well, that my parents would be pleased. We've been together now for forty five years, raised our children, and we've become very wealthy. I earned a good salary but there was always money in Alexander's family. Hurtmoor Estate is huge. I know that I have no right to complain, and I don't mean to appear unappreciative."

"I have a pile of money, Sarah. I don't need it and I seldom use it. I can pay the bills but I'm lonely. I'm with McCartney in that respect. I don't care too much for money. Money can't buy me love."

They'd both grown up with the Beatles, the sound track of their youth. Sarah was transported by the musical reference. "I agree, I do have some money of my own that I inherited from my parents, and I have my pensions, but I don't care about money either. Although I'm with John Lennon today. I need help."

"Yes, we all need a little help from our friends. To get by."

"I had a dream, a figure running through woodland in the dead of night, desperate, running without direction. I seemed to know who it was but when I woke up I couldn't identify the runner. It took me a while to settle down. I felt terrified, drenched in sweat and I was panting, like a lone deer running from a pack of wolves."

"We only ever dream about ourselves," said Cheryl. "You should always listen to your dreams."

Cheryl felt impatient. And she felt concern. When Sarah had talked about being frightened of Alexander, she had seen the fear in her friend. And she remembered a previous reference to Alexander's character. She wanted to encourage Sarah, but she'd picked up the clues, and she wondered how dangerously Alexander's anger might be expressed. She needed to ask. "What are you going to do, Sarah?"

Not for the first time, Sarah was jolted by Cheryl's directness. Her new confidante wasn't one to dance around the issue. "I'm going to tell him that I'm leaving. I'll do that next week, when my bags are packed and I've arranged accommodation elsewhere. Once I've told him, I'll make a swift exit. That's the frightening bit, surviving his first reaction."

Cheryl noted the choice of words and she felt her concern intensify. She felt protective. She admired the courage that Sarah had found but there was something disturbing in the atmosphere, a warning. "Come and stay here with me. I've got room and you can help with the garden."

"I couldn't possibly impose on you like that, Cheryl. So soon after Mark's death. No, you've been so kind, and I'm grateful. I'm going to call my cousin, Martha. She's quite alone and we get along well. I think she'll let me stay for a while." She paused, unsure of her direction. She hadn't yet spoken to Martha and refuge with Cheryl was a much more inviting prospect. "I don't know what comes next. I have no long-term plan. I need a temporary arrangement. Somewhere to lie low until I find my direction."

"You're very brave, Sarah, making such a change, facing such a challenge."

"I don't feel brave. I'm frightened but I must act now. I owe it to Mark."

"You owe it to yourself."

"Yes, and you were right about the dream. It was me, it's exactly how I feel. I'm running away. I'm not sure that it matters where I run to, I have to get away. That's the first task."

Cheryl reached out again. "I'd like you to come and stay with me." She wanted Sarah to understand that her offer was substantial. "Have you no thoughts at all about what the future might hold?"

"I want to live a life that is true to myself and I want to do better with people. It doesn't have to be much of a life, so long as it's mine. That's about as far as I've got. You never know what's around the corner. I didn't see any of this coming. Mark, old friends from school, meeting you. Let alone Greg Whitehead reappearing in my life."

Cheryl vaguely recognised the name. She'd written it on an invitation to her brother's funeral. "Who is Greg Whitehead?"

"He was in the same year group as Mark and I. My first grown up kiss was with Greg. We're having dinner this evening." Sarah surprised herself with her own brief representation of her relationship with Greg, the history and the future. She felt the need to pull back. "We were both staying at The Lion last week. It was just coincidence. Nothing happened. We chatted over drinks in the bar and we arranged to meet this evening. That's all."

For a moment Cheryl didn't know what to say. "So, you're going to have dinner with an old flame, just a few days before you leave your husband?"

For a moment Sarah felt defensive, accused and guilty. "Yes." She waited to hear Cheryl's caution, but her friend stayed quiet. And again, she focused on the environment, the breeze gently moving through the leaves and branches, a blackbird singing. She could draw strength from this garden. She felt that she was accepted here, with her wild rogue thoughts, with desire that had laid dormant for all these years.

"I don't know, Cheryl. The way you describe it, it sounds scandalous. I don't know what to make of it. But I won't turn away. I've never been impulsive, never allowed myself to be guided by instinct. And I know it must sound crazy, a seventy-year-old woman still not able to escape a teenage crush. But there was just one night when Greg walked me home, when we kissed. I lost control, escaped my reserve. He brought something alive in me that night. No one else has affected me like that. Just that one time, I let myself free, and held Greg fiercely tight. The poor young man must have been terrified – Sarah Buxton, who'd never say boo to a goose, was devouring him."

Cheryl encouraged her to continue. "And suddenly he's here again."

"Yes." Sarah had more to say, but she checked herself.

"Don't stop, Sarah. I'm not here to judge you."

"I have no expectation about Greg. I want my freedom. Maybe I'm a fool. It's just that…" She hesitated still. "He hasn't said anything to me, but there's something. I don't know what it is. Chemistry. Biology. Memories. Hope or perhaps delusion. I don't know. I've endured a loveless marriage. I distracted myself with the children and I made the best of my career. And please don't misunderstand me, I enjoyed being a mother. Robin and Scarlet are parents themselves now. I'm seventy years old, Cheryl, and I don't know what it is to be in love."

Cheryl closed her eyes, shielding herself from the pain and power of Sarah's statement. She had no reply.

TWENTY

BUTTERFLIES

GREG HAD HAD time to prepare. A long week waiting for his dinner date with Sarah, trying to make some sense of what was happening and to ask himself a few questions. That had helped him, although the days dragged slowly by and through it all he could feel butterflies in his stomach. Only a few. Light and gentle in their fluttering. But they stayed with him for the whole week and he was glad when Thursday finally arrived.

He decided to travel on his bike. Recent social engagements had involved car journeys and several pints of John Smiths. He'd lost a bit of edge and gained a few pounds. For some reason, he was now working hard to get himself into better shape. He arrived at The Lion late in the afternoon, timing his ride to avoid rush hour traffic and giving himself time to shower and change before dinner.

Chris welcomed him. "I didn't recognise you in your cycling gear."

Greg felt his weight and his age. "I'm not going to have sex with you, Chris."

"That's true. You're early, you've got lots of time. Sarah went to Cheryl's for lunch. I'm sure she'll be a couple of hours yet."

Greg noted with interest that Chris seemed to have full access to Sarah's diary. "We're not meeting until seven. I'll go and get showered."

"Seriously, Greg, you have plenty of time."

"Thank you, Chris. That's good to know. Is my room ready?" He accepted the room key and disappeared.

Greg was a little restless. He wasn't really a dinner date man, and despite his exercise he had no appetite. He went down to the bar just before seven and was surprised to find Sarah had arrived ahead of him.

She smiled and gave a greeting. "Chris said we can eat whenever we're ready. Perhaps you'd like a drink first?"

"I'm not sure that I'm ready to eat yet. I cycled over earlier this afternoon. It's a fabulous day."

"Yes, it is. I spent much of the afternoon in Cheryl's garden."

Greg pulled out a chair but interrupted himself. "Shall we go for a walk? It seems a shame to be indoors. To be honest, I'm really not that hungry."

It was an impulsive suggestion and it landed uncertainly. Both of them fell quiet to consider a change to their arrangement. Sarah felt trepidation creep into her, a warning or perhaps just nerves.

"Yes, alright but give me a minute, Greg. I'll change my shoes."

Once they were out in the sunshine, they relaxed, slowed by the still lingering heat of the day. Greg led them through streets that he hadn't walked on for decades, but this was his home town and his feet found their way. "I like talking while walking. I say different things when I'm moving, find thoughts that would escape me if I was sitting still." Immediately, he judged his statement to be incomprehensible nonsense and he regretted having spoken.

But Sarah responded. "Yes, I'm sure that's true. So long as you don't rush."

"Exactly," said Greg.

And they walked on, slowly.

Suddenly, Sarah's face broke from seriousness and uncertainty. A big smile brightened her eyes and she looked across at Greg, who was also smiling. Neither of them had dared to mention the kiss. Of course, they both had the memory, but until this moment, and for many reasons, their brief moment of passionate union had been left alone, undisturbed. But here they were, outside the entrance to The White Swan.

Sarah's smile was inextinguishable. "The Mucky Duck. I thought you'd forgotten."

"You must be joking! Best kiss of my life."

They stood on the very spot where their walk to Sarah's family home had commenced more than fifty years earlier. There was no hiding place and there could be no form of denial. They were beaming.

Greg was at ease now, his doubts all gone. "Come on, I'll walk you home. Although I've no idea where you live."

Sarah fell into step close beside him and they continued their walk. "I'm afraid I don't know either. Take me anyway."

Bloody hell, thought Greg.

They ambled aimlessly, enjoying the evening sun, sharing trivial observations, their fast beating hearts disguised by slow steps, revelling in the renewal of their intimacy.

Sarah had grown up in a large house tucked away close to the river that ran parallel to the High Street. It had been sold after her parents had died and it had been many years since either of them had walked this path, but they found their way to the footbridge without a moment of hesitation. As they stepped on to the wooden bridge, she took Greg's arm. She'd accepted his invitation to walk and allowed him to choose the direction, but as they traversed the bridge she took the lead, just as she had done on the 25th June 1971.

There had always been gaps in Greg's recollection of that night but now as he felt Sarah's arm leading him on, retracing the same steps, the mist in his memory cleared and it came to him. He'd found the courage to walk her home but by the time they'd reached the bridge his confidence had faltered and without Sarah's lead he would have turned away.

She led him to the same wooden bench on the far bank of the river in front of the house that had been her family home and the two of them sat in the late evening sunshine, remembering.

Greg was pleased to sit. His head was spinning but the memory was full and vivid now. It had been Sarah who'd initiated their kiss and Greg who had eventually ended it, pulling himself free and running for his life. The quiet girl, who had asthma, who allowed herself to be carried along by others, had held him so tight, opened her mouth, breathed his breath, searched for his tongue, pushed her body against him, and he'd been overwhelmed. For years he'd longed for the moment and when it finally came, he'd blown it, run home. Every second of their teenage encounter came clear to him now and he sat quietly, shaking his head, admonishing himself. "I'd forgotten, Sarah. Not everything. I remember the kiss and how much it meant to me but I'd forgotten that I got scared."

Sarah needed more from him. "For the next three months I waited for you. I sat every day on this bench, waiting for you to cross the bridge but you never came. You broke this young girl's heart, Greg Whitehead. Promise me that you won't do that again."

They sat for a while without speaking. Sarah thought back to summer in 1971, remembered herself sitting on a bench by the river, waiting in vain for her young man's return. Even after weeks had passed and she had come to the conclusion that Greg had no interest, still she had maintained her vigil. She was deeply hurt. In the end, university took her away, and she went off to Cambridge without any further communication from Greg.

Greg felt a well of emotion inside him and he felt like a fool. "I wish I could go back to that summer and try again.

You were perfect, I was a fool. I still am. When we spoke last week, I told you about my talent for marrying the wrong people. I'm afraid that's only half of the problem for me, Sarah. For some reason, I also tend to miss out on the right ones. I'm an old fool now, I was just a young fool back then. I can't think of anything that would've pleased me more than to have walked onto the footbridge and seen you waiting on the bench, and yet for some reason I persuaded myself not to come. And I can't explain it to you. I've repeated the same mistakes throughout my life. I'm sorry, Sarah, that I left you waiting on that bench. I know that it's unforgivable but I ask for your forgiveness anyway."

Sarah had enjoyed their walk, their progress. But she was in the middle of so much. A respectable seventy-year-old married woman, walking out with another man, while there was a husband at home who knew nothing of her plans to leave him, or of her clandestine liaison with Greg Whitehead.

"I'll never forgive you, but I may be willing to give you a second chance, if you're still interested. Listen, Greg, I have some changes in front of me. I can't be sure of anything right now and I still have a husband in Surrey." Her thoughts were racing. "But as Mark pointed out, I still have time to go again, and God help me, I intend to. I don't know how long it will take for me to get free from Alexander or to be ready for someone else. Can you be patient for a while?"

"Yes, of course. Take all the time you need, Sarah, there's no rush." Greg was delighted by their rapid progress, but also a little frightened, accepting her invitation and her caution.

For a brief moment, Sarah got sight of the task in front of her, and she felt that she could promise nothing with certainty. "I really do have some things to clear up, but if all else fails, I'll be here again on 25th June next year."

Greg was puzzled, but he answered affirmatively. "Okay, I'll bear that in mind. Perhaps we should get back to The Lion, and grab some food."

But Sarah felt alive, open to new possibilities, stirred by

excitement and fear, and quite unready to retire indoors. She was a woman on the move and disinclined to sit down to dinner. Her appetite was elsewhere and she wanted it all, the glow of the evening light, the breeze playing in her hair, the promise of a new future and Greg Whitehead. Despite her words of caution, she turned her body to face him and, just as she had done more than fifty years earlier, she took him into her arms and she kissed him.

The butterflies that Greg had carried in his stomach, saw their opportunity. Sunlight on water, the wind in the trees, lovers on a river bank. They took flight.

TWENTY-ONE

ON THE ROAD AGAIN

IT HAD BECOME a habit and a need, and for each journey up and down the motorway, Sarah found her thinking space. She took the opportunity to process the developments in her life, to speak to herself and to listen to herself. She was clocking up the miles but the movement in her life was her focus. She smiled as she thought about Cheryl, who had persisted with her offer of accommodation until Sarah had given her acceptance. Then she smiled, remembering Greg's casual offer to drive half way down the country to meet her for coffee. Now she had a place to go, almost three hundred miles beyond Alexander's reach. *Go again, Sarah, you still have time.* Although the prospect of informing her husband about her imminent departure filled her with terror, the presence of supportive friends mattered; she had someone to run to and someone waiting for her.

As she progressed further south, Sarah was planning her actions, previewing the steps she'd need to take, working out methods to prepare herself without detection. She'd thought long and hard and she concluded that her foreknowledge and the element of surprise might be her advantage. She was already two steps ahead of the game and maybe she would be able to make her escape before her unsuspecting husband had time to find and shape his response.

She interrupted her own thinking, somehow looking at herself as if from an external vantage point and she could hardly recognise the woman in the car, who was planning her life, making choices, whose stomach was churning with the mixture of fear and excitement. "I'll find my freedom or I'll die." The sound of her own voice jolted her and the words that she spoke chilled her, but that's how she felt. She would find the courage to fight for her freedom, and if she couldn't succeed, she'd die trying.

It had been close to ten o'clock the previous evening when she and Greg walked back from the river bank to The Lion. They were too late to order dinner but Chris had made them coffee and sandwiches before they retired to their separate rooms. They had breakfast together and Sarah outlined her plan to leave her husband and to accept temporary accommodation with Cheryl. She had arranged to meet Greg on her home turf but she hadn't told him about the enormity of her task, or about the violence in her husband. She wanted separation between the ending of her marriage and whatever might develop with Greg. But he was in her thoughts. Whatever was about to happen, he would be part of it.

In amongst it all, she thought about which clothes to pack into the two suitcases she'd set aside – her survival kit. It seemed surreal to be wondering if Alexander might kill her, while deciding between her dress choices. And even as she drove on the busy motorway, she closed her eyes for a second, swallowing her fear and her foolishness. Two suitcases to be salvaged from the wreckage of her marriage, a sixty kilo luggage allowance to carry across the border to her new life. All of the years behind her, the weight of possessions, milestones and memories, reduced now in her planning to bare essentials. A few changes of clothes, a toothbrush and a travel clock. And rather oddly, as she made her selections, she welcomed the reduction. She didn't want a single item. She wished for a complete abandonment, to walk away from Hurtmoor empty handed. She wanted nothing from her married life, preferring to make her move with empty pockets and open arms.

Sarah had a schedule in mind. Her planning included a time frame. She was tempted to wait until the following Thursday, to maintain her habit, but a week might be too long. She planned to spend the weekend preparing, then she'd meet Greg on Monday and confront Alexander at the earliest opportunity before wheeling her cases to her car and driving away.

Normally, Sarah was able to organise and order her thoughts and she was determined to be thorough in her planning, but even so her thoughts raced from one consideration to the next. She encouraged herself to focus, to keep her eyes forward, and to concentrate on the road ahead.

If Sarah had been less self-absorbed, she might have checked the mirrors more often, and caught sight of the black hatchback that had followed her all the way from The Lion.

TWENTY-TWO
WATCHING

WITH HELP FROM DENNY, Andy had identified George and discovered Greg's home address. During the days following Mark Sanderson's funeral, he took some time to reflect. For many years, and with Polly's support, he'd kept to the right track. He'd made an effort to live a better life, but even still, he didn't fully trust himself. For all of his improvement, he still believed there was badness in him, and he often questioned his own motivations, worrying that he'd find his way back into darkness. He took a stroll around town every afternoon and checked the car park behind The Lion, but everyone seemed to have disappeared. *"They're getting on with their lives, mate. You should give it a try."*

As each day passed, he encouraged himself to re-focus and decide on the best way to approach Greg Whitehead. He had an address in Middlesbrough and the trail to Surrey had gone cold. He ought to have been content, without concern for Sarah Buxton, or interest in George Brand, but they were constantly in his thoughts. Which worried him.

He walked the same route for six consecutive days, eyes wide open, but no new developments. Then, on the seventh day, God found a spare moment to guide him, gave him a little light and he watched with more than mild surprise as

Sarah's Audi came into view. She was back at The Lion. *"Halle-fucking-lujah."* Less than an hour later she emerged on foot and he followed her to the Sanderson house. *"Interesting."* He retraced his steps an hour later, tucked himself into the shadows against a wall and waited. Apart from a newly arrived bicycle, nothing in The Lion car park had changed. It was a hot afternoon, an uncomfortable vigil, but nothing much to see. Sarah returned late in the afternoon and all was quiet again.

Andy waited. A couple of hours later she stepped back out into the street with Greg. *"Where the hell did you come from?"* Greg's car was nowhere to be seen. But Andy's mood picked up – he'd had a week without a whisper. He held his position. This was his territory, his home town, he wouldn't lose them. He waited for them to gain distance and just as he was about to start his pursuit, George Brand emerged from the shadows, once again tailing Sarah and Greg. *"Jesus, it's him again."* This was perfect for Andy, watching George as he watched Greg and Sarah. *"Okay, guys, let's dance."*

Sarah and Greg walked to the town centre, pausing to talk outside of The White Swan, and he smiled as he watched George jumping in and out of doorways to remain undetected. *"I've already clocked you, George, you're rumbled."* They changed direction, walking down to the river close to where Sarah's family home had been when they were at school, George still ducking and diving. *"What a bloody amateur."* Andy was enjoying his advantage, his superior skill.

Then it got really interesting. His former classmates started snogging on a bench by the river and George was filming them with his phone. *"Pervy bastard."* Andy smiled to himself. He had no idea what it all meant but he felt good. He had eyes on them all and nobody knew he was there. Last week he could have been convinced that George was harmless but not now, this man was a potential threat, the enemy. He'd need to find out a bit more about George, maybe take him down.

It was a beautiful summer's evening, perfect for young couples to sit by the river, but Greg and Sarah weren't young, they were his age. Andy was amazed by their bold show of affection. Seventy years old and snogging on a public bench. *"Bloody hell, there should be a law against it. For God's sake, Whitehead, see if you can keep it in your trousers."*

It wasn't a brief kiss. George would have a decent piece of film. Andy got his camera in position and took a few stills, getting all three of them into one picture. Then he followed them back to The Lion, as was his habit now. *"I didn't see any of that coming."*

If George Brand had restricted his interest to Sarah, then maybe Andy would have turned away, kept his focus entirely on Greg, but not after this evening's summer frolic on the river bank. Whatever George was up to, Greg was involved. He made his way home, feeling alive. More alive than he'd felt for a long time.

Usually Andy would tease Pol for a while, hold information from her just for the fun of it. He'd give her the goods eventually, but not before a good wind-up. Not so today, he was bursting. "I'll tell you what, Pol, you're not going to believe this."

Polly prepared for the game. "I'm not interested."

"Oh well, fair enough, I won't show you the photograph then." There was music playing on the radio and Andy got into the groove, tapping his foot, almost dancing.

Polly marched across the room and turned the radio off. "What photograph?"

Andy gave her the story, the walk to The Mucky Duck, then down by the river, George in pursuit, and the kiss.

Polly was fully engaged now, finding questions about every detail, but she was clear where to focus. "So, this guy lives near Sarah and he's filming her with Greg?"

"Affirmative."

"And he's much younger, I mean too young to be Sarah's bloke."

"Well, you never know these days, Pol, but I doubt it. She never struck me as a toy boy type."

Polly considered for a few seconds, then she gave her verdict. "He's been watching, filming. He's working, a professional, he's a private investigator. Has to be. Someone's hired him and someone's paying him. And you, dear husband, need to find out who that someone is."

TWENTY-THREE

GEORGE BRAND

GEORGE COULD LOOK AFTER HIMSELF. No one had ever pushed him around. He was a strong man and he held nothing back, but until Alexander had steered him, he'd achieved very little, drifting from one low paid job to the next without ambition. It was Walter, who managed the whole of Hurtmoor Estate, who had introduced them, and fifteen years later, George had grown wealthy, taking full advantage of the opportunities that Alexander had provided.

Walter had to use whichever workers were willing to pick the produce from the land, mostly a group of cheap imported labour who would work long hours without complaint. Locals tended to be less productive and more demanding. George had grown up a few miles from Hurtmoor without distinguishing himself, but in the farm fields he emerged as a natural leader, announcing his position with his feet and his fists. Walter had brought George to Alexander's attention, worrying that George's authority and his methods might be a potential threat and expecting Alexander to fire him. But Alexander had judged differently. Right from the get-go, he liked George's style.

"What do you think of him?" Walter had said.

"He'd have done very well at St Germaine's College," had been Alexander's cryptic reply.

Alexander tested George, took him off the land for special duties and tested his abilities for administering violent punishment, for reliability and for discretion. George passed all tests with flying colours and with Alexander's encouragement, he developed a network of contacts to support his new career activities. George gained reach into some dark domains, into the local criminal networks, but at the same time he set himself up in business as a self-employed private detective. He stood knee deep in faeces but he smelled as clean as a whistle. This occupation served as a perfectly acceptable and flawless veneer, providing a clean cover over the rotting wasteland where his business activities were conducted, in the criminal underworld that had become his bread and butter. He'd come a long way from picking up the sugar beets in a cold muddy field, and he was doing rather nicely. But even with his independence and his success, he always remained loyal to Alexander, the man who had spotted and nurtured his talents.

Alexander was under no illusions. He'd known for a long time that the distance between he and Sarah would never close. It was far too late to worry about that but keeping up appearances was another matter. The cold atmosphere in their house suited him well enough, absolutely fine so long as no one else could see it. In their private world, they were all done, but the public face needed careful management. Appearances must always be kept up. In the family and on the farm, Alexander occupied a position of leadership and he had no doubt that his control, the power of his leadership, had been built in keeping with the principles that had supported his power at St Germaine's College. His appearance as head of a strong family was a key part of his identity. He wanted Sarah to be seen at his side, everything and everyone under control. There must be no sign of vulnerability, no chink in his armour.

Sarah's initial Thursday excursion had angered him, but the continuing weekly visits to her dying friend aroused his interest and his suspicion. For one day each week, and for one night, she had ventured beyond his sight, escaped his reach. There was something in the air and Alexander was catching the scent. He decided to investigate.

Mostly Hurtmoor House was off limits for George but he'd been up there a few times to meet Alexander, either to receive instruction or to report back. He'd seen Sarah once or twice, although they'd never spoken, but he felt that he knew her pretty well. He'd been listening to her phone calls for more than three years, just monitoring her communications to guard against surprises, and it had given him sight of her local contacts and activities. Mostly he didn't bother to report back to Alexander, as she rarely deviated from her regular routines, but when Cheryl phoned to inform Sarah about Mark Sanderson's failing health, George had given Alexander the heads up.

George was a big fan of cell phones. They made his work easier, and he had several for his own use – a new iPhone on a regular contract and a few burners in the glove box of each of his two cars. They were the tools of his trade, even the ones that didn't belong to him. For example, Sarah's phone gave him access to her calls and he could also track her movements.

He was successful and perfectly able to treat himself to a bit of luxury, but ownership of two cars wasn't an indulgence for George, it was strategic. Sometimes he needed to show himself in fine clothes, but there were other occasions when he preferred to stay hidden. The Jaguar not only made him visible, it made a statement. He didn't want any of his business associates to mistake him for a small timer. On the other hand, the little black Peugeot had a magical quality – it made him invisible.

He didn't even bother following Sarah for the first trip, he just followed the tracker from her phone. She travelled up into North Yorkshire and returned the next day. George made a few calls but everything checked out – Sarah's story was authentic. But Alexander wasn't satisfied. He'd told Mark Sanderson a long time ago to stay away from Sarah and he wasn't about to soften his stance now. Stage four of an aggressive lung cancer was no excuse for disobedience.

So George got busy. He followed Sarah up and down the motorway, watched her wheel her suitcase into The Lion and identified the property in which Mark and Cheryl were living and dying. George had worked with Alexander often enough to know that although his benefactor could be a bit paranoid, often suspecting when there was no need, sometimes his instincts were right on the money. George followed Sarah's every move during her second trip to Stokesley, and although there was nothing untoward, Alexander's nostrils were still twitching as he instructed George to stay on the case.

It got more interesting when Mark Sanderson died. George had listened as Mark's sister delivered the sad news and that's when Alexander's suspicions gained substance, when big questions were raised. Why was Sarah lying to him? Why did she continue her trips to North Yorkshire when Mark Sanderson was already dead and cremated? That was an interesting moment for Alexander and anger had reared up in him, adrenaline surging, and yet he'd sat like a statue, cold and still, calculating. He'd held himself in check, put his anger into temporary storage, and wondered what was afoot. He wanted more information. He'd get the bastards, no need for anyone to worry about that, he just needed to wait while George collected evidence.

He sat still and calm, watched her come and go, timing her arrivals and departures, staying patient. Then early on this Friday morning, he'd received George's video clip: a middle-aged couple sitting on a bench at the river bank. George had zoomed in for the kiss, for the kill, and as the couple broke apart from their embrace, Sarah's face had come into clear focus.

TWENTY-FOUR

MARRIED LIFE

SATURDAY UNFOLDED in accordance with Sarah's plan. She had her own rooms and enough private space to collect her essential belongings together without detection. She spent some time trying to work out when to tell her children, and what exactly she might say to them, wondering how much they had seen of their father's coercive control and how it would be for them to divide their loyalty.

She rehearsed constantly, looking for the phrases that would deliver her message, coaching herself until she felt ready. As ready as she could be. And bizarrely, she went shopping on Sunday morning to get the house stocked up with essential supplies. She fully expected Alexander to be murderously angry, but at least he'd have plenty of toilet paper. In the Tesco carpark, she began the countdown to her rendezvous with Greg – twenty four more hours. She sent him a quick text confirming the time and place before driving back to the house.

She was up early the next morning. It had been a hot night and sleep had been elusive. Sarah and Alexander were able to skirt around each other as they went about their separate lives, walking past each other without interest or acknowledgement. They'd practised for years now.

Nevertheless, she went down early for breakfast, hoping to avoid her husband and for twenty minutes she sat alone with her coffee in the large kitchen, the one room in the house that remained a shared living space.

Everything reminded her of her forthcoming departure, and already she felt herself a stranger in the house. She'd lived here with such unhappiness for so many years and she felt a profound sadness, almost shame, that so much of her life seemed wasted. Now, with her freedom in sight, she wondered why she'd waited so long. *Go again, Sarah, you still have time.*

The sleep that had refused her through the night tugged at her now. She yawned, placed her arms on to the table top and lowered her head to rest.

She awoke to the sounds of Alexander preparing his breakfast, clattering and banging. They had learned to start their days without conversation but Sarah spoke as she reoriented. "Excuse me, I must have fallen asleep." She felt awkward, a bit exposed and quite unaware of how long she'd slept.

Alexander paid no attention to her apology. "How is your friend, Mark? Is he getting better?"

The question caught her unprepared and she felt heat rise in her face. "No, he won't get better." She was panicking. "I must go, I'm getting my hair cut this morning."

Sarah grabbed her bag and went back to her bedroom. She showered and dressed, taking particular care with her choice of clothes, applying an extra touch of perfume before reaching into her bag for her keys, and rummaging around in search of her phone. The unplanned nap had delayed her preparation and suddenly she was anxious and rushed.

"Where have I left my phone?" she asked herself as she ran down the stairs.

Alexander had a brain in his head. He'd been well educated and he was perfectly able to think intelligently. And although he could be roused, driven by emotion, he'd also

129

discovered the value of consideration. Mostly his actions were carefully measured, and administered with cold efficiency, but on this occasion, events had unfolded quickly and he'd moved into the action phase reactively. There hadn't been a great deal of time for strategic thinking. George's short film had pushed too many buttons. The simple truth of the matter was that Alexander wanted to lash out. He was angry, ready to inflict pain, but he had no long-term plan, and no end game.

He'd let things run, sent George out to read the story, but now events were accelerating. George had listened to enough calls, and read all the revealing text messages. His wife, shameless adulteress, was travelling up and down to Stokesley, pretending to visit an old friend who was already dead, to throw herself into the arms of another man. She was laughing at him, taking the piss, popping out to the supermarket and the hairdresser, as if butter wouldn't melt in her mouth.

Sarah marched back into the kitchen where her husband still lingered. She was running late. "I don't suppose you've seen my phone?"

TWENTY-FIVE

A DAY OUT

GREG WAS HAPPY, a perfect example of blissful ignorance. He knew that Sarah had a husband to dispatch, but he had no insight about Alexander's character, and felt no sense of threat. He'd been acutely nervous during his first exchanges with Sarah, but not anymore. They had kissed on the river bank and now he was driving to Guildford, all the nerves gone, feeling secure and starting to enjoy his role as the secret lover of an unhappily married woman, and relishing the prospect of heroic rescue. Greg had never been a man to encourage infidelity, nevertheless, he was excited to be a participant in this clandestine rendezvous. Today Greg was a cool dude, a bad-ass boy.

He laughed out loud in the car, reminding himself of the reality, trying to get his feet back on the ground. They were meeting for coffee, that was all. An hour at the most in a teashop across the road from her hairdresser.

But his mood remained buoyant despite his reality check and he thought about Eleanor and Sue, and how he'd defended his position as a single man, the champion of one person households, happily withdrawn from the complications and disappointments of intimate relationships.

He imagined them teasing him, exposing the frailty of his philosophy, and his own cheerful acceptance.

It had only been three days since they'd sat together for breakfast at The Lion, and if Sarah's plans unfolded in the way she anticipated, and why wouldn't they, then she'd be staying with Cheryl in Stokesley within a few days. They could have been patient adults and waited. Initially Sarah had discouraged him but Greg had pushed his case. He'd told her he enjoyed motorway driving and that he couldn't wait a whole week without seeing her. He could see that she'd liked all of that – his foolish lies and his foolish heart. She'd given up her protest with a grateful smile. Greg turned up the music in his car. He was drumming on the steering wheel, singing along with Tom Petty... 'here comes my girl'.

He arrived in Guildford early which was fine. He didn't want to be rushed and he certainly didn't want to be late. He got his car parked and located the street where they would meet. It was exactly as Sarah had described. The Teapot window was almost directly opposite Donna's Hair World. There he stood and suddenly it hit him, reality. In the car, he'd felt like an excited child waiting for Christmas, free to indulge himself, to mix truth with fantasy, but now it felt different, standing on an unfamiliar street in Guildford, a long way outside of his bubble. It was real.

He was too early and he decided to walk for a while, just to pass twenty minutes before securing a table in The Teapot. With just ten minutes to spare, he made his way back to the cafe and found a table close to the window where he could see the door to Donna's. It was perfect. He would see her the moment she emerged.

A young waitress dropped a menu in front of him. "Can I get you a drink?"

Greg gave his attention, noting her name badge. "Well, that's a very tempting offer, Zana, but I think I'm a bit too old for you." Greg was amused by his riposte and he looked up expecting Zana's smile, but she scowled and shook her head.

He tried again. "Anyway, I'm waiting for my lady friend. She'd be angry if she knew you'd asked me out. She'd probably beat you up." Still nothing. Greg would talk to anyone, there were no age-based decisions of engagement but on this particular morning, Zana met his humour with disdain and he retreated. "Actually, I really am waiting for a friend. Can you give me a few minutes until she arrives?" Zana turned away with a degree of unmasked irritation but Greg smiled. He was waiting for Sarah. He watched Donna's door, and watched the people out on the street going about their lives, in ones and twos. None of them knew who he was or why he was sitting in The Teapot. The smell of bacon tempted him and the scent of a new life invited him. Zana could be as miserable as she pleased, never before had waiting felt so good.

He drifted in his thoughts, and watched Zana clear the table next to him. She looked at him and then up at the clock behind the counter. Greg checked his phone and turned his attention back outside. She was two minutes late – a woman's prerogative. He enjoyed the thought, realising that he was going to have to get accustomed to all of that again – the partner's perspective. Donna's door opened and he rose to his feet to optimise his view, but it was a young man who emerged and Greg sat again. He blew the breath from his lungs, suddenly tensing, and he checked his phone again. He was getting nervous.

The next fifteen minutes were difficult. Five minutes late was almost an obligation, ten was pushing it although acceptable, especially following a hair appointment, but seventeen minutes? He'd caved in to Zana's accusing invitations to order and now there was a latte sitting in front of him. One cup of coffee for one person, occupying one table.

He sighed. The voice inside his head showed no mercy. 'You're an idiot, Whitehead. Who the hell do you think you are, Brad fucking Pitt? Waiting for your lady friend? She's not coming, bud, not interested. You're old and boring. She's decided that she's better off with her dickhead husband.' He felt sick and for a few minutes he thought he would have to find the toilets and throw up. There was sweat on his forehead and shards of broken glass piercing his flesh. It hadn't been easy, to believe there could still be a future, to believe again in the power of love. Or maybe it had been, he couldn't really remember how it had happened. It didn't matter, it had all turned to shit now.

Zana seemed to sense her moment, and invaded his suffering. "Are you going to order some food or what?"

Greg's disappointment flared hot for a second. "No, I'm leaving." He stood up, took a tenner from his wallet and threw it on to the table. Finally, Zana smiled.

Once out in the sunshine, he felt dizzy, too hot and hit by a second wave of nausea. There was nowhere to hide, and he leant against a wall and retched. He puked but not much, just a mouthful of coffee and acid. Passers-by passed him by, giving disapproving glances at an old man who was embarrassing himself.

An hour later, he found himself in a park, sitting on a wooden bench similar to the one by the river in Stokesley. It gave him enough privacy to sit and cry, to inhabit the hollow space of heartbreak and humiliation. And now, with his emotional reserves exhausted, he reviewed the situation, looking for hope. Maybe he'd got the wrong day, the wrong week, the wrong street. Greg knew that misunderstandings sometimes occurred, and he looked around him in all directions seeking explanation. He decided to phone her but it took a while to find the courage. He was afraid to confirm his worst fears, but he made the call and he listened to the buzz of an unanswered phone, then a click and then her voice apologising that she was unable to take the call, asking him to leave a message. He bowed his head and closed his eyes. What kind of old fool was he? He ended the call. He had no message. No words in the world could represent him now. He got to his feet and started walking. He was lost but it didn't really matter. He had nowhere to go.

TWENTY-SIX
MARRIED LIFE

"YES, I saw it on the kitchen table a few minutes ago." Alexander watched his wife rush around the kitchen, following every agitated move. "But it's not there now. I've put it somewhere safe." No, there was no long-term plan but it was time for action and when he'd seen her sleeping at the kitchen table, he'd taken the opportunity to steal her phone. Who wouldn't?

Sarah felt a chill in her spine but she persevered. "I'm running late, Alexander. Where have you put my phone?"

Alexander ignored the question. "No, I don't suppose Mark Sanderson will get better. Dead men seldom do."

That shook her. She had her back to him. Her eyes closed and she froze on the spot, trying to hold her balance while the ground beneath her feet seemed to be shifting. So, this was the time. "Alexander, we need to talk." Sarah turned to face him and she stood firm as he marched across the kitchen with hatred in his eyes. He stood a foot in front of her, drew back his right arm, clenched his fist, and punched her in the stomach. There was real anger in the punch. He threw his whole body in behind his fist, and dropped her into a crumpled heap, gasping and groaning on the kitchen floor.

"What would you like to talk about, Sarah?" Alexander

waited, feeling no need to rush. He'd hurt her, firmly smashed his fist into her abdomen. He found a chair, and watched his injured wife struggling for breath.

Sarah had fallen to her knees, bending over so that her forehead rested on the stone floor. She had anticipated this moment a hundred times, always full of fear. Oddly, now that the reality had arrived, and even though her pain was severe, the fear had gone. She felt helpless and powerless. She knew that she may well be in danger, that her husband might kill her, but she wasn't afraid. The time had come.

She wasn't able yet to change her position, curled over double with her face down when she spoke. "Yes, Mark died two weeks ago." She swallowed as best she could, her mouth dry, and the pain in her abdomen screaming. She rummaged in her handbag and found and used her inhaler, but even then, breathing was still difficult. She wasn't sure how much damage his punch had done but she suspected a cracked rib and feared for her spleen. She raised her head, put her palms against the floor and pushed herself upright. With great effort, Sarah stood. She held on to the side of the kitchen table and took another hit from her inhaler. "I'm going now. Please give me my phone."

Alexander chuckled. "It's over, Sarah. You're not going to the hairdresser, you're not going to meet Greg Whitehead. You're not going anywhere."

All the lines she'd practised, the explanation, the apology, the grown-up conversation, the voice of reason, the art of persuasion, the secret plan that was to be aided by the element of surprise, were all gone now. Alexander appeared to have full knowledge. Sarah had taken an optimistic view, allowed fantasy and wishfulness to obscure the reality of her husband's spiteful anger. Just a few minutes earlier, she had been excited by her prospects for the day and for the future. Now, with her optimism obliterated and her future endangered, she reviewed her situation. The game was changed. She braced herself, ready for spitting anger, cruelty, and recrimination. Although she knew this was just the beginning, that there would be more to come, she promised herself to stand before him and take whatever he would throw at her. Even with a steadying hand on the table top, she needed determination and concentration to remain on her feet, but she would not bow or cower before him, and she held her position. She would go on standing. If he wanted her on the floor then he'd have to knock her down again.

Sarah lifted her head, looking around at cold steel and granite, feeling the weight of silence, taking in the scene. They were husband and wife, married for nearly fifty years, parents to the same children, grandparents, pillars of the community, civilised, educated and wealthy. She wondered what he was capable of, looking into his eyes, glazed with venom, and she knew that it would make no difference what words she chose, that their history and position meant nothing. She looked across at Alexander, who was burning with anger, adrenaline surging through his bulging veins. He was a savage.

Is this it, dear husband?
  You and I, in our late middle age
  Punches and lies
  Cruelty and hatred
  Is this our life now?

Alexander had acted, given his anger expression, and he couldn't allow Sarah to get the better of him. Even after his violent punch, he watched his wife's defiant stance, and he felt compelled to deliver more punishment. He called George, demanding his assistance, and together the two men escorted Sarah across the farmyard into the middle barn, and Alexander locked the door.

TWENTY-SEVEN

CHERYL

CHERYL WONDERED ABOUT HER FUTURE. She'd returned to her home town seven years earlier, exhausted and still heavy with the grief that had threatened to consume her after Graham's sudden death. For almost a year, she stumbled along, gradually recovering, but she never really rebuilt her life. In the end, it had been Mark's failing health that made the decisions and she found her way back to Stokesley. It had worked well enough. Mark had needed to be looked after, and for a while at least, she had found an occupation, a reason to get up in the morning, a purpose.

Now served.

She often looked back, trying to make sense of how she'd arrived at this moment. In the vulnerability of her grieving, she had altered the course of her life, driven partly by a sense of duty but also by default, and even now she wasn't sure whether she'd made the right choices. Too late, she was back in Stokesley and Mark, bless him, was dead and gone. Finally, after all of these years, she had time to think about herself. In some ways, she felt defeated. She'd gone out into the world, borne children, raised them to become independent, travelled to far away places, lived her life. Then she had finished up back in her small home town, in the house that she had grown up in, back to square one. Now, with Mark gone, and her duty done, she could make new choices, determine her own direction.

What's a seventy-two-year-old widow meant to do? She could live with her eldest son in India. Joss worked for a tech company in Bengaluru, and he'd repeated his invitation several times during the past three weeks. Her other children had been equally attentive: Diana worked as an academic in Innsbruck, and Dennis was in New Zealand working for an adventure holiday company. She could sofa-surf between the three of them, play the doting grandmother, take things slow and easy. Something was happening to Cheryl, some kind of release, unburdened by grief and free from her role as carer. Cheryl was only beginning, so early in her journey that she was yet to determine her direction, let alone the destination. She had no clear idea about what the future might hold, only that she wanted something more, something for herself. This retired widow, a seventy-two-year-old small town girl, not yet ready for a sedentary life, wished for adventure. Her conversations with Sarah had reignited her spirit.

As she sat each afternoon enjoying time in her garden, she examined the expectations within her culture, the options for people like her, widowed pensioners. Although she was grateful for her children's interest, she also felt a touch of resentment. She knew that their invitations came from kind hearts, but Cheryl prickled at the suggestion that her life was already spent, that she should accept rich green pasture for a comfortable decline from old age into her own death. What if she wanted to walk in the Himalayas, dance the fandango, or go out and have sex with a stranger? Would those aspirations fit with her children's house rules?

While Mark had lived, these questions never arose. She had had a clear purpose, and she had been fine with that, ready each day to fulfil her role. Now when she got up from her bed in the morning, she had no role, no one to care for, and she felt redundant.

Her new connection to her brother's long-lost friend felt important. She and Sarah had made a connection, talked about their lives, developed a personal and meaningful dialogue in an environment of sisterhood. Cheryl had been forthright, asking questions, demanding Sarah's confidence.

After the children had grown into adulthood, there had been a period when Graham accepted invitations to work in the Middle East and South Asia – a series of short contracts with big pay cheques. Cheryl could have stayed home alone but she wanted to experience new cultures, she had an appetite for life. She'd always felt a need for friendship. She had loved her husband deeply but she needed more, and in the various parts of an ever-changing world, she would quickly identify those who she might befriend. During this period, when she and Graham moved frequently, there wasn't really time for friendships to grow incrementally, so Cheryl learned to cut through social conventions, and she'd taken risks, finding short cuts to intimacy. She wasn't a woman who could be sustained by repetition. She'd never had a small town mentality, and with Mark gone, she felt thankful for Sarah's friendship and almost desperate to break free from her shackles.

The garden always took priority, but there was still time to play the piano or to read a book. Cheryl detested housework and she liked her home environment to be busy rather than ordered. Open books on the coffee table, garden flowers hanging from the ceiling to dry, unfinished craft projects littering every room, and a sink full of unwashed dishes. It was just the way she liked to live. Nevertheless, she prepared a room for Sarah. Not Mark's old room. She'd dispensed with his belongings quickly after his death, but she wouldn't ask Sarah to sleep on what had been his deathbed. She opened windows in every room, left the conservatory doors wide open all through the day, but still Mark's smell lingered. It was in the wallpaper and the carpets, in the bricks and the plaster, in her memory. So she cleaned the spare room, changed the sheets and pillow cases, left fresh towels on the bed. It wasn't fun but it had to be done and when she added a small but carefully chosen selection of books and a vase of fresh flowers, she allowed herself some satisfaction.

Then she waited for the next chapter in her life to unfold, for her next companion. Even though Sarah had indicated it might be sooner, Cheryl felt sure that she'd travel on Thursday.

All of their time together had been on Thursdays, every conversation and confidence. But despite her expectation, she felt impatient, she was waiting. She got as close to organised as she could. A trip into town on Wednesday for groceries, and a well-stocked wine rack.

There had been no recent communications but once Wednesday had been and gone, Cheryl's theory appeared proven – Sarah had waited for Thursday. It was almost midday before she felt the first moment of unease. Sarah's previous arrivals had been late in the morning but Cheryl reasoned with herself. This trip was different, her final departure, and of course the preparations would be a little more complicated. By two o'clock, however, she was restless, constantly checking for messages, but nothing came.

TWENTY-EIGHT

LOST

GREG HAD no memory of the journey back to Middlesbrough and no idea how he'd managed to drive. But he arrived at his home safely nevertheless, and as he closed the car door behind him, he hurried to get inside the house. He needed a safe haven, a place to hide away, to remove himself from the world. He struggled to insert the front door key, unable to stop the shaking in his fingers. He looked at his hand without recognition or ownership, trembling and numb, as he finally unlocked the door. Once inside, his whole body seemed to be shaking, the tension that he'd held in check for nearly five hours on the motorway, rushing now for release.

Time passed. He found himself standing in front of the hall mirror, looking at his reflection. He saw an old man, lines across his face, loose skin hanging from his jaws, thinning grey hair, sadness and shame. An old fool. Somehow, he'd hoped for restoration, anticipating that once back in his exclusive bubble that he'd feel okay, re-engage with the lifestyle and philosophy that had got him through the past months and years, that had enabled him to survive the pandemic. But he found no such comfort and he spoke to his reflection with a heavy heart. "It's gone, buddy, that way of life. You sold it for a worthless kiss. Now, it's all gone." He faced his own folly, knowing that he'd gambled and lost, abandoning his former life, and risking everything. He'd allowed the safety of guarded isolation to escape him, staking everything on the almost forgotten desires of a confused teenager, and although he'd justified his position with sermons and smiles, he knew that he couldn't go back to his previous insular contentment. "All gone." He closed his eyes, trying to shut himself down, looking for darkness. Against his own better judgement, he'd given love another go, and now everything was lost.

More time passed, days went by, and long nights of fitful sleep were broken by desperate dreams. The setting for the dreams varied: a desert, dense woodland or just a wall of bright yellow light, but the theme was consistent... Greg wandering, wounded, lost and alone, unable to find a place to rest, shouting desperately for help, but always unheard.

He ventured out to buy milk and wine. For years Greg had refused to use the self-checkout tills in supermarkets, insisting on human contact. It was a point of principle. Let the people do the work. But now he used them gladly, feeling unable to make either eye contact or conversation. Sometimes he found a few moments of hope, driven by desperation and fuelled by fantasy, allowing himself to remember the kiss on the river bank and inventing innocent explanations for Sarah's 'no show' at The Teapot. They were just momentary distractions. Dead ends.

The days drifted by, and Greg maintained absolute isolation. The severity of nausea started to ease although he still had no appetite. He'd started to shower more regularly, and although he had no wish for company, he was talking to himself. He couldn't find interest in food, and he'd lost half a stone.

"Every cloud has a silver lining," he said as he stepped off the scales, unamused by his quip. He dressed and felt the need for coffee. Greg's wine intake had risen and each morning began with a dull headache and a resolve to get control of his drinking, even though he knew that he'd give himself compassionate permission to delay that intention later in the day. Alcohol had given him a couple of hours sleep after he'd first gone to bed but then he'd awoken at 1.30 in the morning and lain awake for hours. Eventually, when daylight flooded his bedroom, he'd slept again and now, at midday, he was preparing his breakfast coffee.

His phone pinged as he filled the kettle. It stopped him in his tracks. Curious and hesitant, he took in a deep breath, but he couldn't look. He applied himself to the task at hand, adding water to the cafetière, and he made his way into his living room, coffee in one hand, phone in the other. He placed his phone face down on the coffee table, not yet ready to look, and sipped nervously from his cup. His heart rate had risen and his neck had stiffened with tension. The unseen text might have come from anyone. It might be a scam. And maybe it was from Sarah.

He sat back, nursing his coffee and decided to wait a few minutes more. Then his phone pinged again, and he was caught in a wave of excitement and confusion. It occurred to him that Sarah might be waiting for him in a cafe in Guildford, and he sat forward trying to remember what day it was, suddenly panicking that he'd gone to Guildford on the wrong bloody day. With that fantasy occupying his mind, Greg found the courage to pick up his phone. He was puzzled as his head set shuffled the cards into a new order. Both new texts were from Eleanor and he ignored them without even a glance, instinctively following his fantasy and reviewing his messages from Sarah. There was nothing new, and instantly his foolish delusion crashed. He realised that even after being stood up and then suffering an agonising week without communication, he hadn't completely given up hope, still ready to grasp at straws.

His spirit, already injured and depressed, sank deeper into darkness and he cursed himself. He scrolled back to look at Eleanor's messages. *You're quiet, is everything okay?* followed by *I'll phone you tonight.* He'd avoided company, and still felt unready for human contact. He started to compose a message to dissuade Eleanor when his phone pinged again. His small group of telephone contacts had remained silent for a whole week, without a single interruption from either his doorbell or his phone and suddenly he'd got three texts in the space of an hour. This latest communication demanded attention. It was from Sarah.

Greg took in a long slow breath, and felt competing impulses, wanting to look but fearing what he'd find. Of course, he had to look. The words stood before him, clear and still.

I've decided to stay home and work at my marriage. Goodbye, S.

There was no apology, not even a proper name at the end of the message, just cold information. Greg wasn't just hurt by the message, he was disappointed by her tone, and angry that she could be so cold-hearted. Had she forgotten what had taken place ten days earlier? Didn't it mean anything now? She'd picked him up and then dropped him without a care. There was a shift in his mood. He'd been sombre and mostly focused on himself, but now he was angry with Sarah. He hadn't seen this side of her. Perhaps love really was blind. When she'd taken his arm to cross the footbridge, held him close and tight, moved her lips against his own, he could never have believed she could throw him away so easily. It didn't seem like Sarah at all. The pain in his gut intensified. He felt like he'd been punched in the stomach.

He'd forgotten all about Eleanor's messages until his phone started to ring and her name appeared on his phone screen. It was seven o'clock. During the covid pandemic, Greg had developed some quite rigid structure in his domestic routines, chunks of time given to various activities which had helped him to navigate his way through each day of isolation. He'd had time slots for exercise and for housework, an hour of reading and thirty minutes to watch the news on television. Some discipline and order in his home environment while the outside world fell into chaos. In the evenings he would cook himself a meal and once eight o'clock arrived he would allow himself to drink red wine while he watched another box set drama on the telly. He registered Eleanor's call and looked at his watch, wondering how it was that he had a large glass of wine in his hand at such an early hour.

"Hello, Eleanor, what bad news do you bring?"

It took a couple of seconds for Eleanor to form her reply. She could hear the wine in his speech and she experienced a moment of alarm. "Greg, I have no bad news. Nobody died. Are you okay?"

"No, as it happens, I'm not. I died about a week ago."

Again, Eleanor was silenced for a second. "You're frightening me. What on earth has happened?"

Greg closed his eyes, wishing he hadn't answered the call. He'd resolved to keep his humiliation and his shame to himself, ride it out, no need to tell a soul. But he was angry and the alcohol clouded his judgement. "You'll be pleased to know that I took Sue's advice. Anyway, it screwed my life up. If she thinks of any more bright ideas for my future, please ask her to keep them to herself."

He'd sat for days feeling hurt by rejection and the text message from Sarah had been a brutal confirmation of his fate. Eleanor couldn't have called at a worse time, placing herself to receive a build up of emotion combined with alcohol-fuelled disinhibition. She could hear clearly that Greg was distressed, but she also felt ready to defend her partner. "I'm sorry that you're upset, Greg, but Sue always means well, you know that."

The call ended. Eleanor stared at her phone in disbelief and tears ran down her cheeks.

Greg finished his drink and went to bed. He cried himself to sleep as he'd done sometimes as a boy after his encounters with Andy Cooper. He woke later and seeing that it was eleven o'clock, he stumbled out of bed cursing himself for lying in again. It took a minute before he orientated, realising that it was in fact eleven in the evening. He'd got drunk, gone to bed, had a bad night's sleep and woken up again, all before his bedtime. His mouth felt like sandpaper and his head ached, but he didn't care. Then the memory started to form, in fragments at first, until he recalled each word of his conversation with Eleanor and remembered how he'd rudely ended the call. He sat on the edge of his bed, despising himself, breathing rapidly and sweating. He felt his stomach rise and rushed to the bathroom just in time to puke into the toilet bowl. He rested his head on the toilet rim, tasting in his mouth the remains of the day... stomach acid, stale alcohol and the bitterness of heartbreak.

So much for love.

TWENTY-NINE

THE NEW WORLD

THE ORDER OF THINGS, repeated day after day, year after year. The simple predictability of familiar routines, the comfort of a known world. Anchor points holding things in place: BBC news at six, soap operas at seven, curry on Wednesdays, and fish on Friday. It had all disintegrated. Sarah wasn't sure anymore what day it was. She was confused and confined, a prisoner held in the middle barn, an animal, shitting in one corner, sleeping in another.

The barn was a solid enough structure, an open space of about 250 square metres which was used mostly for storage. There were no windows, but shafts of light leaked through here and there and there was an electric light. Sarah had made a temporary home for herself, found a corner free from drafts, made a straw bed and she used a stool as both seat and table at different times of the day.

It had been a few days and she could hardly believe that she'd lost count at such a low number, but it was true, in amongst the pain and the panic, she'd lost track. It had been long enough for her to be reassured that her spleen had not ruptured, although Alexander's punch had definitely cracked a rib. George had attended her three or four times each day bringing food and water and slopping out her improvised toilet.

There had been time for thinking, giving Sarah opportunity to appraise her circumstances and to consider how she might react to them. The first twenty hours had been particularly difficult, suffering and worrying about her abdominal pain, managing her asthma, which had become unusually troublesome, and recoiling from the shock. It had been quite a turnaround, one minute making her way into town to get her hair trimmed and getting ready to meet Greg, then punched and imprisoned by her husband the next. As night gathered in the darkness, and the temperature fell, Sarah had gained a rather grim comprehension of her plight. She wouldn't brush her teeth in her en-suite bathroom, there would be no glass of wine, and no nightdress.

George had brought a bucket, a sleeping bag and some water. No food. She recognised Alexander in that omission. Every aspect of her treatment was a statement of his power and control, a carefully designed campaign to provoke fear and helplessness. That was all he'd give her... the food for demoralising defeat.

So, the first night had been tough, he'd got to her. The physical environment was challenging. Pain and hunger reached significant levels but she could cope with that. She'd been given just enough water to survive, but the psychological injury was harder to bear. Part of it was the shock, the suddenness of the change, having to take in that Alexander knew all her secrets, and then the new dynamics of her marital relationship. Already he had shattered her future, stolen her phone and her freedom. And the fear. She had seen the murderous rage in her husband's eyes, felt the force of his fist. During that first night, she had feared for her life.

On the second day there was silence. George established his schedule – no one spoke a word, but again Sarah was given just enough water, and this time a little food. No clean clothes, Alexander again, but she felt less frightened, down from ten to eight or nine, although her thoughts were all over the place on that day and so it had been ever since.

On day three or four, she started speaking to George, asked him to bring clean clothes and washing facilities. George never spoke but at least some of her requests were granted. With Alexander completely absent, clean underwear and toilet paper were provided and Sarah was able to escape the adrenaline-driven survival state, slow down, and do some thinking.

The first thought, the starting premise, was simple: the marriage was over. The pretence was exposed. People don't make up after adultery, violence, kidnap, imprisonment, humiliation and dehumanisation. All of which demanded the question: what next?

Sarah gave him credit. Alexander had picked up the scent, smelled a rat. He'd scuppered her plans, and taken control. But what next? That was the dominant thought. What was the end game?

No way back, that kept on running through her mind. Where on earth could they go from here?

Over a period of days, Sarah considered the options available to her husband. There was no way back but she couldn't see a way forward either. That was a moment of sinister sobriety. Alexander had a problem but no obvious solution. He couldn't keep her in the barn forever and she couldn't get past the obstacles obstructing her train of thought. Although she'd settled from the panic of the first hours of her captivity, her fear started to grow again. Alexander hadn't shown himself since day one, and Sarah felt the effect of his absence, the terror of not knowing.

With each passing day, her desperation increased, and she appealed to George.

I want to speak to my husband.
Please ask Alexander to come, I need to talk to him.

. . .

She started to put her unanswered questions to him, as a way to show him the futility of their arrangement.

Will you spend the rest of your life doing this?
  When the police come, how will you explain yourself?
  What are Alexander's plans for next month?

George made no reply. It all combined to heighten Sarah's sense of terror. Her husband's absence, George's silence, and the long hours of waiting. She felt the weight of her circumstances, alone and without resources or hope. She didn't believe in Gods and miracles, and she knew that her comments to George would all be ignored.

Sarah wasn't just nervous and frightened, she felt helpless and demoralised. She wanted to see Alexander, felt the need to speak to him, and again she acknowledged his skill for conflict and torture. She had no bargaining power, no trick of persuasion. She was ready to beg for his mercy.

As she stumbled around the middle barn, she could feel herself weakening, experiencing periods of light-headedness and a trembling in her limbs, and she found herself sobbing with her face against cold hard wood. She felt utterly beaten. And in the misery of her defeat, she noticed a scent filling her nostrils. The sweet smell of rich mahogany, a moment of realisation.

The gun cabinet had always been present, the deep red wood had almost turned black with years of dust and grime. It had been built for Alexander's grandfather by a highly skilled carpenter. Even with Mark's recent reminder, it simply hadn't crossed her mind that she was sharing a prison with several lethal weapons. Until now.

Sarah stepped a pace back to view the discovery that had

been with her throughout her confinement. The cabinet stood almost two metres tall, with a slightly bowed door, and it featured a tiny hidden drawer to hold the cabinet key. It had been a game when the children were young, searching for the secret compartment, but always without success. Here she stood, in the same place that Mark had faced her husband at gunpoint, and a cold shiver invaded her as she faced her own emerging thoughts. The cabinet was locked, but there were weapons inside which might defend and free her.

It was quite a moment, resolving to search for the key, finding new hope, and considering how she might make use of the cabinet's contents. Sarah had never joined in the game to search for the cabinet key. Guns held no appeal for her, but with so many hours alone and unoccupied, and with the disconcerting background of fear and an unbearable sense of helplessness, she decided to try.

THIRTY
THE LIMITS OF LOYALTY

GEORGE HAD SHOWN IMPRESSIVE LOYALTY, giving more time than he could spare to carry out Alexander's bidding. First the trips to Stokesley, now guard duty. For Christ's sake. He had other business to occupy his time and he'd already realised that Alexander had no end game – his unfaithful wife wanted to leave him, so he'd punched her and locked her in a barn. It was perfectly clear to George that the master of the house was driven by emotion and that careful thought was yet to make an appearance. George waited until the heat dropped, then he sought the farmer's counsel.

George had been dependent on Alexander's employment in the early days but he'd come a long way since then. These days George owned a Jaguar and he was self-reliant. He was always ready to give a favour to his old friend but his patience had limits. After several days of carrying food to the middle barn and slopping out Sarah's plastic bucket each morning, George was ready to move things forward. Sarah had sewn a few seeds of doubt, asking pertinent questions which echoed louder in the back of his mind with each passing day.

The two men had shared some interesting moments. They

knew too much about each other ever to fall out, but George had no fear and he could speak his mind. "How long do you want to keep her in the barn?"

Alexander was unprepared. He had no good answer. "Long enough."

"Long enough for what? I have other work to do, Alexander. You need to work out what happens next."

"Long enough to make sure that she has nowhere to go."

George spoke plainly, asking his question almost as a challenge, but Alexander appreciated the prompt, his thinking focused and he gained a better sense of his direction. For the first time in several days, his thoughts moved away from what was happening in the barn, and travelled instead up to Yorkshire. He knew very little about Cheryl, just that she was Mark Sanderson's big sister and that she'd offered her home to Sarah as a place of refuge.

George could see the cogs turning. "What are you thinking?"

"You can torch Cheryl Sanderson's house, burn it to the ground." Immediately Alexander felt better. He looked across at George. "That'll sort her out, she won't be so generous with her hospitality once the rafters are on fire."

George nodded, it was fair comment. But he wasn't happy. "That would involve risk for me. You'll owe me a great debt if I set fire to her house. What about Whitehead?"

"I won't forget, George, you know how much I appreciate your talents. I have something in mind for Whitehead, but he deserves a more personal attack. We'll have to be patient." The truth was that Alexander wanted Greg Whitehead dead but with his wife captive in the middle barn, he didn't want to invite any attention to Hurtmoor. He understood that he and George were unlikely to be the only ones who knew of his wife's new romance. Whitehead had crossed him and revenge would have to be taken, but in the current circumstances he couldn't risk a murder investigation. A more measured response was needed and Alexander hadn't yet found the right course of action. "But don't you worry, there's a bullet waiting. I'll give you Greg Whitehead soon enough."

George had enough blood and dirt on his hands already. "I've no interest in him. If you want Whitehead shot, you can drive up to Middlesbrough and deal with it yourself."

Alexander allowed George's response brief attention. George had never refused him before and this wasn't a good moment to discover the limits of his loyalty. George had never spoken to him with such disrespect, and he felt a tension in his temples, with too many rogue elements too far from his reach. He bit his tongue. He needed George onside. "Well, we'll come to that in good time, first things first. Go back up north and burn that woman's house down. The rest can wait."

But George hadn't finished. "I've always been happy to help out, you know that well enough. But you can wait forever. I'm not shooting anyone for you."

Alexander watched George march away and he felt the weight of his trouble. He had more on his shoulders than he could carry in comfort. He had Sarah locked up where she couldn't draw a breath without his knowledge, and he had his foot on her throat, but it didn't feel that way. Somehow, at the moment when his control was tighter than ever before, he worried that she was escaping him.

THIRTY-ONE
WILD CAMPING

ANDY AWOKE to the sound of rain on his tent. For many campers, the sound of rain would be bad news, but not for Andy. It was a tiny, one-man tent, low to the ground in green camouflage, and fully waterproof. Andy was fine with supermarket brands and second-hand cars, but field kit needed to be top quality. It didn't matter how long the rain might last, he'd stay dry. He took a swallow from his water bottle and smiled. It was a magical feeling to lie in an open field and listen to the rain.

He'd spent a couple of days debating with himself about how best to find out more about George Brand. In the end, he packed the car and drove down to Surrey. It was the summer solstice and the nights were short, but he'd slept well. He and Polly had camped out together a hundred times. Always happy times. Polly had retired from camping now, too much arthritis, but Andy's enthusiasm was undiminished. In fact, the move to solo trips had intensified his pleasure. He liked being the lone soldier, just his body and his brain, finding a place in the wild outdoors, surviving in the natural world. He had his military training and he knew what to do. Age didn't change anything.

Even in the rain, Andy loved to be out walking in open

countryside. It didn't matter what weather was thrown at him. When he was out walking, he could escape his past, fully absorbed by fresh air and survival. He'd listened to a radio programme where the practice of mindfulness was discussed, the art of living in the moment, shutting out the noise from what had gone and from what might be coming. He'd heard educated people describe their technique as if it was a mystery, a task of meditation. There was mention of Buddhism, paths towards an enlightened and spiritual land. For Andy it was a more simple and worldly experience. He and Polly called it 'going for a walk'.

He opened the zip of his tent and tied back the door flap so that he could view the target. It was only six o'clock, no sign of life. *"Lazy bastards."* He put the binoculars back into their case and wriggled free from his sleeping bag. He gathered together all the items for his first outing of the day: a spade, toilet paper, toothbrush, clothes and a towel, and made his way down to the river to wash. He had been pleasantly surprised to find a clean river and he stood naked, sheltered by the trees, allowing the cold water to flow around his ankles, squatting to complete his wash, then out onto the bank shaking himself like a dog. *"Lie down."* Then he stood in the light morning rain, which was already giving way to clearer skies, closed his eyes, and breathed in the new day.

He'd arrived in Surrey two days earlier, driving down with a car full of camping gear, his camera, and supplies, fully prepared and equipped to find out who George Brand was and who was paying him to follow Sarah Buxton. He found George's home without difficulty. Denny had provided reliable information, and Andy had been surprised to arrive at a detached house tucked away in smart cul-de-sac. The house ought to have been beyond the reach of a second-hand Peugeot driver, but sure enough, the shabby black hatchback was parked on the drive. But when George emerged from the house, he climbed into the Jaguar that was parked alongside. *"Flash bastard,"* Andy had whispered. He followed discreetly for eight miles to an impressive farmhouse on the outskirts of a leafy village, to Hurtmoor. *"Nice work, Denny."* Later in the day, George drove back to his own home and then later still, he returned again to the farmhouse.

Andy figured that Sarah's home offered the most promise and clearly the rural environment gave plenty of options for setting up camp. He spent a couple of hours walking, surveying the fields and pastures surrounding the farmhouse, getting the lie of the land. It was mostly cattle. There were hundreds of cows but also a few fields for growing food crops, and a river. It was ideal, there were rabbits and plenty of rich green vegetation. Andy could live comfortably here for weeks if he needed to.

He found the perfect location, slightly elevated and giving a good view to the rear of the farmhouse and of the outbuildings, with easy access to the river behind him. He pitched the tent, watched the sun sink into darkness, and slept.

On Andy's second day, he watched and waited, testing the security of his position through a full day on a working farm. Sarah's car remained stationary behind the house, and everything else seemed a repeat of the previous day. George made a couple of trips from the house to the same outbuilding, sometimes carrying a tray and sometimes a bucket. Andy wasn't sure what to make of it, but he'd brought a powerful lens and zoomed in for plenty of shots.

In the afternoon, there was a change. George made the same journey to the outbuilding, but with another man alongside him. Andy kept his camera clicking, getting a few shots of the newcomer. Then he made his way back to his car, deciding to follow George and perhaps get information about the new player. He drove from a back lane around to the front of the farmhouse, and he had to wait for almost two hours, but eventually George's Jaguar pulled out from Hurtmoor and headed back in the direction of Guildford.

George led him into new territory, and Andy was

completely lost, getting sight of a less desirable district. George stopped his car outside a small row of shops, and Andy pulled in to wait fifty metres back along the road. Although Andy had never been anywhere near this place previously, it looked familiar: a betting office, a vape shop and a 7-eleven. George's companion jumped out of the car, and disappeared into the betting shop. George drove on, and Andy followed, disappointed by the uneventful journey, and hoping that George would lead him back into familiar territory. He followed the Jaguar to George's house, and then returned to Hurtmoor. Venture without gain.

The next morning, George didn't show up. Instead, the man who'd accompanied him during the previous afternoon, fetched and carried between the barn and the house. Andy hadn't really gained any clear information and he was puzzled. Where was George? In Stokesley, George had been secretive as he watched Sarah and yet here, in the area where they both lived, he clearly had open access to her home. And now he'd disappeared.

Andy watched for a couple of hours but he was restless. He'd lost his target. *"Sod this. I'm wasting my time."* He packed up his gear and hiked back to his car, hoping that his instinct gave good guidance. He returned to George's house where the Jaguar occupied the drive. But the Peugeot was gone. The battery on his phone had run flat while he camped but he'd had it on charge in the car and he heard a couple of pings as it came back to life. He read Polly's message first:

Well?

"Short and sweet, Pol."

Then he attended to the second message. Billy Walker and Andy should never have become friends, they were galaxies apart. Andy was a man's man, attracted to masculine pursuits. He was a sports fan and a fighter, never read a book in his life, and Billy was a sensitive artist. If he wasn't painting, he'd have his head in a book. But as Billy had found out, art doesn't always pay well and he'd been working behind the bar at The Bricklayer's for more than thirty years. Friday night in The Bricklayer's bar wasn't a natural environment for Billy but it paid the rent, and mostly the trouble stayed on the other side of the bar. But there'd been one occasion, twenty-five years earlier when a punter had aimed his drunken vitriol at Billy, got him in his sights and refused to back off. Billy was restricted, stuck behind the bar, with a shift to finish.

Andy had watched it all unfold, kept his head down and drunk his beer. By then he'd learned to control his aggressive tendencies, and it was only rarely that he'd be drawn into a fight. But it was just like riding a bike, and once you'd got the hang of knocking a few teeth out, you never forgot. He'd been able to see that Billy was frightened, staying safely behind the bar and keeping as quiet as possible. Then, as closing time approached, Billy had had to venture out to collect empty glasses and bottles. His tormentor had seen his opportunity and wasted no time, pushing Billy forcefully against a wall and then moving in for the kill. All the other drinkers had scattered. Except for Andy, who intervened.

The net result was a second conviction for affray, a hefty fine, and a lifetime of gratitude from Billy. It was an unlikely alliance, but the two men had been good friends ever since.

After the black Peugeot had last left the car park, Andy had popped into The Bricklayer's Arms for a couple of pints, and asked Billy to alert him if George made any further bookings. He read the text.

Dear Andy, George Brand phoned yesterday to book a room for tonight. Best wishes, Billy.

Andy chuckled. He liked Billy's style. Polly's approach to text communication was in line with the general population, all economy and emojis, but Billy wrote short formal letters.

"So that's where you've gone. Nice one, Billy."

He sent a message to Polly to let her know he was on his way back home.

THIRTY-TWO

FOUND

GREG HAD TAKEN paracetamol an hour earlier and now his focus was on rehydration. He looked at the mug of steaming tea placed to the right of his glass of water. The two drinking vessels were not the only objects in the room but for a few moments, they were his only focus.

Greg had lived alone for half of his adult life, and he knew how to keep his house. He'd never taken pleasure from housework, not even satisfaction, but it was something that had to be done. Ever since he'd driven back from Guildford, he'd neglected his domestic duties, allowing standards to slip. On the same coffee table there were five empty wine glasses, a tumbler which had once held gin and tonic, two used plates, three small stains of red wine, and half a tomato. He allowed his gaze to extend around the living room, finding more unwashed pots and a scattering of other items waiting to be restored to order. He stood up and walked to the front window to open the curtains. Bright light filled the room, giving him better sight of the mess that his house had become. He picked up the half-eaten tomato and dropped it on top of the overflowing waste bin in his kitchen. It immediately slipped from the top of the pile to join a dozen other pieces of rubbish on the floor.

Greg returned to his lounge, congratulating himself for making a start but he sat back down having decided to clear up the rest of the mess later when he'd recovered from his hangover. His doorbell rang. "Fuck off." He only spoke quietly, but with feeling, nevertheless. Only a handful of people visited Greg's house and never without a prior arrangement. It could only be a stranger at the door and Greg held his line: whoever it was could disappear back to whatever hole they might have crawled out from.

Then his phone rang. It was Eleanor again. He cringed seeing her name on his phone, appalled by the memory of his behaviour, and he felt unable to speak to her. He allowed the unanswered phone to invite a message and breathed a sigh of relief. His doorbell chimed again. "Jesus, give yourself a break. I'm not answering." He could hardly hear himself. His phone was ringing again and the twat on his doorstep was starting to rile him.

He just didn't feel ready yet to face the world, not even friendly faces, he wasn't ready, and he gave silent thanks to no God in particular when the assault of rings finally subsided. But then his phone pinged again, and he assumed it would be a text from Eleanor but he had to look just to be sure, just in case...

Sue and I are standing on your doorstep, where we will remain until you open the door.

"Oh Christ, give me a break." Greg shook his head. He couldn't ignore them, but he definitely couldn't allow them entry. So he made his way along the passage to the front door, trying to manufacture a rationale to send them away.

He unlocked and then opened the door. "You'd better step back a couple of paces, I've got Covid." He paused for a second, trying to read their faces, noting the wide eyes staring back at him. "What's the problem?"

Sue looked him up and down. He clearly hadn't shaved for several days, and his hair was uncombed. The uncoordinated ensemble of denim jeans, pyjama top, one sock and one bare foot, added little glamour. "There was no need to dress up, Greg, we've only called in for a coffee. What symptoms have you got?"

Greg made an unconvincing effort to cough as Sue pushed past him into the house.

"Jesus, Greg," she said as the stale smell of alcohol filled her nostrils. But she was undeterred and found her way into the lounge. "Oh my Lord, what a mess."

Greg followed her into the room. "Sue, I'm unwell, I can't have you in the house. You should have phoned." He watched Eleanor make her entry and regretted his words.

"I phoned yesterday. Remember?" Eleanor marched across to open the window. "But you didn't mention that you were ill."

Greg remembered. He had no answer. They were in the house, and it was already too late. His head was spinning and he sat back down, defeated. "I'm sorry, the house is untidy. I've been a bit off colour."

Sue glared at him. "No problem, Greg. Oh, and by the way, I'm sorry as well. For screwing your life up." She held her stare and gave him a minute to respond, but his head dipped towards the floor. "Go and get a shower. Attend to your personal hygiene. We'll make a start on this lot."

An hour later they sat down in Greg's lounge, now clean and refreshed. He'd showered, shaved and dressed and he sat down in his own front room to accept the hospitality from his uninvited guests.

There was silence. Sue and Eleanor were waiting to hear his story.

Greg tried to speak but already he was fighting a losing battle. He was holding too much tension, feeling too much pain. His chin trembled as his eyes filled with tears. He sniffed back the snot that was rushing through his nose and tried again, but no words came, just more tears and he gave way, allowing his misery to be witnessed.

He cried for a few minutes; it was a long cry, a cry for Sarah.

Both Sue and Eleanor sat quietly, accepting and absorbing his distress until eventually the sobs quietened.

Greg blew his nose, wiped his face, and just about found his voice. "Sorry."

He reviewed the room, noting the change from his earlier assessment. He'd allowed the room to deteriorate into a reflection of his emotions, wretched, dark and miserable, a mess, something once precious, then spoiled. And now, as he looked again, there was order and he was among friends. He was far from cured, but he felt a whole lot better.

He addressed Sue. "You were there that night in The White Swan, Sue, after 'A' levels, when I walked Sarah home. I kissed her." He paused, recognising his inaccuracy. "Well, she kissed me. She was perfect. Of course, I never saw her again. Until Mark Sanderson's funeral, that is." Greg wasn't sure of himself. He was approaching the parts of the story which he was now starting to question. His judgements and misjudgements, his foolishness, and his rejection. He fell quiet.

Eleanor offered encouragement. "Go on, Greg. What happened at the funeral?"

"Nothing much. We spent the evening together at The Lion. Sarah came back up north a week later, visiting Mark's sister, and we met again in the evening. And we kissed again. I read too much into it, I thought, I don't know what I thought. Anyway we were supposed to meet in Guildford. She said she was leaving her husband, but she didn't turn up. End of story."

Sue was outraged. "What? You went all that way and she stood you up? Unbelievable, what a cow. Have you phoned her?"

"I tried, no reply. Then she sent me a text yesterday saying she was staying with her husband."

Sue's anger intensified. "If she turns up for Eleanor's birthday, I'll bloody swing for her."

Eleanor was puzzled, unconvinced. "I never knew Sarah when she was younger but she seemed lovely at the funeral. I'd never have thought that she could behave so heartlessly."

Sue was unrepentant. "She was always Miss High and Mighty at school. Still the same by the sound of it. You're right, Eleanor, she has no heart."

Greg looked at them both. "Please don't. I was a fool, investing so much hope after just a few hours together. I thought it was love. I don't have a fucking clue."

Sue and Eleanor cleaned the kitchen and the bathroom before they set off back to Leeds, clearing away more debris and leaving him an environment fit for a self-respecting man. Greg sat back on his sofa. It would be a long time before the sadness left him but his friends had brought a degree of restoration. He had a different kind of hangover, the tired relaxation that follows a release of emotion. He'd stood before fellow human beings, with his humiliation and shame, and he'd survived. The hurt was no less but now he could face the world again.

He decided not to drink wine that evening, accepting that Sue's instruction to have an early night and a long bike ride tomorrow, seemed a better plan. He still felt fragile and vulnerable but now he had the arms of his friends wrapped around him like a blanket. Comfort and warmth. It'd be a year or so before he'd be able to watch Titanic again, but with Sue and Eleanor alongside him, he knew that eventually he'd get there.

THIRTY-THREE

CHERYL AND GEORGE

CHERYL HAD REMAINED ill at ease all through that first Thursday while she waited for Sarah, and her unease continued on into the next two days. In the absence of information, her imagination offered a thousand explanations, but no matter where her fantasies led her, she arrived with the same bad feeling. She and Sarah had connected and then, at the critical moment, there was nothing. An uneasy quiet. It went on from one day into the next, first expectation, then resignation, and nothing from Sarah. Cheryl felt that she should do something and yet she hesitated, unable to understand her own inaction.

She was a strong character, resourceful and resilient, and usually quite at ease with her own company. But these were difficult days, and she became increasingly aware of how important her dialogue with Sarah had been. Mostly Cheryl had been the listener, a sounding board helping her friend to find a path to a new future. But now, in the empty space and the silence, she felt Sarah's absence as an interruption to her own life, an obstacle to her own future. She had invested something of herself in their Thursday discussions, built a foundation from which both of their futures could develop.

Mark had been part of it, and between the three of them, they had created an intensity, a recognition that life is both precious and fragile. In those final weeks, as the three of them had faced the inevitability of Mark's death, she had felt the coming of new life. Now she felt abandoned and alone, halted without explanation. Mark was gone and now Sarah had disappeared without a word of farewell. She had to reach out. She wrestled with herself for a couple of hours before eventually overcoming her hesitation and sending a text.

Hi Sarah, I hope you're well. I wonder when you'll be coming back to Stokesley? C.

Another twenty-four hours passed and there came no reply. Cheryl wobbled. She entertained a range of emotions, considered explanations, but nothing settled her. The woman who she'd come to know didn't fit with the gaping and prolonged silence. Something was wrong. Cheryl held no religious beliefs, but she had a sense of spirit, a sense of herself in the bigger scheme of things and she trusted her intuition. Something had gone wrong, something serious. No matter what had happened, Sarah would have given some kind of communication.

And finally, late in the evening, she received a reply.

Hi, Cheryl, I have no further need to travel to Stokesley. I won't return. S.

She was stunned. "Really? This is your message? On a Sunday!"

She felt it in her gut, right in the solar plexus, that something had changed. She really was stunned, initially unable to believe that this communication was the conclusion of their relationship. But the next day passed without any further news and she began to accept that Sarah's message was final. She left the room she'd prepared as it was, ready for occupation, and she remained mystified, not just by the reversal in Sarah's intention but also by the coldness of her communication. She went one way and then another, first experiencing disbelief and then bouncing into acceptance. It seemed hard to believe and yet she had confirmation in writing. She went back time and time again to the text message. The dialogue between the two women had been meaningful and personal, and it seemed inconceivable that a brief text message could be the closing words in such a profound conversation. Nevertheless, she reasoned, people can act unpredictably and life must go on. Cheryl was hurt and confused and unsure how to understand Sarah's sudden change of direction. She tried to persuade herself to focus on her own life, but it was difficult. She'd made friends in all corners of the world, and trusted her judgement, but she'd never before encountered a puzzle like Sarah.

George hadn't slept well. Another night on a lumpy mattress at The Bricklayer's Arms and then an hour sitting in the Peugeot had done nothing for the pain in the small of his back. He was feeling out of sorts and impatient when he finally laid eyes on Cheryl. Although he had no interest in her appearance, quite the reverse, he was happy to watch her walk away from her front door as she set off towards the town centre. As soon as she disappeared from sight, he put on his latex gloves, dropped a petrol can into a plastic carrier bag and walked purposefully towards her house.

He moved swiftly once through the gate, around the side of the house and on to the back where he found a conservatory made from bricks, wood and glass. He was delighted by the absence of plastic and he congratulated the Sandersons for their fine taste as he sprinkled petrol on to the wooden frames around the french doors and the conservatory windows. One match, sparked into life by faint friction, then applied to the foot of the door was all he needed. He watched for thirty seconds while the fire spread to his satisfaction, then he left as quickly and quietly as he'd entered. Job done.

George left Stokesley nervously. He knew that he'd taken

a risk with Cheryl's house. As he was driving back to Surrey, with a sense of relief, he made a promise to himself. He'd already gone several extra miles with this crazy journey but here his involvement would end.

THIRTY-FOUR

CATCHING UP

ANDY ARRIVED BACK HOME late in the evening, in time to enjoy a hot meal, and he slept like a log, back in a proper bed. When his head hit the pillow, his intention was to get up early and go out again the next morning, in position and ready to find out what had brought George back to town, to follow the Peugeot one more time.

Andy had talked to Polly but neither of them had a rational guess or an explanation for George's return to Stokesley, and he felt himself pulled into a situation that he really ought to abandon. So, they'd agreed that this would be the last look. Unless George Brand gave them reason to reconsider, Andy would get back to his original mission.

Unfortunately, the combined impact of a series of short sleeps in a tent and Polly's warm body beside him, was underestimated. He slept late, cursing and stumbling as he rushed now to get dressed. "Bloody hell, Polly, why didn't you wake me?"

Polly rolled over and groaned, still half asleep. "When?"

Andy gave up on the conversation. He threw some cold water against his face, picked up his phone and set off for The Bricklayer's Arms. He checked his watch and hoped for good fortune, but when he reached his destination, breathless and already sweating, the black Peugeot had gone.

"*Shit, fuck, and bananas.*" He would leave it now. He'd given George a pretty good look but it was becoming a less than merry dance. He phoned Polly. "I've missed him. Get the kettle on, I'll be back in twenty minutes. I need some breakfast."

"I'm still in bed. That's twice you've woke me up. Have you checked The Lion?"

"Why?"

Polly roused herself. "Give me strength. Usually when George hits town, Greg and Sarah are staying at The Lion. That's the main reason, pet." She killed the call and sank back into her pillow.

"Yes, fair point," said Andy, mostly to the fresh morning air. Already the sun was climbing in the sky. Andy walked slowly but he followed Polly's direction and made his way to The Lion.

Again he drew a blank. Neither Sarah's nor Greg's cars were in the car park. "*Thank you and good night.*" Andy walked away without a thought. This part of the game was over. He'd had a trip out, seen a bit of rural Surrey, but George and Sarah could get on with whatever they were up to without Andy's further interest. "*Bollocks to them.*"

But even as he let his distraction run loose, he was walking in the wrong direction, towards the Sanderson house. "*Where are you going, Cooper? Go home and get some breakfast.*" But he continued. He'd followed George from The Lion to the Sanderson house a week earlier and his feet knew the route.

"*You're wasting your breath, mate, time for a bacon sarnie.*"

Suddenly he broke into a trot, wondering what he was witnessing. There was black smoke rising above the Sanderson's roof. "*What the hell is that?*" His legs were in better shape than his lungs and he arrived at the back of the house quickly, but breathless. The conservatory was burning, glass panels were popping and already the inside of the conservatory was starting to burn. He took a few steps back and looked up at the first floor windows, trying to see who was in the house although there was neither sight nor sound of human presence.

The fire was growing but Andy was calm – his army training had kicked in. Eyes everywhere, assessment then action. He followed the hosepipe from the tap on the back wall out into the garden. He opened the tap and saw a jet of water rise from the side of the greenhouse. He ran out to retrieve the hosepipe and it took him about two minutes to put out the fire. Then he stood in the midst of the scene, breathing the fumes from burnt paint, listening to the hiss of water and fire, and then to the sirens growing louder, drawing ever closer.

A neighbour called out to him to stand back and told him that the fire brigade were on their way. The conservatory was filled with black smoke and Andy decided not to wait. If someone died in the house, he'd never forgive himself. He kicked hard against the conservatory door, running through broken glass and thick smoke and on into the house. He went straight up the stairs, systematically checking all of the first floor rooms, then back down to repeat the exercise on the ground floor. The house was empty. Andy was coughing and he staggered back out into the garden where he was greeted by three redundant firefighters.

"There's no one inside. The fire's out." Andy was breathless and still coughing but he was calm. A fireman steered him towards a garden seat and gave him a bottle of water.

For the next hour, Andy was questioned, first by the firefighters and then by the police. It was an awkward situation for him. Ever since his army service, he'd developed a healthy respect for people in uniform. Except for the police. Firefighters were comrades, the police were the enemy. While the questions were put to him, Andy paid only brief attention, trying to make sense of what had happened. He had a few questions of his own. So he was economical as he spoke to PC Banton, disinclined to share the purpose of his walk around town. He had no reason to mention that he'd been trying to find George Brand in a black Peugeot. *"Plod can dig their own dirt."*

PC Banton approached Andy for a second interview, checking that his story held firm and hoping for some new information. She'd been on the radio and learned about his police record. "So, Mr Cooper, you've been a bit of tearaway in your time according to my sergeant back at HQ. How was it that you happened to be on the scene just at the moment when the fire got going?"

Andy was unimpressed. "That's right, constable. I'm rotten to the core. Almost certainly the culprit. Are you going to arrest me?"

Cheryl's neighbour was even less impressed than Andy. She'd watched him break through the door to conduct his search. "Oi, hang on, love. Leave him alone. He put the fire out, the man's a hero. Where were you when it all kicked off, back at the station filling in forms?"

Andy appreciated the support and raised his eyebrows, inviting the PC to give an answer. None came, just a sigh.

Andy didn't know what to do. The fire was out and George was long gone. Cheryl Sanderson hadn't been in the house and still hadn't returned and he had no idea how to understand this unexpected turn of events. The simple task of discovering Greg Whitehead's address had become surprisingly complicated. He had a quick word with the senior fire officer and left the scene. He felt the need to consult Polly.

Polly smelt him before she saw him. "I hope you haven't been up to your old tricks."

Andy had told her about his own activity as a young

arsonist. It had just been for a few months when he was ten years old. When something really frustrated him or when anger seemed to be trapped inside him, he would start a fire and watch it burn. It started with public litter bins, then a couple of old tyres. At times of unbearable frustration, it seemed to calm him. Then he took a leap, went out to old Grundy's farm and burned a haystack. It was way out of control and finished up spreading across into a large outbuilding. Six fire engines had been needed for almost three hours before the blaze was extinguished. It had frightened Andy and brought an end to his fascination with fire. No one else knew until he told Polly, forty years later.

"No, I didn't start the fire, I put it out."

Polly got the bones of the story. She stripped off his clothes and sent him up for a shower. An hour later, she had questions to ask.

But it was Andy who asked the first. "What do you make of it, Pol?"

Polly wasn't ready to judge, she was puzzled. "Why did you go to the Sanderson house?"

Andy took a defensive position. "Don't you bloody start, you sound like the filth." He glanced up in time to catch Polly's expression. "I walked to The Lion as you suggested. Nothing there and I just walked from there without really thinking much about it. I couldn't believe that I'd slept in, and I was trying to catch up, but there was no sign of George Brand, or anybody else. It was the last call before I gave up and came home. I didn't expect to find the house on fire."

"So you never saw George?"

"I didn't see anybody, Pol."

"But he was definitely at The Bricklayer's last night?"

"Yes. Well, I didn't actually see him, but he had a room booked."

"Well, you need to check with Billy." Polly watched him nod. "Now."

Andy sent a text, and Billy replied promptly.

175

Dear Andy, Yes, he was here. He checked out early this morning. BW, Billy.

Polly took a few seconds to put it together. "George was there last night and he left this morning, and the Sanderson house gets torched. That's some coincidence."

"Who knows? Maybe it was a coincidence. Why would he travel up here and set fire to the Sanderson house?" Andy put the question to Polly but he was also asking himself.

Polly wouldn't be deflected. "No, George was involved, although I haven't got a clue why. He's up to something."

Andy took her point. George's actions were beyond explanation. He knew that something had been driving him. He hadn't travelled to Surrey and camped out on a whim, but now Polly had found the words to match his intuitive understanding. "I think you're right, Pol, he's creeping me out, but it's nothing to do with us, and anyway he's gone again now. I'm done with him."

Polly ignored his resignation. "Do you know Cheryl Sanderson?"

"Not really. I can remember her from school, but she never had anything to do with me. I don't think I've ever spoken to her."

"Did you talk to her this morning?"

"No, she wasn't there."

Polly shook her head. "So, he set fire to an empty house."

Andy was more cautious. "Someone did."

They both sat quiet for a while. Andy had been invigorated by his mission and he'd enjoyed tracking George, but today things had got serious. Maybe it was time to withdraw. He had Greg's address and whatever was going on with George, it was unlikely to help him.

"But yes, either someone attacked an empty house…" Andy paused.

Polly was impatient. "Or what?"

"Or they thought someone was inside."

"Well, it's Cheryl's house, but he was following Sarah."

"Neither of them were there, Polly, and why the hell would he burn an empty house? Why would anybody?"

"Well, you're the expert. Why did you burn old Grundy's barn?"

Andy knew that it was mostly just impatience and curiosity but he felt hurt nevertheless. "I wish I'd never told you. I'm going to step away, Pol. It's all got a bit weird. I don't need any of this."

"You can't stop now." Polly was starting to panic. "Why didn't you tell the police?"

"Stupid young copper, worse than useless. A waste of a uniform. And what would I have told her? That I've been following someone I don't know, for reasons I'm not sure about, who I haven't seen do anything wrong. That would've impressed her."

"Oh well, perfectly reasonable then. No need to give critical information about the perpetrator of arson and attempted murder, not when the copper's under thirty and wet behind the ears. And a woman. Jesus, Andy, you test me sometimes."

"We don't know who set the fire. I'm not about to make wild accusations."

Polly was exasperated. "You're the one who's just spent days camping in Surrey. Go back to the house, find out whether Cheryl's back, and see who she thinks might have torched her house."

Andy nodded. Polly was the better judge, and he accepted her instruction. "Right, well, you can come with me. No time like the present."

THIRTY-FIVE
CLOSE TO A HOME

CHERYL AMBLED her way back from the library. It was almost July and the midday sun delivered all its glory, drenched her in warm light, and she felt recharged, ready to go again. For the first time in several days she had escaped her lonely vigil, stopped waiting, and followed her own path. But her easy enjoyment was interrupted by her own thought, which repeated in her head, this time spoken with Sarah's voice. Go again. You still have time. They were her late brother's words, given to incentivise a friend. Perhaps now they were a parting gift from Sarah.

Cheryl had always enjoyed libraries. Books were important but so was the atmosphere of quiet contemplation and learning. For Cheryl, reading and personal development were one and the same thing. She had set out early to the library, looking for a new story, a place to start the rest of her life. It had done her good to get out from the seclusion of her home and garden. She'd greeted a dozen or so passers-by with smiles, chatted while she shopped on the way home – made a bit of space for herself.

She was content to let her thoughts drift, almost back home and anticipating a cold drink under shade in the garden, when she turned the corner and saw the fire engine.

Instinctively, she quickened her stride, although she felt that time had slowed down. There was a small gathering of her neighbours across the road from her house. Her house.

"My God," she said to herself, "it's my house."

Jennifer Hansen had enjoyed the whole show from up close, from the privileged position of a next-door neighbour, and it had been entertaining. She'd seen the smoke and dialled 999. That had been exciting, but then Andy had entered the scene, unhesitant and courageous. She'd watched him at work with the hosepipe and then his dramatic foray into the burning and smoke-filled house. She spotted Cheryl's approach.

They weren't soul sisters but they were neighbours. Jennifer knew about Mark's death and she went forward to meet Cheryl. "It's alright, the fire's out." She took hold of Cheryl's outstretched arm, first pulling it towards her and then taking her hand.

Cheryl accepted Jennifer's help, drinks, food and the offer of an overnight stay. It was a strange afternoon, beginning with shock, and then veering towards mystery. The firefighters and the police had been perfectly clear – Cheryl had been the victim of an arson attack. Petrol had been poured onto her conservatory. They had asked her repeatedly who might want to harm her, who had she argued with, but she had nothing in response; she was a woman without an enemy. Or so she had believed.

It had been a hectic couple of hours but she'd reacted with impressive pragmatism, notifying her insurance company and arranging some emergency repairs. She'd spent time talking with the police and now she'd got herself kitted out for a short stay with her neighbour. But despite her attendance to the practical agenda, she remained distracted. Either an arsonist, unknown to her, had randomly chosen her property to burn, or she had been deliberately targeted, the victim of a violent attack. The same questions invaded her consciousness repeatedly. Why? Who?

No one would give her the name of the passer-by who had saved her house from serious damage, and no matter how far she searched, Cheryl was quite unable to come to terms with the day's events. Why?

She had asked the young police officer who had promised to investigate, and she'd asked Jennifer, who seemed entirely occupied by her own distraction. Jennifer was critical of the police for lack-lustre investigation and of the fire service for a slow response. Her attitude changed when she described Andy's involvement, giving full respect to the passing stranger who'd put out the fire and searched the house single-handedly, all before the fire brigade had entered the street.

The two of them collected a few things from Cheryl's house. Just an overnight bag with a few belongings to get through to the next morning. Jennifer brightened as she spotted Andy and Polly crossing the road. "Here he is, Cheryl, the man who put the fire out."

Cheryl was unprepared. "Oh, hello. I owe you my thanks. How fortunate that you were close by and how brave of you to act so swiftly." She was unsure of herself, unable to invite him in for coffee and surprised by his appearance.

Andy looked at her. He'd seen her at Mark's funeral, and he had a vague memory of her from school. That was all. "No problem." He hoped that Polly would do the talking. "This is Polly. Not too much damage, I hope."

Cheryl felt it immediately. This man had come in good faith but he carried an awkwardness, not quite an apology, but she could feel it: this man had something to say. "Mostly smoke damage, and the conservatory will need some repairs. But not too bad. You prevented serious damage. I'm very grateful. The fire officer said that you must have arrived very soon after the fire started. That was very fortunate. A few minutes later and the damage could have been much worse."

"Yes, well, that's good. I just wanted to check that you were alright." Andy gave his polite reply but then fell quiet, searching to find the right words, desperate to know but unable to ask.

The four of them were all infected by unspoken words, each of them waiting for someone else to speak and wondering who would signal the way forwards. It was a pregnant pause, more complicated for Andy and Cheryl who were both trying to look beneath their polite pleasantries, both aware of their reticence and their curiosity, and looking for a way to expose the hidden agenda.

It was more straightforward for Jennifer. She felt an attraction to this rather masculine hero even though she could see that Andy was at least twenty years her senior. He could put her fire out all day long. She resented Polly's presence. She and Polly filled the uncomfortable silence, talking about the hot weather, each of them instinctively disliking the other beneath their polite and pointless exchange, while Andy and Cheryl exchanged uncertain half glances, waiting.

Andy found himself and spoke to Cheryl. "I'm Andy, Andy Cooper." He reached out and shook her hand. Cheryl stayed quiet but distant memories were breaking through. She knew him now. Ordinary kids at school were easily forgotten, with only the brilliant, the bad and the ugly remembered. She couldn't be sure how bad he'd been. Bad enough.

In Jennifer's eyes, he was far from ugly. "Please come inside, Andy. I'll make us all a brew."

Cheryl's thoughts were racing. Andy Cooper, former school bully, had become a good citizen. He of all people had walked by her house at the moment the fire had started and now he was back, and Cheryl could feel it from him – Andy Cooper wanted to speak.

"No, I won't come in, but thanks anyway." He was stuck. Jennifer wasn't the first woman to take a shine to him. Something about him seemed to be attractive. As a younger man, before Polly, he'd filled his boots, but those days were long gone. The idea of drinking tea while Jennifer fussed around him held no appeal, and he knew that Polly would be riled. He turned to Cheryl again. "Do you know me?"

Cheryl responded without hesitation. "I remember you from school."

"Oh dear," replied Andy.

"What?" said Jennifer, suddenly feeling excluded. Neither Andy nor Cheryl responded to her question. They were focused on each other, eyes locked together.

Polly took her chance. "No, we haven't come to drink tea." She'd finished with Jennifer and turned her attention to Cheryl. "We wanted to be sure that you're okay, and you know, to find out what happened." She looked at Cheryl's bag. "You're having to move out then?"

Cheryl felt appreciation for Polly's contribution and noted her enquiries with interest. "It's not too bad, thanks to Andy, but the smell of smoke is overpowering. Jennifer has offered me her spare room, but I'll be back in my own house tomorrow." She handed her bag to Jennifer. "Jennifer, I want to show Polly and Andy the house. I'll follow you in a few minutes. Is that alright?"

It wasn't. "Yes, of course," said Jennifer, broken hearted.

Cheryl led her guests to the front door and then on into the house. She'd opened doors and windows to create an air flow through the house. Apart from the conservatory and the smell of smoke, there was no damage. She invited them to sit at the kitchen table.

"Andy said that the fire had been started deliberately." Polly put her remark on the table, beside a vase of smoke scented flowers.

"Yes, apparently. Please forgive me, I think I'm affected by the shock of it all, and I'm trying to understand why. Why did the two of you come here this evening? And why, Andy, were you walking along this street when the fire started?"

Andy was disarmed and somehow relieved at the same time, but still not ready to reveal his story. "Why do you ask, Cheryl?"

"Because someone set fire to my house this morning and I'd like to know why. If I'd been at home and if you hadn't come along, it could have been very much more serious. I'm very grateful for what you did, Andy, but I need to understand what happened. It was a deliberate act, targeted. It appears that someone tried to kill me this morning. I'm uncomfortable with that knowledge."

"No, I'd be the same." Andy cleared his throat and he asked her again. "Do you know me?"

"No, not really. I remember you were unpopular but I never knew you."

"I was in the same year as your brother Mark. I was a twat, pardon my French, a bully."

Polly prickled defensively. "That was a long time ago. He's different now."

Andy continued. "I went to Mark's funeral. He was a good guy. I'm sorry."

"Yes, he was. Thank you." Cheryl looked at him, sitting at her kitchen table, trying to find his way.

"That's where it started." Andy was doing his best, feeling his way towards a connection, but his dark history impeded him.

Polly helped him along. "That's when he saw Sarah. We thought you might be interested."

Cheryl was fully engaged now. "And why would that be?"

"Well, it's just that Sarah Buxton was up here recently, visiting this house, and the man who was following her stayed at The Bricklayer's Arms last night. Just before your house was set on fire. Coincidentally." She watched as Cheryl followed her signposts.

"Do go on."

"A man who stayed in The Bricklayer's Arms last night has been following Sarah Buxton for more than a fortnight. This morning someone set fire to your house. We thought you should know."

The Sanderson house was a semi-detached shrine to suburbia, worship for anonymity, compact but not cramped, a substantial garden albeit long and narrow, built from red bricks with clay tiles on the roof. It could have been anybody's house and it could stand unnoticed in any town, but in this moment Cheryl felt herself to be in an extraordinary place, a place of intrigue, her childhood home, a hiding place, almost a refuge, and then a hospice, and now a crime scene.

She looked back at Polly, flooded now by the events of the day and unable to contain them. Tears came, rushing for release. She managed to speak, nevertheless. "I'm sorry, it's been a difficult day."

Polly took her hand. "Take your time."

But Cheryl pressed on. "It's a lot to take in. Everything was fine when I went into town this morning. Who is the man you're speaking of? Did he start the fire?"

Andy had sat back when the crying began, that was Pol's territory, but he leaned forward again now. "We don't know. There's no direct link to the fire and we can't think of any reason for him to burn your house down."

"But you know who he is?"

"It was a man called George Brand. He lives in Surrey, just up the road from Sarah Buxton." He paused for a moment, giving Cheryl opportunity to speak but she was unmoved, waiting for more. "I've been keeping an eye on him for a couple of weeks while he's been following Sarah. I was meant to follow him this morning but I slept in."

Cheryl's face creased with confusion. "But you were here just as the fire started."

"I was trying to catch up. I'd drawn a blank at The Bricklayer's and at The Lion, and so I came here. I didn't see anyone. Whoever started the fire had already gone. George had followed Sarah to your house previously and I was worried that Sarah might be inside the house this morning. That's why I went in and searched."

It was a lot to take in for Cheryl, but a good cry and some new information was helping her to focus. "That's helpful. Knowing who's trying to kill me feels a bit better than not having a clue. I was expecting Sarah a few days ago but she didn't arrive."

For the next twenty minutes they exchanged information. Andy told her about his original intention to find Greg Whitehead and the subsequent and unexpected involvement of George. Cheryl was astonished. She'd offered refuge to a new friend, an innocent and generous accommodation. Now, after a trip to the local library, her house had been torched. A few questions had been answered but new ones had arisen.

Cheryl listened intently as Andy described his active investigation, following George, watching the farm in Surrey, watching her house. Plenty of detail but one glaring omission. She had heard Sarah talk about Alexander and as they each shared their intelligence, the question pressed for expression. "When did you last see Sarah?"

"When she came to visit you. Her car's back in Surrey but I haven't laid eyes on her for a while now."

"You've been looking for her, and I've been expecting her," said Cheryl, "but neither of us has seen her. She seems to have disappeared."

Andy surprised himself with his next comment. "I think she may be in danger." He looked at Cheryl, afraid that his speculative remark may have been over dramatic.

Cheryl waited forever, considering her reply. "So do I."

THIRTY-SIX

SEARCHING

ALEXANDER HAD ALWAYS REFUSED to show her the gun cabinet's secret compartment. It had been a game for the whole family. The children would start off with optimism and energy, enjoy a period of hope and the possibility of victory, but after a few minutes, frustration would surface and the cabinet was never opened. Sometimes Alexander would allow them to half see as he replaced the key but it made no difference, the key seemed to disappear as if by magic. It was as close to a few minutes of family fun as they ever got, Alexander enjoying his position and power, the children captivated by the mystery, and Sarah wishing in vain for her husband to soften.

It was just Sarah now, playing all by herself. She searched for hours each day, running her fingers lightly against the darkened wood of the cabinet, feeling every rise and fall in the grain, the bumps and knots, but the key remained hidden. She'd started with random searches, choosing her spot on impulse, feeling with her palms and then light scratches with her nails. Nothing. Then, after a couple of days, she became more systematic, starting at the top and working slowly down towards the bottom, pulling her fingers in all directions in her attempt to reveal the key. Still nothing. She maintained her effort for longer than her children had done, but the end result was the same – bewilderment and frustration.

She had asked herself the question but as yet she had no answer. What would be the right thing to do with a loaded gun for a seventy-year-old woman held prisoner in the grounds of her own home? She had her doubts. Alexander was comfortable with guns. They had always been a part of his life. He'd shown her how to load a shotgun during the early years of their marriage, trying to persuade her to shoot clay pigeons, but she'd felt no interest, always uneasy with such destructive weapons. She wondered what on earth she would do if her searches succeeded. Would she be able to take a gun in her hands, and point it at another human being? She hadn't even managed to shoot at a clay pigeon. Could she pull the trigger? Shoot to kill? She had no answer.

Sarah wondered if she should devise an alternative plan, dig a tunnel, send smoke signals out into a moonlit night, seek to engage George, or his recent substitute, in negotiation. But even with her doubts and her questions, she dedicated many hours to her task and still the cabinet refused to reveal its key.

Each search would last for twenty or thirty minutes, then Sarah would rest, lie back into her straw bed and allow her thoughts. Even that was challenging. There were a whole bunch of rogue thoughts ready to invade when she closed her eyes. Initially Sarah had expected release. She understood that Alexander was enraged, that he'd lashed out, but she expected that after a while, he'd realise that the situation was unsustainable. Then she'd feared for her life. With no way back and no way forward, she could only see one solution – her own disappearance. But her captivity was into the second week and despite her repeated requests to George, Alexander still hadn't shown himself.

And through it all, day after day, Sarah had only one intention. She was determined to open the gun cabinet.

George had enlisted help from one of his men. Her water

and occasional fragments of food were now delivered twice each day by a nameless stranger, who wouldn't even look at her when she spoke. Sarah's world was the inside of a windowless barn, solitary confinement. Her spirit faltered. She'd tried to negotiate with George, spent hours searching the gun cabinet, waited patiently, again and again. She didn't know what else she could do or even what day it was anymore.

She had maintained her focus, held on to a faint hope, but after days of fruitless searching she was worn down and she felt herself beaten, broken, crying into her sleeve, sometimes shouting out, begging. Her sliver of hope had turned into a brick wall. Dirty clothes soaked in sweat stuck to her dirty body, her resources spent and her resilience exhausted. Alexander knew his work – she was wretched. When her keeper came to leave water, she made no move, no effort to disguise her distress. Her dignity and pride had shattered. She'd given her resistance, tried to be strong, but now she collapsed.

THIRTY-SEVEN

NEGOTIATION

ALEXANDER HAD RECEIVED a brief report each day, initially from George and more recently from Phil, who had taken over the fetching and carrying to the barn. He'd bought himself some time to consider his options and, as it turned out, he had plenty of time, but not too many options. He and George had taken care of things up north, but the problem in the middle barn was yet to be solved.

The truth of the matter was starting to disturb Alexander. He'd tasted the satisfaction from lashing out, administered punishment to the foolish woman who'd dared to act against him, but the future for his good lady wife was uncertain. If only she'd had the sense to carry on with her life, appreciated her good fortune. This thought refuelled his anger. Sarah had brought this on herself and now she'd suffer the consequences.

The farm was large, almost four thousand acres. He had extensive areas of land only accessible to the farm workers. Some areas close to the river were never disturbed, with clumps of trees and reeds, and steep grassy banks. Alexander could bury dozens of bodies without fear of detection. He knew his land. But the more he thought about it, the less this option appealed. If he buried Sarah, he'd have to invent a story to explain her disappearance to the rest of the world, including their children. He told himself that he could do it if he had to and the family would have no choice but to believe him. But it would be some story to swallow – Sarah, stable and sane, a professional background in mental health, disappearing without warning and without a trace – Alexander wasn't convinced. So when Phil reported a change, describing Sarah's emotional distress, Alexander thanked the Lord above for this small mercy. Right was on his side and so was God.

He questioned Phil, who was clearly uncomfortable with his role. He pressed the poor man to give details of his observations, to compare with previous visits, and the emerging picture pleased him. He'd done it a dozen times at St Germaine's, delivering a daily programme of soul-destroying abuse, watching hearty resistance crumble into pathetic pleading, and he knew then that he had tamed any rogue aspiration. The future would bring whimpering obedience. He decided it was time for a chat with his wife.

And now he came. Phil opened the doors and Alexander looked from the entrance. Sarah didn't move, didn't even turn her head to see who had entered. Alexander smiled and stepped inside, gesturing to Phil to close the doors and then to stand back on guard. He walked slowly across the barn to speak to her.

He walked right up to where she lay, curled in a foetal position, facing the barn wall. Alexander pressed his foot against the back of her hip, and waited while she turned to face him.

There was a brief moment of eye contact, then he spoke. "I wonder how you like it here, living in the barn?" He waited, allowing her the chance to reply, but he was neither surprised nor disappointed when she remained silent. "You've been a fool, Sarah, running up and down the country, planning another life. Did you forget that you are my wife?" His voice boomed and echoed. Still no reply. "You stink, lying in your own piss. You're a filthy animal. You've betrayed me, lied to me, taken me for a fool. You will never leave this farm and never be forgiven. But I may allow you to survive. That's one possibility. One of two," he added. He looked at her again, enjoying his power, looking down at her cowed figure, too broken and too frightened to speak. Alexander had spent several days feeling troubled, wondering if his rash and angry confrontation had left him in a tight corner. Despite his position of dominance, he was still far from comfortable. The reeds by the river waited as a last resort, but maybe he could bring her back to order, tame her wild and wayward instincts, put a leash around her neck and lead her home, make her into his dancing bear, a shell without spirit, beaten, silent and submissive. He had a moment of opportunity. "Perhaps your stay here has helped you, taught you a lesson. We'll see. You have a think about it, make your decision. You can resume your duties as my wife, so long as you comply with appropriate conditions, or..." Alexander paused, searching for the right words. "Or not. Sleep on it, Sarah."

THIRTY-EIGHT

DREAMING

SARAH HAD FELT DEFEATED and quite helpless, and during those hours from the middle of the previous day until late into the night, after Alexander's strange visit, she had lost her dignity and her spirit, unable to stand on her feet and without the will to face the world. Demoralised and exhausted, she had sunk into deep despair, unable to even look at her husband.

After Alexander left her alone to consider the choices he'd offered, he sent food. She couldn't remember the last time she'd eaten something that almost resembled a proper meal, and she took the food slowly, chewing each mouthful of a cheese sandwich a hundred times. It took her an hour to finish the sandwich, and then Sarah fell into a deep sleep. With her acceptance of defeat, she no longer needed to stay alert and she slept for twelve hours, eventually waking just before dawn after a vivid dream. She felt rested and took time to recall her dream: she had been crawling on hands and knees in a ploughed field, neat lines of furrowed soil, dark and moist, and bathed in sunlight. She was searching, for understanding and for something else. It had seemed incongruous. Such well tilled and fertile land but not a single plant growing. And she'd continued her search until finally a single green stem appeared on the other side of a glass door and all she had to do was to push open the door to reach the stem.

She awoke still carrying the mood from her dream, and although she felt unhurried, she knew what she had to do. The sunrise was still an hour away, and the darkest of the night had passed. In just a few days in her new environment, Sarah had learned to track the cycle of the day by subtle changes in the shafts of light and dark, moving as hands on a clock. She lay on her back in her straw bed, fingers entwined at the back of her head and she examined herself, taking an interest in her wellbeing, physical and psychological. Her asthma had remained under good control and the pain from her cracked rib had started to ease, just a little. Food and sleep had been much needed. For the first time during her captivity, Sarah had properly rested and filled her aching stomach. The despair lifted. During the previous day she had sunk to a desperately low point, overwhelmed, hungry and beaten, but now it had passed.

Even before dawn, Sarah resumed her task, once again running her fingers across every inch of the gun cabinet. It felt different in the dark. In the absence of any visual distraction, she could sense the physicality of the object more intensely. She caressed it, held her soft skin against the unyielding structure, rested her cheek and forehead on the cold smooth wood. In the darkness, her dislike for the cabinet seemed to be gone and her fingers found new patterns of movement, more flow. She pushed into the wood, pressing her fingers, moving her hand and pressing again.

Then her heart missed a beat. She felt it in her finger, in her heart and in her throat all at once – a faint click and an inward movement. For a second, she froze, afraid that she might make a wrong move and lose her progress, and she allowed the wood beneath her finger to push back. It was such a delicate spring, both the sound and the movement barely perceptible, and her appreciation for the woodwork grew further. The carpenter who had created this cabinet was a very different man to its owner. Sarah knew in that moment that the cabinet had been built with care and sensitivity. Its construction had been a labour of love. The cabinet maker clearly had a passion for wood, just as Alexander loved the guns and the power. She refocused, another application of gentle pressure, then she slowly drew her finger back, holding the slight depression in the surface until the tiny drawer came away into the palm of her hand. There was still no light. Sarah felt the shape of a small metal key resting neatly in the dislodged drawer.

THIRTY-NINE
NEW RULES OF ENGAGEMENT

ALEXANDER HAD LOST HIS RAG, a perfectly understandable reaction under such gross provocation. Nevertheless, he'd got himself into a sticky situation. Not that Sarah had given him much option. But things were coming back to him now. George had been back up north, wreaked a bit of havoc, and Sarah's new life had been flushed away before she'd made a start. Shit to the sewer.

He congratulated himself for delivering an effective mixture of reward and punishment. Unpredictable switches, first offering hope and then snatching it away again. He'd continue with the same method, and when he next visited Sarah, she would be begging to stay. He knew the technique and he'd chosen his moment, waiting for Sarah's collapse into demoralised helplessness, and then appearing in person to view her misery and to offer his options. He'd given her time to make her decision, made it simple for her: yes or no.

In truth, Alexander also needed some time. An evening to think and a dark night to dream. Time to slow down. He'd almost got it all closed down. He'd got in front and he wanted a few more hours to let it all settle. He'd taken some risks, acted rashly, and hurt people. For a while he'd lost control but he'd got through, and now he collected his thoughts, and reflected. He'd reacted to his wife's dishonesty and he was without regret. She had wronged him and he'd administered the requisite punishment. Any self-respecting man would have gone the same way, although as Alexander thought about it, he recognised his exceptional and brutal efficiency, bringing her to her knees, ready for repentance. Excellent work.

He cooked bacon and eggs. His GP would disapprove but today was a big day. Anyway, he told himself, it was hardly a full English, just a good farmer's breakfast. He hadn't specified a time for his return to the middle barn. He'd let Phil complete the morning routine before making an entry. He didn't want to smell her shit while she grovelled in apology and he could use the time to get a padlock fixed to her bedroom door. Maybe get George over as additional back-up. Alexander was in a charitable mood, ready for phase two.

But for all of his satisfaction, the whole affair had troubled him and he was relieved that the shift back from the middle barn to a locked bedroom was about to occur. For Alexander, this was an important step. Until Phil had reported Sarah's collapse, Alexander had found himself in uncertain territory, and he was relieved to regain a position of control, to re-establish something close to his rather perverse idea of normality. He didn't examine this progression too closely, nor did he look too far into the future. One step at a time.

He drank coffee. The whole kerfuffle was bothering him. Cooking his own bacon and eggs, brewing coffee, pots to wash. House shit. He wanted her back, a more submissive and attentive version of herself, and he smiled. Nearly there.

He spent a few minutes preparing himself, forming a clear idea of what he'd say. He decided to manage without George, who had become surly, instead briefing Phil in preparation for a minor role in the move from barn to bedroom. Alexander wanted his house brought to order. The events through Sarah's descent into insanity had disturbed him, but with George's able assistance, he'd closed down her escape route, and now he could begin a closely supervised period of re-training. He'd experienced headaches and some chest pain during these past couple of weeks but today he was on better form. He was pleased by the opportunity to resolve the problem in the middle barn, to feel a sense of control returning. He walked across to the barn with Phil – it was time to talk to Sarah.

One shot.

Who knows how a lion feels, hungry but driven to survive, pushed to the edge of risk and reason. Who knows? Who knows when a life is lived? And who the hell knows what a person might do – cornered and threatened, injured and armed?

After several days of being treated like an animal, Sarah had got closer to her base instincts. She'd learned about hunger, dropping into panic and then deep depression when food had been withheld, experiencing nausea and light-headedness, losing concentration and sometimes stumbling into moments of wild disorientation.

Sarah had experienced a range of moods in the space of the last twenty hours, moving from desperate submission into sleep and dreams. Then her calm search and the key discovery. Now she waited, alone with her thoughts, speaking to herself as she prepared for another moment of confrontation.

Yes, okay, you had your moment of victory,
Enjoyed the spoils of war.
Good luck to you, my husband.
Things change, move along.
I opened the gun cabinet.
How about that?

Touched it with searching sensitive fingers, a lover's hand, triggered
the reflex.
We wait now, the shotgun and I, to find out.
Who will live and who will die?
Who's hungry today?
Who's the lion?

One shot. No breakfast for Sarah this morning, just water and a clean bucket. It didn't matter, Alexander had sent food yesterday after his visit. That was a foolish mistake. Her husband was good at cruelty, heartless and brutal, but he was no lion, and he'd never learned about hunger. He'd half starved her, taken her to the brink, into compliance and helplessness, and celebrated victory. Then, at the moment when he should have sunk his teeth into her throat, he'd fed her.

She had reminded herself of Mark's timid encouragement, of Cheryl's support, and she thought about Greg, wondering how he'd reacted after her 'no show' at The Teapot, and she remembered her own resolve and determination.

I'll fight or I'll die.

She waited, crouched in long grass, patient, still, and ready.

The established early morning routine was repeated. She caught the smell of bacon when the barn door first opened but no food came, just a clean bucket and fresh water. And then more waiting.

Eventually he came. Phil opened the barn door, stood aside to allow Alexander entry, and then stepped back into the shadows to stand guard by the doorway.

Sarah didn't move. She was sitting on the floor with her back against the barn wall and she kept her head bowed as he advanced.

He picked up an old saw horse as he moved closer, placing it a few feet in front of her, then used it as a seat. "We can end this foolishness now. We all make mistakes, none of us are perfect. I hope that you've come to your senses."

Sarah felt the hairs on her neck stand to attention. This was the moment. Her mouth was dry. She considered his question, asked herself. "Yes, I believe I have."

Alexander wasn't entirely convinced by her response. A little more clarity was needed. "What on earth were you thinking, Sarah? You put me in an impossible position. I won't forgive you for that but I will be generous. We can bring it to a close right now, move you back to the house, and see how you get on. A probationary period if you will, and if you behave in a fit manner, then you'll be allowed to resume your duties as my wife. Is that clear?"

Now she raised her head. She knew that she could never go back, in that respect she was clear. "Yes, that is clear." She looked up at him. Eye contact.

He was still not satisfied. She'd given compliant answers and yet he detected recalcitrance – he felt the need to test her a little further. "You've made the right choice, Sarah. Phil and I will escort you back to the house."

"What are my choices, Alexander? Please tell me again. I've forgotten." Sarah's request for clarification was delivered to signal her challenge and she held his gaze for a second. But really she was asking herself the question, wondering how desperate she'd become.

Alexander felt a tiny nagging doubt grow into something much more substantive. Already she was wayward. He could feel the colour rising in him, his contentment evaporating, but he held himself. He'd give her clarity now though, he was in no mood to play games. He stood up from the saw horse and he raised his voice. "You have one choice. To obey your husband and to keep the house, and to keep your filthy whore's mouth shut. Are we clear now?"

Sarah nodded, holding her head high, unflinching as he towered over her. "You're wrong, Alexander. Do you really imagine that I could stay with you, keep your house? I won't, I can't live in that way any longer. I'd rather die." She could see his agitation. "So it's you who must choose. What will you do now?"

She spoke boldly but she was frightened. Frightened of everything that might now happen, of what Alexander would do, of what she herself might do, and most of all of what she might fail to do. More than anything in the world, Sarah wanted to find a way out of the barn without violence or injury. She had opened the gun cabinet and she had a loaded shotgun hidden in the straw by her feet, but now she'd found some fear, and once again the question that she asked of herself, was directed to her husband. Quietly she prayed that he would come to his senses, because in that moment she couldn't persuade herself to fire the gun. Her fear held her, and despite her defiance, she felt unable to move, almost frozen.

He was unprepared for this scenario. His self-control fled, replaced instantly by blind rage. "There's a reed bed at the bottom of the south field. I suspect that some of my ancestors are buried there. You'd be in good company. So to answer your question, I choose to open the gun cabinet, blow out your brains and bury your dead body by the river."

Sarah had invested great effort to stand before him so boldly, pushed herself, found some courage, and then some fear. But as the conflict accelerated and with Alexander's tolerance expired, she felt something else directing her. Psychobiology intervened. She no longer had capacity for thinking and doubt, adrenaline surged through her veins, delivering desperate fear. She had moved beyond reason into a more primitive place, to the core of her instinct for survival. Without any conscious thought, she found movement, reaching into the straw around her feet and pulling out the shotgun. It had been more than forty years since Alexander had shown her how to use this same gun and even then she'd paid only scant attention, but it fell into place easily, the fore-end sitting into her cupped left hand while the forefinger of her right hand found the trigger. She raised herself to her feet and the gun butt to her shoulder, pointing both barrels at her husband.

Phil shifted nervously over by the door, looking first to Alexander and then out into the farm yard, but neither viewpoint gave him instruction. He stood motionless with crossed fingers.

Alexander was in a state of disbelief, unable to process the new order of things. He was the dominant figure, the person in charge, beyond challenge, the man who called the shots, and he really was struggling to believe the evidence before his eyes. It was simply too big a shift in his cognitive apparatus, too great a reversal to be real.

He watched her closely as she started to move with slow sideways steps, keeping the shotgun in place and maintaining her aim as she edged along the wall, gradually getting closer to Phil and the barn door. The two of them turned like a wheel, husband and wife for nearly fifty years, watching every move, separated now by just a few metres, by murderous hatred, by mistrust, by a universe, and by a gun.

Alexander shook his head, and forced a grin. He ruled in this place, this woman with the gun belonged to him. He stepped a pace forward, testing her, watching her tense up and tighten her grip on the weapon. But she didn't shoot. His grin grew more confidence.

She flinched when he stepped closer. One squeeze of the trigger now and she'd spray lead shot into his chest, probably killing him. Just one shot. She was breathing rapidly and she started to shake. Her whole body was primed for action but she remained still, holding a gun to threaten another human being, but unable to pull the trigger, while watching Alexander regain his position and re-establish control.

"You're pathetic. You couldn't persuade yourself to shoot a fucking clay pigeon. Look at you, you're shaking. You haven't got it in you, Sarah." He held out his arms, palms upturned. "It's now or never. I'll tell you what's about to happen. The stock of that gun is solid oak, a hundred years old, hard and heavy. I'm going to take the gun from you and I'm going to batter you with it, slam that old piece of wood into your nose and your teeth, break a few bones in that pretty face. That's how it ends. The last taste in your mouth will be your own blood. I won't waste a cartridge on you. There's no need. So it's now or never. Go ahead. All you have to do is pull the trigger. I'll stand still, you can't miss."

Phil watched as the two figures shuffled sideways with synchronised steps – dancers in the hay. And he winced as he listened to Alexander's challenge. To Phil, it seemed an unnecessary provocation, and he wanted to shout out, to ask Alexander to stay quiet, but no words came. Phil could feel it in his bones – this would not end well. Phil wasn't an exceptionally bright man, but he could see that he was in a bad place. For a moment, he held his position beside the door. Then he took two slow steps out into the farm yard, where his pace quickened. And then he heard the gun fire. He froze, his feet rooted to the ground and he stood for a few seconds, confused by his own inertia, until he realised that he had to look. He couldn't walk away not knowing.

FORTY

AMBULANCE CHASERS

ONCE ANDY and Cheryl had shared their concern about Sarah, the 'do nothing' option was removed. Cheryl had to deal with the fire damage and Andy already knew the territory. Polly had given clarity to the nature and limits of his mission. The three of them were in agreement: they were worried about Sarah and the mission was to lay eyes on her. End of story. That had helped Andy. He'd almost got to a stage where he didn't know who to follow or why, but now he was back on track. They all shared a sense of unease about Sarah's disappearance, and it was Andy's job to find her. There were unexplained loose ends and it was turning out to be a strange story, but if Sarah was seen alive and at liberty, then Andy could return home with his mission accomplished.

He had set out early and he arrived back at George's house at ten thirty. *"Both cars back on the starting line."* He found himself a parking spot with a view of the exit road, to allow himself a few minutes rest before driving out to the farm. *"I'll catch you later, George."* Cheryl had offered a radical shift in strategy. She had complimented Andy on his survival skills and on his record for observing others without detection, but she had questioned his approach, suggesting

203

that a week of wild camping might be a less effective method than ringing the doorbell. He'd had to accept that it was an interesting idea and now that he'd checked in on George, he intended to give it a try.

Andy had negotiated with Cheryl. They had talked about involving the police, a perfectly reasonable step to consider, but when they had thought it through, they had found no faith. They had no actual evidence of George committing a crime and nothing more than intuition to support their concern for Sarah's safety. Andy had already had more encounters with the police than he cared to recall, and he wanted one last look at his friends in the south without the bungling interference of Mr Plod.

Cheryl hadn't objected, impressed that Andy had already located and identified George. She was happy for him to continue the investigation. Polly had imposed the time limit and the conditions: one day to complete the mission. If Sarah's whereabouts remained hidden then they'd give their information to the police and withdraw.

That suited Andy. Another twenty-four hours to uncover the mysteries. He would either find Sarah or he'd return to Stokesley with a clean conscience, having exhausted all search options including the new 'ring the doorbell' approach.

He'd asked Cheryl to phone Sarah and predicted that she wouldn't answer. Cheryl followed his suggestion and he was right – one ring and then straight to the answering service. Then he'd told her to keep ringing Sarah's number throughout the morning while he travelled and he checked his own phone now to see if Cheryl had sent a message. Nothing. He sent her a text: *I'm back at George's. Both his cars are both parked on the drive. Any news?*

The reply came immediately: *Still no answer.*

Andy had no reason to watch George. He'd just wanted to satisfy his curiosity, and check that George had returned home. He dropped his phone onto the passenger seat and was about to start the car when he looked up to see George emerging from the cul-de-sac in the Jaguar. *"Good morning, George."* Andy couldn't resist. He followed cautiously, keeping plenty of distance between them, unconcerned when George's car moved out of sight for a few seconds. They were travelling a familiar route, heading out to the farm, but he was jolted from complacency when George took a detour into a lane off the main road. Andy knew the lane as he'd checked every access point to the farm, by car and on foot. His interest grew and he wondered why George had changed his approach. He was uncomfortable, suddenly feeling exposed as he followed along a narrow lane. George's car came to a halt alongside the same gate that Andy had used to access his camping site. A familiar figure emerged from the hedge and jumped into the passenger seat of the Jaguar, the same man who Andy had photographed coming in and out the barn, and then George drove briskly on. *"Interesting."*

Andy drove on and parked by the gate. He'd catch up with George later. Or not. *"Stay with the mission, no distractions."* He was back at his own access point for the farm and decided to walk up to his viewing position. The doorbell option would have to wait. He walked slowly at first, increasing his pace when he heard sirens in the distance. By the time he reached his viewing point at the top of the rise, a police car and an ambulance had driven into the farm premises. Andy watched in amazement as a second ambulance arrived. *"Yes, good luck waiting for an ambulance, unless you happen to own half of Surrey of course."* Two bodies emerged, carried on stretchers from the same barn that George and his unidentified companion had frequently visited, and taken into the two waiting ambulances, which left the scene with lights flashing.

Andy decided on a strategic retreat, sensing that this was an inopportune moment for ringing the doorbell. He felt unsure again about whether his mission was completed or indeed exactly what his mission should be now. George and his buddy had made a discreet exit just before two bodies were taken away in ambulances. *"What the hell has happened here?"*

He drove without a care for his direction. He just needed some distance from what appeared to have become a serious crime scene. *"What was that? Who was that?"*

He stopped the car and wandered out into a field of broad beans, looking for a place to think. What had happened? What had he allowed to happen? And what was he going to do now? He thought again about going to the police, and he was tempted to drive home. He wondered about going back to George's house. But none of these options fitted the brief, his mission to get eyes on Sarah.

He used his phone to find the nearest hospital with an Accident and Emergency service, and forty minutes later he parked at the Royal Surrey County Hospital in Guildford and headed cautiously towards the hospital entrance, just in time to see George enter the building. Andy noted with interest that George was alone again. *"Jesus. He just keeps turning up. Wherever this goose chase leads, George appears on the scene."*

There were boards behind the reception desk, listing the various hospital departments and some kind of colour code which was lost on Andy. There were coloured lines on the floor, which made no sense to him. As luck would have it, George seemed to understand. Andy was easily able to follow. George was a big man and he had metal tips on the soles of his shoes. Andy, guided by shape and sound, followed. *"Here we go again."*

Five minutes of walking through hospital corridors led to a dead end. There was a gathering of uniformed people around the staff entrance to A&E, including NHS clinicians, security staff and several police officers. Most of the corridors had been crowded, giving plenty of cover, but this seemed to be the end of the blue line. Andy and George had this corridor to themselves. George clocked the uniforms and did a swift about turn. Suddenly he was walking back towards Andy, giving him an anxious moment as he remembered their close encounter in Stokesley, but George walked right past him. Andy breathed a sigh of relief. Then the steady rhythmic clicking from George's shoes fell silent. *"Fuck."* Andy needed to think quickly. He felt himself caught between a rock and a hard place, between George and the police. None of these people were his friends. And now George had rumbled him. Both men turned together, like gunfighters ready to draw their weapons. Andy had no fear. Facing the enemy had been his profession, combat was in his nature, and of course the police were just down the corridor.

They were six or seven metres apart. Andy grinned extravagantly. "Good to see you again, George." He was first to draw and raised his camera ready to shoot. "Say cheese." He got a great shot, saluted George and resumed his walk down towards A&E, listening again to the rhythm of George's clicking heels. *"Moving a little faster now, George."*

Andy realised that whoever had been stretchered out from the farm would be in good hands and he didn't wish to distract the doctors and nurses from their work. Of course, the police were involved now.

It had been a feature all through the story, a simple objective being complicated by unexplained events. Each time that Andy anticipated quiet, there was noise. And everywhere he went, there was George. There was a group of five blue plastic chairs in a line against the corridor wall, close to the A&E entrance, but still several metres short of the gathering of uniformed workers. Andy lowered himself into a seat and took a breath. He didn't have a clue what had happened or any clear ideas about how to find out. Two bodies carried into ambulances and two sightings of George. He was perplexed.

A nurse walked briskly along the corridor. Andy chanced his arm. "Bless your heart, nurse. I'm Andy Buxton, Sarah's brother. Can I go and see her?"

She answered with brisk economy. "No visitors in A&E. Not since the pandemic."

"She'll want to see me."

This time Nurse Jenkins was less tolerant. "She's not conscious."

FORTY-ONE
THE BIG BAD WORLD

FOR THE FIRST time in several days, Greg awoke without a headache and emerged from his bed into a house restored to order. Sarah had given him a rollercoaster ride, blown him from the safety of solitude into a precarious social world, and then abandoned him. It had hurt, made him ill, given him real pain, and he'd fallen apart, consumed by alcohol and self pity, unable to face his own humiliation.

Then angels came. Sue Berry, from school, so pretty and always unsure of herself, now so honest and assertive, insensitive and impressive in her pursuit of humour and truth, and Eleanor, soft and curious, accepting everyone, comfortable with unconventionality and generous with support. These were the friends who'd hammered on his door, swept his floors, and held his hand. He had been in desperate need of the generosity and kindness from his friends. They had picked him up from the floor.

He was up very early but already bright sunlight signalled a fine day to come and he felt appreciation for Sue and Eleanor as he made coffee in a clean kitchen. His thoughts moved beyond his miserable rejection, beyond his front door. He wanted to go somewhere.

The Covid pandemic had made Greg's world a smaller

place, confined him, and he had never pushed himself to reclaim the lost territory, becoming content with his reduced lot and happy enough to live his life indoors. But today, rather oddly, he wanted to go out, to be in the big bad world. He switched his television on, to catch up with some news while considering his options for a bike ride.

Ten hours later his flight landed smoothly on the runway at Josep Tarradellas, Barcelona. Breakfast television had screened a feature on cycling in Spain and Greg had felt invited, almost targeted, while he had imagined himself sending a selfie to Eleanor from a cool bar on the beach in Barcelona. What better way to thank the two of them for their support and guidance. It had been a long time since he'd travelled abroad and even longer since he'd acted on impulse. He stepped out from the air-conditioned arrivals lounge. It was late in the afternoon, but still the searing heat shocked him. Greg had heard that Barcelona was pretty good for cycling and was aware that he could take a train ride a hundred kilometres north into the foothills of the Pyrenees, but he hadn't focused in on the details. "Hey, don't sweat the small stuff, like checking the fucking temperature."

It was seriously hot, even for Barcelona at the end of June, climate change hot, and Greg was disorientated, almost dizzy with the bright sunlight and the heat. He stumbled to a shaded spot, took off his jacket and found his way to a bus bound for the city centre. The bus had air-con and the ride gave him half an hour to recover himself and get himself organised, packing away his jacket and finding new pockets for essential documents. By the time he disembarked in the centre of Barcelona, he was back on track and determined to dive into the first hotel that he found.

The walk from the airport terminal to his bus stop had been more than enough to dissuade him from hauling his bags around town looking for the perfect location. His original intention had been to spend a couple of days cycling around the city and then to head north into more scenic territory. He just hadn't been ready for Barcelona, and he stood in the shade, looking in all directions to spot a hotel. The sheer volume of people caught him unawares, and already the crowds and the heat had combined into an oppressive force. His wish to cycle in the city evaporated. He revised his plan, deciding to stay overnight in the city and travel north the next morning.

He wasn't sure whether he could see a hotel, but he set off nevertheless, back into the bright sunlight. After walking a hundred metres, he was already sweating heavily, but he saw the sign he'd been seeking, and to his relief, the steps up into the Hotel Catalonia were just a few metres away. He bumped against someone. Greg turned to see who he'd collided with and started to make an apology, but suddenly there was a flurry of activity. The man who he'd bumped against had spilt his drink on Greg's shirt, although Greg hadn't really noticed as his shirt was already drenched in sweat, but then another man lent a hand and the two of them were apologising profusely and wiping around his chest to clean up the spillage. Then a woman stepped forward, shouting at both of the men, admonishing them and pushing them aside so that she could help with the clean up.

Greg was confused and crowded. These people were trying to be helpful but they had invaded his personal space. "I'm fine, it's okay. I have a clean shirt."

For a moment, reassuring and helpful hands seemed to be all over him, then a final set of apologies and the three of them were gone. They had appeared from nowhere and they disappeared with equal mystery.

A passer-by spoke to him with concern. "Are you okay?"

Greg felt self-conscious. "Yes, yes, I'm fine, just a spilled drink. Thank you." He remained motionless, held by his confusion and he looked again at the passer-by, who seemed unconvinced. Greg felt the need to offer further information. "I've just arrived. It's a crowded city, but everyone seems very friendly."

The concerned citizen smiled kindly and walked on. Greg found his feet and dragged his bags into the Catalonia. He felt much better once his room request received a positive response. His heart rate started to settle, the air-con soothed him, and he accepted a welcome glass of water as he checked into the hotel. Greg had been an enthusiastic traveller for much of his adult life, always fascinated by a new culture and a new country, but this was his first trip abroad since the pandemic, and he seemed to have forgotten that hot countries were indeed quite hot and that iconic cities can get quite crowded in high season. He'd found the last fifty minutes stressful and he was grateful for the opportunity to relax again and to get his bearings. He gave Martina, the hotel receptionist, his details, looking forward to a shower and a clean shirt.

"Oh, and I just need your passport number, Mr Whitehead."

Greg dived back into his bags without any clear idea where he'd stored his travel documents. "Just give me a minute, Martina. It's in here somewhere."

But it wasn't. Greg could feel himself growing anxious as he began a third search through his bags. "It has to be here. Passports don't just disappear." He'd addressed his comment to Martina but as he heard his own words, he flashed back to the kerfuffle that had taken place out on the street, to the group who had surrounded him with their searching and soothing hands, and to their sudden disappearance. "Shit, I've been robbed."

The hotel staff were helpful. Luckily, Greg had his wallet secreted away deep in his luggage. He'd paid over the odds for a thousand euros at the airport and thankfully all of the cash and his credit cards were inside his wallet. The muggers had taken his passport, and that seemed to be all they'd got. He went to the police to report the theft and he was issued with a crime report. Even the police were friendly. Already he was on first name terms with the young uniformed officer who had patiently ushered him through the procedures.

"Okay, Greg, we're done. Put the report in a safe place. You'll need it when you apply for a new passport, and I'll call you if anything turns up. What's your cell phone number, please?"

Immediately Greg felt another wave of anxiety, as he searched his memory, trying to recall when he'd last looked at his phone. He'd had it on the bus from the airport, since then nothing. "We may need to amend the report, Mateo, it seems my phone was also stolen."

Greg couldn't sleep. The whole episode just kept on replaying in his mind. He wasn't sure whether he'd been scammed, conned, mugged or robbed, but either way it felt bad. He was angry with them, whoever they were, vultures preying on the vulnerable. Bastards. He'd behaved like a brainless dickhead tourist, struggling with his bags, eyes everywhere, desperate not to offend or question, and three scumbags had done him over, taken him, mauled him, invaded him. Even after his return from the police station, he couldn't stop thinking about what had happened. He spent time hanging around outside of the hotel, willing them to return, to try again with another sweating tourist, and he'd be ready, but they'd gone, scored their phone and run for the hills. It was a shitty memory and it kept Greg awake and on edge the whole night.

And it stayed hot. A painfully sleepless night was followed by another day of hassle in the scorching sun, but even with online form filling and liaison with the British Consulate, he still made time to plan his journey to Girona. His emergency documents would be delivered to the hotel in Barcelona but he could easily pop back on the train to pick them up. He felt desperate to get free from the city and to breathe some mountain air.

It had been hot and hectic and it had challenged Greg,

tested his metal, but he'd come through and as he navigated his way forward from the mugging, he regained a sense of himself as a seasoned traveller. He'd survived a traumatic welcome without too much trouble and was already setting up his next destination and adventure. The routes for cycling around Gerona gave great options, with beautiful landscapes and no need to go crazy, climbing big mountains. He was a victim of crime and he was buzzing.

He only considered buying a new phone for a few seconds, realising that he had no one's contact details and no wish to communicate. After the fun and funerals in North Yorkshire, he felt freed, released from the unexpected dramas involving old school friends and bullies, and after a few hours he found his phone-free status quite liberating. No longer glancing to see if Sarah had sent a text, no more dodging Eleanor's calls, Greg was on the road, walking on new paths, playing catch me if you can.

Gerona didn't disappoint him. Even as he emerged from the train station, he knew that he liked the town. He got a feeling of the history from the architecture and the heat was a few degrees lower than in Barcelona – less oppressive. He checked into a hostel where cycling gear could be hired and where he'd be able to talk with other riders about which routes to take.

As it turned out, the Hostel El Manillar had pretty good rooms and facilities although Greg quickly became aware that he was the only guest aged over thirty. He'd got used to the age gap back home. Most men of his age bought motorbikes, the easy riders, delusional Peter Fonda's chasing dreams from fifty years ago. But Greg had great thighs. Even as a boy, his strength was in his legs, and he could really ride a bike. He'd always cycled and he'd done some road racing during his university years. He knew how to ride a bike, confident in his cornering, and trusting of the mechanics. He didn't mean to be competitive, and he didn't really want to be, he just couldn't help it. He wanted to go faster, further, and he didn't like to be left trailing. Right through until Covid, he'd taken organised tours with groups of keen cyclists, often through some spectacular landscapes, and he'd always been able to keep pace with the younger guys.

During the pandemic, he kept up regular cycling but he became a solitary rider, and after the pandemic he continued to ride alone, restricted to the area surrounding his home. But now he was in Gerona, drinking Sangria and wondering what pace would be expected on the forthcoming ride. He'd signed up for a group ride starting out the next morning – three hours through gentle slopes between the town and the coast. It was good Sangria. It was always good in Spain.

Greg had missed these things. This was the lifestyle he'd chosen: the freedom to act on impulse, to be home and safe in Middlesbrough for breakfast, then to dine out in Barcelona in the late evening, after being mugged. The jug of Sangria sparkled in the evening sunlight. Greg's table was outside the hostel's front entrance, positioned to appreciate the social grace of hot countries, siestas and life on the street. He took it in, the big world that he could be a part of, the Pyrenees, a different pace of life. He was sitting on the street in the middle of town but he enjoyed a glorious view of magical light skipping on the river, tall buildings, movement and colour.

Having found such a vibrant place, he breathed it in with relish. He felt himself unwinding, felt the trials of the previous twenty-four hours slip from his shoulders, carried away by the wind and the river. Sometimes he allowed his eyes to close, taking in the sounds and the smells of the lives lived here. He felt restored.

"Is it okay if I sit here?"

Greg looked across at the young woman who'd spoken. "Yes, please do. It's a fine evening."

It was a small hostel, with fifteen bedrooms, and large

communal kitchen and living areas. There was a garden at the back where the younger riders seemed to gather. Greg had opted for one of the two small tables at the front of the hostel. His new companion, a stranger, might have sat out in the garden or she could have chosen to have her own table but for reasons which weren't apparent to Greg, she wanted to share his table. Maybe she'd clocked the Sangria.

"I'm Stella, I just arrived today. I'm just here for a couple of nights, and I don't know anyone."

"Hi Stella, I'm Greg. I travelled up from Barcelona earlier today. I haven't really got my bearings yet but I like it here, in Gerona, at El Manillar, at this table. Please, take a seat. Would you like a glass of Sangria?"

They spent twenty minutes sitting together, making polite conversation and drinking Greg's Sangria before Greg said good night and retired to his bed. He had missed some sleep and he hoped to catch a few dreams before the sixty kilometre ride tomorrow.

Greg slept well and was the first rider ready for departure. Antonio, who would lead the group, informed him that there were seven more riders to join them, they would take a break after thirty-five kilometres and be back in Gerona before midday. Three pairs arrived in quick succession and Greg was slightly disappointed. He had guessed that there'd be no one of his own age on the trip but he'd hoped for at least one other solo traveller. He remained undeterred, Antonio seemed knowledgeable about bikes and about the local area, and the weather was perfect.

Antonio asked the group to wait for a few minutes to give the last rider a chance to join them although they had already passed the scheduled departure time.

Stella ambled into view. "Oh, you're all very early." She turned to Antonio. "How long before we start?"

Greg smiled. He didn't normally react well to poor timekeepers but today he was all charity and acceptance.

Antonio took the opportunity to make a point. "Actually, you're late. We've all been waiting for you." He turned to the group. "Okay, let's get moving."

Stella glanced across at Greg, unable to suppress her grin, enjoying being the naughty child. "Hey, you're everywhere."

"Yes, I try to be. Good morning, Stella."

The cycling was sensational. A couple of hills sorted the cyclists from the tourists and Greg was impressed to note that it was Stella who was the only rider able to stay with him for the climbs. They stopped at the top of last hill to wait for the others to catch them up.

"Wow, we blew them motherfuckers away. You have great legs."

Greg understood the compliment. "You too." Who the hell was this woman, drinking at his table, riding like the wind, and speaking so freely. "You're a rule breaker, Stella, a natural anarchist."

She turned to him with a beaming smile, clearly satisfied by his assessment. "Only when I'm on holiday."

The stragglers arrived at the top of the hill, panting and sweating, and after a short rest, the group set out to complete the final ten kilometres back into town. The sun had climbed high in the sky and the temperature sapped the riders' energy through the last section of the ride.

Greg had already had a good work out, proved his point, and he was content to pedal lazily right into Gerona, where he anticipated a shower and lunch, and another jug of Sangria, but he arrived back at El Manillar to good news – his emergency documents were waiting in Barcelona. He took the shower but skipped lunch, taking a taxi to the station and boarding a train back to the Hotel Catalonia.

• • •

His return to Barcelona felt very different. He'd got the hang of things, knew exactly where he was going, and as he jumped from the train, he looked along the platform, watching the newcomers sweating in the heat and struggling with luggage, eyes wide open, and he could see what an easy target he'd made of himself a few days earlier. He wished his fellow travellers good fortune and went to collect his documents. The city felt fine to him now, but even so, he couldn't get back to Gerona quick enough.

He took a siesta on the return train journey and got back to El Manillar just before eight o'clock, starving hungry. Stella had reclaimed her chair at the small table and she greeted him with curiosity. "Where were you all day? Leaving me all alone."

"Hi, Stella. I had to pop back to Barcelona to pick up some documents." Greg was reluctant to say more, embarrassed by his naivety when he'd first hit the city. "I need some food. Do you know any of the local restaurants?"

"Are you asking me to have dinner with you?"

Greg was taken aback but he coped. "Absolutely."

"Well, that would lovely, and yes, I know some great bars."

El Puente Rojo wasn't an easy place to find. Stella led him along narrow cobbled streets, deep into the heart of the old town. Greg feared that she would take him to a loud bar filled with people half his age, but he needn't have worried.

"My father used to drink here with his friends, more than thirty years ago. The tourists don't come here and the Ollada is the best in town."

Greg couldn't believe his good fortune. There was a guitar player at the far end of the room, the smell of food, and a room filled with the goodwill of the local people. He felt privileged to be there and appreciative of his companion. "Good work, Stella."

They ordered drinks and food and found space to sit at a table close enough to hear the music. Greg was fascinated, enchanted. He'd learned to play guitar as a teenager and although he'd never progressed to a high standard, he'd gained an appreciation of musicianship and he always loved to listen to live music. The guitarist was tall and skinny, with a long prominent nose pointing to the elegant fingers that looked so easy in their constant movement. He was surprised by the style. It was distinctly Catalan, classical and folk music all at the same time. The waitress didn't walk from the kitchen to the tables – she danced, simple steps in time with the music.

For a while he sat spellbound until suddenly he remembered his manners, wondering how long it had been since he had last spoken to Stella. "Sorry, I didn't mean to be rude, the music is fabulous."

"The people here would have thought you rude if you had ignored the music. Don't feel obliged to talk to me if you want to listen."

They did talk, and they listened, to the music and to each other. The food tasted every bit as good as the aromas had promised. Everything, including the Sangria, was intoxicating.

"Did you grow up in Gerona?"

"No, in Cadiz, my mother's town. My father grew up here."

The music, the cycling, and the town had all caught Greg's interest, but as the evening grew late, his interest settled on Stella. So, he asked his questions.

"Are you here to visit relatives?"

"No, I just broke up with my boyfriend, so I needed the mountains, to be in my father's land, and to cycle."

"I'm sorry about your boyfriend."

"Thank you. I had hoped that he was the one. For a while, he was. We reached the end, probably a year ago, but I didn't want to see it. He found someone else." Stella released a sigh and sat quietly, subdued by the telling of her brief tale. "And what about you, what brought you here?"

"It's a long story."

"Good, I like long stories."

And so he told her. Gave her the whole show. From Janey's funeral to Andy Cooper and Sarah. She wanted every detail, gave her full attention and Greg responded, giving chapter and verse of his reunions with school friends and foes, and describing the foolish old man who thought he'd found love.

"And that was the end of it, Stella. She sent me a text message a few days later saying she'd decided to stay with her husband. End of story."

"Pah! It's not possible."

"I swear to you, I've told only the truth."

"No, you are mistaken. This woman, Sarah, who kissed you when you were younger, who waited for you on that bench by the river, who kissed you again. No, that woman could not send you that text message. It's completely impossible."

Greg chuckled. The naivety of youth, the certainty, untarnished and unshaken. "People aren't always the way we think they are. I should've known better. To be fair, it's been the story of my life."

Stella shook her head. "No, Greg. Don't be so British. You're in southern Europe now. You have to feel it, remember that kiss, go to it now and feel it again." Her eyes burnt into him. "Show me the text message."

He had to confess now. "I don't have it. I was robbed in Barcelona, and they took my phone."

"Oh my God."

"But I can remember the message. She didn't even sign her name, just an 'S'."

"Well, you tell me, Greg, does that message sound like it came from the same person who kissed you?"

"I take your point, Stella, but when the evidence is right in front of your eyes."

220

"Sarah didn't send that text. If you don't believe me, go to her and ask her to her face. My God, the British."

"What?"

"It's true, emotionally illiterate."

They stayed too late, and drank too much alcohol. It was Stella's night, her last night. All she had to do the next day was to get out of bed and get a train back down to the south of Spain. They stumbled back through the cobbled lanes to El Manillar. Stella went off to her bed while Greg sat out by the river. He was exhausted and quite drunk, but not yet ready for the night to close. Stella had charmed him and he spent a few minutes reflecting on the time they had spent together. He wondered at her refusal to accept Sarah's message. She'd been so sure that she'd made fun of his emotional ineptitude. She was crazy and he thanked his lucky stars that he'd met her.

FORTY-TWO

GRIFFIN

DI GRIFFIN HAD BEEN at the station when the call for an emergency response had first come through, and he'd made his way to Hurtmoor with mixed feelings. He'd bumped into Alexander MacDonald at local fund-raising events, and Griffin hadn't been particularly impressed, but he was clearly well connected and the emergency caller had reported an injury from a shotgun. That was the full extent of his knowledge, but it had been enough to persuade him to allow the ambulance to pass his car – best to give the paramedics first access, but he'd followed close behind and accepted a farm worker's guidance to pull up behind the house.

The lone worker had offered direction. "They're in the middle barn."

DI Griffin had looked to where the worker was pointing and watched the ambulance crew run forward. He'd paused for a second, puzzled by the man's directive. There were just two barns, one to the left and one on the right, nothing but fresh air in the middle. He'd made a mental note, even before entering the 'middle' barn and without yet knowing what crime had been committed. This man, the only man left standing, was a suspect.

There had been nothing much to see, no damage and no visible intruders. He'd felt cautious as he approached the barn and held back, deciding first to question the farm worker. "Who's in the barn?

"The two casualties – my employer, Alexander MacDonald, and his wife, Sarah."

"And who are you?"

"I'm Walter Rathbone, I manage the farm. I'm mostly up at the milking station." Walter had pointed across the field to the huge sheds where the cattle gave up their milk. "I hardly ever come down to the house, but I heard the shotgun."

DI Griffin had shown his ID. "I'm Detective Inspector Griffin. Any other witnesses?"

Walter was an honest man. He knew about cattle, but immediately he'd felt reticent. He'd worked for Alexander for more than twenty years but had never got close to him on a personal level. He had never set foot in the house. Alexander hadn't said anything directly but Walter seemed to have got the message just the same: he was there for his work, and in all other respects he was excluded. He'd offered a guarded response, sensing it was hardly the ideal moment to be pulled into the privacy of the family. "I haven't seen a soul and I witnessed nothing. I heard a gun and I came to investigate. End of story."

Definitely a suspect, thought DI Griffin. "Did you call 999?"

"Yes, but someone had already called it in."

"Have you got some ID?"

Walter had taken his driving licence from his wallet.

DI Griffin had glanced carelessly. "Don't go anywhere. We'll need a statement." A second ambulance had arrived as he walked into the barn, but he kept clear of the activity, allowing the paramedics to administer first aid, content to observe and to listen. He'd taken the opportunity to liaise with colleagues, requesting the Forensics Team and more investigating officers.

The two ambulances had left in tandem, one following the other to the Accident and Emergency department in Guildford, Alexander in the lead ambulance, and Sarah following in the second. DI Griffin had watched them speed away, and still he'd wondered – where was the criminal and what was the crime?

FORTY-THREE

A BETTER MAN

ANDY STARTED on the return journey home late in the afternoon with mixed feelings, still not able to free himself from the tangle of events that he had witnessed at the farm, and still feeling himself engaged in battle, despite his retreat. He made no further communications to Stokesley, deciding instead to think while driving, to replay the morning's drama and to make some sense of the latest and most startling twist to the developing story.

But there was more on his mind than that. Of course, he was curious about exactly what had taken place and his sense that Sarah was in danger was more alive than ever, but he also wanted to examine himself, trying to work out why he was travelling back and forth to Surrey, and why he cared what happened to Sarah. *"Why are you doing this, Cooper? What's the pay off?"*

Andy was looking for peace, an end to conflict. He wanted peace within himself, a way to silence the critical commentary of his own life, and to emerge from his darkness. He knew that he'd come a long way, and moved some distance from the angry young man who had punished himself and others. War had changed him, Polly had worked miracles, and he'd had months of counselling. He was closer than he'd ever been but until he'd honoured his promise to Janey, he could progress no further. One final hurdle before his race was run.

Andy had always told himself that he neither wanted nor expected forgiveness. He wanted to put the record straight. Explanation would be his best apology. But as he looked at it all again now, he recognised a more selfish motivation, one which he'd failed to acknowledge previously. His lifetime of misdeeds had created a prison cell for him, and through acts of repentance, he hoped to gain release. It wasn't just the promise to Janey, there was more. Andy wanted to be able to forgive himself. And yet for all of his endeavour, he still faced a locked door. Still not free.

He was trying to be a better man, to earn something close to self-respect in the later stages of his life. He'd put the fire out at Cheryl's house: that was a good deed. Perhaps that was the motivation for his interest in Sarah, to show the world the best of Andy Cooper. He was trying to rebalance the scales, to outweigh history, but he was up and down, and certainly not content. He'd fallen short in his attempt to talk to Greg Whitehead and he felt that he should have done more to protect Sarah.

He drove forward while allowing his thoughts to travel back. The episode in Surrey played on his mind. The dramatic appearance of police cars and ambulances seemed to suggest that whatever had been building, had come to a climax. Maybe it had, but Andy didn't feel that way. Sarah's well-being was uncertain and the end of the story was missing. *"You're worse than useless, Cooper."* That was his conclusion. He was trying to see the good in himself, trying to push away the negative thoughts, but as he drove on, the balance settled unevenly, with the darkness gaining ascendancy.

He arrived back in Stokesley and entered his own house with no clear understanding of any of it. He was tired and in need of Polly's perspective.

She gave a familiar welcome. "Oh, you're back."

"No, Pol, I'm still in Surrey." He walked to the fridge,

grabbed a cold beer, and took a long drink straight from the bottle.

They settled down and Andy described his trip to the farm and on to the hospital. He concluded that the nurse's indiscretion served as confirmation of Sarah's continuing existence and indeed of her safety, but neither of them were satisfied.

"I'm not happy but I'm done with it. I'll go and see Cheryl in the morning and she can follow up if she wants to, but I'm finished."

Polly nodded her assent. She had a sack full of unanswered questions but it was clear that the answers wouldn't come from Andy. "Fair enough. I'll come with you to Cheryl's." Polly had no direct involvement, no reason to care about strangers from Surrey, but all the same, she felt she was involved right up to her neck. Andy could pull back if he'd really had enough, but she was already looking forward to another meeting with Cheryl. It was better than EastEnders.

The meeting with Cheryl the next morning was inconclusive. There were still just as many unanswered questions and no clear way forward. Andy announced the ending of his pursuit. Polly wanted to know more about what had happened on the farm but she accepted her partner's position, and Cheryl was unsettled. The three of them shared the frustration, all of them dissatisfied, but unable to see the way forward. Cheryl said that she'd try phoning the hospital and they exchanged numbers, agreeing to share any new intelligence.

The meeting with Cheryl only intensified Andy's feeling of anti-climax. He was left at a loose end, hanging around in the house without purpose or occupation.

Polly could see that he was struggling. She had to hang tough when Andy's mood sank low, and try to get him up on his feet again. Sometimes she would put an arm around him,

227

and sometimes she kicked his arse. "I want you out of the house tomorrow, you're getting under my bloody feet."

Andy gave no reply.

"Are you listening to me?"

Still no reply.

"You can go to Middlesbrough and see Greg Whitehead, get the whole business wrapped up."

And he did. He travelled to Middlesbrough the next morning with renewed determination, walking to Greg's front door without hesitation, but his call went unanswered. He'd called unannounced so he had no right to complain, but he returned to Stokesley in a low mood, more frustrated than ever. "I give up, Pol. He was probably watching me from a bedroom window. Why would he give me a hearing? I can't say I blame him."

Polly would have been happy for him to give up, but she knew him well. He needed some encouragement, that was all. And she knew after all of these years that Andy wouldn't rest until he'd done Janey's bidding. "I agree, you give up, love. You're wasting your time."

"Are you serious?"

"Don't be so bloody stupid. He can't stay away forever. Get a good night's sleep and go again tomorrow, and the next day, and the day after. I didn't marry a quitter, Andy Cooper. You'll keep going until you find him."

FORTY-FOUR
TOGETHER

TWO LIVES that had become inextricably entwined. The relationship between Sarah and Alexander was an unhealthy tangle, twisted and bent, and yet they seemed to be inseparable. First they had become strangers, losing the habit of civil communication, and then enemies, reaching the point of open hostility in the middle barn, but they had remained together through it all.

And so it continued, travelling in convoy at high speed to the hospital, and stretchered inside to receive medical assessment in neighbouring bays. They were both sent for surgery on the day of their admission, and now, twenty-four hours later, they were both starting to catch up with their own events, wondering what recovery might look like.

For Sarah, the process was slow. She had felt herself drift in and out of consciousness in the barn and in the ambulance. Throughout the morning after her operation, she felt the same way.

An ambulance came for me
I've been unconscious, I think
And here I lie, in a hospital, I think

229

I'm drowsy, in and out of sleep
It's the drugs, I think

The paramedics had given first aid – painkillers and anti-coagulants, and an ice pack to the side of her head and face where there was ugly swelling and heavy bruising. Then she'd been rushed into surgery, but even though a further twenty hours had passed, she had just a few small flashes and fragments of memory of her hospital experience. That didn't concern her. She was searching back a little further, through a fog of drugs and dizziness, trying to pull it all together, desperately trying to remember what had happened in the middle barn.

She could remember so many of the seemingly insignificant moments from her ordeal in the barn. She knew how it had started, and she had clear memory of the time she'd spent locked away, sleeping in the straw, and using a bucket as a toilet. Her return to awareness came slowly, but as the morning progressed, she gained more clarity. Then quite suddenly, the fog lifted, and she remembered Alexander taunting her. At that moment, she'd almost given way, feeling herself unable or unwilling to commit an act of extreme violence, reclaiming her humanity, but his final words, the relish in his tone, the perverse and bloodthirsty grin on his face, the violence in him, had all rallied together and it had refuelled her. She'd been hungry and desperate, without time to consider consequences or alternatives, and when he'd told her to shoot, she'd given him her obedience. She'd pulled the trigger.

One shot. Bang.

Alexander was wounded. The lead shot had taken lumps out of his shoulder, blown it to pieces. The neurosurgeon had been up to visit early in the morning and talked him through the complications of brachial plexus injury. She had done her best to repair nerve damage, but she had warned him that recovery would be limited. Shoulders were more complicated than Alexander had realised. He would never regain a full range of abductor movement, elbow flexion would be compromised, and even his hand movements may be limited. That conversation had been a less than ideal start to his day, but he didn't dwell too long over his recovery prospects. That would have to wait. Alexander had more pressing concerns.

Although Alexander emerged from his post-surgery slumber with a sore and immobile shoulder, in some ways he was ahead of Sarah. He refused the offer of painkillers, preferring to stay fully alert. By the middle of the morning, he was sitting up in his hospital bed with clarity of mind, preparing for the day ahead. He knew damn well that the lunatic who his wife had become, had shot him. And now he'd gained a pretty good idea about the damage she'd done, but after that, he knew nothing. He'd been assigned a private room in the neurosurgery ward, and he was being treated like royalty. Word had already reached the ward staff that Alexander was a personal friend of the NHS Trust Chair. Alexander didn't just accept privilege, he felt himself entitled. He'd experienced privilege throughout his life. It was normality for him, but this morning he felt uneasy. He needed information and he had identified a few loose ends which would need to be tidied up. He needed to see George, and with kind assistance from Nurse Collins, he made the call.

George wasn't happy. He'd been spooked the previous day, when he'd caught sight of police uniforms in the hospital corridor. That was bad enough, but then he'd seen the guy dressed in camouflage, a familiar albeit unidentified face, in the same hospital corridor at the same moment, grinning like a Cheshire Cat, greeting him by name, and taking photographs. He'd racked his brains, searching through the memory banks, until finally he placed him. In Stokesley, close to The Lion. George had returned home in a hurry. He'd spent half the night listening to local radio, hoping in vain to hear news of his former employer. He was anxious. There was someone out there who knew too much, but he heard no reports of a shooting. It had been a long night, but finally Alexander phoned him, requesting his presence at the hospital.

George's thoughts came in a rapid jumble as he drove to visit Alexander. He just wanted to get clear of the whole mess. He'd returned from his house-burning excursion feeling relieved that his work in Stokesley was all done, and happy to leave Phil taking care of things at Hurtmoor. And perhaps his wish for withdrawal had persuaded him to take his eye off the ball. Phil wasn't a strategist, but loyalty and obedience more than compensated for deficiencies with intelligence and integrity. He could follow orders, but thoughtful action had never been on his job description. Mostly George kept him closely supervised while he did his dirty work, but for once he had left him alone, running back and forth between the house and the middle barn. And it had gone badly wrong. Surely, he'd earned a break after the risks he'd taken. He'd put his feet up, allowed himself to relax, but then his phone had rung, and George had listened in disbelief as Phil described his morning's work.

He'd felt it coming. Alexander had no good options and George had wanted to distance himself before things went pear shaped. Then suddenly he was creeping along the back lane, hoping to God that no one spotted his Jaguar as he stopped to pick Phil up, and drove on, following the ambulances. Now it was a mess. George was nervous.

He drove to the hospital in two minds, angry that he still seemed to be up to his neck in Alexander's domestic dispute, and relieved that his recent criminality appeared to be undetected. By the police, at least. He also wanted to find out how badly Alexander had been injured and to discover the extent of Sarah's injury, but at the same time he felt reluctant to show association. Already, even before he'd heard a word from Alexander, George was fantasising about a new life. In a different country.

It was all going through George's head as he entered the hospital building. He stopped in the entrance lobby to clear his head, and he sent a text to let Alexander know that he was approaching. He was greeted with expectation and a sense of urgency. "Close the door, George. Now, come and sit down."

George complied. "Jesus. What the hell happened?"

"Sarah shot me. I didn't see too much after that. Phil was there. So you tell me, George, what the hell happened?"

George hesitated. Over many years, they had been close, partners in crime, but that meant nothing now. George had blood on his hands, petrol cans, buckets and spades in the boot of his car. Phil, dozy bastard, was equally vulnerable. But Alexander was squeaky clean, and George didn't trust him. He never had.

He spoke quietly. "Phil whacked her with a spade. Then he phoned 999, and then he phoned me."

Phil had panicked. It really was that simple. He'd almost slipped quietly away, but then heard the gun being fired. He'd turned and started to retrace his steps back towards the middle barn. The spade leant against the barn wall. He'd walked past it each time he'd entered the barn, and he'd picked it up without a thought as he'd re-entered, with the gunshot resounding. His employer was down on the ground, calling out in pain. Sarah, the prisoner, stood motionless with the gun still in her hands. Phil hadn't wanted to be there. These were not his problems, and he'd panicked. He'd made no conscious decision but he'd acted nevertheless, taking hold of the shaft of the spade and slamming the back of the blade against the side of Sarah's head. She'd fallen.

Phil had surveyed the scene, reviewing it all… the two injured bodies and his own participation. Not just that morning but over the past days, he'd been an active player, and he'd committed a series of serious crimes. At that point he had decided he could walk away. Too damn right he could. He'd gone back out into the yard and leant the spade back against the barn wall. Then he'd phoned George, who would know what to do, who would be calm, who could think in tight situations.

It all came as valuable information to Alexander, but still he wanted more. "Where is she now?"

"She's here." George hesitated again, mindful of Alexander's wide eyes. "In the hospital, as far as I know. I followed the ambulances."

"How is she?"

George held his palms to the sky. "I've no idea." George lowered his voice to a whisper, and he got to the point. "What's the story?"

"There is no story. Sarah shot me." Alexander gave graphic description of the mess that Sarah had made of his shoulder. "There's nothing more."

George was unimpressed. "What about Sarah? How are you going to explain her injuries?"

"I can't explain it. I'd been shot."

George almost chuckled as he watched Alexander's indifference. "You don't think the police might ask questions? What's Sarah saying?"

Alexander was dismissive. "You leave all that to me, George. I'll talk to the police. I know the Chief Constable."

George was unconvinced. It was a tense discussion. Neither man knew exactly what Sarah would say, but George was in no mood for sacrifice, and he made himself clear. "Well, that's good for you, but I've never met him. I'm not going to prison, not for anybody. You need to make this all go away."

"Calm yourself, George. Retain your dignity, man. You follow my instructions and we'll all be fine."

"You can shove your dignity straight up your arse, Alexander. Someone's been following me, taking photographs. I haven't got a clue who he is but he knows my name. He took my photograph, and he's watching me. If I go down, you're coming with me. Make no mistake. Talk to your people, and get it sorted."

Alexander focused. "Who's watching you?"

George told him about the man dressed in camouflage clothing, making appearances in Stokesley and in Guildford. Alexander wasn't yet threatened, but this was unwelcome information. He had believed that their manoeuvres had been unobserved. He'd got his story straight, and he was getting all of his ducks in a row, but the thought of a rogue figure, unidentified and beyond his control, bothered him. He felt it in his skin. Even as they sat exchanging urgent whispers, the site of his injury seemed to inflame. He was starting to get itchy. He issued his orders with precision and economy, bringing the discussion to a close.

George accepted his instruction quietly. But he was unhappy, ruffled by the power that his former employer still seemed to hold, even from a hospital bed with a shoulder full of lead shot, and he resolved to cut himself free now. He would carry out these last instructions and all of his debts would be more than repaid. He would owe nothing more.

While George made his way furtively through the hospital corridors, Sarah remained quiet and motionless, receiving hydration through a drip, and heavily sedated. She had received one blow. One strike from the blade of a spade had hit Sarah on the right side of her head and face. The impact had knocked her out cold but the lower jaw received the most serious injury. If Phil had delivered the blow with more heart, she would have sustained brain damage. How lucky was Sarah? She was taken for x-ray and the damage to her jaw was revealed. It was a mess.

The surgery had been prolonged and complicated. A feat of engineering, requiring access through the inside of her mouth, then reassembly with metal plates and screws, and more metal around her teeth to ensure realignment. Sarah had bitten her tongue, six or seven times by the feel of it. She fluctuated between numbness and pain, dizziness and sleep, but slowly she made her way back to awareness.

She'd received traumatic injury and still she wasn't too sure how badly she'd been hurt. Very slowly, with enormous effort, Sarah turned her head a few degrees to the right, and she groaned as the pain filled half of her face and all of her mouth. It was a wilful action, a voluntary movement, executed independently, and it gave her a view of the sky. Lazy clouds drifted slow and high, and she wondered exactly where she was.

For all of her confusion, she knew where she wasn't. Her confinement in the middle barn was ended. She was on the other side now. After weeks of waiting for the moment of confrontation, wondering how it would be, she'd arrived and moved on. Not quite in one piece. She seemed to be explaining to herself, in her thoughts and in her dreams, and in all the confusion in between. Just trying, even with the headaches and the drugs, and a face full of pain, to understand what had been happening in her life. Sarah was awake again and starting to expect that she might have to explain to one or two other people.

I'm Sarah Buxton, and I'm alive
I surprised you, Alexander,
With my courage
I surprised myself

As the day progressed, Sarah lay quietly with her thoughts. She felt pain. Unable to eat or speak, the inside of her mouth felt like broken glass and barbed wire. Sometimes she drifted into sleep, sometimes she was awake, often she felt drowsy. In her sleep, demons dragged her back to her prison in the barn, until she woke again with her heart pounding and her head full of terror. They were the worst moments, but in wakefulness her experience was quite different. Even with the unmistakable sense of confinement, Sarah felt cared for. She was hurt but she was being treated well. That was her perception. After two weeks of dehumanising imprisonment, in fear for her life, she'd been rescued, and now, through her tiredness and the sedation, she felt soft hands, the overwhelming sensation of being cared for, held in the arms of another. She was safe.

Somehow, although I know that I'm in trouble, I feel very safe
Like a child might feel safe in a war zone or in a famine,
In its mother's arms
Safely cocooned and surrounded by danger
I haven't felt this safe for a while

Sarah needed to get herself woken up. Alexander was already half way to having her hanged.

FORTY-FIVE
SHIPS AT NIGHT

ELEANOR WAITED for a couple of days after she and Sue had carried out their rescue mission in Middlesbrough, leaving Greg to himself and crossing her fingers. Then she sent a text, bright and cheerful, just to let him know she was thinking about him. The message hadn't demanded an answer and none came. Fair enough. She tried again during the next several days, composing her messages with carefully chosen words, a gentle instruction to respond. But no response came.

Eventually, Sue suggested a less sensitive approach and she sent her own message, threatening another dose of tough love.

I assume that you're feeling so sorry for yourself that you won't accept my calls. If you don't reply to this text, we'll be knocking on your door again in the morning.

Less than twenty-four hours later, Sue and Eleanor drove from Leeds to Middlesbrough and they were sitting on a bench in Greg's front garden. They had rung the bell, hammered on the door, and phoned repeatedly. Greg wasn't home.

"There's something wrong, Sue. I can feel it."

To an extent, Sue shared her partner's concern, but she

wasn't fully convinced. "He's probably out riding his bike, Eleanor. Either way, he's not here, and we should go home."

"No, we're here now. Let's wait for a while." She looked around at the debris that had collected in Greg's front garden. "We can tidy around. I'll take a walk, and find some coffee. You wait here in case he comes back." Eleanor turned and set off before Sue had chance to protest.

They picked up the litter and drank their coffee, waiting for more than an hour before Eleanor was prepared to give up the search. The concern that had prompted their journey was greater than ever but they were defeated. Eleanor pushed a hand-written note through the letter box before returning to Leeds.

Andy arrived about twenty minutes later, parking on the street and then marching to the door to ring the bell, as he'd done on the previous day. Still no answer.

He'd expected no different but still he was disappointed. *"I'll be back."* He turned from the door to begin his exit. Another wasted journey. But he slowed down as he walked towards the gate. Yesterday when he'd walked this path, there had been litter in the garden. Not so today. *"Someone's been busy."* He walked over to a bench and sat, assuming that Greg had spent some time in the garden, and that only bad timing was obstructing his search. So he waited, expectantly to begin with, but after an hour or so, he found his way back to hopelessness. He sighed with heavy disappointment. No sign of Greg. He made his way back towards the gate, almost walking straight past the wheelie bin, but then he stopped. *"That's moved since yesterday."* He lifted the lid and looked inside, where two coffee cartons sat on top of the pile of rubbish. *"Jesus Christ. Make your own bloody coffee, man. Much cheaper."*

But he was puzzled. Do people go out to buy coffee then return home for consumption? Two cups? It didn't seem to add up. He picked up one of the cartons, and tipped a few drops of cold coffee into the palm of his hand. He dipped his head to take a sniff. *"I'm smelling the coffee here, Whitehead."* He held onto the coffee carton and walked back to the garden bench. Finally, he felt that he was getting close. It was the only sign of life he'd found and he wasn't going to miss an opportunity. He took pen and paper from his bag and wrote a note – I'll be back tomorrow at midday. See you then. He carefully rolled the paper into a thin strip which he inserted into the opening in a coffee carton lid, pointing up to the sky like a straw, and left the carton sitting in the middle of the bench.

Sue and Eleanor arrived back at Greg's late the following morning, after more unanswered phone calls and with ever increasing concern for their missing friend. They were unsurprised when no one answered the door and made their way to the garden bench. Eleanor had brought sandwiches. They were prepared to wait.

They both looked at the coffee cup placed conspicuously on the garden bench, and then at each other. Sue spoke for them both. "He's here." Eleanor nodded. "A bit weird though, don't you think? After we'd cleared up all the rubbish. It looks like one of our cups. Why would he do that?"

Sue was impatient. "Well, have a look."

Eleanor pulled out and then unrolled and read the note. "What time is it?"

It was almost an hour later when a car pulled up outside Greg's house and a figure appeared at the garden gate. Sue anticipated Greg's arrival and it took a second or two before she adjusted and was able to recognise Andy Cooper. She spoke quietly, mostly to herself. "Well, look what the cat's dragged in."

They were never friends at school but today they were

particularly disappointed to see each other, both of them momentarily believing that their search for Greg had ended in success, and then a mutually uncomfortable recognition.

Sue folded her arms and stood up from the bench, all defence.

Andy felt his heart sink. He knew that Sue was seeing the teenager that she, and pretty much everyone else on the planet, had despised. Including himself. He had to deal with this from time to time but it didn't get any easier. "Sue Berry."

"Andy Cooper. What are you doing here?"

"Minding my own business, Sue. What about you?" He looked up to see her disapproving grimace, and his spirit flattened. He understood now where the coffee cartons had come from and he worked out that, despite the garden party, Greg wasn't home. He turned and began to walk away. "I'll go. If Greg shows up, please give him my regards."

Eleanor watched the exchange between the former classmates. She'd heard the stories about Andy, but she had her own view, based on the incident in The Lion when Andy had been overwhelmed by emotion. She certainly wasn't going to allow him to leave. "Andy, please wait for a moment."

Andy swung back around to deliver his reply. "I didn't come here to be judged by Sue Berry. I don't need it, believe me. Enjoy your coffee." He walked back out to his car.

Sue stood her ground, happy to see the back of him.

Eleanor ran out on to the street after him. She appealed to him. "Please, just five minutes of your time." She hesitated, unable to see his face, but he paused and after a couple of seconds he turned to face her. She managed a moment of eye contact and she pressed herself forward. She smiled and walked right up to him, her hand extended in greeting. "I'm Eleanor and I'm glad to meet you." She held her smile, and then his hand.

Andy made no comment but he accepted the handshake and waited to hear what Eleanor had to say.

"We all seem to be looking for Greg. Maybe we'll find more success if we collaborate. At the very least we should compare notes. Come back and sit down." Eleanor stole a conspiratorial glance over her shoulder, and continued in a whisper. "I'll ask Sue to buy coffee. She'll be fine. Just five minutes, please."

Andy wasn't hugely attracted to the idea of coffee with an unfriendly Sue Berry, but Eleanor's invitation to compare notes made sense. "Okay."

"Thank you." Eleanor led him back into the garden. "Andy has very kindly accepted my invitation to stay for coffee, Sue." She turned to Andy. "How do you like your coffee?"

"Americano, a double shot, black."

Eleanor completed the order. "I'll have a flat white. As quick as you can, Sue."

Sue felt herself dismissed like a schoolgirl. She accepted the command but not without a word for the workers. "Un-fucking-believable!"

Andy enjoyed Sue's withdrawal but already he was reticent. He allowed Eleanor to guide him into a garden seat, but he stayed quiet.

Eleanor's position was quite different. She felt relaxed and ready to talk. "I assume you wrote the note?"

"That's right, yes. And you and Sue were the coffee drinkers?"

"Yes, we live in Leeds. It's quite a long drive so we hung around hoping that Greg would turn up. But he didn't. When did you last see him?"

Andy still felt unsure. He was evasive. He knew his reason for seeking Greg Whitehead but he knew nothing of Sue Berry's motivation. He diverted the conversation, making small talk until Sue returned with the coffee. She appeared to have got past her initial offence but for a moment, a tense band of hesitation held them in check.

Andy wasn't prepared to sit and squirm forever. He was

yet to discover the nature of their business but he wanted it done. He went back to where he assumed it had started. "I recognised you at Janey's funeral, Sue. I remember you both. I'm good with faces."

Sue had started to settle but she still had an edge. "I recognised you. I was surprised to see you, there. Janey would have felt the same way."

Andy almost bit back but he caught himself. He almost stood and walked but he sat tight. "Janey asked me to go, as it happens, Sue." He left it there. His reticence intensified, and he looked at Sue, who was silenced and disarmed. He turned to Eleanor. "When did you last see Greg?"

Eleanor smiled. So this was the infamous Andy Cooper, throwing back her question, the one he'd refused to answer. "It's almost a week ago. I've been phoning and sending text messages, but he hasn't answered, so we drove over."

Andy didn't know what to do. No mention of Sarah or Cheryl, and no reference to events in Surrey. "Well, that's pretty weird. I don't have his number. I've driven across for the last three days. I need to talk to Greg, but he's not here so I'll get back to Stokesley. Can you give me a number and if I find him, I'll give you a shout."

Andy Cooper and Sue Berry exchanged numbers. Sue was amused. "I never saw this moment coming."

Andy, less so. He said a brief farewell and departed. He wanted to get Polly's perspective. It should have been the simplest task but he'd found yet another complication. Each time he looked for Greg Whitehead, he seemed to find someone else, and where the hell was Greg? Not at home and not answering his phone.

FORTY-SIX

TEAM GRIFFIN

TWENTY-FOUR HOURS HAD PASSED since Griffin had been sent to investigate the Hurtmoor incident. That's what his Chief Superintendent had called it, and indeed what he continued to call it. So, the Hurtmoor incident it was. Griffin was an experienced policeman. He knew the ropes. He routinely reported to his Chief Inspector. All good from DI Griffin's point of view – accountability, support and scrutiny. That arrangement seemed to have worked well for everyone for the past twenty years. Until yesterday afternoon when Alexander MacDonald was shot. In the Hurtmoor incident. Now the Super wanted direct reports.

It was an odd set of circumstances, quite unlike any of Griffin's previous cases. A serious crime had been committed, the Chief Superintendent was paying full attention, and so far, he'd been given no human resources. It had appeared uncomplicated. The force was overstretched and despite the Super's keen interest, no additional personnel had been allocated. DI Griffin was on his own, it seemed. Usually, he would be leading a team of officers in a case where a shooting had occurred, but Chief Inspector Richardson had left him pretty well on his own with this case. He had support from Forensics and PC Ellis as chaperone, but that was the full team. DI Griffin wasn't entirely comfortable, but at least PC Ellis seemed full of enthusiasm.

Griffin had left Hurtmoor with very little information. Walter Rathbone had given him nothing. The Forensics Team had taken some bits and pieces, including the shotgun, and they'd left the area of the barn where the bodies were found, cordoned off. Rathbone had locked the barn behind them, and had seemed comfortable for the police to hold the key. Griffin had taken a long look at the crime scene, which seemed to suggest that Sarah MacDonald had shot her husband, and then received a debilitating injury.

He'd had some time to consider the knowns and the unknowns. Alexander MacDonald received a gunshot wound in his left shoulder. Sarah MacDonald received a closed blunt force injury to the right side of her head and face. That was the Hurtmoor incident. Both of them had needed surgical procedures, which prohibited the opportunity to question either of them. Griffin had waited.

PC Ellis wasn't officially part of the investigating team. Protocols instructed half of her working life, and she hated them, preferring the old fashioned methods like thinking for oneself. Nevertheless, protocol dictated that a chaperone must accompany the investigating officer for interviews with vulnerable people in hospital beds. Griffin gave her a few additional duties, his best attempt to keep her mindfully occupied and her ego intact. And very quickly, she demonstrated her usefulness, making calls to the hospital to facilitate access to the MacDonalds. As it turned out, it would be several days before Sarah would be well enough to be questioned, but Alexander was almost ready to speak with them. He'd invited them to visit in the afternoon. That was good news. Finally, Griffin would get an account of events, something to report to the Chief Superintendent.

It was clear to Griffin that not only was PC Ellis efficient and helpful, she was also as keen as mustard. DI Griffin was more than happy to keep her on board. The two of them entered Alexander's room at two o'clock.

"Mr MacDonald, I'm Detective Inspector Griffin. This is Police Constable Ellis. How are you?"

Alexander gestured an invitation for his visitors to be seated. "Good afternoon, Inspector. I've been better."

Griffin and Ellis took their seats. "Yes, I'm sure." Griffin was pleased to receive a cordial reception, and aware of the need to proceed with thorough professionalism. "Because you are injured and in hospital, you're considered to be a vulnerable person. PC Ellis is here for your protection." He gave a friendly smile. "She'll make sure that I don't take any liberties while I question you about the incident at Hurtmoor, yesterday. And I've asked her to take notes as a record of this interview. Does that sound okay?"

"Yes, fine."

"We want to know exactly what happened yesterday. I'm hoping that you can tell me."

Alexander had got himself prepared and he responded without hesitation. "I'm afraid that Sarah, Mrs MacDonald, shot me. There's not that much more that I can tell you, Inspector." He was fully aware of the opportunity to get his version of events on record, pleased to establish his innocence, and content in the knowledge that he and George were already ahead of the game.

Griffin was unsurprised by this statement, but it brought a little more colour to his cheeks, as he now felt the need to caution Alexander, who was both victim and witness. It all felt rather delicate, balancing the personal and professional politics, but he went ahead with the caution, albeit apologetically.

Alexander appeared to accept the formality. "How is Sarah?"

Griffin was surprised to hear the concern in Alexander's voice, and relieved that he didn't have the knowledge to provide a satisfactory answer. "She received an injury. At present, I don't have reliable information. I'm sorry. I should know more by the end of the day. In the meantime, perhaps you could tell me a bit more about what happened yesterday in the barn."

"I'll do my best. It's quite sensitive. I hope I can rely on your discretion. Sarah has been unstable for several weeks. I think it may be a bereavement reaction. One of her old school friends died, and it has clearly affected her. She's been irrational, subject to unpredictable mood swings."

Griffin watched him, every twitch and blink, while he composed himself. There was no doubt in his mind that this man was genuinely upset, and sympathetic to the woman who had shot him. "I know this must be difficult, but please continue."

"This really is very sensitive. Normally, Sarah would never have behaved so oddly. She seemed to lose her moral compass. And her judgement. I wish I'd asked for professional help, but we're a very private family, and I thought I could support her through it. I should have known better. I didn't realise how seriously disturbed she'd become. I was thinking about it this morning. I think she must have had some kind of psychotic episode. But what do I know? I'm a humble farmer, and hindsight's a wonderful thing." Alexander bowed his head and sighed, performing his act of sympathy with growing confidence as he watched Griffin swallowing every word.

"I'm sorry to press you, Mr MacDonald, but please continue." Griffin listened with more than interest as Alexander MacDonald described his wife's descent into madness, how she'd been affected by the loss of a friend, and how her behaviour had become wayward, to the point where she'd thrown herself at another man. She had apparently become a woman driven by fantasy and headed for a fall. Alexander painted a picture of himself as protector, trying to introduce moderation, asking Sarah to slow down, but she'd reacted with hysteria, unable to listen to reason, issuing

247

threats and making wild accusations, and eventually shooting him in the middle barn. He concluded his account with a flourish of tragedy and regret. "I tried to protect her. She was a danger to herself. I should have asked for help. I'm afraid I underestimated her struggle."

It was a compelling story. Griffin felt more settled, and again he asked for more. "I wonder if you know how Sarah sustained her injury?"

"I've no idea. I really can't imagine. Until I spoke to you this morning, I knew nothing about that, but I'm desperately keen to know. Whoever it was may well have saved my life. I guess that's how you people earn your wages, practising the art of crime detection. Please do your best, Inspector, and keep me informed."

DI Griffin left the hospital with PC Ellis, feeling much better. It was a sad story, but he had a pretty good grasp now of what had happened. The Chief Superintendent would be delighted. Griffin was making progress, although there were still a couple of unanswered questions, but DI Griffin had a pretty good idea about where the answers might be found. As they made their way back to the car, he wondered if he'd have this one wrapped up before the end of the day.

PC Ellis jumped into the driver's seat. "Where to now, Guv?"

"My name isn't Guv. You've been watching too much television, Constable Ellis."

"Apologies, Inspector."

"That's better. Well, Alexander MacDonald could not have delivered the blow to his wife, and we can assume that Sarah didn't strike herself down. Who does that leave?"

"Walter Rathbone."

"So, to answer your question, we'll go to Hurtmoor."

Ellis was excited. For the first ten months of her police career, she had felt like a junior clerk. It had been all paperwork and no action. Now, she was assisting a senior officer to investigate a serious crime. She was content to accept restricted participation, but she was getting involved.

"Will we arrest him?" She wasn't really asking the question, she was making a suggestion. She wanted to announce herself as an active, crime-busting copper, to take Rathbone back to the station in handcuffs.

"We'll see." Griffin was also excited, but a bit more cautious. "He's in the frame, Constable, and there was no one else on the scene, but we'll need evidence. We'll need to take him down to the station, but let's see what he has to say."

PC Ellis was full of nervous expectation as she drove out to Hurtmoor. She hadn't yet viewed the crime scene, nor had she met Walter Rathbone. They parked at the back of the house but the place was deserted, and DI Griffin phoned Walter, requesting his presence. The two police officers walked across to the barn while they waited. Ellis was keen to look inside. While Griffin reached into his pocket for the key, Ellis walked ahead and opened the barn door.

"Wait a minute. That door should have been locked." Griffin had felt more relaxed as the day had unfolded but he tensed up now. "I saw Rathbone lock it, and I tried the door myself to make sure. It was definitely locked."

That was enough to send a shiver through PC Ellis's spine. "Oh my God. The perpetrator must have returned to the scene of the crime. We covered this at the academy." She looked inside the cordoned area, protected by a circle of yellow tape, and at the crude outlines drawn on the barn floor – Alexander MacDonald and his wife, Sarah. For a moment, Ellis was lost, unable to think. She read from the tape. "Crime scene. Do not enter."

DI Griffin was also taken aback by this development. "Yes, indeed, except that someone already has. So, we'll need to get Forensics in again. Step back please, Constable."

They both stepped back with light feet, until they stood together just inside the barn. Griffin's memory had always been patchy. He was dreadful with names but a reliably detailed visual memory had assisted his progress through the ranks. Not quite photographic, but not far from it. He took a few seconds now to review the scene, allowing the events of the previous day to replay in his mind's eye. The paramedics had divided into two units to treat both casualties. They had worked impressively, attending to their patients with calm focus. Then he remembered the bucket. One of the ambulance crew had interrupted her work to reach across and move a yellow bucket to a more distant position. It had caught his attention, puzzled him that she should turn away from her patient, in an emergency, to move a harmless plastic bucket. As Griffin reviewed the scene now, the bucket was gone. As far as he could remember, that was the only discrepancy from the previous day. It was just a yellow bucket. It hadn't appeared significant the previous day, but now that it was gone, he wondered.

"There was a yellow bucket in here yesterday. The Forensics Team must have taken it." Griffin felt a chill. He heard a vehicle out in the yard. "That'll be Rathbone," he said. "He's never too far from the action."

FORTY-SEVEN
BLUE SKY THINKING

WHEN GREG EMERGED FOR BREAKFAST, having slept late and missed the morning ride he'd planned to take, Stella was already gone. It had been a great night and he was disappointed by her departure. He spent the morning nursing a hangover, taking a rest day. He pottered around the place, and chatted with some of the other guests. It was almost time for lunch when Antonio delivered the note.

"Stella asked me to give you this," he said, passing a folded piece of paper to Greg.

Greg opened the note:

Hey Greg
  Thanks for dinner, and for being the friend I needed.
  Message me when you find the truth about Sarah.
  Un beso, Stella

Underneath, she had written down her mobile phone number, an email address and a postal address in Cadiz. It was just a few words, crazy, but it meant the world. He spent a few more days at El Mallinar, joined a couple of guys from

Barcelona on some testing circuits, and spent his evenings in the garden at the back of the hostel, fully immersed in the social scene. There were some fine people who embraced him gladly into the heart of their group, but the memories that he took back to England were all about Stella.

Greg's exit from Spain was less stressful than his arrival. A few days cycling had improved his mood. He was relaxed and a little reluctant to bring an end to his trip. He looked down from the aeroplane window to say a last farewell to Barcelona and then, for the first time in a week, his thoughts turned to home. Distance had given him a different perspective, and he was able to look back without the same sense of involvement, to be an objective observer of his own recent past.

He thought back to Janey's funeral, and immediately he noticed how the passing of time had re-ordered the significance of recent events. Andy Cooper had filled his head after the brief drama in The Lion. Andy's appearance had disturbed Greg for a period of several days, and yet during the last two or three weeks, Andy had dropped off his radar. Greg found his observation perfectly acceptable. He'd been curious for a while but not anymore. Andy Cooper had made an appearance and then crawled back into his hole. All fine with Greg.

He thought about Sue Berry. At Janey's wake, Greg had been pleased to say hello again after so many years, but he hadn't expected her to become a close friend, or to become a part of his life. Nor Eleanor for that matter. And then of course, Sarah Buxton had come along. She had seemed to knock the whole world off balance, throwing emotional bombs, making false promises, and disappearing without a proper goodbye. And then Stella, for Christ's sake. Where did she come from, all young and Spanish? Greg couldn't think about her without smiling. They had flirted playfully, but they had both recognised the nature of their encounter. It was never going to be sexual, but somehow they had made an intimate connection. They had revealed themselves, shared their secrets and their vulnerability in the mountain air, built a bridge across the age gap, and rode together.

He wondered what life was waiting for him now, and what kind of a man he was now. He'd felt something stirring within him right after Janey's funeral, something changing, and he'd felt apprehension, watching as the walls he'd built around himself, had begun to disintegrate. He was going back to the same house in the same town but it would be a different life, lived in a different way. The coming of the change had provoked anxiety, but not anymore, Greg was ready to accept the dangers and the rewards from human interaction. Bring it on.

He landed at Leeds/Bradford airport at midday. He considered driving to Leeds to pay Sue and Eleanor a surprise visit before returning home, but his instinct pushed him towards home and he set out for Middlesbrough.

He pulled the car over to park on the street outside his house and immediately caught sight of movement in his garden. He advanced from his car with stealth and urgency up to the garden gate to discover the intruders. The reception committee appeared busy in his front garden, but he was undetected, and able to eavesdrop.

"Andy wasn't so bad." The frustration and concern for Greg was unresolved and yet Eleanor's focus had shifted. "How strange, that we should bump into him in Greg's garden."

They'd eaten their picnic and were waiting out time, having decided to stay until three o'clock before heading back home to Leeds.

"He was bad at school, El."

"He wasn't very talkative though, and he didn't really tell us anything. Still not to worry, he has your number, no doubt he'll be in touch."

They had spent enough time now to feel quite at home in Greg's garden. Sue was doing a bit of weeding while Eleanor re-ordered a group of potted plants. Neither of them noticed Greg standing at the garden gate.

"Typical, gone for a week and bloody squatters have moved in."

They took twenty minutes to catch up. Eleanor gave Greg details of the numerous missed text messages, unanswered calls, trips to Middlesbrough, and the accompanying anxiety. Greg described his trip to Barcelona and the loss of his phone. He'd arrived home in good spirit. He was grateful for their concern, and cheerfully apologetic as he told his Spanish tale.

Andy Cooper's entrance into their conversation was an afterthought as Sue realised that she should really let Andy know that Greg had been found. She decided to run her realisation past Greg. "Andy Cooper was here earlier. Apparently he's called round for each of the last three days."

"To my house?"

Sue saw the opportunity to avenge her wife's coffee errand. "Yes, Eleanor invited him in for coffee, didn't you, El. Her and Andy are bessy mates."

"Hey, it was you who exchanged numbers."

Greg's smile had slipped, and he spoke with urgency. "No seriously, guys, what did he say?"

Sue outlined the series of crossed paths in his garden, their coincidental searches, and then she asked him directly. "So what do I do? It's up to you, Greg. I won't phone him if you don't want me to."

"It sounds as if it won't make a huge difference, if he's knocking on my door every day." Greg paused as he heard himself recognise the inevitability of another encounter with Andy. "No, leave it just now, Sue. If he turns up here again, I'll hear what he has to say, but I'm not setting it up for him. I need to get myself a new phone."

Eleanor had been friendly with Andy. She had the social skills, and she'd been genuinely interested to meet him, but she was still reviewing their conversation, still trying to figure him out. "I'm sure he means no harm, but he was definitely holding out on us. I could see the cogs turning but he said almost nothing."

Greg wanted more. "What do you mean, Eleanor?"

"I'm not sure. We were both looking for you and we were supposed to share information. He said he wanted to talk to you, that was all."

"Well, Andy seems to promise more than he delivers. I'm sure all will be revealed in the course of time."

Greg spent an hour in the garden before he unloaded his bags from the car and opened his front door. He'd reflected on his flight home, wondering how it would feel to return to an empty house, and he was pleased to have been welcomed into his own garden party. But he felt no disappointment when Sue and Eleanor prepared to depart. During his flight, Greg had thought about Andy Cooper's disappearance, and now he was back in view and actively seeking contact. He needed some time to think again. He opened his wallet and re-read Stella's note. He'd dismissed her dubiety in Gerona, but he was back in Middlesbrough now, and he wondered – what was the truth about Sarah?

FORTY-EIGHT

WHAT ABOUT THE CHILDREN?

ROBIN WAS heir to the estate. He was well educated and well heeled. He resembled his father physically, with the same colouring and a strong muscular frame, but his personality was quite different. Robin was less sure of himself, and more accommodating than Alexander. While Walter looked after the farm production, Robin dealt with the supermarket chains and pratted about with diversification projects that never reached fruition. He obeyed his father. That was the main thing. There was an element of fear involved – Robin had learned long ago not to cross or question Alexander – but he knew how his bread was buttered and he was happy enough to accept the advantages that come with a multi-million-pound estate. Que sera.

He was waiting at the hospital while the surgeons did their work, and back at his father's bedside again soon after the police had departed, getting the story. The same tale that Alexander had told to Griffin and Ellis an hour earlier. Robin gasped repeatedly. For forty-five years, his family had been a model of respectability. Of course, Robin had seen some of the flaws and cracks. He knew that his parents' relationship was imperfect. He'd seen some pretty vile moments, but such was family life. His mother was the rock. And now this.

Not an easy listen. He'd had some testing moments growing up in his cold family, many challenges, but nothing that prepared him for a shoot-out between his parents in the middle barn. Alexander was emphatic. Sarah would never return to Hurtmoor. She was no longer a part of the family. There was sadness somewhere in Robin, but he accepted his father's story, and he understood the implications. He would stand by his father. That was all he could do. He phoned his sister, Scarlet, relaying their father's instruction that she visit.

Scarlet sat for almost an hour on her sofa, with her coat buttoned, and her car keys in her lap. Robin had barked his father's instruction. She had been summoned. He'd phoned her the previous evening to tell her about their parents, both in hospital with serious injuries, and she'd thought about nothing else, but still she was hesitant.

She was horrified by the plight of her parents. There had never been a stain on the family name, and never a scandal. They weren't an emotionally demonstrative family, but there had been no serious divisions. She knew her father's authoritarian nature well enough. He was the head of the family, and she'd always accepted that without question. The balance of power in her own marriage was quite different to her parents' generation. They had married when 'the man wearing the trousers' tradition had still been the dominant narrative. It hadn't been a battle ground but her father had always been in charge.

She had never seen her father strike her mother. That would have been a line crossed. But no, there had been no mysterious cuts or bruises. There had been incidents, with angry scenes, harsh words, and humiliations. Scarlet tried not to dwell on such moments, but she'd never witnessed an act of physical violence.

She loved her father and she only ever wanted to win his respect, earn his love. She was always striving for his approval, and never questioned his judgement or his authority. She had wanted to be the equal of her brother in her father's eyes and yet she always fell short. Alexander had time for Robin. He took him out on the farm, taught him to shoot and ride with the hunt, gave him privileged access through doors that were closed to Scarlet. She spent her childhood trying to prove herself worthy of a father who never gave the recognition that she so desperately needed. What a confused set of emotions it had given her. He was her hero and at the same time her destroyer, and somehow, she'd tied herself into a spiral of dissatisfaction, forever trying to please a man who refused to be pleased. The more he withheld, the more she wanted. She had always obeyed him gladly, in the hope that he'd smile upon her, but she was doomed by biology and she was always denied.

Her mother had never denied her.

Scarlet had married Jerry, a quiet man who exhibited none of her father's traits. He worked in the city and demanded little of Scarlet. He was an unassuming man, reliable and inoffensive, and sadly, she never loved him. She was forty-three years old, with two teenage boys, Richard and Alex, who worshipped their grandfather. Alexander had never found time to spend with Scarlet when she'd been a child but he more than compensated with her boys, who were included in every aspect of the farm's annual cycle of activity. Already it seemed they were Alexander's boys.

And these were the considerations and complications that Scarlet must now navigate a path through. Robin, it seemed, had already taken the easy option, and accepted his father's word without a moment of doubt. As far as Robin was concerned, his mother had thrown her life away. Her foolishness was a matter of regret, but he could never and would never forgive her.

So Scarlet was alone with a strong emotional connection to each of her parents, one who had shot the other, and now she must decide. Whose bedside would she sit by?

And what of her mother? Her father's wife. She knew of no crimes from Sarah, who had been as solid as a rock, always there with sympathy and smiles, the softer parent. Scarlet had thought about all of this when the news had come. Her mother had never let her down, and never disappointed her. She had always been there to offer comfort when Alexander had looked past her, the parent who had given encouragement and recognition. What of her?

Sarah had given herself as a mother without much thought. Her children had been the best part of her married life. She wasn't a tactile parent, or gushing with emotion, but she was dependable and attentive. And Scarlet had felt such need for her father that she took her mother's love for granted. She had never had to work for it, and perhaps she'd underestimated its value.

She decided to visit her mother first. It wasn't an act of defiance, nor was it a taking of sides. It was strategy. She decided to visit her mother before her father forbid her. It wasn't difficult. Sarah was sleeping, aided by sedation after her complex surgery. She'd been knocked apart and put back together again. Scarlet sat with her for a while, then she walked to the ward where her father waited.

It was six in the evening by the time that Scarlet arrived at her father's room. His last visitor in a busy day. Four pellets had found their way into Alexander's shoulder through four separate entry points. They were removed quickly after his admission. They had penetrated deeply, blasting the shit out of his left shoulder and upper arm, leaving chunks of flesh exposed or flapping, but the doctors had patched him up quite nicely. He pointed out to Scarlet that if her mother had controlled the gun more ably, he'd be dead, and he watched her wince as the information penetrated. Robin had already relayed the full story. There was no need for further discussion. Scarlet was relieved about that, and pleased that her father had taken strong painkillers. For a while he slept. She was glad to sit with him, peacefully, although she wondered how long the peace would last.

After an hour, she watched his eyes open, and he smiled.

As it turned out, her father was less instructive than she'd anticipated. He had plenty to say about his wayward wife but he didn't demand Scarlet's loyalty. Well, not exactly. He described Sarah's madness, her hysteria, her affairs and her murderous violence, but he stopped short of asking Scarlet to choose. He did talk about her boys though, their right to inheritance, and their security within the family. Despite her earlier sense of foreboding, she was pleasantly surprised. Her father didn't shield her from the facts, but he displayed more human sympathy than she had ever seen in him previously, and she left with more hope than she'd anticipated.

FORTY-NINE
BUCKET AND SPADE

ALEXANDER HAD REACTED IMPRESSIVELY for a middle-aged man with a shotgun injury. Even at the moment of his hospital admission, while his shoulder had felt like it was on fire, he had found presence of mind, and asked for Robin to be called. Now, three days later, he was back in control, directing traffic from his hospital bed. George had sent him a text the previous day: *All done.* It was just two words, but exactly what Alexander wanted to hear.

Of course, George had a key to the middle barn. He'd unlocked and the re-locked the door many times during Sarah's imprisonment. Alexander had sent him to Hurtmoor straight from the hospital on the day after the shooting. It was a high risk move, mostly for George, and George completed the task with only a couple of hours to spare, but it had had to be done, and it had delivered a big reward. George had collected a couple of key items – a bucket and a spade.

Alexander had given a fine performance in the police interview, with repeat showings for each of his two children. He had them all swallowing the same sad story, a tragedy, with himself as an innocent victim. He had a couple of different faces for his role. Sternly unforgiving for Robin, and

261

compassionate benevolence for Scarlet and the police, and they were all responding exactly as he'd hoped.

Robin had passed judgement in accordance with his father's wishes. He completely ignored his mother. She was gone from his life. Poor Robin, addicted to his father's poison, and now a motherless child. He was visiting every day, updating Alexander about the farm, including the visits from the police, which had become more interesting by the day. DI Griffin and PC Ellis had been back up a couple of times, and some members of the Forensic Team had also made a second visit.

Alexander listened to that information with satisfaction. It must have been pretty close, but George had been ahead of the game. All was going along very nicely. And then it got even better.

Robin brought unexpected news. "I hope you're ready for this, Dad. The police have arrested Walter. I only heard yesterday, but apparently he's spent the last two days in the cells."

Alexander was startled. "Walter?"

Robin gave his interpretation of the brief information that he'd got from DI Griffin. "Walter was the only other person at the scene and it appears that he clattered Mum. Why else would they hold him?"

Alexander needed clarity. "Exactly what did Griffin tell you?"

"That Walter wouldn't be at work because he was helping with the police enquiries. They must have arrested him."

Alexander smiled. George had been unhappy. This would cheer him up. And Phil. He looked across at Robin. "Rathbone of all people. I didn't know he had it in him."

And each day, Scarlet came. Directly from Sarah's bedside. It was perfect. He wasn't pushing Scarlet. Not yet. Each day, Scarlet gave updates about her mother, and Alexander listened without judgement. He wanted to know. He had a good grip of the situation, and Walter's misfortune was an unexpected bonus. Scarlet's contribution would help him to maintain position. He'd established a flow of information from all key sources.

For several weeks Alexander had felt the strain. There had been times when he had felt unsure of his direction, when his iron grip had seemed to weaken. He wouldn't let that happen again.

FIFTY

THROWN TO THE DOGS

The surgeon has been very kind, protecting me
Today he spoke, preparing me
To be thrown to the dogs

THE HOSPITAL STAFF had indeed given some protection. For five days, Mr Barnard had kept her safe. He'd rebuilt her jaw and supervised the post-operative care. There were no exceptional complications and already Sarah was starting to use her mouth, taking nutrition drinks through a straw, and uttering one or two words. Sarah's recovery period would extend for several weeks yet, but it would be rest and healing from here on. There would be some follow-up appointments but the essential surgeon's work was all done.

Through it all he had shown no judgement, his bedside manner warm and cheerful, the health agenda being the only focus. He'd treated her well, behaving with impressive professionalism. Until today, when he was apologetic. Mr Barnard explained to Sarah that she'd need to stay in hospital for a few more days. He wanted to see the swelling reduce further and to keep an eye on the alignment of her jaws as she started to gain more movement. He gave good information about the process of rehabilitation, the progression from liquid meals back to solid foods, and then he told Sarah that the police would come later to ask some questions.

Then he startled her, shifting almost imperceptibly from professional etiquette. "Yes, I understand that the police must do their work, ask their questions, but of course talking will be very difficult for a few days yet." Then he leaned forward, getting close enough to lower his voice. "But they're impatient to question you and they'll give you pen and paper to write your answers. Take your time, Sarah, I wouldn't say too much if I was you, not until you've seen a solicitor." He leaned back and found full voice again. "So I'm afraid you'll have to put up with the frustration and be silent for a while. We can't have you undoing my work."

Sarah nodded her thanks, and she felt a shiver, watching her protector walking away. She wondered what came next. She accepted Mr Barnard's suggestion, glad of the opportunity to think, to stay quiet, and watch the story unfold. Before the afternoon ended, police officers came, asking inevitable questions.

DI Griffin had waited patiently to interview Sarah MacDonald, keeping himself busy first with Alexander, and more recently with Walter Rathbone. Walter was a puzzle, in up to his neck, and denying all knowledge, but today Griffin had a bigger fish to fry. Finally, access to Sarah had been granted.

Sarah had a small room to herself within the orthodontic ward and she'd become aware of the permanent police presence just outside of her door. She was sitting up in her hospital bed, expectant and uncertain. She'd heard Mr Barnard's advice and she'd had a couple of hours to determine her strategy.

"Good afternoon, Mrs MacDonald. I'm Detective Inspector Griffin. Your consultant has explained that talking is difficult for you. Nevertheless, I have to ask some questions. I have a pen and paper, or you can use our word board. Whichever suits you best."

He and Ellis each took a seat, one on either side of Sarah's bed. PC Ellis reached across to place a pen and notepad on her tray table, and held the word board up so that Sarah could see it clearly.

"I'm taking an audio record of this meeting. And PC Ellis will take notes." Griffin looked to Sarah for affirmation. He'd seen her lying in a crumpled heap at Hurtmoor, but now he was able to get a proper look, and for a moment, he paused. She looked very poorly, with savage bruising covering almost her entire face. She looked old and vulnerable, so much so that Griffin was not only reminded of PC Ellis's formal role, but also obliged to explain it to the suspect. Sadly, and inevitably, that moment of humanity was followed by formal caution.

"You don't have to say anything, or to write anything. But it may harm your defence if you do not mention when questioned something which you later rely on in court. Anything you do say, or write, may be given in evidence."

Sarah had heard the words many times before, but always on television. Hearing them spoken live, and directed at herself, was a bit different. She nodded and her eyes settled on PC Ellis. The sight of a nervous young woman prompted her to think about Scarlet. Despite her serious injury and Mr Barnard's kind caution, Sarah's tongue was held by consideration for her daughter. The conversations that she would have during the next few days would determine the shape of things, clarifying her position in the family and before the law. Sarah was grateful for Scarlet's daily visits, but she hadn't yet talked to her about what had happened in the middle barn. Scarlet had talked to her about Alexander's injury. Sarah was catching up. But today, and for all the wrong reasons, she would accept her surgeon's advice and say very little. She wasn't protecting herself, she was looking after her daughter. Until she'd explained to Scarlet, she would hold her swollen tongue.

"I'm investigating the events at your home on the morning of 25th June." He looked at her and waited while she nodded her acknowledgement. "And I want to hear your account."

Those words provoked anxiety. Suddenly, she felt tired and unready. She nodded again, aware of the pulsing pain behind her eyes, the tender soreness of her mouth, and the heart pounding in her chest.

"Your husband received a shotgun wound. Do you know how that happened?"

A tear filled her left eye. She nodded again, and reaching for the notepad, she wrote: I shot him. I'm sorry.

DI Griffin was affected by the silence and the simplicity of her response. She didn't look like a violent criminal. He really didn't want to ask the next question and he didn't understand his reticence. It didn't really matter, he had to ask. "And did you shoot the gun by accident or was it deliberate?" DI Griffin had ordered his words carefully, offering the accidental option first.

Sarah wrote: Deliberate. She couldn't stop herself. It was just a word, but she was fragile and frightened, feeling desperately alone. Her shoulders began to shake and her face filled with tension and pain. Crying was the last thing that she needed. Almost every muscle, joint and nerve in her face seemed to be involved. It was agony.

DI Griffin looked over his shoulder to PC Ellis. He felt bad. He was a good copper, a decent man, and he took satisfaction from his work, catching the bad guys. But interviewing a seventy-year-old woman while she recovered from facial surgery, who had always been a highly respected, law abiding member of the community, reading the silent confession of a woman who was broken physically and emotionally, while still in her hospital bed, bandaged and bruised, shaking tearfully, felt bad. Really bad. He wanted to hold her hand, to dry her eyes. But that wasn't his job.

He closed his eyes for a second, while he tried to swallow his discomfort. "Mrs MacDonald, you've said something very serious. I must remind you that I'm recording this interview. You've written that you deliberately shot your husband. Is there anything else that you should tell me?"

Sarah was overwhelmed, without the strength to continue. She wrote: Not today, thank you.

Griffin had no choice. He spoke gently as he performed his duty. Sarah was informed that she was now held under arrest, facing criminal charges including attempted murder, and invited to speak in response, while under caution. She was concentrating on controlling herself, minimising her movement while tears rolled across her cheeks. She nodded at the farcical invitation and she almost spoke, just to say that she couldn't, just to complete the farce.

PC Ellis spoke, growing into her role. "We'll let you rest. We will need to ask some more questions, and take a full statement, but that's enough for today." She stopped the recording and reclaimed the notepad and pen from Sarah's bed.

The two police officers walked from the room. The gun had been fired by Sarah MacDonald. That was what Alexander had told them on day one and what Sarah had now confirmed. She had confessed to the crime.

Sarah watched the two of them walk away. She wasn't sure whether it hadn't gone to plan, or whether she'd had no plan. Either way, she was wobbling. It'd been a tough couple of weeks.

FIFTY-ONE
VISITING TIME

SEVERAL DAYS SEEMED to drift by, and Cheryl was unable to settle. After Andy had reported back, describing the arrival and departure of emergency services vehicles at Sarah's home, she had hoped that more solid news would follow, but nothing came. Cheryl was restless, and even with the distraction of builders repairing her conservatory, she couldn't escape her anxiety, not before she had a clear and reliable report about Sarah.

Her phone calls to the hospital had produced no result. The switchboard operators had diverted her skilfully, refusing to give confidential information to an unidentified caller, and Cheryl's frustration intensified.

The builders were constantly present, but she felt isolated. After an eventful period of social activity and intrigue, suddenly she was alone. She paced around her home and garden without focus or application, until her impatience pushed her into action. Cheryl booked a hotel room and drove down to Guildford. She was done with waiting. It was visiting time.

As it turned out, her timing was less than perfect. She arrived at the hospital the day after Sarah had her brief encounter with DI Griffin, and had been formally arrested.

With consideration of Sarah's health and family status, the Custody Officer had granted special dispensation for Scarlet's visits to continue. Sarah would be able to see her daughter and allowed access to legal representation, but no other visitors.

Cheryl entered the hospital full of uncertainty and determination, walking along every corridor, from one unit to the next, acting the role of a confused old woman, peering through glass door panels into each ward. Until she saw the policeman, seated in the corridor. For a moment, she was halted but she pressed the buzzer and bluffed her way inside the ward. She strode past the police officer, who showed no interest, sitting motionless by the door of a private room, away from the main bay of the ward, and approached a gathering of nurses and administrators behind a counter to ask about the visiting times.

"I want to see Sarah MacDonald. What are the visiting hours?"

These were unusual circumstances, but Nurse Henderson was fully informed. Nevertheless, she hesitated for a second as she glanced across the corridor at the seated police. "That's not possible at the moment. Are you a relative?"

Cheryl had travelled a long way. She had found Sarah. She was frustrated to be halted, having got so close, and for a moment she protested. "I'm Sarah's closest friend and I've travelled from Yorkshire. I must see her."

Scarlet had been surprised by her father's tolerance, allowing her to visit Sarah without objection, to the extent that she had made her incursions into what she'd expected to be a war zone, quite comfortably. But the tension had ramped up again with her mother's arrest. Her arrival today had been delayed while she arranged legal representation for her mother. She entered the ward just in time to hear Cheryl's claim, curious to identify the intruding stranger.

Cheryl recognised Scarlet in a second, even though they had never met before, so strong was the resemblance to Sarah.

She did her best to explain herself, giving her phone number, and imploring Scarlet to call her at the first opportunity.

Cheryl's visit to the hospital was the first sure step to uncovering the mystery of Sarah's disappearance. At least, she hoped so. Cheryl had just a couple of minutes alone with Scarlet. There had been an awkward moment while the two visitors introduced themselves and exchanged brief information, but Cheryl arrived back out into the corridor feeling relief.

The basis of the instinctive sense of danger that she and Andy had shared throughout the last two weeks had become more substantial. Sarah was hurt and she was in trouble, and now she was found. Cheryl left the hospital with mixed emotions. There were still gaps to be filled, but she'd got much closer, and already she was willing Scarlet to call.

FIFTY-TWO
FAMILY THERAPY

THE EXPERIENCE IN HOSPITAL, involving reconstructive surgery to her lower jaw, had never been on Sarah's bucket list, but at least her injuries had given her the space and time to think. The period when she had been shielded was over now and the flow of people in and out of her room gained pace. Initially there had been no expectations of communication after she'd emerged from surgery, still drowsy, listening to half heard phrases and peering through the mist at unrecognised faces. As she found her way back to clear sight, she felt herself to be a passive observer, powerless, and looking to see what was left of her life.

Despite all of her troubles, her injuries and her crimes, more and more her thinking space was occupied by her children. In many ways, Sarah felt that she'd lost Robin before he'd grown to manhood, stolen from her by MacDonald traditions, boarding school and the harsh lessons from a cold-hearted father. Her son had made no communication. His absence spoke for him – Robin had already chosen Alexander.

Even before her imprisonment in the middle barn, when she'd been planning her departure, Sarah had worried about how Scarlet would judge her. She was reluctant to expose her children to the truth about their father, and for that matter, the truth about herself. She was afraid that Scarlet would also have to choose which parent to believe and to support. For Robin, it had probably been straightforward. It seemed inevitable now that each of her children would lose a parent, but for Scarlet, the choice would be more complicated. As a child, Scarlet had risked her life in a desperate attempt to win her father's approval and, although Sarah despised her husband, she was reluctant to ask her daughter to sever the relationship in which she'd invested so bravely.

When DI Griffin and PC Ellis had interviewed her, she had been very tired and restricted by pain, but she could have said more. She could at least have begun to tell her side of the story. The police would return later for a full statement, but Sarah was determined that Scarlet would hear it first.

For Scarlet, it had been a stressful twenty-four hours, but nevertheless, the news of her mother's arrest had pushed her from hesitation into action. She'd liaised with the Custody Officer and recruited a legal team on Sarah's behalf.

Even before her encounter with Cheryl, she knew that today's visit would be different. Each day Scarlet had sat by her mother's bedside, and she'd given the same courtesy to her father. Mostly, she'd sat quietly. Her father had said his piece but Sarah had remained silent. Over the series of visits, Sarah had progressed to full consciousness and although speech was clearly still painful, it was increasingly possible. Today, Scarlet and her mother would need to talk.

Formal arrest had introduced a new formality around Sarah, and Scarlet felt nervous entering her mother's room, slightly hesitant, but the conversation in waiting pushed her forward.

Sarah continued to feel sharp pain from even the slightest movement in her face. It hurt to speak, to eat and to smile, and her tongue felt as if it was twice its normal size. She now had some wire holding her jaw together, and her face was very badly bruised. So although talking was just about an option, Sarah was happy to listen while Scarlet gave her news. So far, Scarlet had mostly talked about the boys and about Jerry. Safe territory.

They were well practised, flitting around the same agenda each day, while waiting for the real conversation to begin. Scarlet was afraid to hear it from her mother's mouth. Once the questions were asked, there could be no turning away.

She took her seat, and sat for a moment without speaking, trying to slow down and to compose herself after a busy morning. The silence brought tension. They could both feel it. Scarlet told her mother that she had appointed a local solicitor, Don Johnson, to work with a barrister called Roland Salt, who was a close friend of her husband. She told her mother that Salt would successfully apply for bail, and watched as Sarah turned to look at her in grateful acknowledgement. Then she heard herself ask the first real question.

"Who is Cheryl, Mum?"

Sarah's communication was improving. She'd learned effective use of gentle head movements and sometimes she used a pen and paper, but now she was learning to speak again. It was painful and each time she spoke with economy and minimal movement. Her voice sounded quiet and had acquired a distinctly nasal tone. "A good friend."

They had begun. Sarah wrote down her next comment: I think this is as good a time as any. We can't talk about the weather forever.

"No."

There was a long pause while Sarah wrote: I'll have to tell you things that will be difficult for you to hear. About your father. I've always taught you to be honest and I won't hide from the truth now. I hope that you can take it, and I hope that we can survive it.

Already there were huge tears spilling from Scarlet's eyes.

"I don't know if I can, or if we can. I guess we're about to find out. What on earth happened, Mum?"

Instinctively, Sarah spoke again. "I shot him," she whispered, and then she wrote: I'm guilty of that. I'm glad now that he's alive. Luckily, I'm a poor shot. I hope that one day, you'll forgive me.

Scarlet felt a wave of relief and a deep sense of disturbance. They had overcome their nervousness, and moved into scary territory. Sarah's words, spoken and written, suggested that her intention had been to kill Alexander. Scarlet wiped the tears from her face and sat back in her chair, making room for more of her mother's narrative.

Sarah was writing quickly: I needed to get out of the barn, away from the house. I was frightened.

She was struggling to know how much to say, wondering if there was a form of words that would leave her daughter with both parents. She allowed Scarlet to read her message and then their eyes met.

Scarlet could feel something coming, pushing and wriggling to find a way through her mother's caution, and she offered encouragement. "What did he do to you?"

With each newly written sentence, Sarah took them closer: I'd been locked in the middle barn for almost a fortnight, using a bucket for a toilet, starving, and sleeping on a straw bed. I needed to escape. I was hungry and very frightened.

It felt too much for Scarlet. She sobbed. Tears streamed from her eyes, and she reached out and took her mother's hand, just for a second. Although she knew instantly that her decision was made, she was unable to stay. She stood, and hurried out of the room.

Scarlet was lost. She left her mother's hospital bed feeling some kind of mental paralysis, as if her capacity for thought and judgment had frozen. For the past several days, she had tried to occupy a position of delicate impartiality, but it was never going to last. Her mother had been arrested and now she'd found her voice. The uneasy peace had ended. Guns were firing. She ran from the hospital seeking cover, forgetting about her car, and wishing she could forget everything. She made her way into the Japanese garden at Stoke Park, a place where she might calm herself. As a young woman, she had escaped the family tensions into an early marriage and tried not to look back, leaving her parents' home with damaged self-esteem but also a resilient constitution. Her task through childhood was to learn to live with disappointment, to always be second, a forgotten straggler behind Robin. But she had never lost her courage.

Now, she reflected on the extraordinary circumstances that were almost too much to face. Her mother would be judged in court, by strangers, without reference to the times when Alexander had given his orders, announced his punishments and delivered his humiliations. She and Robin had the benefit of an inside view, front row seats in the family stand. It had never been a sporting contest and there was only ever going to be one winner. She'd looked away, held her hands before her eyes, discounted the signs and symptoms, offered herself alternative explanations, making attempts to pacify or distract. She'd found all manner of ways to deny the evidence of her father's brutality. But as she had read her mother's words, she'd been forced to look again, eyes wide open.

She hadn't asked her mother any questions. One simple statement had been enough to expose the family secret that had been right in front of her all of her life. *I was frightened. I was very frightened.* Those few words had turned Scarlet's world upside-down. She didn't need the detail… she knew that her mother was truthful and she'd seen her fear a thousand times. Sarah had been so frightened that she'd shot Alexander. She shuddered as she recognised the ugly truth. Her father had terrorised her mother. And in that moment when her mother's words were spoken, she knew that whatever sorcery had held her family together, it had lost its power. The spell was broken and the family disintegrated.

Scarlet had raised her children in accordance with her

mother's example, treating Richard and Alex equitably. They were growing up too fast, shaping themselves now, learning too much from their greatly admired grandfather. Scarlet had feared that her father would take no interest in her children, and she'd been delighted when he gave them generous attention. They had passed the gender test that she and her mother had failed every day of their lives.

That would be another test. Her boys were old enough now to decide for themselves, growing into confident youth, already knowing better than their mother. Would they find a corridor to walk between their grandparents, find doorways to them both, or would they follow their mother, and make a choice. What does a mother say to her teenage kids when their grandparents start shooting each other?

She'd phoned Robin the previous evening and asked him directly if he considered his father to be a misogynist. He'd dismissed her, wondering if she'd gone the same way as his crazy mother. The family was in trouble. She and Robin had never been close but they were sister and brother, the same blood and bones. They hadn't argued on the phone. It was the same as ever, she asking for recognition and Robin thoughtlessly dismissive. Scarlet was almost two years younger than her forty-four-year-old brother. Theirs was an unbalanced and unsatisfactory sibling relationship, without warmth or even much respect, but at least they had endured. Until now, the time that they must proceed in opposite directions, follow different parents.

Robin had been tasked to recruit a nursing service and domestic help for his father. Alexander was to be discharged from hospital. It was his own decision, taken against his doctor's advice, but keeping him in prime position to direct operations. Scarlet had also tried to dissuade him, but without success. She had made her hospital visits as a dutiful daughter, attending both parents. There had been no time to think about her own needs. Finally, in the tranquil garden, she closed her eyes, felt warm sunshine, and gained a sense of herself. She felt the need for a break from her parents. Scarlet walked from the Japanese garden with a heavy heart. Her family was broken. She needed some space, to feel the air around her, to talk to Jerry and the boys, to be in a healthy place. She needed a couple of days. And maybe she'd phone Cheryl.

FIFTY-THREE

SARAH, THE CRIMINAL

SARAH HAD FELT VERY low in mood during the first couple of days in hospital. In the days that followed, she'd been up and down. She was yet to discover Scarlet's choice but at least they had talked. Sarah didn't know how to comprehend her daughter's sudden departure, or whose truth Scarlet would believe. Time would tell. She hoped that there would still be opportunities for more discussion as time passed. It wasn't until the following morning, when a nurse informed her that the police would come at eleven to take a statement, that Sarah remembered – Scarlet's first question had been about Cheryl. Now, as she tried to prepare herself to speak to the police, she found some comfort from her friend's reappearance. Somehow, Cheryl had bridged the gap between Yorkshire and Surrey. She felt better knowing, hoping, that her friends in the north were out there. Somewhere. She faced a rocky road ahead of her, and she would need her friends.

Don Johnson arrived unannounced at ten thirty, and introduced himself, explaining that he'd be with her through the police interview. He wasn't really ready for Sarah's account of events, but he coped. His job today was to ensure that his client didn't dig herself into any holes that would

279

weaken her defence or her application for bail, and then to report back to Roland Salt.

She watched as DI Griffin and PC Ellis arrived promptly at eleven o'clock. They took their seats, one on either side of her bed. The same two police officers in the same chairs, a small audio recorder, and the hi-tech pen and paper. Greetings and introductions were exchanged, although Griffin and Johnson had known each other for many years.

DI Griffin started with a reminder that she remained under caution, and proceeded immediately to his most pressing question. "It appears that someone struck you with a blunt instrument in the barn behind your house, after you had fired the shotgun. Do you know who struck the blow?"

During the next twenty minutes, DI Griffin listened and read with interest as Sarah revealed her side of the story. After a long and painful period of silence, Sarah was finally able to give her version of events. She gave verbal responses when one or two words were needed, and wrote the longer answers. She was pleased that Don Johnson was present, but she managed herself perfectly well. When she completed her statement, and it had all been agreed, she spoke her longest sentence of the week, to be sure that the nature of her defence was clearly understood.

"I shot my husband to save myself."

The statement was signed and the police departed. Don commended Sarah, offering warm encouragement, but beneath the surface, alarm bells were ringing. He had no idea what the truth might be, but if Sarah's story was to be believed in a court of law, she'd need persuasive evidence on her side.

He kept those thoughts to himself and turned to a more hopeful agenda. "Your daughter has appointed a barrister. The two of us will work together. If you're able, I'll arrange for us to attend the local police station tomorrow. They'll charge you with attempted murder, and we'll apply for bail. Successfully."

Clearly Don Johnson was on her side and in a way, Sarah felt heartened, but his words brought the serious reality of her situation into sharp focus. She felt a sudden surge of anxiety as she recognised herself as a criminal. "And then what?"

"Back here, but we'll lose the police guard, and you'll have the same entitlement to visitors as other patients. Please don't ever talk to the police without my being present. You can call me any time. This will be a long process. Months will pass before we go to court. I'll talk to Roland, and we'll work out the best way forwards. Get yourself well, Mrs MacDonald."

Sarah gave thanks and watched him walk away. The rescue team had arrived, but Sarah was more afraid than ever.

I'll be charged with attempted murder
At least I tried.

FIFTY-FOUR

LAW ENFORCEMENT

THE POLICE STATION was always busy, and Griffin enjoyed his time at HQ. It was the engine room, the place where the strands of evidence got weaved together. He liked the hustle and bustle, and the sense of shared purpose. PC Ellis had driven them back from the hospital after taking Sarah MacDonald's statement, but neither of them had said very much in the car. They both needed a few minutes to process the new information, to find a fit for the new pieces in the puzzle.

The Chief Superintendent had arranged a lunchtime 'progress report' meeting before they'd gone to the hospital. Griffin was impressed – sandwiches and cake from an external caterer. He'd gathered his thoughts, and he was confident that real progress had been achieved. He had information from the Forensics Team, and from both MacDonalds. He collected PC Ellis and joined his Chief Inspector and the Chief Superintendent, with a spring in his step, already salivating. He viewed the cake and sandwiches, but began his report with an empty plate.

"We took a full statement from Sarah MacDonald earlier today. She's admitted to shooting her husband. Her prints are on the gun and all over the gun cabinet. The forensic evidence is consistent with the accounts given by both parties. So that's a slam dunk." Griffin paused, looking up to see the Chief enjoying a ham sandwich, and then continued. "She's spoken to her solicitor, and she's given us quite a story." Griffin outlined the flavour of Sarah's explanation. He wasn't sure how to judge her tale of woe, and he was interested to see what his senior colleagues made of it. But he was getting nothing back from his audience, who appeared to be more attentive to the sandwiches and cake. He'd been investigating violent crimes for more than ten years. In his experience, self-defence was rarely successful as a full defence. He'd never heard of a case where such a defence had been accepted after a shooting. But it appeared that Sarah MacDonald intended to give it a try.

Chief Inspector Richardson held a neutral line. "Well, that will be a matter for judge and jury."

The Chief Superintendent asked a question. "Does she have back up from witnesses or from the forensic report?"

Griffin answered without hesitation. "No, sir." He decided to leave it there. The only rogue thought that was playing on his mind was the yellow plastic bucket, which seemed to have disappeared. He'd almost forgotten about it, but Sarah had described the same artefact, claiming to have used it as a toilet. Griffin had expected the bucket to feature in the forensic report, but there was no such reference.

Chief Inspector Richardson picked up a second slice of cake, and diverted them. "What about Rathbone?"

Griffin was confused by Walter Rathbone's denial. "Yes, that's a strange one. He's clearly in the frame, but he flat out denies involvement. And Sarah MacDonald can't remember seeing him at all. She's reported another person present in the barn, who she cannot name. Rathbone's been granted bail. We expect that Sarah MacDonald will also have her application granted."

The Super again asked about forensic evidence.

"Nothing. We haven't found a weapon, yet, but we'll keep

looking, and the circumstantial evidence should be enough. Despite Mrs MacDonald's information, there was no one else in close proximity." Griffin looked again at the platter of sandwiches. He watched as all three of his fellow officers re-filled their plates, while his own remained empty.

Chief Inspector Richardson needed clarification. "What's strange about it?"

"Well, if he holds his hand up, he'll be covered in glory. You know, neutralising an armed attacker, but that doesn't seem to have dawned on him."

The Chief Superintendent offered advice. "Yes, well, these..." He paused for a few seconds, chewing energetically, and searching for an acceptable term. "... rural people. They might know how to grow a cabbage, but they wouldn't survive for five minutes in the middle of town. No street craft." He abandoned his determination for appropriate language. "Country fucking bumpkins." He looked directly at Griffin, but still managed to locate another sandwich. "Have you pointed it out to him – the simple solution to his problem?"

"No, sir."

"Give the poor creature a steer." He appeared satisfied. "Okay, we're done. Keep at it, Griffin. Find the holes in Sarah MacDonald's story and either find something to pin Rathbone down, or show him a more intelligent strategy. Either option is fine with me, but the CPS may want a bit more than circumstantials, no matter how strong. You know my mantra: evidence, evidence, and more evidence."

Griffin was tempted to offer and alternative mantra – cake, cake, and more cake. It was only five hours since Griffin had enjoyed a hearty breakfast, but he left the Super's office feeling faint with hunger. His suffering wasn't helped by the sight of PC Ellis wiping her mouth with a serviette.

"Pop down to the canteen and grab me a sandwich, Ellis."

PC Ellis felt for him, to an extent. "Yes, Guv," she replied, suppressing her laughter and already out of the door.

FIFTY-FIVE

BACK TO HURTMOOR

FOR THE FIRST few days of her parents' hospitalisation, time had seemed to pass slowly. Scarlet had sat in her visitor's chair, often in silence, waiting for developments, but from the time of her mother's confession, first to Scarlet and then to the police, changes came more rapidly.

Nevertheless, she stayed home for a couple of days. Don Johnson and Robin kept her informed with phone calls. Twelve days after their admissions, both of her parents left hospital for the first time. For Sarah, it was just a short excursion to the police station where she was formerly charged with attempted murder, and granted bail. Then she was returned to the hospital. Alexander's departure was permanent. Robin drove him back to Hurtmoor and introduced him to the new team: nurses and a physiotherapist from the private healthcare sector, and Cath, the domestic help.

Scarlet had spoken at length to Roland Salt, and to Cheryl. During a twenty minute telephone conversation, Cheryl had given a series of startling insights. It had almost been too much to take in, and Scarlet was unable to judge either the reliability or utility of Cheryl's information, but she would come back to that in due course. First, she would follow

Alexander back to Hurtmoor, and for once in her life, she would challenge her father.

Scarlet could manage Robin, and if not, she could manage without him, but it was quite a different matter with Alexander. She felt the weight of her task, the finality, and just as her mother had done, she felt that she must face him for the moment of severance. It was just five minutes in the car, although it took her more than an hour to find enough courage to start the journey. A four mile drive with a crash waiting at the journey's end. And while she prepared herself to walk away from her father, and from all of their shared history, she reflected on the many years when all she had wanted was to be close to him.

Throughout her childhood, her earnest determination to win favour had almost always met with failure and frustration, but there had been one success, one golden moment. Alexander's interest in his children was both considered and careless. He knew that Robin was the heir to the estate, the one to be groomed into his role, and to one day walk in his father's footsteps. For Alexander, his role as father was to ensure that Robin was prepared, shaped in his father's image. It was different with Scarlet. She was less important. She could find work if it pleased her, but not on the farm. She was a girl and there was no place for her in a man's world. And it really made no difference that she out performed her older brother academically and that she worshipped her father. No level of achievement or dedication could alter the fact of the matter. She was female.

But there had been that one glorious moment when she'd won through. On the occasions when the four of them spent time together as a family, Alexander would set the children against each other in competitive play, and of course Robin, the older child, could outrun his sister. He was taller and stronger, a more confident child. That was always the pattern of things. Scarlet would give her best, then bite back the tears when her brother triumphed.

They went away each year on holiday, mostly to walk in the Lake District. It was 1989 and they rented a cottage close to Kendall. A stream ran at the back of the house and the children swung on a rope tied to the branch of a sycamore tree. They would swing out over to the middle of the stream and then back to the bank where they could safely release themselves to land again on solid ground. And of course, Alexander made it into a competition. Who would be the first to launch from the rope across to the far side of the stream? They had both shown excitement when the competition was announced and took their turns on the rope with renewed focus. But the view from the high point in the arc of their swings was frightening, too high above the shallow, stony stream, and although they displayed an appearance of interest, neither child relished the challenge. Sarah had chastised her husband, pointing out the danger, and he'd laughed as he assured her that neither child would be foolish enough to attempt the feat. He was just playing with their fear.

Scarlet watched her brother, at first expecting him to succeed, but she was surprised as she saw fear in him and she took her turn with the rope with a little more interest. Even today, she could still feel the pounding heart in her chest, as she recalled the jousting in her emotions, fear and courage fighting for ascendancy. Somehow she had risen to the moment. She let go of the rope just before it reached full height, and she seemed to glide like a hawk, keeping still and relaxed, almost entranced. And then it was as if she woke from a dream, still in the air, and she screamed as she fell to the ground. And then it was done. She rolled in the grass and sat up with her hands held in front of her mouth, disbelieving of her own courage and success, of victory. She'd won.

Ten-year-old Scarlet took off her shoes and socks, blood trickling from her knee, and walked calmly back across the stream to join her family, listening to her father teasing Robin because he'd been beaten by a girl, outdone by his little sister.

Even then he attended mostly to Robin, ensuring that his humiliation was painful, making him pay the price for failure, and making sure that he would never want to lose again. But in amongst it all, as Scarlet stepped from the stream, he'd ruffled her hair and said, "Well done, Scarlet." She stood there glowing. After years of frustrated endeavour, she'd gained his approval. She had reflected on that golden moment many times as she'd grown older, realising that even then his praise had been intended to taunt Robin, but on the day she had felt like an Olympian. It was the only time. She seemed to have spent the rest of her life trying to repeat the experience, without success.

Scarlet felt herself torn, and even in her middle age, she could still feel the little girl inside her, craving his approval. But she wasn't a little girl anymore, and she had made a very grown up decision.

She and her father sat down, waiting for Cath to bring the tea tray into the room. Scarlet asked about his injury and she was pleased to find the house in such good order. She crossed her fingers, hoping that he'd behave well enough to keep Cath content in her new role.

"I went to see Mum."

"Did you, indeed?"

This would be challenging. Scarlet had no script to follow. She hoped that the right words would find her. "Yes. The blow that she received did serious damage, but the surgery went well, apparently. Mr Barnard is happy with her progress."

"Is that why you've come, Scarlet, to talk about your mother?" Alexander made no effort to disguise his irritation.

"I'm not sure what I want to say, Dad. I've been wondering, worrying about what happens next, trying to figure out how we all deal with what has happened." Scarlet trusted herself, she was good with words, never clumsy, sometimes deeply hesitant, but naturally articulate. She'd laid out the agenda, and now she side-stepped, taking them back to the time when they had almost felt like a proper family. "Can you remember our holiday in Kendall? In the cottage by the stream."

"Yes, I can remember. You were very young, nine or ten, I think." He had no idea where the conversation was heading but the sharp edge had gone from his voice. "You leapt from the rope into the grass on the far bank. I haven't forgotten, Scarlet. I thought you were either more courageous than I'd realised or just stupidly unaware of the danger." He smiled. "In the end, I realised that you'd probably let go by accident. You were lucky to find a soft landing."

She was stung by his interpretation. "No, it was neither accident nor misjudgement. I was terrified, swinging back and forth, looking down at the shallow water running over the stones and the rocks. I could see the danger clearly. I thought that I'd die if I fell short, and I expected to fall short. My heart was racing, but that's how desperately I wanted to please you, to make you proud of me, to be your daughter. I was ten years old and I risked my life. And you decided it was an accident."

"It was a long time ago, Scarlet. Memory is often unreliable."

This was her father, even now unwilling to give her credit. "Are you proud of me, Dad?" She asked her question without a fanfare. Nevertheless, it was a big one.

Alexander's brief respite ended, and he moved back into irritation. "Pride comes before a fall. There's no room for conceit in this family."

Scarlet had always been the good scholar. She loved learning, always keen to apply her intelligence, she was the family problem solver. Even as a young child, she would find ways to deflect household tension. When his father's voice was raised, Robin would clear out of the way, get himself beyond earshot, but not Scarlet. She'd find her way into the line of fire, stand between her parents, inventing aches and pains, announcing urgent needs. She was full of fear but unable to walk away and leave her mother exposed to Alexander's venomous vitriol.

Here she was again, frightened and in a familiar position, standing between her parents and still trying to fulfil her fated role. She'd heard enough of her mother's story to make her own assessment. It was perfectly clear to her that both of her parents were in big trouble. The facade had been removed and the desperate reality of their marriage revealed. But with all of her skills and courage, she could see no solution.

"No, of course. I wonder what we have got room for in this family." She had proceeded with care, stopped short of the tipping point. Now, she would have to let go of the rope, pray for safe landing, and accept her father's judgement. Of course, Scarlet already knew what was coming, and she was braced for a fall. "We're in a terrible mess, Dad. I spoke to a friend of Jerry's recently, Roland Salt. He's a barrister. If this all goes ahead and into court, the accusations, investigations, and legal processes, it'll be a nightmare. I don't know what to tell the boys. They're asking questions and I don't have any answers."

Neither had Alexander. He sat quiet, feeling the weight of his predicament, the consequences of his angry reaction. Just for a few seconds, then he snapped back into reality. He pointed to his injured shoulder. "It was your mother who fired the gun." He had no doubt that Sarah was culpable but he'd arranged early discharge to strengthen his position, to get back into the seat of his power. "This barrister, Salt, I'd like to speak to him."

Scarlet wondered if this was the moment of finality, and she braced herself again. "He's representing Mum."

Her wondering was quickly resolved. Alexander had heard enough. "Well, now we're clear. Your mother tried to kill me but you've decided to support her. I'll tell you what you can say to the boys. Tell them they have no grandfather and no inheritance because of your foolish and misguided notion of loyalty. Now get out of my house."

After Scarlet's departure, Alexander fumed. The preservation of the MacDonald estate had always been his first responsibility. As far back as he could remember, that message had been drummed into him. The family tree stretched back through centuries, and this land, his farm, had been hard-won by Alexander's forefathers. Family was everything: the family name and traditions; family wealth and inheritance; the family line. Blood and land passed through the generations. Power and position preserved.

For decades, Sarah had followed his instruction, accepted the world and the ways that she'd married into, and delivered the next generation. For forty-six years she'd done her job. Not perfect, but adequate. Now, not only had she gone crazy and turned against him, she'd infected Scarlet with her insanity. Alexander had never been a huge fan of his daughter, but with Robin twenty years into a childless marriage, Richard and Alex were important. They were the future.

He was perfectly confident that he'd come through this messy business unscathed, but for a moment he was filled with negative energy, burning with anger. He reviewed Sarah's descent into madness. It had started with her running back to Yorkshire to watch Mark Sanderson die. She'd lied to him, deceived him, cheated on him. Shot him. And yet he found himself abandoned by his daughter. Well, so be it. His wife lay in a hospital bed, charged with attempted murder, and Scarlet had made her choice. And he resolved there and then to recruit his own counsel, and to throw all of his power, money, and influence to crush Sarah. Scarlet would forego her inheritance, and spend years making prison visits. But even with his resolve fully refuelled, still his anger burned.

Cath had heard the raised voices, and watched Scarlet walk from her father with tears flowing. She was shocked. She thought she'd won the jackpot when she was given thirty hours a week to carry out domestic work at the MacDonald home. She was up to her neck in credit card debt, but with the income from this job, she could see a way froward. This was day two, and already her new employer was beginning to frighten her, but she couldn't afford to lose her new job, and she crept back into the room to collect the tea tray.

Alexander waited until her hands claimed the tray. The movements from his left arm were still hugely restricted, but his feet were fine. He kicked the tray from Cath's grasp, scattering and shattering the crockery. "Who the hell asked you to enter the room?"

Cath froze. Alexander was shouting at her, bristling with aggression. She felt cornered, frightened of him. "I'm sorry, I thought..."

"You're not paid to think, you're here to clean my house according to my instructions." He stepped in closer and shouted. "Do you understand?"

Cath didn't dare lift her gaze in acknowledgement. "Yes. I apologise, Mr MacDonald." He was just a couple of feet from her. She could smell his halitosis.

Alexander stared at her, his eyes glazed and full of fury. "Get this mess cleaned up."

Cath watched him walk from the room. She was shaking with fear, crying as quietly as she could manage. She had already exceeded her agreed finish time to clear up after Scarlet's visit, trying to create a good impression on her new boss, and even though she was trembling with terror, she cleaned up the broken crockery, before quietly slipping out of the house. She'd spend the evening looking for enough courage to persuade herself to walk back in for her next shift in the morning.

FIFTY-SIX
UNPLANNED HOLIDAY

THE UNEXPECTED COFFEE with Sue and Eleanor had allowed Andy to return home with at least a glimmer of hope. Not that Greg's discovery was any closer but at least someone else was looking. He seemed to have been chasing shadows for weeks and making little progress. He was glad to spend a couple of days at home with Polly, but from time to time his thoughts went back to Surrey, and he answered with keen interest when Cheryl phoned with an update, confirming that Sarah was indeed at the hospital in Guildford. They scheduled a catch up meeting.

Andy approached the Sanderson house remembering his previous visit, sitting in Cheryl's kitchen with the smell of the fire still present. Cheryl invited him into the house and took him through to the newly repaired conservatory.

"Hello, Andy. Thanks for coming."

"Hi, Cheryl. How are you?"

"Very well, and finally, I have news of Sarah."

"Hallelujah. How is she?"

"She received a nasty injury, but she's recovering. She's at the hospital in Guildford. But that's the least of her troubles. It's quite complicated." Cheryl delivered the whole story, concluding with news of the criminal charges.

Andy was genuinely shocked. "Whoa. I could see that something must have happened, but I didn't expect that. They'll put her away, Cheryl. No question."

"It's looking that way, I'm afraid." Cheryl took a deep breath. "I'm going to ask a favour."

"Ask away."

"Sarah's daughter, Scarlet, is organising her mother's legal team. She's asked me to attend a meeting with the barrister, but really it's you she needs to speak to. You followed George, and you have the photos."

Andy was starting to wonder what might be expected from him. "Right. So when's the meeting?"

"The day after tomorrow. In Guildford."

Andy was curious, but also uncertain. He'd interrupted his trips to Middlesbrough, taken a couple of days to recharge, but he intended to resume. "I'm not sure, Cheryl. I've hardly seen Pol these past three weeks, and I'm still trying to catch up with Greg Whitehead."

"It'll just be a couple of days, Andy, and Polly could come with us." Cheryl had almost forgotten about Greg. Nevertheless, she felt interest. "Where will you be seeing him?"

"I've been calling at his house in Middlesbrough but he's never at home. Another of the disappeared."

Cheryl was distracted and she enquired further. "How strange, first Sarah and now Greg, evading your detection."

"I know, it's weird. Sue Berry from school turned up at his house a couple of days back. She's looking for him as well."

Cheryl felt curious but she found no connection and she got herself back on track. "Listen, Andy, we were right. Sarah was in danger, and she still is. Clearly, she had reason to shoot Alexander, but that's of little interest to the police. The barrister has been clear – without evidence to support her story, Sarah's defence is unlikely to succeed."

Andy picked up Cheryl's alarm. "I hear you, Cheryl. I'll talk to Pol. If she's up for it, we'll go to the meeting."

Cheryl was relieved. She had felt some tension when she'd spoken to Scarlet, which she couldn't understand, but she hoped Andy's contribution would be received with more warmth. "I've rented a house for a few days. I'm not sure I can do this alone. I do hope that you and Polly can travel with me."

Andy was unready for this development. He thought that his interest in Sarah had ended. He was all over the place, one minute searching for Greg, now God only knows, but Cheryl was persuasive. She had a natural authority about her. He'd rather refuse an order from Major Ferguson than disobey Cheryl.

"Give me an hour, Cheryl. I'll have a chat with Polly and I'll phone you back."

The conversation with Polly moved to a rapid conclusion. A few days earlier, she had sent Andy out in search of Greg Whitehead, but Cheryl's news had shifted Polly's priorities. While Andy prevaricated, she had no hesitation, instructing Andy to phone Cheryl, while she started packing a suitcase.

Andy made the call. Twenty-four hours later they were more than half way to Surrey. He'd already developed a healthy respect for Cheryl, although he hardly knew her, but as he listened to her hatching plans to trap George and to incriminate Alexander, new aspects of her character were revealed. Cheryl, it seemed, was prepared to take risks and to bend rules. This seventy-two-year-old widow was without shame or hesitation as she outlined her ideas to confront the enemy. Andy couldn't help himself, he was right behind his commanding officer. There were several occasions when he answered her with a sharp, "Yes, sir," and a couple of times he almost saluted her. They were headed into battle and Cheryl was planning for victory. Andy had started the journey with scepticism, but by the time they arrived in Guildford, he was more hopeful.

Polly was beside herself, her first time riding in the back of a Mercedes and planning to eat a salad. She'd never felt so posh. She missed some of the strategy planning up in the front of the car, and she guessed that egg and chips would be off the menu until she was back in Yorkshire. But what the hell, this was her first holiday since she and Andy had spent a long weekend in Blackpool just after they'd first got together. Andy was still drinking heavily back then, and he'd thrown up several pints of strong lager after an ill advised flirtation with the big dipper. But hey, it's the journey that counts and this one included the soft leather seats in Cheryl's Mercedes, ensuring comfort and promising more than the funfair.

A couple of hours later, Polly ate her salad without complaint. She lay in an unfamiliar bed with way too many thoughts for sleeping. One way or another she'd grab a slice of pizza tomorrow, and she wondered what else the new day would bring.

Cheryl awoke in an unfamiliar room. She felt keen to get busy, but the meeting was scheduled for two o'clock, and she decided to take the opportunity to visit Sarah at the hospital. Although Scarlet's request had persuaded Cheryl to travel back to Guildford, her first priority was friendship. She wanted to be there for Sarah, to offer support in a moment of crisis.

She sat with Andy and Polly for a light breakfast, feeling slightly apologetic – she would leave her colleagues to their own devices through the morning. She spent several minutes outlining her thoughts, explaining that she would visit Sarah in the hospital to get a first hand account of the current state of play. She suggested that Andy and Polly might scout around while she went to the hospital. She hoped that would be enough to satisfy them. Polly was fine. She wanted to tour the territory in which Andy had already become familiar. She wanted to see the farm and to take a look at George. Until now, she'd seen events unfolding indirectly. Today would be different. Andy was less impressed, but he held his tongue. At least Cheryl would get the full story.

Cheryl took a taxi to the hospital. She had gone rogue for her first visit, but with Sarah on bail, the process was straightforward. Finally, she would hear from Sarah, find out how their dialogue had been interrupted.

Sarah was dressed and sitting on her bed. The strange shape and colouring to her face was grotesque but clearly her recovery was proceeding. She moved carefully but was perfectly able to stand as she greeted Cheryl. They stood facing each other. Sarah had never really been a hugger, but she held both of Cheryl's hands for a second or two, her speech checked, not by the surgery but by a well of emotion. She ushered her friend into a seat and gently lowered herself into the remaining chair. One deep breath and she found her voice. "It's good to see you, thanks for coming." She took Cheryl through the tale. It hadn't been too difficult writing her statement for the police, but this was a very different experience, speaking directly to a supportive friend. She knew that her ordeal was deeply disturbing. Flashbacks intruded into her dreams every night, taking her back to her trauma with an intense feeling of reality. She was more able to hold them back during the daylight hours, but today, as she described her experience to Cheryl, the intensity of her emotions was frighteningly powerful.

It was a stuttering narrative, broken by tears and sighs. Sometimes she hesitated to settle herself, sometimes just to give Cheryl a moment to take it in, and sometimes to write when her mouth complained. At times, the depravity of her recent experience threatened to overwhelm her, but she found a way to tell it all, her first steps towards psychological recovery.

Cheryl was a strong woman, robust physically and emotionally, but even so, the power of Sarah's astonishing story was inescapable. She was profoundly affected. She had anticipated neither the severity nor the scope of Sarah's injuries. Her friend's long road to recovery would be challenging, physically and psychologically. She wanted to give reassurance, to make everything come right again, but she remained silent, feeling utterly powerless. She hoped that the meeting with the barrister would give encouragement, but the harm received by Sarah would never be undone. It was a sobering moment for Cheryl. She desperately wanted to offer a helpful response, but as she'd listened to Sarah's tiny voice emerging from a fragile mouth, she realised it was already too late. The processes in the police and the courts would unfold, and verdicts would be reached, but the ordeal that Sarah had suffered would never be erased. She felt angry, and she revised her aims. Of course she wanted freedom for Sarah, but more than that now, she wanted Alexander brought to account.

Eventually she managed a verbal response. "What can I do to help?"

"I'm worried about Scarlet. She was upset when I last spoke to her. She thinks the world of her father."

Cheryl was cautioned as she realised that she wanted to hang Scarlet's dear father. Perhaps she'd stumbled into the source of the tension between them. Time would tell. In the meantime, Cheryl had her own story to tell. She gave a brief summary of Andy's reconnaissance, and talked her through the photographs of George, north and south. Each of the two women gained new information, and a better understanding of the sequence of events. Suddenly the time was gone and Cheryl left to make her way to Don Johnson's offices.

While Cheryl made her hospital visit, Andy acted as tour guide, taking Polly out to view Hurtmoor, and then back to Guildford to take a look at George's house. Andy noted with interest that the black Peugeot was gone from the drive. He'd sensed that Hurtmoor was occupied, but there was no sign of life at George's. For Andy, that was the only point of interest during the whole morning. Polly was happy, again enjoying the novelty of riding in a Mercedes, and getting live sightings of the places she'd heard Andy describe.

The meeting was a bit formal. Six attendees with limited knowledge of each other, but the exchange of information made each of the participants more knowledgeable. Roland Salt chaired the meeting, and he was good. He kept them on track. Clearly, he would be an effective man in the law courts. He was almost brutally efficient, economic and focused. Cheryl had been right – Andy was the key contributor, and there appeared to be links between his photographs and Sarah's description of events. Polly, Cheryl and Don Johnson all gained a coherent picture of events, and they felt hope. Scarlet remained poker-faced. Andy wasn't feeling it, and neither was Salt, who turned to Andy.

"Does Alexander appear on any of the pictures?"

"No."

"It's not going to help us. There are a series of images showing George Brand and Sarah in the same towns on the same days. No wrong-doing is documented, or even suggested."

He turned his attention to Scarlet. "Your mother has already told us who she thinks must have hit her. Now, we have some photos of him, but we don't know who he is."

He turned to address the meeting. "It's early days, and at present we are still early in the police investigations. They appear to have charged the wrong man for Sarah's injury. My point is that there are many possibilities and a whole lot of unknowns. But right now, I'm concerned. In some respects, some of Andy's pictures support Alexander's version of events. She appears to have got involved with another man. She went to a friend's funeral in Stokesley. I don't mean to discourage. George Brand may well have something to contribute. Who knows? But you're paying me to defend Sarah, and if we went to court tomorrow, with everything we have on the table, we'd struggle. A good prosecuting barrister would attack Sarah, suggesting mental instability and moral corruption." He looked directly at Scarlet. "Your father's legal team will be very confident. We need much more than Sarah's unsupported testimony. If she's going to withstand the opposing counsel, we need to have a winning case. Right now, we're nowhere near."

FIFTY-SEVEN

MOVING TO THE FUTURE

FOR A PERIOD OF WEEKS, events had unfolded rapidly, with each day bringing new developments, but as the summer progressed to mid-July, the pace slowed. Sarah was discharged from hospital to continue the next several weeks of her recovery at Scarlet's house, with the criminal charges weighing heavy. Her bail conditions allowed a degree of short-term comfort but the passage of time had delivered no further signs of hope. Despite Scarlet's attentive care, Roland Salt was preparing her for the inevitability of conviction and the probability of a long prison sentence. She did her best to show a brave face with her grandchildren close by, but alone in her bed during the hot nights, she felt the hopelessness of her plight. Alexander, as always, would win the day.

Alexander had paid a price. His family was split in half with Scarlet taking her mother's side. Forgiveness wasn't within his nature, and he'd recognised immediately after Scarlet's final visit, that her choice represented an irreparable breach, but he was confident that the damage would be time limited. He'd been stung by Scarlet's behaviour, and he'd given Cath a hell of a week while his angry response lingered. But as the days and weeks passed, he settled, and formed plans to reach out to Richard and Alex. That would be poison to his crazy daughter – watching her precious children cross to his side. Sarah could enjoy the illusion of release while on bail and in the company of her grandchildren, but his legal advisors reminded him often that her reprieve would crash into a brick wall when the court proceedings commenced.

The teenage boys still needed their mother, and Alexander was able to see that, in the short term, the boys could do little else but stand by their grandmother. He decided to be patient, to bide his time, play the long game, recognising that as they moved to adulthood and independence, they would develop a more mature understanding of the value of a large farm estate in Surrey. As young adults, looking at a multi-million-pound inheritance, and with their grandmother in jail, a convicted criminal, they would be tempted to review their position. Alexander would make damn sure of that, and he'd be ready to forgive their adolescent show of loyalty to their mother. He could wait.

He knew well enough that despite the damage to family relations, his position with the legal processes was secure. He smiled to himself as he thought about the ease with which he'd managed the police enquiry. Alexander had the advantage of good breeding, an education at St Germain's and Cambridge. He was a man endowed with self-confidence and fully in charge. The Chief Constable had given reassurance throughout, apologising for DI Griffin's intrusive questions, and providing regular updates as Sarah's prosecution proceeded. Alexander could manage a dozen over-weight detective inspectors, with their second rate state educations and their greasy spoon diets. They were inferiors, common people, people he could manipulate with ease. His moments of concern and anger were hidden from DI Griffin, while he acted out sympathies that in reality were anathema to him. He had given easy answers to DI Griffin's questions, deflecting him without a trace of tension whenever George's whereabouts was mentioned.

Alexander had no difficulty justifying his casual relations

with truth and morality. The punishments that he'd given in response to Sarah's outrageous disloyalty and infidelity were fully deserved and no one's business but his own. In Alexander's world view, the police should have no involvement in domestic disputes. Self-respecting husbands, heads of families, should be left alone to do whatever was necessary to keep their wives in order. If Sarah had had the sense to accept her wrongdoing, he'd have given her a second chance. He'd offered her an opportunity for repentance, but she'd poured scorn on his generosity, chosen her own foolish and murderous path. Well, so be it, she could rot in a prison cell, and Scarlet would have to watch her mother's misery, and her children's change of heart.

As the weeks passed, DI Griffin also became more settled. Sarah MacDonald had maintained her rather unlikely story of kidnap and imprisonment but neither witness nor evidence had emerged to support her version of events. He was good at his work. He remained curious about the unexplained injury to Sarah, and he was frustrated by the disappearance of George Brand. Sarah's shattered jaw and Andy Cooper's photographs of George were left as untidy loose ends which offended his professional pride, but his superior officers and the Crown Prosecution Service were quite content that the charges related to the shooting of Alexander MacDonald were rock solid. And Griffin could live with these outcomes. He had no choice but to do so. He'd been pleasantly surprised by the generosity of Alexander's attitude. The rich farmer had suffered a serious gunshot wound and seen his family shattered, but he'd consistently demonstrated compassion. Even weeks after the Hurtmoor incident, he seemed reluctant to see his estranged wife prosecuted, asking repeatedly if Sarah might be excused, pointing out that she she'd been knocked into temporary insanity by a bereavement reaction. Griffin had hoped that the perpetrator of Sarah MacDonald's injury would be discovered, and that George Brand might reappear to answer his questions, but both areas of hope had been dashed. No new information had emerged, Brand was nowhere to be found, and although Sarah seemed an unlikely criminal, the evidence was clear. He'd secured the key conviction and he could do no more.

FIFTY-EIGHT

ELEANOR'S PARTY

IT FELT to Greg that he'd been the last invitee, but as he re-read Eleanor's message for the fiftieth time, he already knew that something was wrong. Eleanor had made a late change to the arrangements, informing Greg about a change of venue and a reduced group of guests. The original intention to party all night had been revised to a quiet lunch. Something was clearly wrong.

Greg had been in good form, cycling and socialising, and the moments of sadness from losing Sarah, were reducing. He'd found something in himself, something of his old self, but also something else. He'd escaped his post-Covid hangover.

For several weeks, ever since the trip to Barcelona, he'd been able to step out into the world, to talk with strangers. But today, 28th August, the day of Eleanor's party, he wanted to crawl back into his bed. He'd picked something up, something between the lines of Eleanor's increasingly brief messages, disguised in triviality, but he'd seen it clearly enough, and now, as he travelled ever closer to Leeds, it sat like a lump of lead in the pit of his stomach, still gaining weight.

He pushed it away, desperate for distraction, and he

reflected on his recent meeting with Andy Cooper. After the aborted approaches, zig-zagging through crossed paths, he and Andy had finally managed to meet. Andy had driven over to Middlesbrough a week earlier and delivered a brief letter, asking if Greg would meet him, and Greg had responded positively.

They'd met by the river in Great Ayton two days later. It had been a forty-five minute journey for both of them, Andy on foot and Greg cycling. Greg had arrived almost thirty minutes early, and he'd taken the opportunity to reflect, recalling their last meeting in The Lion after Janey's funeral, and hoping Andy would manage better on this occasion. He'd met Sue and Eleanor on the same fateful day. Greg had reviewed the weeks that had followed, remembering something stirring inside him, a vague feeling of anticipation. Then there had been the second funeral, and Sarah Buxton of course. Even though he'd come a long way, Greg still shook his head when he thought about Sarah, embarrassed by the recklessness of his heart, and shocked by the coldness of hers.

It had been painful, but he felt no regret, no wish to retreat back into his exclusive and solitary world. Somehow, the deaths of old school friends, and his misplaced trust, had freed him from the shadow of the pandemic. He was back in the bigger world now, making new friends, taking holidays abroad, and cycling on new paths.

Even with the camouflage clothes, he'd spotted Andy's approach from fifty metres. Greg stood tall, waving his arms. Andy had waved back in acknowledgement as he approached.

Greg invited him to sit. "Hello again, Andy. I understand you've been looking for me, and I remember that you wanted to explain."

"Yes. Sorry about The Lion. I'm a bit flaky these days. And I'm sorry about stalking you. You know, sitting in your garden." Andy had indeed been a bit flaky, struggling to find his words and spending too much time apologising for nothing much. He'd started again. "Are you, are you well?"

"I'm fine, thanks, going to too many funerals, and I was bullied as a child, but otherwise I'm good."

Andy had made no complaint. "Fair enough. Yes. I was sorry to hear about Janey dying. I spent a bit of time with her during the last two or three years before she got ill," Andy had said, taking a glance to see how he'd landed.

Greg reacted with curiosity, and puzzlement. The idea of Janey hanging out with Andy seemed unlikely. "Oh, right."

"It's a long story, Greg. You'll need to indulge me. I might take a minute, if you'll bear with me."

"You have my attention. I'm all ears."

"When we were young, I don't know, probably six, I lived round the corner from Janey. We were friends. You know, good mates, playing together in the street, in and out of each other's houses. Then she lost interest, didn't want to know me. There was no reason as far as I could see. We didn't fight or argue. It was like she just got fed up with me. I was sort of upset, I was just a kid but you know, I had a lot going on. Then you two were big mates."

"Right." Greg had become a bit touchy as he followed Andy's story. "My fault, was it?"

"No. Please, Greg, bear with me. But no, none of it was your fault. And there's no excuse for my bullying. I'm not asking for anything from you. Janey said I should tell you the whole story. I told her that I would. She wanted you to know. All of it. And she wanted me to ask you a question. We talked about it all, and she knew you'd come for her funeral."

Greg's interest had been won, and he'd stayed silent.

Andy continued. "I was angry, confused, I suppose, not just with Janey."

Greg's irritation had prompted another interruption. "No, not so much Janey, it was more with me."

"I don't know about that. I bullied you, I don't think I

was angry with you. That was the problem, I wasn't angry at anybody really, I was just angry. I had a chip on my shoulder, that's what people said. There was some shit going on for me, that's as good a way to say it as any other. I was angry, and I didn't know what to do. Something bad happened and then Janey fell out with me. I knew when I was giving you a hard time that I was being a bastard, and I knew what everyone thought about me. One big barrel of laughs."

"What was the question Janey wanted you to ask?"

"You remember Janey's mum, Gwen?" Andy took in a deep breath. "I'm just going to have to say this, Greg. She used to play with my willy. I was only about six. It happened quite a few times."

There followed a period of silence. A wilderness. For a while, neither man had known what to say and they'd let the river talk, just idle chatter to the wind and the trees, but it had filled the space.

Greg had been able to remember Andy's previous attempt to tell his tale and he decided this time to wait, giving Andy some time.

Andy had been nervous, and quite unsure about how Greg might view his disclosure. It was a big deal, to tell another person about his experiences of abuse from childhood. Even still, the same as it had always been, it felt like a badness in him. Not a badness done to him, but in him. All his life he'd carried a stain, and it was no small thing to say it out loud. He'd been in control of his emotions, but he'd waited nervously. Greg had turned his head to look directly at Andy.

"She wanted me to ask if Gwen did the same with you. That's the question, and I promised her that I'd ask you. She wanted me to tell you the whole tale. I hated myself, but that's what happened. I used to think about it back then, and I always wanted to ask you, but you know, we were six or seven, and I finished up bullying you. I don't know why. I wish I hadn't, but I can't take it back. I'm deeply ashamed, and I'm sorry."

Greg had been stunned. "Did Janey know? I mean, when it was happening."

"We were too young to understand. Both of us, but she picked something up, and she knew something was wrong. Enough to fall out with me, which stopped me from coming to the house, but it wasn't until years later that she put it all together."

Janey never got to see what had gone on between Gwen and Andy. She and Andy were young children. Gwen would send her to the corner shop on an errand while Andy was left in the house, alone with Gwen. It had happened too many times. Janey started to get a knot in her stomach as soon as Gwen sent her off to the shop, and she had often sensed a reaction in Andy when she returned. Nothing much, it was as if Gwen had sucked the energy from him. That's all. Throughout the whole of her adult life, she had never felt sure whether her decision to fall out with Andy had been made with conscious calculation or whether it had been driven by instinct. Either way, six-year-old Janey had ditched Andy as a friend. It meant that he wouldn't come to the house anymore. Her betrayal had been her best attempt to protect him.

But that had been the limit of her insight. It wasn't until she was away at university that she looked back at her mother's strangeness. Gwen seemed to have struggled to recognise that there were boundaries in relationships and that some people were children. It was only when Janey gained her adult form and some distance, that she'd wondered how far Gwen's inappropriate behaviour might have extended. Only then had she dared to consider that her mother had taken a sexual interest in the little boy who had once been her best friend.

"But the two of you talked about it in the end," Greg had said, feeling slightly hesitant, and allowing the impact of

Andy's story to penetrate. He would never have guessed. Andy had shown him a new window into the world he'd inhabited, made in stained glass, distorting and obscuring the view into rooms where bad things happened. A dark world for those who were tainted, the unworthy, the young lovers of Gwen Tasker, the victims and the abusers. Andy Cooper.

"We became close friends again, really close." Andy had held himself under control. He'd already told Greg everything within his obligations. But as he'd remembered Janey, he'd filled up. "It broke my heart to watch her fade away."

Greg had sat quiet for a moment, thinking about Gwen, travelling back in time, placing himself in the Tasker's house, searching for memories. He'd shuddered, hearing Gwen's teasing voice, feeling her hand on his cheek. Janey had always been in attendance. She'd protected him for every second by staying close and she'd protected Andy with rejection. And now she was dead. And the bully was sorry. And what on earth was he meant to make of all of that.

"No, Gwen was odd, but she didn't abuse me."

Andy had nodded, his task completed. "Thank God. Gwen used to send Janey off running errands. I dreaded those times, left on my own with Gwen. Jesus, I was a little kid, she was a grown woman. I'm glad you never had to go through it."

Again, Greg had been silent. Silenced. He had no training for such a conversation. His memories of being bullied would never be changed, but his ill feeling towards Andy had already gone. He'd wanted to speak, but he simply didn't know what to say.

Who would have foreseen this moment, the school bully and his victim sitting quietly, settling into a new understanding of what had happened to them. Gwen Tasker, the fire starter, and long dead, would never see the dying embers, the last remains.

They'd sat by the river for a long time, and for several

minutes neither man spoke a word. Eventually, Greg had pulled two bottles of water from his backpack, and handed one bottle to Andy. He'd raised his own bottle and moved his hand towards Andy, inviting his participation, and they'd bumped their plastic water bottles.

"To Janey."

"God rest her soul."

For a minute or two they'd both stayed quiet, chewing the cud. The silence had seemed to suggest to Andy that their conversation had ended and they should either say farewell or talk about something else. "I wanted to tell you earlier but you're a difficult man to find. I came over a few times but you were never home."

Greg explained that he'd been cycling in Spain, and then Andy had talked about his love of wild camping. It was small-talk, and they weren't about to plan a joint holiday, but the subscript was more important. They were starting again, as adults with some understanding of their complex shared world. Meeting each other as equals for the first time. He'd looked at the man beside him with an appreciation that even the previous day would have felt impossible. He was glad to know the good man that Andy Cooper had become.

Small-talk would have felt like a crime after what had just passed between them. There was nothing more to be said. So they had said goodbye, awkwardly, neither of them knowing whether it was the end or a new beginning. Greg had watched Andy walk into the distance, and then he was gone. He'd seemed to melt into a hedge. Greg had waited for a while at the river's edge, anchored to the spot, unable to turn away from the running water. There must have been more important days in his life, but none that he could recall. He'd had his three score and ten, watched his daughter's birth, and cycled all over the world, but that afternoon, talking to Andy, topped the lot. In the space of two hours, his understanding of his own life had altered.

• • •

Suddenly he met the traffic on the ring-road, and his mind returned to the present. Again, he reviewed recent communications from Eleanor, all from Eleanor, none from Sue. There had been no invitation to the house or to stay overnight, just a postcode for the restaurant, a neutral venue, a place primed for early escape. Eleanor's messages had focused on Sue, including references to medical appointments, tiredness, abdominal pain and weight loss. Greg had been waiting for weeks now to hear what diagnosis emerged, but no information came.

His sat-nav announced successful arrival and Greg found a space in the carpark behind a distinctly unglamorous Moroccan restaurant. There were just a couple of other cars, Eleanor's ten-year-old Saab, and a white van, without a man, but Greg's eyes were drawn to the bike wedged between the back wall and a half-filled skip. It was a decent road bike, and he thought about Stella, and then about Sarah, grateful for a few seconds of diversion.

He regained focus and checked his watch. He was five minutes late, and suddenly he knew. Before too long, there would be yet another funeral.

Tears were forming. These two sensational women, who had invited him into their lives, were waiting for him. No one else would be present. Sue had waited more than half of her life to find and free herself, and now her time was running out. He walked slowly, feeling afraid and steeling himself both at the same time, getting himself ready to wrap his arms around his dear and dying friend.

FIFTY-NINE

SARAH AND ANDY

ROLAND SALT really had been concerned when he'd first recognised that Andy's photographs offered no help, but six weeks later his concern had grown to the point of despair. He'd invested some hope in George Brand turning up, but that too had come to nothing. He went back, looking for a new angle, anything to get some movement, but every avenue became a dead end. Eventually, Salt shifted his aim, recognising the hopelessness of Sarah's defence, and moving with increasing emphasis to a duty of care for his client. Salt was shifting from barrister to psychologist. He wanted to move Sarah towards acceptance and closure, and it was Salt who suggested getting Andy and Sarah together. Through it all, they had never met. They'd spent days in close proximity, Sarah inside the barn and Andy outside, and Salt just thought they should give it a try – maybe, somewhere in the mix, something helpful would emerge. It was Salt's best attempt to provide a form of therapy.

This time Andy's invitation came directly from Scarlet, and it was personal. She phoned him and she mentioned that it was Roland's suggestion, but she also said that Sarah wanted to thank him. Early in September, Andy made the trip. He'd got himself into a better place, made his peace with

Greg Whitehead, become a better man. He travelled by train so that he could complete the round trip within one day. It would be a long day, but he'd be able to sleep on the return leg – which seemed a better option than falling asleep at the wheel of his car. Scarlet, bless her heart and her purse, paid for first class tickets and she met him at the station.

Sarah was up and down. In some ways, she felt that she'd reached the position she'd sought for many years. As it had turned out, she'd taken detours through a dangerous route, sustained injuries along the way, and now faced a lengthy prison term, but she had found her way to some kind of freedom, albeit late and wounded, and probably temporary, but for the time being, finally she felt something close to ownership of her life. During these past weeks, talking to Scarlet, and sometimes alone with her thoughts, she had started to make sense of this period of chaos, pain and turmoil, of the years in a lonely wilderness, and of the way that the Covid pandemic had affected her.

The weeks she had spent with Scarlet were precious. More than that, they were transformational. The support from her daughter had given its own form of healing. Both she and Scarlet had needed the time to reset their relationship. Sarah had spent several weeks in her daughter's home as houseguest. Just a few weeks, but during that time they had developed their dialogue, and spoken with an ever increasing appreciation of the new context for their relationship. It had taken a series of steps, testing the ground, and allowing Alexander's absence to penetrate, but they had reached a point where they were able to talk more openly than ever before. They had built the foundation for a new connection.

Even as she adapted to and nursed her own severe injuries, Sarah had been able to see the challenges of her daughter's adjustment. Scarlet had lost her father and she had grieved. She'd struggled for a while with radical swings in her mood, sometimes angry, sometimes sad, and often confused, but as the days and weeks had passed, Scarlet realised that a burden had been shed. The drive to please her father had gone. Now, perhaps she could please herself.

Richard and Alex had surprised Sarah. She felt that she hardly knew them, and anticipated friction as they too had to find reception for the family crisis. But they had adapted with fierce and protective reactions, taking their mother's side without a moment of hesitation, and giving Sarah warm welcome in her new lodgings. Sarah had been convinced that her separation from Alexander would come at a higher cost to the family, and that she would be outcast. The reverse had come about. Robin had made no communication and seemed to be gone, at least for the time being, but the support from Scarlet and the boys moved her to tears. Even Jerry had become closer – to Sarah and to Scarlet.

Neither Sarah nor Andy had ever thought about meeting, a fact that seemed extraordinary when they finally met. She waited in shade in Scarlet's garden and stood from her chair to greet him, and Andy stopped in his tracks. She walked across to him. Sarah Buxton thanked the school bully and shook his hand.

Andy's chin was already shaking. It was worse than the time at The Lion with Greg. He hadn't managed a single word, but he looked at her, and of course it was Sarah, but she looked so small. She looked old. They were both tearful, suddenly overcome by the power of the experience they had shared, albeit from distance. Andy would always work hard to hold back tears, but when they broke through, they came with a force. He had sat up on the rise out at Hurtmoor for hours, watching through binoculars and taking photographs, full of tension, wanting to see Sarah safe. Finally, he'd found her, and the release of tension was really quite dramatic. They both remained standing, neither of them able to speak, but words weren't needed. Somehow, to see one another, was sufficient.

They did talk. Andy and Sarah, nervously hesitant, talked about their experiences. They each had different perspectives:

Sarah inside the barn, Andy watching from afar. The arrival of emergency vehicles and the hospital admission. Andy had watched it all. Taken the photographs. Now he could place Sarah into the story – see inside the barn.

Sarah found some comfort, knowing that someone had looked for her. It would be an exaggeration to call it closure. They both now had an understanding of trauma, and they both knew there was a long journey ahead. But they were able to help each other forward, filling in some of the gaps, replacing guesswork with first hand accounts and the beginnings of resolution.

Andy and Sarah talked through the whole chain of events. Two hours of conversation and three pots of tea. They wandered in and out of a dozen topics as they swapped personal histories, and their experiences of the pandemic. It was just one meeting and there was no expectation of future contact. Really, they were strangers meeting for the first time, but their time together was an experience of intimacy. Andy was reminded of some of his sexual encounters when he was younger: urgent needs and naked bodies, giving everything, trusting a stranger. He was a man driven by emotion, always able to speak openly, and women liked him. He had such a low opinion of himself that he could never understand why anyone would take a liking to him, but throughout all of his ups and downs, he'd never been short of female company. He knew the value of a good partner. Without his better half, Andy was nothing. Without Polly, he'd have already died a miserable death. He'd learned from a lifetime of experience, that his misdeeds had tarnished him. Yet, even at his worst, drinking heavily and fighting in the street, women had forgiven him, given themselves to him. In the end, Janey had accepted him. And Polly more than anyone had demonstrated how the power of love could look past imperfection and foolishness.

More than once, a one night stand had been a survival kit, a way to get through a dark night. And somehow, that's how this intense encounter with Sarah had felt, but without the sex. They had bared their souls, needed one another, accepted each other, giving and receiving comfort. They had both taken something from an afternoon encounter, drinking tea in someone else's garden, and then moved on.

When all had been said, they were left with nothing but politeness and small-talk. For Andy, there had been some significant steps, progress at last. He'd honoured his promise to Janey, made his explanation to Greg, and he and Polly remained on friendly terms with Cheryl. For the first time in his life, he felt himself to be acceptable to his peers. "Has Cheryl told you about her plans? She's off to Nepal in a couple of weeks, to walk in the foothills of the Himalayas, and already talking about extending her holiday, even before she's set off. She's a character, that's for sure."

Sarah appreciated the diversion. "Yes, she's very adventurous. I'm going to house-sit for her while she's away. I need some time away from Surrey, and I've always loved Cheryl's garden." Sarah gave only the bare bones of an explanation. The decision to accept Cheryl's offer of accommodation had triggered a review of the past several months. Just a few months earlier, from out of nowhere, she had heard Mark's call, and she'd driven back to her home town for the first time in decades, to drink tea with Cheryl and sit by Mark's bed. Now she would live in the house where Mark had died, and where Cheryl could no longer reside, sensing the house and the garden as a spiritual haven, a place to seek further recovery while waiting for the ordeal of the trial. For the later stages of this extraordinary year at least, she had a place to sit and wait.

Andy paused, surprised by Sarah's announcement. He wondered about Greg Whitehead. Neither Greg nor Sarah had made any reference to the kiss by the river back in Stokesley, and he decided to let it pass. He'd spent most of his life trying to claw back some self-respect, and now that he was finally gaining ground, he had no wish to risk a clumsy insensitivity.

Scarlet left them alone, refusing Salt's instruction to listen to every word. She served them with tea and sandwiches, and when the time came for Andy to leave, she insisted on driving him back to the station. They made polite conversation in the car. Scarlet explained that she had to make a short detour to drop a couple of bags off at a local food bank.

Andy was tired. The motion of the car rocked him almost instantly to sleep. Scarlet stopped the car, jumped out and delivered her donation, and returned to complete the journey. She gave the car door a slam, bringing Andy back from his slumber. He glanced quickly across to her, and apologised as they recommenced their journey. He was in unfamiliar territory and yet as they drove away, he had a feeling of deja vu. Then he realised that he had been to this place before. The vape shop and the betting office were right alongside the car. George had dropped his buddy here. Andy had forgotten all about it. Until now, when he remembered.

Scarlet drove on to the train station, thanking him for his time, and wishing him well, as he jumped from the car.

Andy woke early after a poor night's sleep. He'd stood on the station platform late on the previous afternoon, first watching his train pull in, and then watching it pull out again. He hadn't been able to persuade himself to get on board, so he'd checked into The Station Hotel. Today, he'd hang out at the betting office, maybe pick a winner.

He checked out from the hotel and found a cafe, where he drank a pot of tea, ate a fried egg sarnie, and made his way to the spot where he'd last seen George's companion. There were roads and alleyways in several directions, and Andy was tired. He went into the betting shop, where he bought coffee and sat on a large sofa. Bookmaker's premises had moved along since Andy had last thrown away a tenner. His sofa offered a fine view out on to the street. It was twelve thirty before his target came into sight. He walked right past Andy, and placed a bet. Andy listened to the exchange of greetings, and picked out his target's name – Phil. After that it was easy. Andy followed Phil for two hundred metres, and watched him unlock his front door and enter his house. He made a note of the address, then took a walk round to the back of the house, where George's Peugeot was parked. *"Back in the game."*

He took an Uber back into town, dropping him right outside of the police station. Andy had some new information, and he entered the station hopeful that DI Griffin would take up further investigations.

Griffin was good enough to pop out to hear Andy's news, but he showed little enthusiasm. He'd moved on, working now on new cases. "So what do you want me to do? Please don't misunderstand. I appreciate the information, and we'll add it to the file, but you've given me a man's Christian name and his address. That's all."

Griffin wasn't entirely at ease with Sarah's injury still unexplained. The charges against Walter Rathbone had been dropped, and Alexander had welcomed him back to work at Hurtmoor, but the case against Sarah looked strong. Griffin was an experienced copper, well aware that too many crimes remain unsolved, but able to live with limited success.

Andy was exasperated, to the extent that he wasn't quite able to keep his mouth shut as he watched DI Griffin turn and walk away. "Very impressive, Detective Inspector. We could have used you in the Falklands," but Griffin disappeared without response.

Andy stood back out on the street, and he was angry. *"For target practice."* And as he stood, he felt adrenaline surging through his veins. Andy Cooper, a man trying to find the best of himself, and desperate to be reformed, wanted to hurt someone. Suddenly he felt that his fists were on fire, and desperate for a target. Nothing else would settle him.

He travelled back out towards the train station full of trouble, hot under his collar, fighting against unwelcome impulses, and five minutes later, he was hammering hard on a stranger's door.

Phil opened his front door with energy, ready to demand explanation for the excessively loud knocking, but the speed and aggression of Andy's intrusive entrance gave him pause for thought, and by the time Andy had him pinned to the floor with pressure on his throat, Phil had lost sight of his objection. Survival seemed to be a more important consideration.

During the next thirty minutes, Andy pressed his advantage, prodding and slapping, with the occasional back-hander, and a kick to break the boredom, and he laughed at Phil, humiliating and dominating his opponent. Bullying. Flat out, nasty bastard, bullying. It came all too easy, and he delivered his brutality with practised expertise, until Phil begged for mercy. By the time he dragged his victim into Guildford police station, Phil had confessed his violence into a voice memo, directed Andy to the boot of the Peugeot to find the bucket and spade, and fully described the involvement of George Brand and Alexander MacDonald. It was a game changer, but Andy felt sickened. Years of hard work, the therapy and the apologies... all of Polly's support... and in the space of fifteen minutes, he'd undone all of his progress, reverted to type, found his twisted violence. He'd needed the worst of himself to deliver a good impact on the world. The world would be fine now. Andy was wretched.

SIXTY

SARAH

I'M SARAH. *It's almost mid-winter, short days and long nights, a time for regeneration.*

DI Griffin was kind enough to visit me before I left Surrey to house-sit for Cheryl, and he gave a full account of the rapid progress that led to Alexander's arrest. Apparently, Andy Cooper made a somewhat unconventional citizen's arrest. DI Griffin spoke to the paramedic who'd given me first aid in the middle barn. She had felt the need to move the yellow bucket, my toilet. She'd been clear and succinct in her explanation – it smelled of urine. The forensic team had found the bucket and other key items of evidence in the boot of a car, including a spade that had been used as a weapon against me.

DI Griffin explained that Alexander was shocked by these developments – he'd become comfortable and confident, but then once he'd been made aware of Phil's collapse and confession, and he'd been formally charged with several serious crimes, he'd sent word to his accomplice in Spain, lashed out full of anger and spite, informing George Brand that he was safe to return, and George was subsequently arrested at Heathrow Airport. DI Griffin seemed satisfied.

It was kind of him to speak with me, but it was Andy Cooper who unlocked my prison cell. I see Andy from time to time, and I've become friendly with his wife, Polly. I will be required to testify when the cases against Alexander, George, and Phil, are heard. The prospect of a long legal process frightens me. I hope that I'll find courage, but really I see no value in punishment. That's how I feel, as I sit here in winter sunshine, in Cheryl's garden.

I needed to come here. I needed solitude, to look back without any other witness, and to make decisions about my future. Cheryl's invitation to house-sit was perfectly timed, exactly what I needed – a therapeutic environment and the chance to be alone. Cheryl's garden comforts and contains me. I'm content here, able to confront the frightening images that intrude into my dreams.

And now Cheryl has offered an extended stay, with an option to buy. I'm not sure about that. Maybe I should buy Cheryl's house, or maybe I should follow her to Nepal. Perhaps I'll wait for mid-summer and sit on a bench by the river. Big decisions are for later. For now, I'm happy enough house-sitting, enjoying temporary lodgings with no permanent fixed abode. The arrangement seems to fit my uncertain needs perfectly well. The future will show itself, all in good time.

So much has changed, and now I'm back where I started, in the place I once ran from, getting reacquainted with familiar surroundings. There are good days and bad, but slowly my injuries are healing – my shattered jaw and my damaged spirit. I escaped Alexander, and I remind myself daily of that monumental achievement. I have no doubt that it is better to live a lifetime with trauma and injury, than to live for another minute with Alexander.

It's early still, and the memories are too close, but I can feel progress. Small steps on a steep hill, but I'm getting there. I'm fortunate to have been well supported in my hour of need. Scarlet, Jerry and the boys, and Cheryl of course. They have been wonderful. With these people in mind, I can be alone.

I think about it every day. All of it: the traumatic imprisonment in the middle barn, the hospital, the police, my family and my friends, and Greg Whitehead. Every day, I'll spend time sitting in Cheryl's magical garden or out by the river where I once lived, allowing my thoughts and feelings. Sometimes the feelings are very powerful, and I find myself shedding tears that I can't understand. I *challenged myself to learn the language of emotions and I'm learning faster than I might have expected. A series of events and conversations have brought me to this place, taken me into new emotional territory. It can feel overwhelming, and yet I celebrate every tear, every moment of uncertainty, my fear and my fortune. I'm free to feel it all.*

ACKNOWLEDGEMENTS

Thanks to my early readers: Meg Ashley, Les Cameron. Andy Prescott, and Julie Prescott. Thanks also to Maggie Bellew for grammatical corrections and feedback. Big thanks to Gillie Hatton for guidance and editing.

ACKNOWLEDGEMENTS

ALSO BY TIM PRESCOTT

WHO CARES WHO WINS

A gritty psychological thriller

"... a thoughtful and extremely well written gripping, page turner."

Danny Hutton needs to fight for his turf in urban Teesside when his life and livelihood are threatened.

Danny is one of a group of children who grew up together in the care system. No one else is there for them so they look out for each other, emerging into adulthood unprepared and unhealed, sometimes making questionable decisions. But their bonds hold firm and even in the face of serious threat, they stand alongside one another.

Danny survives against the odds, channelling his darkness to gain power in a dangerous underworld. He's in a world of trouble - facing an intimidating rival at the very moment when his past starts to catch up with him.

Emina was an innocent teenager in rural Albania, until she became a victim of people trafficking, deposited in the North of England as a sex worker.

Close friends and a longing for love, lead Danny into uncharted territory. He's chasing too many shadows, covering too many cracks. He can't be everywhere... something has to give.

A gripping psychological thriller with heartbreak and humanity.

Available in paperback and Kindle on Amazon.